FALL OF HONOR

FALL OF HONOR

A Tale of the Persian Wars

DAN LYONS

Waterside Productions

First Printing, 2024

ISBN-13: 978-1-962984-10-2 print edition
ISBN-13: 978-1-962984-11-9 e-book edition

Waterside Productions
2055 Oxford Ave
Cardiff, CA 92007
www.waterside.com

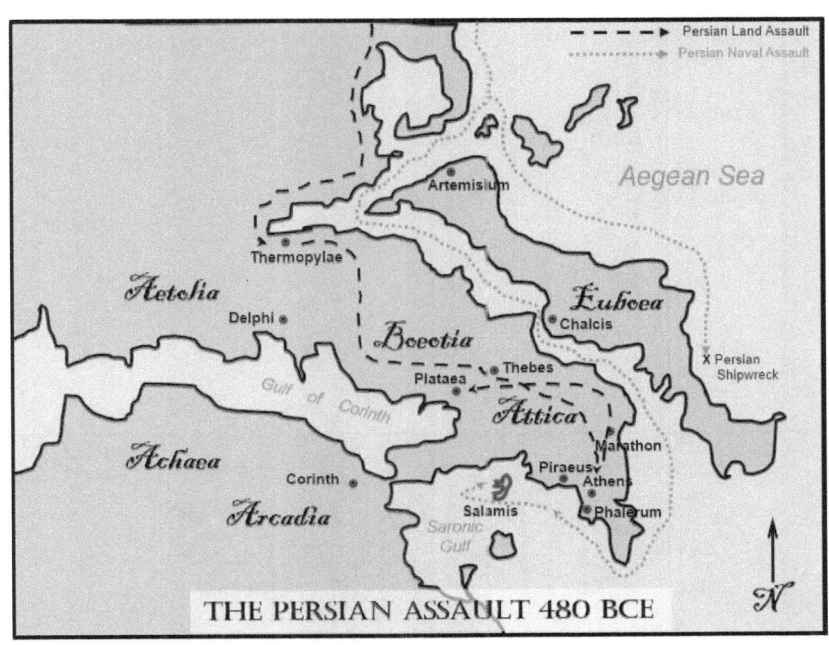

THE PERSIAN ASSAULT 480 BCE

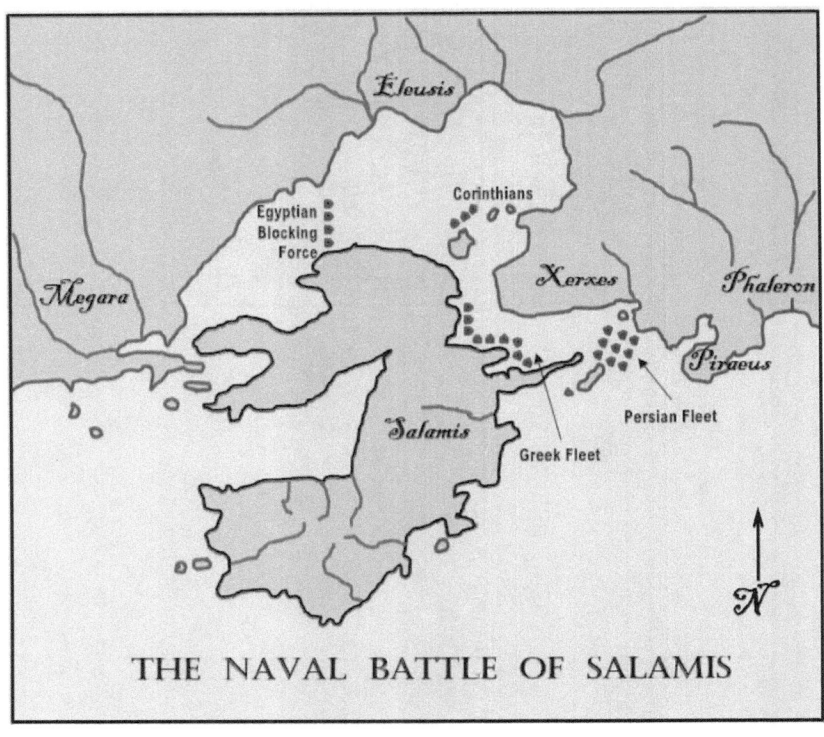

THE NAVAL BATTLE OF SALAMIS

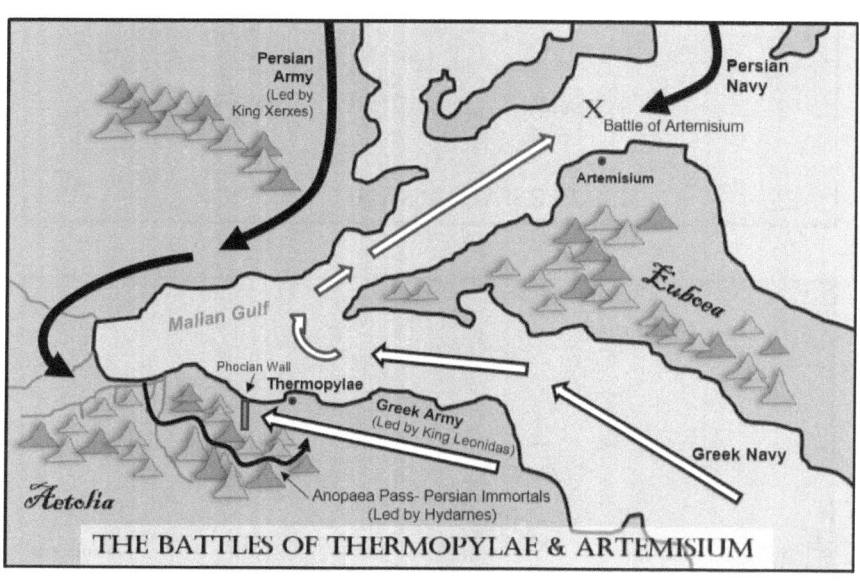

THE BATTLES OF THERMOPYLAE & ARTEMISIUM

"Any sailor knows that the ocean is driven by the deep currents. *Fall of Honor* is an exciting, page-turning story about strategy, tactics, bravery, and leadership. But mostly it's about people and their relationships. Relationships of trust and confidence. And any sailor also knows that those are the deep currents that drive history. I recommend that you dive in to this story."

Admiral John Richardson
Chief of Naval Operations (2015–2019)
United States Navy

"*Fall of Honor* is much more than just another historical novel. Lyons brilliantly weaves a treasure trove of leadership lessons as told through the eyes of Persian and Greek leaders in pursuit of victory and their way of life. This masterful and eye-opening analysis of human behavior, strategy, and the complexities of decision-making processes reorients the reader through the battles, flourishes, and charismatic performances of legendary leaders. A compelling and riveting read!"

David Smith, Associate Professor in the Johns Hopkins
Carey Business School and coauthor of *Athena Rising:
How and Why Men Should Mentor Women* and *Good Guys:
How Men Can Be Better Allies for Women in the Workplace*

"In *Fall of Honor*, Dan Lyons has crafted a thoroughly enjoyable page turner. Adding to a historical setting already full of lessons for the ages, Dan has given us truly rich characters and a story that teaches us again the power of inspired and unselfish leadership and the destructiveness that follows selfish intent. Through the journey, we are reminded that righteous causes will always inspire great sacrifice; personal honor, once lost, is very difficult to reclaim; and greatness and integrity are built one decision, one day, and one generation at a time."

Lori Reynolds
LtGen (Ret.) USMC

CONTENTS

PROLOGUE

Great forces stir in the Eastern Mediterranean in 480 B.C. The huge and powerful Persian Empire, formed decades earlier by Cyrus the Great, has swallowed all before it in an overwhelming rush of military mastery. Egypt falls to it. Ionia in Asia Minor, filled with ancient colonies of Greeks, succumbs yet lies restive under the yoke of Persian oppression. Their attempts at resistance and calls for help from their mainland Greek allies prove futile.

In the early months of the year, the Great king of the Persians, Xerxes, son of Darius, casts his eye upon the Greek mainland, then forms an expedition to conquer all the free Greeks and bring them under his heel. Ten years earlier, his father, Darius, had sent a smaller force to invade and conquer the Greek city-state of Athens, partly in retaliation for the help Athenians had provided the Ionian Greeks, and partly to extend his grip on Persia.

Many, even in Athens itself, are sympathetic to the tyrant's aims. They chafe under the new and unstable power of the Athenian democracy, and long to return to the days of their oligarchical power. But at the battle of Marathon, the Greeks turn the Persians back, though many in Athens flee and find themselves seeking assistance at the court of the Persian king. It is an uncertain time. A time when loyalties are questioned, and the battle between the power of the state and the power of the individual has never been more fervent.

Darius had vowed to subjugate the Greeks. But upon his death, the mission has fallen to his son, Xerxes. The new ruler demands samples of earth and water, the ritual symbols of submission, from the Greek city-states. Some comply. Most do not. In Athens and Sparta, the two leading powers of Greece, warriors throw the Great king's emissaries into pits and kill them.

Enraged, Xerxes speeds his preparations. His army, numbering in the hundreds of thousands, crosses the Hellespont and enters Europe. When the strait itself seems to erupt in a storm to protest this violation, the king scourges its waters in punishment. An enormous navy cruises alongside the advance of the army. Man, and it seems nature, cower before the might of Persia.

In Greece, the fractious city-states meet to discuss strategy at Corinth, on the isthmus between Athens and the Peloponnese, where Sparta reigns supreme. They decide to defend the narrow pass at Thermopylae, in Northern Greece. They send five thousand soldiers led by Leonidas, a Spartan king, and a large naval force under another Spartan, Eurybiades, and an Athenian named Themistocles. The navy takes station between Thermopylae on the mainland and Cape Artemisium on the northern tip of the isle of Euboea.

The Persians find them there.

CHAPTER 1

Northern Greece, in the year of the Athenian Archon Calliades,
480–479 BCE

Lysis

"Enemy in sight!" The lookout's shrill cry echos across the surface of the sea.

Soon, I see them, hulls up on the horizon, bare masts outlined against the powder blue sky. Above their flashing oars, fluffy fish-scale clouds spread low on the water, heralding the gods' intent to tip the weather. The clouds cover both Cape Artemisium on the isle of Euboae off to my right and Thermopylae, or the "hot gates," on the mainland to my left. Now, though, where we are, the sea is flat. An offshore cross-breeze runs across the deck and caresses my forearms, helping to cool the sweat drenching my body, as it runs down my chest and soaks the yellowed linen tunic that presses against my girt breastplate of layered linen.

Anxiety builds within me like the strain of an anchor cable, taut, and stretched to the breaking point. Kneeling on the foredeck with my shield resting against the forward bulwark, I watch our bronze-beaked ram casting the sea to the left and right, its frothing passage marked by an angry wake that speeds down the sides of our trireme battleship. The sea whirls and spins under the sharp measured cadence of 170 wooden oar shafts. They bite the water and drive the ship relentlessly forward..

My fingers hurt. I turn my head to glance at the beautiful eight-foot spear in my right hand, its sharp iron butt-spike resting on the deck of our trireme. I grip the lance so hard that my tendons bulge with the effort.

"Relax, Lysis!" I hear from my right.

Hippocrotes. Of course. Always the easy one. Never rattled, never at a loss.

"We will be in battle soon enough," he says, grinning. "Better save it. Besides, I hear we have a surprise for the barbarians."

I loosen my grip, feeling my fingers stretch. He is right, as usual. In a while, we will be in it— our first real fight, the first time we will meet the enemy face-to-face. There is time enough for fear.

I close my eyes and focus on my sensations, willing my frozen muscles to relax, trying to remember the lessons I learned as a child at the Kynosarges gymnasium. *Breathe, focus, stay above the fear. See fear in the distance, like the dark summer storms that roll over Mount Hymettus, flashing, awesome, but something outside of who I am.* I am not skilled at these things, as my irritated teacher never ceased to remind me, and I find my mind wandering, slipping in and out of the fear, resisting my call to focus.

The threads of my thoughts weave back and forth as the great ship surges beneath me, and I rock with the ebb and flow of its power. I think of home, a few days in the past but in this moment as distant as a year. I think of my uncle and my mother, standing on the quay at Munychia, waving goodbye as the fleet set sail, hiding their fear in the poised pride of the Athenian with a guise worn by many who nevertheless trembled beneath for love of their sons.

I remember, too, the archon Calliades. It is in his time, this time, that the Persian enemy comes, crashing like a tidal wave over the shores of Hellas from their vast and teeming lands to the east, bent on destruction and conquest, driven by the arrogance of the undefeated. He had arrived at the port to wish us well, overseeing the solemn sacrificial rituals that had sent us on our way, good omens mixing with ill, in a confused sense of the gods 'wishes.

Calliades had waited on the dock, huddling with the other generals not sailing with the fleet; staying, preparing the city and the port for the coming storm. Their multi-colored himation cloaks flapped in the breeze as they gave final warnings and instructions to Themistocles, the navarch, commander of the fleet, and the leading citizen of our great city. I assume they bid him the best of luck and encouraged him to bring the fleet back home, intact and victorious.

And, of course, I think of Andronica. Dear, sweet Andronica. Impulsive as usual, she too had come to Munychia, running along the curving breakwater leading a host of others, separated from her parents who had fought to stay her flight. She followed our ship all the way out through the narrow water gate, past the crenelated battlements as we slipped into the open sea. She waved to me wildly, her chin thrust forward, dark hair flowing in the offshore breeze, her long, deep blue tunic clinging to her form like the morning sun on the hills: illuminating, revealing, caressing.

But most of all, I think of my father, that ghost who exists for me in shards of memory only. It is his armor I wear, his spear I carry, his honor I have sworn to uphold. He had not come to see me off. He had not come to give his blessing or beam with the pride of a man who had raised a warrior citizen. He had not done so for many years, for time out of mind.

He had been lost at sea when I was but a boy. All I have of him are my child memories and the stories told by others; by my mother, her older brother, and their friends. But I do not need those stories. I know my father. I know who he was. A hero. A champion of Athens, a warrior beyond compare. I remember him that way. I remember how he swung his great sword and hefted the huge round shield that had so terrified me as a child, demonstrating the proper thrust and parry of the hoplite in battle. I remember how he knelt in front of me and held my shoulders in his strong hands and with that distinctive lift of his eyebrows and piercing gaze promised me he would always be there when I needed him. We would fight together, he told me, side by side in the Phalanx of our city. I remember the warmth of his skin and the safety of his embrace when I told him "Father, I will fight with you!"

I cling to those memories, as I cling to my spear, and strive to live up to what I can no longer see, or touch, but what I can feel with every fiber of my being.

It is these memories that calm me, that bring me back to myself. I inhale and taste the salt in the breeze. My lungs fill with the scent of the ocean and the pungent smells of a warship at sea. The deep, woodsy smell of pitch and oak, the musty scent of wet canvas and coiled lines that melds with the odor of urine, of tanned leather, of horsehair plumes, cornel wood, hemp, wool, and linen. But more than anything, the overpowering stench of unwashed men. One hundred seventy rowers strain at the oars beneath me, their every exertion pushes sweat from dirtied pores, their refuse oozes up from the hold washed away by the breeze but always there, waiting to roll upon us all like a tide.

Nine other hoplite marines besides myself kneel on the oaken deck of the forepeak, and contribute to the stink. At the same time, four archers space themselves behind, seeking already the protection of our shields. They, like me, ooze fear, anticipation, and determination.

Swaying with the rhythm of the ship, I open my eyes and feel the rowers lock their blades forward at the furthest extent of their reach, levering and sending the ship so it leaps ahead with the surge of power unique to a trireme.

"Better?" asks Hippocrates.

I nod. Yes. Better.

I look at him, my closest friend for these last ten years and almost a brother, the solid rock of competence and strength against which I have measured my growth to manhood. He smiles, brown eyes gleaming with excitement, ready as he always seems to be for the fortunes or misfortunes that come our way. It was not for him to feel the fear I struggle to keep at bay. We'd met in the Kynosarges, the gymnasium, when I had begun my tenth year. An enthusiastic bundle of energy, competitive, strong, and aggressive, he seemed to have sought me out.

A decade later, I am taller than he and leaner. But muscle layers his thick body, and he wears a rich, dark beard. My beard has barely started, and fine hair lay on my face like wisps on a willow. We have both keep our bodies at full strength by way of the gymnasium, he in the Pankration, me in the pursuit of the Pentathlon. He is popular with both men and women, a natural leader, confident, brash, and powerful. I recall our last night on shore in the rat's nest old Patrocles, our marine captain on *Winds of the Gods*, likes to call a "gentleman's drinking establishment."

"Lysis! You dog!" Hippocrotes shouted above the din of a packed house of sailors and marines. "Tell this miserable excuse for an Akamantian who's the finest Pankratiate in Athens!"

Hippocrotes enjoyed riling up the other tribes in Attica—any other tribe, as long as it wasn't our own. No, his loyalty to our tribe, Kekropis, was undying. Though he came from the city, and I from the plains below Mount Hymettus, we share the same tribal bond.

I threw up my hands, looking puzzled. "Athrodes? Nicias? Perhaps Appollophanes?"

He roared, and amidst the laughter of the crowd, threw me in a headlock that I did not bother trying to escape.

"Who's the finest?" he yelled.

"Could it be Anaxilaus?" I gasped.

A further indignant growl, and he released me.

"Hippocrotes, of course!" I said, bowing. "Was there ever a doubt?"

He laughed and returned the bow. "Only among our enemies!"

I feel lucky to have him, especially as we approach the Persian dregs. He was a good man to have in a fight, as my father liked to say so many years ago.

The enemy draws closer, picking up speed.

Miretus, trierarch of *Winds,* calls out to the oar master, "Attack speed! Prepare to form in station!"

Three levels of rowers make up the powerful thrust of the swift trireme, sitting one above the other in the efficient arrangement first perfected by the Corinthians in the days of our fathers. I had rowed among their number for a time, holding down an amidship's seat as a thalamite on the lowest, or least skilled level. It had been part of my military training as an Ephebe, part of the necessary experience every Athenian male citizen goes through from the ages of 18 to 20 years, sweating then as they do on this day.

I had seen the big triremes many times before. As a child, I had walked among the ship sheds of the Piraeus and counted out the paces with Hippocrotes as we measured the impressive length and the tapering, narrowed beam of the vessels that lay quiescent under peaked roofs. "Almost 140-feet long," my uncle had once said, "and every foot a work of art." We had often watched as the big ships surged from the harbor, oarsmen swinging in sharp unison, or as dusk settled on land and sea and the trierarchs brought their charges in with echoing commands bidding the rowers, "Up, oars!"

The rowing itself I remember too well, having completed my training a few months before. I can still feel the raw and bleeding blisters that hours on the end of an oar had brought to even the toughest fingers. Soon enough, that torn skin turned to the hard and calloused hands of old veterans, but I was spared that path.

For me, it was the armor of the hoplite marine rather than the sweating confines of the thalamite bench, hemmed in and blind. I serve above decks instead of as a slave to the cocky thranite who leads each triad, wetted by the sweat of those above and the seawater that leaks through the dubious seal of the leather askoma.

Miretus, a weathered veteran of many years at sea, seems pleased as the ship picks up speed, oars snapping to the water, cadence increasing to the rhythm of the pipes. His tanned skin sits like a ragged cliff face beneath the riot of graying hair that blows free in the breeze above his eyes, a study in concentration. From him, I turn back to the fore, watching the approach of the enemy, with greater confidence, feeling the strength of our ship, and the courage and competence of our leadership.

The Persian fleet—a formidable collection of Phoenicians, Egyptians, Cyprians, Ionians, and it appears, hundreds of others—spreads out before us much longer than our line and rows down upon us with the utmost determination. Once more, despite the reassuring presence of my shipmates and fellow marines, I feel myself tense, palms sweating, heart pounding. I look left and right.

We are in a long line abreast, leading another long line in a column behind us. It seems to me if we rowed straight on, we will be first to engage. But I suppose everyone must feel this way.

From the curving sternposts of our ships, colored pennons fly, snapping above each of the trierarch's chairs. The bows of our vessels are painted brilliant reds, blues, and greens, with the eye of Athena under the forepeak gazing upon the enemy. The oar blades match the ships' paint schemes, together forming a moving rainbow that enlivens the visual splendor of our force. I had witnessed this scene many times in peaceful maneuvers, but never before in the presence of the foe. It is at once breathtaking and terrifying.

We are closer yet, our faces set in stone-like concentration. We lean forward, all eyes fixed upon the enemy. I can make out the swarms of marines on the Persian decks, even down to the bows that stand ready to draw. Then, as the enemy slice through the wind and sea, charging forward, surging to contact, Miretus and a host of voices in our fleet roar the command.

"Form station! Hold water! Back larboard side!"

At once, our ship slows to a halt, the oars on both sides flail in the water. Those on my right stop, pushing against the momentum of the hull, while on my left three banks of rowers strain to back, rather than row. In an instant, we are pointing at an angle to the enemy attack. Those ships to either side of us have done the same. The entire fleet duplicates our maneuver, and forms a circle in the middle of the bay with prows pointing outward, sterns inward toward the second row. It is an amazing feat in the face of a full-blown attack, and we execute it with nary a nicked blade or battered hull.

The Persians stop in confusion, sweeping around the edges of the circle. We sit in place, gazing outward, surprised ourselves. We watch the Phoenicians, Ionians, and Egyptians swarm around us like sharks, unable to crack the circle and seeing no exposed sides while they expose their own soft underbellies. I can hear them shout over the surface of the sea, their frustrated insults falling, for the most part, on deaf ears.

"Cowards! Come and fight! Do you fear us?"

I can understand their insults only because of Hippocrotes. He had taught me the Persian tongue as we grew, roaming over the hills of Attica or spending long afternoons perched above the assembly that met on the Pnyx, listening to the endless debates on the proper way forward for the city, our polis, and voted on by all. He had moved from the East when he was young, he said, and had learned the language from his parents. He'd been amused by my interest in Persian and more than happy to be my "pedagogue."

Close up, I see that what other mariners had said about the barbarian ships is true. They are smaller than ours, but quicker. They knife through the water sharply, not like our own solid but unspectacular hulls Their decks hold what seem to be almost twice our number of marines and archers. I am reminded of this as arrows thwack against the hull or slice into the water, companions to the enemy's taunts. I gaze upon the spectacle with awe; my stomach knots as I wait for the next move. *What did the fleet commanders have in mind? Were we to sit here until nightfall and let the invader parade past our bows?* I feel as if I am standing on the stone balbis, the starting blocks at the Panathenaic games, with my toes curled around the cool rock and my frame expecting the starting command, ready to explode off the line and race the 600 feet of the stadion.

In answer to my unspoken question, Miretus once more barks his commands. "Full speed! Crew to attack positions!"

Winds of the Gods explodes into action. Oars churn the water, and the three banks of rowers —thranite, zygite, and thalamite— steady to the task, hurling their bodies against the bending elatai oar shafts and stand with all their weight hard against the footboards.

The transition nearly knocks me off my feet. In moments, our heavy ship is once again underway, the lead thranites setting a frenetic yet disciplined pace driving us forward with increasing speed. Bracing myself against the bulwark, I turn to see Hippocrotes.

"Here we go, brother! Follow my lead. Time to get into the fight."

I turn back, watching the startling change in the situation catch the enemy by surprise. Contempt for their Greek foe had led the

Persians to circle closer and closer, their weather-stained sides vulnerable to a well-placed ram thrust. Miretus and the rest of the fleet rush to gut the enemy's entrails.

I pick out the ship our tetrarch aims to assault. It labors from right to left. I eye the painted blue monster. It trails seaweed on the waterline; her captain recognizes the danger too late as we race forward. Shouts and curses roll across the water separating our two warships, and the enemy vessel picks up speed. With its dancing oars and rakish hull, the swift Phoenician ship is put hard over, attempting a turn to larboard, trying to come into us to ram us in our starboard bow if she can.

"Should have turned away," Hippocrotes says of the enemy.

It would have been the wiser course. She had reacted too late. Miretus adjusts his course, and there is no doubt who will strike first, and with power.

"Brace!" comes the cry from the tetrarch's chair, and we throw ourselves upon the deck moments before our surging ram pierces the larboard bow of the enemy vessel with a deafening thunder.

No practice, no visions, no amount of storytelling can have prepared me for this moment. Our whole ship shudders and shakes as the heavy, bronze-sheathed ram snaps the solid ribs of the enemy like the dried bones of a sheep. I can hear the groaning of our foe's timbers and the inrush of the sea into her belly as we settle in place.

"Up, shields!" shouts Patrocles. "Archers to the fore!"

I struggle to my feet, keeping the large shield at shoulder height and locking with the shield of the neighbor on my left and Hippocrotes on my right. Behind me, the archers notch and draw their bows, releasing on command and firing on the enemy ship, her decks packed with soldiers trying to regain their footing in the unstable world of their wounded home.

"Prepare to withdraw!" I hear Miretus roar over the cacophony that erupts all around me: screams, shouts, pleas for help, curses against the gods, the crashing of bronze upon wood, the moans of the stricken, the thrum of bows and the rat-a-tat of arrows against bronze-faced shields. Our deckhands run to the bow and add their weight while the rowers stand and push for all they are worth against their oars, driving their blades into the unforgiving sea, bent on freeing us from the tangled thrust into the enemy.

"Rock! Rock!" shouts Miretus.

And we do. Up and down as our archers draw and loose, while the enemy recovers, their bowmen unloading a hail of return fire which we do our best to fend off. *Winds of the Gods'* ram had driven far into the bowels of the Phoenician and seems unwilling to leave her prey. Nevertheless, we rock her loose, even as the dying barbarian vessel begins to heel toward us, its hold filling with the sea, its frantic rowers clawing their way on deck. Our oarsmen have found purchase against the ocean and lever us back clear of the wreckage, bringing us into a relative calm in the raging battle.

I look up and over my shield, my bronze helmet filled with sweat, my body with fiery energy. We are clear! We have done it! Our first action with the enemy, and there they lie, the once-mighty barbarian, rolling about in the sea, frantic, drowning like terrified rats. I scream with elation and raise my spear with a fierce thrust. Beside me, I can hear Hippocrotes do the same, even as a final few spent arrows whistle overhead.

"Quiet, you fools!" shouts Patrocles. "Keep your mind!"

I grin, despite my discipline, and look at Hippocrotes, who winks; a broad smile creases his strong face.

"See, Lysis? Not a fear. We will drive the men of Xerxes back to their ports faster than Zeus can mount Aphrodite." He slapped me on the back of my helmet, laughing. "Then you can come see my sister, eh?"

Though used to Hippocrotes' brash impiety, even amid the battle, I feel my face flush. I envision Andronica with the light of the rising moon reflected in her lustrous dark eyes. She and I had gone to the hills above the city a few nights before the fleet departed, intent on stealing whatever time we could, knowing it could be a long while before we saw one another again.

"Lysis," Andronica had said, leading me under a large, gnarled plane tree that sheltered a moss-lined stone grotto, "how many days since we first met eyes?"

"Since you were younger than this summer grass," I answered. "A long time."

Her dark moon-frosted hair glistened, and those eyes, moist and round in the shimmering light, the deep windows to her soul that had welded my heart to hers from the moment I gazed upon them looked up at me. She stretched her lithe body and reached her arms around my neck, pulling me closer until her lips brushed mine, as my own arms encircled her waist, drawing her willing body to my loins. She sighed, kissed my cheek, and whispered in my ear.

"And in all that time," she breathed, "have you always thought of me? Have I always been yours?"

"Always," I said, feeling the surging course of my desire. "You have been forever in my dreams."

"And you in mine," she replied, pulling me to the gentle grass as a soft breeze stirred the charged air around us. She turned her gaze to mine. Once more she seemed to reach to the deepest pool of my thoughts, no more constrained in her questing than the gentle and incessant fall of waves on the beach.

"Lysis" she said her soft hands entwined in mine, "The enemy has come. Are you afraid?"

Afraid? I pulled her close to me, my fingers slowly tracing the lines of her form; feeling the swell of her breasts, the firm plane of her belly, the curve of her hips.

"Afraid? Yes, I'm afraid" I said. "Afraid for you, afraid for Athens, afraid for my country. Yes, I know fear."

She stood up then, gently pulling her hand free. She faced me, her eyes never leaving mine. Her fingers went slowly to the ties that drew her tunic together. She released them. The woven cloth fell almost languidly from her, gathering with a sigh at her feet. She stepped free and once more came to my side.

"I am not afraid" she said,

And then I knew there would be no more waiting.

"Lay with me, Lysis, Lay with me and come home to me. You are my life. I can love no other."

"Nor I, my dear sweet love, nor I."

11

She gazed at him with a frank stare, unencumbered by doubt

Lysis

And we did lay together, in the hills above a city girding for war, even as the nightingales trilled in their leafy homes. We shared love as the pale evening stars winked above, blanketing the heavens with certainty.

But on this day, in savage strife, as far away from the soft embrace of my love on that warm summer night as I can have ever imagined, Hippocrotes notices my glazed look.

"Get back here, you lecherous dog!" he shouts. "Dreaming of my sister that way! That will not do, will not do at all. Why, when we get home, I will have to—"

"Quiet!" snaps Patrocles. "Eyes clear to the shores, or I will do the work of the enemy for him!"

Hippocrotes feigns hurt, but his eyes twinkle with oafish mirth. "Yes, commander!" he barks. "I obey!"

"Best that you do," responds the captain. "May the gods give you the might to do so."

In the midst of this joust, Miretus has ordered *Winds* put hard over to larboard. We swing around, gliding by the last remnants of our sinking foe, and follow another Athenian galley into the maw of more combat. We surge past a duo of triremes locked in a death grip, bow to stern; Persian marines attempt to swarm the decks of their Greek rival. I come back to myself as an arrowhead plants itself in the deck by my feet, splintering the hard oak and drawing a further exclamation from Hippocrotes.

"Bastard's probably jealous you have got my sister, too!"

That draws a nervous laugh from those around us, yet Patrocles shakes his head in disgust. "Keep your shields up and heads down!" he orders. "Straight to the eyes men!"

And we do. Miretus veers from the stern of the trireme ahead of us and sets course for a beleaguered Cypriot vessel that lay dead in the water. Her oars thrash like the legs of an overturned beetle, caught as it was in a mass of dueling warships, unable to get to clear water. We have them dead to rights, as Miretus aims our vessel like a well-thrown spear, straight amidships of the enemy.

"Victory for the *Winds!*" bellows Hippocrotes, serious once more and bracing himself against the deck.

I also brace, planting my shield in front of me and dropping to one knee. I have a better sense of the maneuver this time, so when it comes, I am ready. Still, the wave of fear I feel as we once again hurl ourselves at the enemy is no less unnerving than before.

The angry and terrified shouts of the Cypriots rise when we plow into their exposed flank, splintering the hull, and embedding ourselves, it seems, all the way through to their keel. The stricken battleship settles upon our ram, the damage catastrophic and mortal. Again comes the command from Patrocles.

"Up shields!" he cries. "Archers, release!"

We rise to our feet, our helmets barely peeking over the rims of our four foot shields. Behind us, the thrum of taut-strung bowstrings scream the release of our first flight of missiles. We are not one-sided in attack, however.

The enemy has also found their footing and their courage. The air fills with the whir and slap of iron and bronze, the clatter of wooden shafts skittering against shield as the hiss of death hangs in my ears. A startled cry behind me indicates one of our bowmen has been hit, and I hear his body thud to the deck. However I quickly return my focus to the larboard side, where the Cypriot marines are beginning to gather. *Winds* has driven so far into their vessel that our catheads and forepeak are flush and even with their main deck. If they want, they can climb directly at us. And they seem to want. Miretus notices.

"Get out, men!" his voice rising above the din that rends the air. "Crew forward! Break us from here!"

Every available hand races forward and begins to drive the bow down, even as *Winds'* rowers respond to the trierarch's crisp commands.

"Back us out! Back us out! Everything you have got now!" His voice carries with it an overtone of anxiety new to him. "Faster!" he implores. "Faster!"

In the tight-knit ranks of marines on either side of me, I feel the beginning wavering of uncertainty. Something is not right. On the Cypriot, the enemy let loose a cheer and begin to clamber over our bow. They hold their odd wicker shields forward, and as their archers lay down a withering hail of arrows, they rush to the attack.

"Advance in force, men!" commands Patrocles. "Take them down!"

I hear Hippocrotes growl as we lock shields and move to cut down this foe.

A scream erupts on my left. Nocias, a tall, rangy hoplite whose family live close by my own on the slopes of Mount Hymettus, is hit. The barbed head of an arrow is buried in his neck, and as I turn, spurts of his blood blind me. His gurgling gasps follow him to the deck as he collapses in a heap. Then his spear pitches forward, and he rolls onto his shield, face-up, eyes a paroxysm of pain and fear. I turn further, sensing the obvious: that arrow has not come from our front.

Yes. There it is. Another vessel has pulled alongside to larboard and is upon us. With no intention of ramming, this Cypriot trireme shatters our larboard oars and lays alongside. Before we can order a turn, their numbers explode over the rail and advance among us.

"Back, men!" screams Patrocles. "Flank left! Second rank, reform in line!"

But it is too late for such a maneuver. Now it is hand-to-hand. The enemy wields huge axes with deadly effect, smacking them onto our upraised shields with terrifying force. With Nocias' death, I lose contact with the marines to my left, and see to my right only the invaders attacking, piercing and breaking our lines. I move closer to Hippocrotes. He has lost none of his comforting surety.

"Push them out Lysis like the dung of Poseidon!"

Disoriented, I follow his lead, raising my spear high and striking at the face before me, the broad iron head slashing right through the shield of my target to find soft flesh underneath. A piercing screech follows, and my shaft sags under the unsupported weight of the first man I have ever killed.

But I do not have time to carry its weight on my mind. I do not have time for anything. I wrench the point free and strike again at a different target, this time missing my intended victim, who stumbles to my right only to be impaled by the descending stroke of Hippocrotes 'bloodied weapon.

"Hah!" he laughs. "Keep feeding 'em to me, Lysis. I will clear these decks!"

Just as he says, the threat to our front is routed; those not struck down by our spears jump into the sea. But my hairs on end tell me the battle to our rear is not at all over, in fact it is desperate. Our second rank of marines has managed to turn and fight, protecting our exposed backs, but they need us to join their frenetic effort.

In the rush of fear-filled energy that suffuses me, seeing what lay in front becomes difficult. My stomach tightens in terror as I swing my shield to face the Cypriot onslaught along with the *Winds'* sailors, rowers, and marines locked in a titanic struggle to the death. The foe swarms in as I search my thoughts for answers: *Where had they all come from? This could not be one ship!*

I feel a large presence to my left, and as I press forward, this time to Hippocrotes' right, I sense another calamity. The deck lurches and shifts beneath me—the ship moves upward, heaving to larboard, and groans. I lose my footing and land with a thud as does Hippocrotes who rolls on top of me.

The Cypriots had rammed us.

Hippocrotes pushes himself off, enraged. "The gods be damned! Enough!"

With that, he flings himself back into battle, jumping over those still off-balance and wading into the Cypriots like a rabid animal, plunging his spear into the hearts of the enemy with reckless abandon.

"Hippocrotes!" I shout. "Rally to Hippocrotes!"

I scramble up behind him into the fray. Behind me, I hear old Patrocles. "Form line, men!" Keep your heads now!"

But there is no room to form the line. There is no chance. The decks on either side of the center passageway are filled with hacking, slashing bodies. The impact has flushed our rowers from the hold. They arm themselves with whatever they can, and lay into the enemy with unbridled ferocity. I hack my way through to where Hippocrotes is causing havoc amidships and, turn my back to him, continuing my defense.

"I am here!" I shout through the commotion. "I am here, Hippocrotes. I am at your back!"

"And I yours, Lysis! Stay with me!"

Around us, the battle intensifies. I can sense, and see, my friends and fellow marines, the archers, deckhands, officers, and rowers of *Winds of the Gods* fighting, unwilling to admit defeat, unwilling to let the barbarians lay claim to even a part of Athens.

Though we fight like lions, an end to the onslaught never appears. I see Patrocles taken by three men at once. He falls, his head nearly severed by an ax. Miretus, too, meets his fate by the trierarch's chair he so loves, pinned to the stern post by a host of javelins, he hangs there like a slaughtered goat. Under a weight of numbers no bravery or skill can diminish, the attackers drive Hippocrotes and me back to the bow. Axes dent and gouge my shield, and their force and power numb my shield arm, though I make their bearers pay with their lives. My spear is hacked and splintered, and I throw it to the sea, drawing my father's sword instead to lunge and slash at the mass of bodies to my front and side. I can hear my old friend roaring behind me, but despite his passion, he defends himself with more and more desperation.

"Back!" I hear him gasp. "Back, Lysis! We must use the bow to protect us!"

I understand him. If we can make it to the bow again, we can present only three embattled sides to the enemy.

"Let us go!" I cry as I spring forward. I leap over the bodies of the slain, and slip in the rivers of blood that pulse from the crawling wounded and the emptied hearts of the eternally dispatched. Hippocrotes follows with a shout.

The violence of our attack has cleared a path and we make it to the forepeak, gasping as we turn to face those who thirst for our

'Hippocrates'

deaths. I hear Hippocrotes' raspy breathing, and in the lull, before the enemy strikes again, I survey him. He is weakened. With shield battered into splinters, spear gone, and sword broken, blood oozes from cuts on his arms, and a feathered arrow protrudes from his right thigh. Yet, he returns my gaze and winks, his familiar smile reappearing.

"You are not looking too fine, Ephebe," he says. "Can you still remember who's the best fighter in all of Athens?"

"Is it Demonthenus?" I reply. "Perhaps old Heros?"

He stares at me, dark eyes intense, still filled with life.

"Hah!" he says. "You have always known it was me!"

Out of the corner of my eye, I watch a tall, broad-shouldered Cypriot marine step forward and rear back, hurling an ax through the air. I open my mouth to warn Hippocrotes, but all seems to move in slow motion— except the whirling, double-bladed weapon. Hippocrotes senses it, however, whipping his head around, his eyes a blur of motion as the remnants of his shield come up to defend him. My mind seizes on the notion that Hippocrotes will be alright, that he will make it, even as my deeper thoughts know it won't be so.

The ax grazes the top rim of his shield and continues in, embedding itself with a sickening thud in his left shoulder, near where his neck joins the collarbone. The force of the blow sends Hippocrotes staggering back. He drops his sword, and his hand flies to his neck, grasping at the ax head, trying for its removal. He falls then, right to the deck, his back slams against the forepeak. The remnants of his once-proud shield, shattered beyond recognition, falls to the oak. I cry aloud, my grief and anger overcoming the terror of my situation. Then I step in front of him, my shield held high, my hammered arm trembles with exhaustion.

The Cypriots let out cries of their own. The great warrior is down, they will finish it now. I stand in front of my fallen friend, sword at the ready, my breath comes in heaving gasps, tears of anger mix with sobs of grief. Then I hear his voice behind me.

"Lysis," he gasps, "listen to me. Don't look around. I'm done now, listen."

I can not turn anyway as the Cypriots advance. Behind them, the final desperate resistance of my fellow marines ebbs, and it appears I will be the last.

"Lysis—" Hippocrotes' voice falters, growing weaker as death stalks his youth. "I never told you...meant to...never could. I never told you—"

He is going, almost done. Through my tears, my hurt, my fear, I still sense his dying urgency. "Hippocrotes!" I croak, "What?"

"Lysis, I'm sorry...so sorry. Look. Look in the old chest in my room...the old chest...look..."

And there is no more. His words barely register, but in their ending a power courses through me I have never known. Upon his death, a vehemence beyond imagining fills me, a desperate animal energy emanates from the core of my being, and I spring forward to the attack.

Archers raise their bows and release. I shrug them off. Marines hurl their javelins and swing their axes. I brush them aside. From within me, a fire arises, a mounting tide of power. My friend dead, I am alone. Despair descends upon me like the dousing of the day's last light, but it does not crush me. No, it does not crush me. I wade further into the mass of the enemy. My sword a blur of motion, I cut down all before me. The enemies' blood pools in a lake at my feet.

And yet, of course, it can not last. A sword tears my helmet from my skull, another hacks my shield to bits, and my Father's sword shatters in my hands. My head roars as I find myself, at last, forced to the gunwale, pressed to the edge, gasping for air. Then comes a blow to my chest. I feel my balance desert me. I am pitched overboard through the remnants of our splintered oars and into the rising sea.

I splash into the warm water's welcoming embrace with little resistance. My chest compresses, my mouth opens to the stinging salt water. I taste the briny bitterness and know life will end here, in the sea, after everything.

I have lost my heavy armor. My linen breastplate, slashed and shredded as it was, acts as my anchor. *It will be enough* I think, and

I begin to sink like a stone. *It is better this way. It is better that I do not have to tell Hippocrotes' parents of his death. Better than admitting I could not live up to him, or to my father.*

My chest begins to fill with the dense salt water, and with no breath, I begin to thrash. I think of Andronica, alone and at home. *What will she think when she hears? Will she grieve and find another? Does it matter now?* I struggle, my body's reflexes kick in. I am young, not ready to die. *Will I not fight for a while for my life?* I kick more and feel my arms begin to move, reaching up toward the light and pulling. *Why bother?* I think. *It will be so easy to die.*

I relax then. *Yes. Easier this way, not struggling. No more. It feels so much better now.* I close my eyes.

Then, a disturbance beside me. Something else there. Someone else there. An iron grip on my arm. Then another. I open my eyes. *What was it? What was this? Could not they let me die? I did all I could. Who is this?* As the light grows brighter above me, my mind leaves me, and blackness closes in.

CHAPTER 2

I awake, yes, a living, moving thing, but my body aches and throbs from head to toe, and my eyelids are heavy, crusted, and sticky. The dried residue of the sea coats my body. I will my hand to move, order it to wipe my face, to clear my sight. I cough, then retch, and finally choke, feeling fluid in my lungs. When I moan and roll to my right, warm, viscous liquid drools from my mouth onto wood.

Wood. I am on a ship again. My ears are clearing now to noise, all around... people. They are speaking. But they are not Greek. No, no Greeks. No Athenians.

I struggle to raise my head, rolling onto my back again, as the noise grows sharper.

"He lives," comes a voice.

But it is strange, this sound. Yet I know what it says. I can understand.

It continues. "Put him there Tabazus, against the mast. Let me speak to him."

I feel hands lifting, dragging, propping me up. Then they let go. I raise my arm to wipe my eyes again, and again, until they open. I am on the gangway of a trireme in fading daylight. On either side, rowers swing together. They move in rhythm but without enthusiasm.

A man eyes me. He kneels on the deck, arms crossed on his enormous knee, with his dark, thick beard thrust forward. His twisted tree trunk arms show muscles and cuts. He wears a purple tunic, dark trousers, and a purple felt cap, filigreed around the narrow brim with fine gold thread. An ax—glistening, sharp, and deadly—hangs on his belt.

DAN LYONS

"You fought well, barbarian scum," he says. "As did your friend."

I hold his gaze, my throat dry and constricted.

"He can not understand you," the man Tabazus says from behind me. "The barbarians cannot speak a civilized tongue."

The big man stands up. "No?" he asks, looking over my shoulder. "But Demaratus can."

"Because we taught him! Besides, he's a Spartan, not like this Athenian animal."

The big man looks amused. "Remember," he says, "I was on the plains of Marathon and it was no easier then. Those 'animals,'" he continues, "dealt us a heavy blow today. Perhaps we can learn their ways."

I hear a derisive snort from Tabazus. "There's nothing they have to teach us. They only had luck from the gods today."

The man shrugs. "As you wish."

I clear my throat, swallowing hard. "I can understand you," I say, imagining every word before I speak. "What do you want with me?"

He looks pleased. "You see, Tabazus? He can speak." Again, he kneels, watching me. "We are a civilized people," he says, voice rising. "We honor those of great courage and skill, even if they are our enemies." He pauses, looking around where there must be more gathered whom I can not see.

"I brought you from the water because of these things," he continues. "You will see that we reward men like you for your efforts. You will be grateful I have let you live."

I say nothing but meet his eyes with a frank stare. He laughs.

"Tabazus, I don't think he believes me!"

"I wouldn't if I were he," replies Tabazus. "Cyrus the Persian promises death."

I presume my captor to be Cyrus.. His face softens.

"Nothing more than they deserved, Tabazus, you know that. This man, on the other hand—" and he points at me, "—this man deserves better."

"Well, we have no lodging for him here. Best put him ashore. Perhaps you can reward him there?"

24

Cyrus stands tall again, stretching himself to his full height, a magnificent warrior. "Tabazus, yes, and I'll do more. I will introduce him to one of his kind, more or less. I will let Demaratus see that courage does exist outside of Sparta."

"He will be loathe to see that," says Tabazus. "Demaratus thinks mighty old Sparta invented courage, honor, discipline, and even warfare itself."

"We shall see," replies Cyrus, who turns away. "Feed him squid and olives. He will need his strength."

A short while later, a deckhand gives me not fish and fruit but the dregs of wine from a darkened old leather wineskin, along with two handfuls of cardoons and leeks, good considering their time since harvest. I wolf them down, my body once more obeying its instincts. My heart and mind, however, are empty of emotion, devoid of caring. My life feels worthless yet I live only because it is apparent the gods will it so.

The ship sails ashore before twilight descends. Cyrus and other marines help me to my feet, lift me over the side, and force me to keep moving. I can not stand, much less walk as I stumble down a long beach, gritty and hardened by the hot summer sun. I feel as if the Olympic wrestling champion, Milo of Croton himself, has hammered me to the ground in incessant falls. My arms bear slashes from glancing blows in the heat of battle. My bruised chest aches, but, remarkably, it seems I have no broken ribs.

Despite my woes, what catches my attention is where we have landed; the mainland. Mountains along the coast to either side tower over the shoreline, and a large plain lay in front of us, stretching to the foothills and disappearing out of sight to my right. The plain tapers down to a narrower strip of land that hugs the looming heights inland and skirts the sea to my left. On this plain, an army lay encamped. But it is not just an army. No, it is more like a large city, or a nation. In every direction, campfires sprout like barley on my father's farm, their rising smoke and flaming bases whip in the fitful breeze of day's end.

Men and animals lay on the land like a pestilential horde, filling every flat and fissure, every hill and valley, as far as the eye can see.

For the time it takes to gauge this wonder, the pain and hurt leave my body, all of the apathy flees my soul. This is something so new, beyond anything I have ever dreamed or thought, even in my darkest nightmares, as existing upon the face of the earth, such that my mind fills with it and questions pour forth: *How could this be? Where have all these people come from? Can this be the army of the Great king Xerxes? How can Athens, or indeed, all of Greece, stand against this?*

Cyrus notices my discomfiture.

"You see, young Athenian, how happy you are to be alive, to witness such a thing," he says. "Never has there been such a gathering. Never has there been such an armed host. Indeed, what can even courage like yours do to prevail against this might? This is why you will be like so many others who have seen fit to join our ranks. Yes, join, rather than be crushed."

My knees buckle, and the men on either side grip me, and laughing, raise me up. Still, they have misjudged. My reaction is one of physical pain, not the fear I feel for Athens and myself. I stagger, hurt, though still with the combative fire I have possessed for all my life.

We come to a tent along the shore deep within the lines of the enemy. The sharp affair formed of marine canvas stands square supported by long poles and taut lines extending to all sides. Guards surround it, their short javelins planted in the earth, their demeanor stone-like. At the entrance, Cyrus bids me to sit.

"We will wait here," he says, "for the arrival of your fellow Greek, Demaratus, the Spartan."

We sit in silence, Cyrus gazes into the falling darkness of the ocean.

"Do your people like the sea, Athenian?" he murmurs.

"I am a marine," I answer. "But yes, we are seafarers."

"And your gods, do you fear them?"

I hesitate, feeling for a moment a surge of homesickness, remembering both the excitement of the Panathenaic procession in the city and the humble prayers offered to Hestia around the hearth of our home.

"Some we fear, others we love, but we carry all in our hearts. I know Athena will protect me, as she looks after all."

"If there are more of your like, I will be hard-pressed to get back to my home before year's end."

"There are more like me," I reply.

He grins. "So be it."

Silence returns between us while the tent guards prepare a fire. They work with the same sense of purpose with which they stand their posts. After, when the last vestiges of Helios' chariot disappear from the twilit sky, a single torch makes its way along the beach, bobbing up and down, a lone light against the blackness of the sea and separated from the mass of movement that is the Persian army. It comes closer, a form becomes visible, illuminated in the glow of the torch. A man steps into the firelight and strides with force to where we sit.

He wears a warrior's mien, dressed not in the tunic and chiton of our kind, but rather caparisoned as a barbarian of the Persian court. His long red robes trimmed with gold hang to his ankles, and soft leather shoes cover his feet. He is older, his long hair graying yet still full. He looks at both of us, taking in my poor outfit, cuts, and defiant stare, then smiles.

"Cyrus," he inquires in a rumbling bass. "What have you dredged from the sea?"

"A gift, your lordship," replies the Persian marine, rising. "An Athenian soldier we took today off Cape Artemisium."

"It looks like he has had a poor time of it," the man replies.

"Yes, my lord, but I can guarantee you he fought like a lion possessed. There were many of my men pulled to the heavens because of him."

The man's dark bushy eyebrows raise. "Thank you, Cyrus," he replies. "I am sure you have learned much from him already concerning the enemy's dispositions?"

"No, my lord. I thought you would delight in that more than I."

"Perhaps," he says, then turns to me. "I am Demaratus, son of Ariston. Welcome to the camp of the Great king."

27

I remain silent.

He snaps his fingers toward the guard, who stands outside the tent entrance "Bring me a chair," he commands, imperious, used to being obeyed. The soldier ducks inside, emerging a moment later with a camp chair, reeking of Eastern opulence. Demaratus arranges himself on its red silk cushion. "So you have no tongue? Our marines have cut it out? A pity. We could have shared much."

Cyrus smiles.

"He can speak our language, my lord. He is...reticent."

Demaratus looks up. "Thank you, Cyrus. I will speak with him now. You may return to your vessel."

"As you wish, my lord." Cyrus bows, inclining his head and nodding as he sweeps by me, "May your gods protect you, Athenian." Then he strides into the night, his ax slapping against his hip.

Demaratus muses, "The gods, yes, the gods indeed." He leans forward in his chair. "Would you prefer we speak Greek?"

"I can speak either," I hiss. "But I fear I have nothing to say to the likes of you."

"The likes of me?" he chuckles. "And what likes are those?"

"The likes of a traitor to his people," I shoot back, "a lap dog to the barbarians." For I have heard of Demaratus, the former Spartan king, now gone over to the enemy.

His face turns to stone. "You understand little, my friend, I could have you killed where you stand right now. You would be wise to remember it."

I fight to suppress my rising anger. I unclench my fists and exhale as taught at the Kynosarges with Hippocrotes and I all ears, fidgeting at the enforced stillness of our exercises. I think of old Menilus, our doddering pedagogue. *What would he say I do now?*

The Spartan traitor notes my change. "Good, now, we can speak. What is your name?"

"Lysis, son of Androcles."

"And your home?"

"Athens."

"Ah, Athens," he breathes. "How interesting. I have heard of an Athenian named Androcles. "But my memory," he hesitates. "No, it's gone. I can not raise it. It will come to me."

I remain stone-faced.

"Well, Lysis, son of Androcles, do you know why you are here and not at the bottom of the strait as supper for the fish?"

"No," I spit. "I presume an 'honorable' man saved me."

The Spartan absorbs this with little expression. "Ah, yes. Cyrus," he hesitates "An intriguing man, Cyrus. He does tasks for me, from time to time." He leans back in the chair, crossing his arms in front, crushing the finely spun Persian robes. "Indeed, you are here because of a task assigned him," he continues. "Well, perhaps not you," he smiles. "But one like you."

I feel my body tense.

"Tomorrow, this…." He hesitates, obvious disdain crowding his features, "army goes into battle against the men holding the pass. We have marched for months around the littoral of the Aegean, supported by our fleet, as you have found, and are confident of victory. Many states have surrendered to us, and many still will. Yet, the Great king knows nothing of those whom he attacks."

"Though he has you to tell him!" I exclaim. "Have you no tongue yourself? Or are your counsels steeped in lies?"

"How very Athenian of you," Demaratus says. "Of course, the Great king listens to me. And I have had much to tell him, but I have not been home for many years, and times and alliances change. Besides, I admit I have never understood the Athenian mind, though I have journeyed to your home on occasion. You will help me understand, which will then help the Great king."

I bite my tongue, willing back my sharp rejoinder. The gods have given me this chance, for whatever reason, and I know it is better to live.

"I take by your silence, you agree?" he asks. "Good. In the morning, you will travel with me and speak of what you know to his Lordship. I fear his first lesson on Greek fighting prowess will be an instructive one."

I feel it wise to keep to myself the truth that the Persian fleet had already tasted Greek fighting prowess off Cape Artemisium, and, according to my Persian captors, were driven off.

Demaratus signals his guards, and in a moment, they hustle me away a plethron or so and chain me like a dog to a post amidst the decadence and smell of the Persian host. I lay down, exhausted, hungry, and hurt, my wounds throb, my chest bruises make it difficult to breathe. I turn my eyes to the night sky, cloudless and lit with the gleaming white from thousands of heaven's stars. *If the gods are real and live among those brilliant lights*, I think, *they have conspired to land me in this wolf's den.*

For a moment, I allow myself to bathe in self pity. But then I remember with unbearable sadness the faces of my friends and shipmates, now dead. Tears come to my eyes, and despair comes upon me like a wave. *Where was Hippocrotes now? Was he standing already on the banks of the Styx with no coin for passage? Was he a lost soul among many lost souls, alone and wailing? Where were Miretus, and Patrocles, Nocias, and so many others?* All that I had, all that I knew, gone.

Once more, my heart turns to Andronica and home. I can see her dousing the final lamps of night in the blue-columned house by the Dipylon Gate and retiring to her small room above the beautiful courtyard where the crocuses and lilies she attends to thrive. *Was she thinking of me as well? Did she know I might never come home to her again, and that my promise to her was worth no more than my father's had been to me?*

I think of our Greek warriors in the pass, blocking the only practical way of invasion into the heartland of our cities and lands, blocking the way to Andronica, to my family, to Athens. How can they hold against this vast sea of humanity, an ocean of men whose fires flicker for miles and mirror in numbers those stars above. What did I know of the Greeks who barred the way to the enemy at the pass of Thermopylae? I search my memory, and recall the loose talk that had circulated at our fires when we beached at night; the confident assertions of overwhelming force that would be brought to bear in this narrow place, where none but the slimmest could navigate; surely, however, no Athenians were among them.

In this campaign, we have seized the moment, with our fierce soldiers either on our ships or back at home. Yet, I worry that if the Greeks in the pass do not hold, what will happen to my beautiful Athens? What will happen to Andronica?

I had heard men speak, of course, of Leonidas, the great Spartan king who commands his men in the pass. And every Greek, whether Corinthian, Theban, or Athenian, knew of the fame and fearlessness of Spartan warriors. But I do not think, as Demaratus seems to, that I can understand my own people, much less the Spartans to answer such riddles as what makes them who they are; what makes them think they can hold the pass; who was this king that he could inspire them so?

And here is Demaratus, a traitor to his own. Were the Spartans then, nothing more than human— frail, and at times soft? Maybe this task is but a fool's errand, an exercise in overweening pride. "I do not know," I mutter to myself, before exhaustion overtakes me.

CHAPTER 3

Demaratus

The arrogance of the man. By all the gods, the arrogance of the lot of them! These Athenians may be Greeks, but there's a reason they're not Dorian. I should have him executed. But he may prove useful for what I have in mind. Cyrus is rarely wrong. The Athenian came to me tonight, in rags, plucked like flotsam from Poseidon's grip, his life spared by my orders but he is oozing self-righteous anger so common to his people. Where does that come from?

It has always puzzled me. They rule themselves without the benefit of discipline, without adherence to a common code or set of laws handed down from forefathers. What is civilization without the strong presence of ancestors? They are impulsive, these Athenians. Bold, it is true, but boldness without deliberation. Indeed, a nation of children. They worship at the shrine of individualism, their "collective" action stinking of vanity, of a need to appear grander, even when the whole needs to be so much greater than the sum of the parts.

And that is where my people are superior. Our Dorian ancestors set for us a code of living that created the perfect crucible to forge the unique strength of our nation. Tested through the many years of our training, those found wanting fall by the wayside. We are like iron, hard and tempered by fire. But by choice and circumstance, I am no longer part of the Spartan state, I suppose. My Spartan people are no longer "mine." I am no longer part of the flesh and blood of the Spartan state. Even in the pages of this journal, I find these truths difficult to write. But they are so.

Before we arrived in this place, Xerxes had heard from one of our scouts that the Spartans were preening themselves in front of the wall. As is our Spartan custom, the men had been combing their long hair, oiling their bodies, and exercising naked. The king called me to his side to explain these strange habits. I assured him these men were preparing to kill or be killed, and not to be fooled by either their languor or their approach. He laughed at me, as he can do when in that mood, but I wished him to know the truth. I told him if he could still laugh at the end of the day, he could have my life.

I watched Leonidas and the king's guard preparing in front of the wall two days ago. I felt again the loneliness that has been my burden these past few years. Oh, to be leading those magnificent men myself, as I was born to do!

But such has not been my fate. For the circumstances of my birth were my downfall. And to be deprived of my birthright at the moment of my entry into the world was a crueler irony than even vengeful gods could have envisioned. I sit here in barbarian excess, wishing to be somewhere else: a place and a way of life I chose, of my volition, to abandon.

But perhaps it will not be that way forever. With a victory here, this army will continue its march forward, into central Greece, through the Athenian homeland, and into the Peloponnese itself. When we come to my Spartan lands, the gods may allow me to return and claim the kingship again. The kings who shamed me and sent me away will both be gone by then. Our friend Leonidas took care of the schemer Cleomones years ago. If the gods smile on me ever again, I will feed my sword the blood of the wretched Leotychides and return to my inheritance. That is what I wish for, when I feel this way.

But there are other times I know the gods will never let me return. I listen to the young Athenian who reminds me that though my fate is mine alone, many know of my choice. And for that, there may be no forgiveness in the hearts of my countrymen. It is in those times I sense another final outcome. I will remain where I am, a prisoner of my past, a stranger to my people, and a guest to my benefactors. In that case, there is nothing more to it. I must see to the defeat of both my Spartan countrymen on this day and of all the Greeks who were my countrymen in days long ago. I must assure myself of their fall, that I will once again share their fate.

But perhaps there is another way.

Lysis

I awake to the sounds of an army coming to life. The sun has not yet risen, but the air is heavy with the promise of heat. All around me, soldiers and servants stir, commanders bark, horses neigh. I feel as if my entire body has suffered repeated beatings. Bruised and battered as I am, however, I can still feel the uneven indentations the rocky bed has ground into my back.

I moan and sit up against the thick wooden post, prying open my eyes and dragging the shackles across my lap. Looking down, I notice gashes and rents in my tunic and splotches of blood across my chest; perhaps mine, perhaps someone else's. I suppose I had been in too much shock to have taken notice the day before. But clarity is returning as the morning's pallid light presages the dawn.

I remember the night before, the haughty face of the Spartan traitor, his sharp questions, my tart retorts. I remember my last moments on *Winds*. The surprised look on the face of Hippocrotes when the ax felled him—his strange, final words: "Look in the old chest in my room." They make no sense to me and perhaps never will as the black winds of despair shred my heart.

I am the last survivor of my ship. Separated, detached— but not yet dead and buried. I wonder what the new day holds for me, even as the barbarians start their morning fires, converse in their accursed tongues, and perhaps wonder the same thing of me. The answer is not long in coming.

Demaratus

This morning was the fifth day since we arrived in front of the pass. After dawn, I found the Athenian chained to a post and left to roll in his filth. That would not do, of course. One does not see the Great king looking like a wild boar in a mudflat. "Unshackle this man. Wash him, attend to his wounds, and supply a proper tunic. Then bring him to me," I ordered the guards.

They did, and Lysis appeared in front of me once more, resentful but under control.

"Lysis, son of Androcles," I asked, "do you feel better with the morning?"

"The morning does not cast a different light on where I am."

"No, but at least you are alive to see it."

He said nothing.

"Today, Athenian, you will have the great honor of meeting the mighty Xerxes, king of Asia and commander of the vast army you see before you. I expect you will show more sense in his presence."

I motioned to the guards, and we moved toward the encampment of the king, some ways back from the shore in an open space near the high ground. As we walked along the shoreline, I could see a small portion of the fleet drawn up on the beaches across the bay. The main force still held in place by the Athenian and allied fleet based off of Cape Artemisium. I fell into deep thought, trying to find an alternative plan to offer the king.

Until and unless we dislodge their ships, we cannot force the Greeks to move. The pass is narrow, one hundred feet at its greatest width. The mountain on our right flank is impassable, begging the question: do we outflank the Athenians by sea or go right at them? But we cannot flank them. Nor can we attack the enemy on a broad front.

The king would rather not fight at all, and keep his army fed and rested. He continues to expect Leonidas to retreat in fear and wishes to let the fleet do the work, especially in these narrow quarters.

I agree. While Xerxes has not had direct experience with our Spartan way of fighting, he is wary, as he should be. It is true that the Persian forces have an immense advantage in numbers,, but the close in fighting this situation demands will favor the Spartans and their allies..

The Greeks in the pass are armored and wield eight-foot spears. The shorter lances of the king's Asian levies cannot directly engage, and their wicker shields pale against Spartan bronze. Yet, even though we outnumber them one thousand to one, we still have to fell each Spartan one at a time. And there is Leonidas, of course. They will not dislodge him. If he is there, and if he fights, it is because he means to stay.

I know this. But does the king? While he is cautious, he is confident. No, arrogant. He has brought this grand army across hundreds of miles, from the Hellespont to the Hot Gates, supported and supplied by the fleet on sea and an immensity of foot soldiers and cavalry on land. It is a formidable force. Can we be defeated? It is hard to see how. So perhaps Xerxes sees with clear eyes. Yet I know my people. Even certain death will not still their sacrifice.

With these thoughts in my head, we approached the imposing tents of the king. The Athenian held up well, taking it all in, his eyes sweeping back and forth, noting the size and composition of our forces. Despite his situation, he did not seem intimidated. Though he is the enemy, and an Athenian, I could still feel pride at his bearing. After all, he is a Greek. Besides, that name nagged at me. Androcles the Athenian. I cannot remember from where I know it, but am certain I will come to place it.

Lysis

Walking along the beach on the way to meet Xerxes, I can not see through the morning mist Cape Artemisium to my right. The Athenian fleet is there still, holding position. Even if I can not see them, I know they are there. My heart swells with a longing to be among them once again.

The enemy army is enormous. Not one of hoplites, like my people, but a mass of men armed with lances and bows and caparisoned in bright colors and odd dress, unfamiliar to my eyes. They wear long trousers that cover their legs from hip to ankle and sleeved, colorful tunics. Variegated sandals and boots of all shapes and sizes cover their feet. I also see Greeks amongst this army, or perhaps

Ionians. Sandaled and robed in short tunics, they stand out more for their armor, similar to my own. Seeing this discourages me: we had gone to war two decades ago to protect these Ionians from the depredations of the Persians. Have they forgotten? I can make out no sensible order in the throng, but they stretch along the shore and spread out over the plain to the distant mountains.

Demaratus strides in front of me. He walks as a king, yet even I can see he is not content in his place. I had detected his melancholy, even through my fear the night before. Though most in Athens pay little attention to life in Sparta, I know of this warrior. The Spartans are ruled by two kings at the same time. Demaratus had been one. Cleomones the other. Somehow, Cleomones had deposed Demaratus over a question of legitimacy. The details were hazy, but after that, Demaratus had left for Persia. I thought it the work of an angry god that he could now find himself serving the Medes. His antipathy against his Spartan brethren must have been substantial.

At the camp of the Persian king, hundreds of guards ring the mass of tents that make up his traveling court. They dress in purple tunics trimmed with red and wear tall, red, conical-shaped felt caps. Their weapons shine in the early light.

The rising morning breeze stirs a host of woven pennons. They flutter from the tent poles making up the king's quarters. Messengers hurry in and out of the large awning, which covers a group of richly dressed barbarians to our front. The group parts to reveal a low-lying table strewn with documents and maps, behind which sits the king. He is indeed an imposing sight. His long hair hangs in braided ringlets on both sides of his head, and his beard is thick, dark, and tightly wound. He wears a magnificent gold and purple box-like crown above a thick neck and powerful shoulders. Robed and trousered, the folds of his lavish golden cloth hang to the ground. All of which appear to make minimal difference to his court being held in the field. Nevertheless, he carries himself like a warrior, and one used to commanding without dissent.

Demaratus approaches and bows to the king, then acknowledges the other generals surrounding the king's table. I feel my back begin to stiffen, my throat to close. I resolve, however, to show none of this to the enemy.

Xerxes inclines his head toward Demaratus and looks beyond, fixing his gaze on me. "And what have you brought to me this morning, Demaratus, my friend?"

The Spartan glances toward me, then set his eyes back on the king. "An Athenian captured yesterday in the battle off the cape, your Highness."

"An Athenian!" replies the king, his eyes hardening. "I have a special place in my ribs for Athenians." He rises from his seat and advances in my direction as his courtiers bow before him. I draw myself as tall as I can, holding my gaze steady.

"Demaratus," he said, his eyes boring into mine, "did you make clear to this Athenian why we are here?"

"No, your highness, I did not."

"Perhaps then a lesson is in order."

The king circles me, his robes drag in the dust. I keep my eyes fixed forward, trying to calm my pounding heart.

"Athenian, we have brought this great host to the shores of your native land to avenge our honor."

I remember when Xerxes had sent his envoys to all the Greek states demanding submission and the traditional tokens of earth and water. We Athenians had shown our contempt for the summons by throwing the envoys into a pit and having them killed. I also remembered that Xerxes' father, Darius, had lost a vast army at the battle of Marathon against us ten years before. We Athenians, supported by our tiny ally Platea, had routed them, killing over ten thousand. I deem it wise, however, to heed Demaratus' warning and keep my presence respectful.

"Yes, your Highness," I reply.

"You understand? Hmmm...an Athenian with knowledge, how unusual. You must know then that we will not spare Athens. We will lay waste to your city, your lands, and your people. We will leave nothing for even the crows to fight over. Even should we let you live, Athenian, you will have nothing to go home to."

I turn my head and face the Great king of all Asia. "Yes, my lord. I know that. But I also know that we will resist you to the best of our strength."

Xerxes' face reddens with fierce anger. "Demaratus!" he yells. "Why did you bring this insolent hyena in front of me? Bind him! Take him to the sea and feed him to Poseidon!"

Soldiers seize me by my legs and begin dragging me away. I can feel my wounds opening again, and the pain from them makes me gasp.

Demaratus, steps forward and addresses the king. "Your majesty," he speaks softly, casting his eyes downward so not to offend. "I had thought to have this Athenian for the work we had spoken of earlier. He is suitable...perfect...for the task. Time is of meaning here. I beg of you my glorious king, might you come to a different mind?"

Xerxes' demeanor shifts as fast as wind appears in a desert storm. He stops his raging and steadies a cold stare on Demaratus. "As you wish it," and turns to the soldiers. "Release him." Xerxes moves his gaze past Demaratus and onto his courtiers, all of whom bow in fear before him.

The soldiers release me and thrust me forward to stand behind Demaratus while Xerxes arranges his robes and seats himself once more behind his map table. Glancing up at Demaratus, he asks, "What is the name of this Greek?"

"Lysis, son of Androcles," replies Demaratus.

From behind the king, my eyes catch a startled movement as a fierce, pug-nosed, short, muscled warrior lurches forward, spilling his wine onto the king's robe.

"Fool!" snaps Xerxes. "Do you wish to take his place at the bottom of the sea?"

"My Lord," the man stammers. "My life is not worthy. A thousand begs for your mercy."

"A thousand?" screams Xerxes.

"Ten thousand begs for your mercy. My Lord, this man, this Androcles the Athenian—"

"For ten thousand I will not have you beheaded where you stand! This counsel is over. We attack as planned." With a ferocious wave of his hand, he dismisses the gathering. They bow, retreating before his winds shift; the fierce warrior sears me with fiery eyes.

Demaratus

The young Athenian almost got himself killed. And what was that matter with Medarnes? He acted like he had seen a ghost. It was that name again, Androcles. I must remember to ask him about it when I get the chance. Xerxes put the fear of Hades in him though! That was a royal sight. It is disgusting how these men debase themselves before him, but it is the Persian way. Yet again, it is understood that people who displease the king disappear. They seem to be competent enough, except for all of that. It is not the Spartan way, of course. It appears the king has realized the truth about Leonidas. The Spartans will not leave. Now we will see.

I dragged Lysis away from the encampment and held my temper in check. Due to his outburst, I did not have the opportunity to brief the king on what I intend to do with this man. It will have to wait until later in the day. I knew, however, that the king was to inspect the Greek positions before the assault was launched, and so I will speak with him then.

"Lysis," I said, "Do you have a death wish? Are you so slow-witted that you cannot take good advice?"

"No, but I am my own man. Xerxes can kill me. You can kill me. But I make that choice, not you."

"Well, indeed, you almost chose your end," I replied, growing irritated. "Hear my words Athenian, today we will attack the pass with a great chance of success. Many will die, including many of my countrymen. I would prevent that if I could."

Lysis seemed wary. "You would prevent that? Do you not wish for it?"

"I wish for victory, not for death. We hold here because we await the retreat of the defenders of the pass. We hope the sight of this army will persuade them to leave."

"It seems that you would know far more than I about that likelihood."

"That is true. I doubt Leonidas will leave unless he has good reason. I intend to give him that reason."

Lysis was intrigued. "Why do you speak to me of this? I am but a feather in your fan. And I will not betray the land of my fathers."

"I will not ask you to. I only wish you to deliver a message to Leonidas, a message from me, Demaratus. He will understand the contents."

Lysis paused for a moment, studying me. "I am not worthy to stand before Leonidas. Another more brave than I can present your message to the great king."

"That is not so," I replied. "I do not know of another. I have vowed that this tablet will be guarded, that it will not be dishonored. I need a man who will die rather than betray his word."

"Sire, why do dare think I am that man? I could run away once I am safe within Leonidas' lines."

"You will not because you are a man of honor. You are here and alive because Cyrus believed so. I see that in your steady chin, in your shoulders held wide. You will deliver my message and return to me and I will ensure your safety. That is the bargain. Will you take this oath?"

Lysis paused, holding a firm stare onto my eyes, and then, "I will."

Lysis

The sun is halfway up the morning sky by the time Xerxes and his generals arrange themselves on a rise near the mountain face to view the Greeks' positions. As I wait for Demaratus to offer his counsel to the king, I see him point to me several times, and then to the blocked pass. It is a lengthy gathering. Several of the king's aides attempt to speak, but the king appears impatient and dismissive. He grabs the wax tablet from Demaratus and reads it. He then snaps it shut before handing it back to him. The pug-nosed warrior I had seen earlier says nothing, but turns his eyes to me.

My father's name, Androcles, means something to him, and to the king. Something unpleasant. I will have to be careful.

Demaratus breaks from the group and strides toward me. He looks pleased. Sending my guards out of earshot, he says, "Athenian, I have arranged for you to carry a message from myself to Leonidas. It is in this wax tablet. You will also take this." He produces a scroll of rolled papyrus sealed with the king's mark. "It is Xerxes' last demand that the enemy give up the pass."

"That is also in your letter?" I ask.

"What is in my letter is for Leonidas alone. You need only do two things. Deliver the letter to him. And tell him this from me: 'Gorgo's way will turn the key.'"

"Gorgo's way will turn the key?"

"Yes. Tell him and observe his face for secrets he does not wish to reveal."

I agree, curious, and ecstatic to leave the claws of these barbarians. There is no lack of want to escape. I feel immense temptation to disregard Demaratus' confidence in my honor and stay on the Greek side of the pass at the first opportunity. But honor is a concept dear to our family, and I know I must return.

While we talk, the Persian forces gather in their ranks to begin the assault. They shout commands in their barbaric tongue and whip lines of infantry into position. Rows of archers and slingers take positions behind the initial wave of spearmen. It is frightening, and also a spectacle of beauty. I can not help but notice that enthusiasm did not fire the men in these first columns. In their strange trousers, knee- and wrist-length tunics, wicker shields, conical helmets, and short spears, they do not jabber among themselves or emanate the proud spirit of an undefeated force. Instead, they appear nervous, hesitant to face their enemy.

Demaratus notices my gaze. "Medians and Cessians," he says. "Not the king's best troops, but he prays they will be sufficient."

"And what do you think?"

The Spartan turns, fixing me with an intense gaze. "We will see," he replies. "Now, get on your way."

I need no further prodding. Escorted by several of Demaratus' guards, I leave the forming crowd. There is order now, though the whole affair seems far more chaotic than I am used to in preparing for battle outside the walls of Athens or on the decks of *Winds*. As I brush by the lead troops, their strange, deep and musky smell overwhelms me. Sweat pours from every bearded face, soaking every colored tunic.

But in their ranks, I sense something else, too. The scent of fear. That was a scent I remember well. It gives me satisfaction and makes me realize, as if for the first time, that this mass, while large and intimidating, is made up of mere men after all. They are not invincible. We pass through the last few ranks, the soldiers parting to the shouted commands of my guards, and in a few moments, I stand between the warring bodies. To my front, the familiar phalanx formation of our kind stands awaiting the Persian assault. I can now see for myself where the fear originates.

The Spartans form the majority of the battle line, their distinctive scarlet cloaks and Lambda-painted shields exude a gallant aura. They stand shield overlapping shield, their right hands gripping a forest of brightly pointed spears that glisten against the blue sky. They are backed by Tegeans and Mantineans, who stand proud and tall, perhaps growing in spirit with their proximity to the long-haired Spartans. I can see Theban plumes and shields also where the high stone wall meets the sea, a square-faced tower that bristles with archers. As I move further through the Persian's ranks, I recall again how terrifying it is to rush such an assemblage. The Corinthian bronze helmets of the warriors cover all but their eyes and nose, and their tall horsehair plumes make them all appear well over six feet. Giants, they seem. I had trained for this way of war. But what must the Persians be feeling?

Silence settles across the plain as I approach the line.

"Come no further, Persian!" a voice booms. "What say you?"

I look to the left in the direction of the voice. A man steps from the center of the line and swings towards me. Hair flecked with gray streams from his helmet and stirs in the morning sea breeze. Yet as he comes closer, his eyes glint, hard and unyielding. He stops a few feet from me.

"Speak!" he demands.

"I am not Persian. I am an Athenian marine, captured yesterday in the sea battle off of the cape. I have personal messages for king Leonidas from Xerxes and Demaratus, the Spartan. I am here on my honor to return to the Persian camp. Where may I find the king?"

"You have found him," he says. "Your guards remain where they are. Come with me."

Leonidas turns and leads me through a line of stolid hoplites who part as he approaches, eight ranks deep and bristling with their eight-foot iron-tipped cornel wood spears. We stop near the wall, and I find myself surrounded by his protective guard of red-cloaked warriors.

Leonidas removes his gleaming bronze helmet— one of the old style Corinthians, the ones with room for the ears to hear. A helmet like my own, like my father's. He reveals a handsome face marred by a crooked nose, broken perhaps in some fight in years past. His rugged cheeks and square jaw bear long wear and many worries. His piercing grey eyes gaze upon me, noting my fresh slashes. "What is your name, son?"

I draw myself up, once again in the presence of royalty, yet I cannot help but note the difference in my spirit. "Lysis, son of Androcles."

"And you were with the fleet?"

"Yes, your Highness. The enemy captured my ship yesterday and slew the entire crew."

Leonidas nods. "The tears of many mothers will fall with this news. Tell me of the battle on the sea?"

I feel the escort all around the king lean forward to hear. "I am not certain, sire. We were overrun, but from what the Persians have said, I think we were victorious. I think we can hold as long as necessary."

I can sense a collective sigh.

"We yearn for good favor from the glorious gods. Now, what is your message?"

I hand him both Xerxes' papyrus scroll and Demaratus' wax tablet. He breaks the seal on the scroll first and moves further away for solitude, back toward the wall, where he reads it.

"Hmm," he breathes. "It seems the Great king offers us our lives in return for our surrender." He looks around at his sentries. "What say you men? A fair trade?" Laughter and grim smiles greets this remark. "Indeed," says the king. "These Persians are mighty warriors. Some say their archers are so many, their arrows block out the sun."

"That may be true, your highness," I blurt out. "I saw at least ten thousand lined up behind these troops you see in front."

There are low whistles that greet my report, and I can see heads turn and look at one another.

"Well then," a voice interjects, "so much the better. We will fight them in the shade!"

The king leads the laughter this time. "Dieneces," he says. "As usual, you do yourself and your city honor! Let us see what shade the morning brings! Now, Lysis, what of this other message?"

I join in the general laughter, all the while feeling my heart lighten. These men were every bit as courageous as their reputation had told. They bear no scent of fear.

"It comes from Demaratus, your highness. He says to tell you 'Gorgo's way will turn the key.'"

The king pauses, looking at me. "He said that?"

"Yes, your highness."

"Give me a moment, then." He opens the tablet, reads the lines in the wax, and reaches to his sword belt to remove a wrought iron dagger. Taking the knife, he begins at the top of the tablet and scrapes away the layer of wax, shards falling to the sand at his feet. When finished, he replaces the dagger and stares at the wooden face of the tablet.

"Interesting," he says. "An interesting proposition."

Raising his eyes to his now-quiet companions, Leonidis strokes his chin, deep in thought. Slamming the tablet shut and handing it to me, he says, "Lysis, I will not write you a response. Say this to Demaratus. 'It is not in my power to do as you suggest. Were it so and it were happier times, perhaps it could be different. May the gods protect all the Spartans.'"

"Yes, your highness," I reply. "I will deliver him your message."

"As for Xerxes," he smiles, "We will deliver him the answer ourselves."

Turning then, he replaces his helmet and leads me back through the line. As he passes the men in the ranks, they acknowledge his presence with raised hands, nodding heads, and eyes that glint adoration. He returns their affection, calling out their individual names and exhorting them to stand tall on this day. We come to the front rank, and he offers his hand.

"Now Lysis, be off. May we meet again." He fixes me with his sturdy grip, his eyes bore into mine. "You have done well," he says. "The gods have saved you for some special task. They will give you a chance once more to serve your country."

I bow, overcome with emotion. Then I turn and make my way back across the silent plain, with the Persian guards at my flank.

CHAPTER 4

Lysis

Walking back toward the Persian forces seems the longest journey of my short life. Only moments before, I had been in the presence of a true leader of men. I had been embraced and found worthy within eye blinks of my arrival, without knowing how. It just was. Leonidas had, by his presence, drawn from me my natural nobility. He had reminded me of all that was valuable in my being.

I approach the enemy line with a heavy heart, knowing I can do nothing to help my true king or his brave soldiers. An ordinary man or army could not stop Xerxes and his troops. Leonidas, however, seems as no ordinary man, nor was the aura of strength that glows from his men an ordinary spirit. Perhaps miracles can happen. Perhaps the gods wish it so. I do not know. I only know my role as a prisoner, a spectator. I would be as I had been during my journey to Olympia to watch the games there: an observer of supreme effort in an atmosphere of unbridled truth and passion.

Demaratus waits for me behind the lines. He seems to know the answer without me uttering a single word.

"What was his reply?" he asks.

"He will fight."

He nods. "And to what I sent?"

I tell him of the king's response. He appears for a moment to shrink, to shed for but a breath his upright mien and assume the years of his life. He straightens and, letting his gaze stray toward the allied line, places his hand on the hilt of his sword.

"Be it so. I will tell Xerxes." He turns on his heel and strides to the Persian king, who awaits him on the rise. I follow, unsure of what to do but not wishing to stand alone amidst an attacking force. I can see Xerxes' angry gestures to his commanders, and them rushing off, ordering their army forward. In the press, as I approach the hill, I catch sight of Pug Nose and my sense of unease sharpens. He had been watching me, and he is agitated. Under the full sky in the light of day, it appears to me that his dislike has darkened to hatred. When he sees me looking at him, it is as though any bonds that tied him to inaction burst asunder. He lurches forward, hand on his sword, vitriol coalescing on his broad forehead.

Several men seize me at that moment. They shove me through the advancing troops. Someone in the crowd jeers at me, yet other men interpose themselves between the two of us, as a wave of troops surge forward. I can see pug nose, pinioned and restrained and can hear his howls of frustration as my captors drag me away. They keep me moving until I am near the shore and a distance both from Medarnes and from Demaratus. When they loosen their grip, they set me in front of a Persian courtier of some magnificence. Though his dress and attitude seem Asian, his face, lined, scarred, and battered seems somehow familiar.

Demaratus

Leonidas' response was, I suppose, to be expected. Still, I had hoped he would see reason. But it is not over. Nevertheless, I need to be careful. I must ensure the contents of that message remain as they are now: unknown in this camp.

Today was one for the scribes. After the Athenian returned and I gave Xerxes the Greek's reply, his anger ignited. At once, he ordered the attack. The first of our Persian troops surged forward as a sky full of arrows descended on the upright shields of Leonidas and his defenders. It was a classic Persian assault and a classic hoplite defense. The problem for our side was the narrowness of the pass. As I had warned Xerxes, on such a narrow front, we could not take adequate advantage of our numbers.

The Greeks wielded their spears with methodical and brutal efficiency. I could see the constant, almost rhythmic, up and down thrusting of the eight-footers. They mowed our troops down like a scythe gathering the harvest. The onslaught of our bows paused while our forces were engaged, and when they were driven off, the hoplites raised their four-foot shields and deflected most of the shafts. The war raged like this all day, assault after assault launched against the line. I could see, in the interval, fresh troops rotating from the gate in the Phocian wall, replacing the exhausted Greeks who had begun the battle. The wall had been built by the Phocians to protect themselves from the depredations of their neighbors in Locris. On this day it was serving a deadlier purpose. Leonidas, it appeared, was using his resources wisely.

The Medians and Cissians fell by the scores. Seeing our attacks not gaining headway, the Great king ordered my closest friend, Hydarnes, to his side. Hydarnes commanded the famous "Immortals," the bravest of our army. Xerxes ordered Hydarnes forward, hoping his magnificent warriors would bring an end to the enemy. I had known Hydarnes for the last ten years, and had never seen him this concerned. As he passed me, he paused for a moment. "Demaratus," he said, "these Spartans of yours fight well. I will have to pay closer attention to your incredible stories."

Upright, proud, and brave, the Immortals moved forward, a mass of disciplined infantry. I was awed by the sight. They would face the same brutality as their predecessors, but I thought perhaps their spirit would push Leonidas from his position. They stepped over the bodies of the men who had gone before, charging to the fore. But they had no better fortune. Though Hydarnes' men engaged with power, pushing into the Greek line, the battle soon resumed its former course; however, it was the king's best troops now doing the bleeding..

The Greeks then feigned retreat and opened a gap between the forces. Sensing victory, our troops rushed in disorder to finish the assault, only to find Leonidas' disciplined phalanx execute an about-face and effect a horrific slaughter. I rushed forward and tried to make our officers understand the fate that awaited, but it seemed they became mad with blood lust and grief and would not listen to reason, and certainly not from a Spartan. So I waited, and I watched. I saw with admiration and envy the way Leonidas commanded his troops, being at all times in the center of the fight, his distinctive red-and-white-striped plume dancing back and forth as he led his men time and again into the press of battle. Their spears broke, their swords nicked and dulled, and new ones appeared. Their men fell. They bled. They died. But through it all, Leonidas rallied and fired commands, willing his men to push ahead, husbanding his strength to become their strength as well.

We, on the other hand, were extravagant with our troops. At first, they charged the fearsome Greek line with commendable bravery. However, as our losses mounted and our attacking forces were made to climb over piles of our dead, courage turned to hesitance; hesitance turned to fear; and fear, as it is wont to do, spilled over into mulishness. As the sun dipped over the mountains, Xerxes ordered the final assaults by whipping our men into the fray.

They obeyed, cursing their officers, but they obeyed. They hurled themselves into the fight like cornered animals, snarling and caught between two hells, only to be impaled as if by the horns of wild boars. It was a shameful waste of men. But to the Great king, warriors were like the sands of the shore— countless, endless, and with no cost. During the course of the day, Xerxes sprang from his seat at least three times, by my count. Whether it was anger, frustration, or anguish he was feeling, I could not tell.

As night fell, it was over. The Immortals withdrew. The Greek line remained unbroken. The bodies of our slain lay piled high in the sand. In the west, the sun's last rays glinted on the horizon, and the sea lapped the shore, polluting its waters with the blood of the fallen.

Lysis

"You are Lysis, the Athenian, son of Androcles, are you not?" asks the scarred Persian.

We stand by the shoreline, waves rolling at our feet. I hear the cheers of the Medians as they move to the attack beneath the merciless sun. My questioner wears his grey hair cropped short exposing his sharp and hooded eyes. His lips hold a bitter twist, perhaps drawn to that look by the two deep and unpleasant scars that run across his face from ear to nose. His commanding presence speaks of a life accustomed to power and its exercise.

"I am. And you sir?"

"That is for another time. For now, it is sufficient that you are safe." His Greek is perfect, with even the distinctive Ionian lilt of a native Athenian.

"Safe? Of what concern is my safety to you?"

"Concern enough." For a moment, I think I can see a flicker of emotion ripple across his scarred visage before he continues: "Soon you will be in great danger here. And not because you are a prisoner of the king."

"I am a prisoner of no mortal."

"You do not understand. The man who came at you as you were being brought here—"

"Yes."

"He would kill you if he could."

"As would many others."

He hesitates, stroking his cleft chin. "He believes you are the son of a man he has reason to hate."

"He is mistaken. My father was Athenian and died when I was young."

"Did he?" his lips curl in a tight smile. "And who raised you up from boy to man?"

"My mother raised me in my uncle's house," I say, irritated. "What is this to you?"

He turns and strolls up the beach for a moment as the sounds of battle begin to roar in the background. "This man who hates you, his name is Medarnes," he continues, facing me once more. "He believes your father killed his father many years ago in a fight over land on which they both wanted to grow harvests."

51

I am distracted by the noise and begin to feel faint as the sun climbs toward midday, heating my injured body like coals for forging swords. Even so, the Persian's insistence demands my attention. "Unless this Medarnes was a metic and settled in Athens for a time, what you say cannot be possible."

"There is much you do not know about your family," he replies, ignoring the screams of the wounded that now fill the air. He pauses and searches my face. "You have eyes that like those of the woman in whose womb you grew. I can see her in you," he says, then spins and paces the shore again.

"Follow me," he says over his shoulder.

Surrounded by his guards, I fall in alongside, my heart pounding. What did this man know of my father? How did he know of my mother? We walk in silence for a few minutes, as the din of battle carries its screams through the air. Just as Leonidas had promised, he is giving Xerxes his answer.

"How much do you know of your father?" he says, breaking the silence.

"Only morsels, I suppose. I have been told by my mother and uncle he was a wealthy man. My family owned large estates north and east of the city. They grew olives and grapes. My father had some influence in the city."

He seems to pause in his step. I look over. His visage is stern, his eyes far away.

"And how did he die?" he asks.

"My uncle told me he died at sea. He was on a trading visit to the East..." My voice trails off. I remember my mother's anguish and the sorrow in the house the day we received the news. I was eight years old.

The Persian notices my distraction. "What happened after that?"

"The state seized our lands and estates. My mother told me Father owed people a great deal of money. My uncle took us in after that."

Eyebrows raised, he allows a grim smile to form. "That is what you believe?"

"That...and, other things," I reply. Memories crowd my mind's vision, images of flailing fists and bitter words. "Traitor's boy, traitor's boy!" playmates' taunting jibes rang in my ears. I shut them out again, slamming the door on the past as I had done so many times before.

"Did you know my father?" I ask, forcing my sight to leave my mind and onto the man before me.

He stops and turns. "Yes," he pauses. "I knew your father, and your mother."

I let out an involuntary gasp. "How? When?"

"We were partners in harvesting grapes for wine. I spent a great deal of time with your father."

I am stricken with a flood of emotions. What was happening? Could the gods, as Leonidas had said, be leading me on a path of their design?

"This surprises you, then?"

"Of course!" I sputter. "I had no knowledge of my father trading with the Persians."

"Times were different back then. Your father had alliances with many people. You speak Persian, Lysis?"

"I do, not well. I understand what is said and can make myself understood."

"And where did you learn it? Not from your father?"

"No, I grew up with a boy who taught me. His family traded with the East." I think then of my friend lost to afterlife, his body a mass of arrows, slipping into the sea. My stomach spasms and once again, the blackness descends. "His name was Hippocrotes."

"Ah," grunted the Persian, his body tenses. "And when did you meet this boy?"

I am puzzled. What did this matter? "I met him at the Kynosarges gymnasium when I was ten or so."

He pauses again, and then adds under his breath, "Ten years ago."

"Where is this boy now?" he probes.

"Dead," I reply. "He was killed in battle only a day ago."

He turns back toward the sea, and I see his shoulders relax. "I am sorry. There is much you should know of your father, but now is not the time. It is sufficient that Medarnes is no longer in a position to harm you. I'm sure he is engaged in battle at this moment. Perhaps he will not survive. Besides, I would wager that you will be with us for seasons."

It is maddening, this refusal to give me news. "This Medarnes, what does he think happened with my father? Does he have reason to hate me?"

"He has reason. But now we must get you back to the Spartan. He will be worrying where his prize messenger has gone."

Demaratus

I have returned from the war council. The king was in a terrible mood, and the experience was like a jackass' kick to my head. Our losses were heavy from the day's fighting. Hydarnes reports over two thousand casualties amongst the Immortals alone, but he will make up that loss. They are known as the Immortals because their numbers never vary—there is always another to take the place of the slain.

Nevertheless, we face an intractable problem. Word from the fleet also is not good. We lost many ships in a storm off the island of Euboea, after they tried to sail up behind the Greek vessels. We will get no relief from our fleet. The Greeks continue to deny us the opportunity to flank them from the sea. Our scouts in the mountains report of no merciful gods in their attempts to find ways around to Leonidas' rear. Thus, our only course of action is the same each day: a frontal assault.

We learned a few things, though. We will be wary of Leonidas' fake retreats. Also, if we give them no rest, they will find it harder to rotate in fresh men. We killed many of theirs today, no doubt of that. The king asked what I thought, though the others seemed resentful of my presence. It is as if after ten years, they are just noticing I am a Spartan. I told him I believe the Greek force in the pass to have between three and five thousand men with few

Spartans among them. Perhaps, save the king's guard, I suggested three hundred total, maybe, plus their supporting Helots. But that is enough to hold us for quite a while, especially if they are receiving any reinforcements from the landward side.

I repeated my assertion, made some days prior, that we would be wise try to work our way around the Greek fleet and land on the Peloponnese where we would be more threatening to Sparta. With that threat, I reasoned, the Spartans would have to focus on defending their homeland and leave the defense of Northern Greece to less able soldiers. But I was shouted down again by the court's counselors. Even after today, the council still believes they can beat Leonidas here, at the pass. Alas, they lose sight of the treasure. We must divide to conquer. What we do now unites.

And so, tomorrow, we will attack again head on. We will try to keep the pressure on, even more so than today, and give Leonidas no relief. Maybe it will work. It is a strategy. Yet, is it the best one? I think not.

When I returned to my tent, Medarnes approached me. He had been in the thick of it. "The Greek son of a whore slashed right through my shield and cut me across my shield arm!" he said, waving a bandaged limb "I sent him to hell though. Went right under and took out his legs. This one was not wearing greaves."

He spoke, still as intense as a viper, coiled tight from the stress of battle, yet, I am sure he later slept the drugged sleep of the victor over death on this day. And he had something else troubling him.

"This Athenian of yours, this son of Androcles, what do you know of him?"

I continued walking, looking out to sea. "He is a prisoner, captured by the navy. He has been forthcoming in his knowledge of the enemy and helpful in the exchange of messages. There is little else I know. Why do you ask?"

"Do you not recognize the name, Androcles the Athenian?" he asked, the agitation evident in his face.

"There is something to his name. I cannot place it."

Medarnes stepped back, stomping his foot hard on the sand. "You, above all men, should know! You knew my father! Androcles was one of the Greeks who came seeking aid from Darius!" He ran his hand through his oiled and blood-smeared hair. "The Great king, as was his decision, gave land and money to these exiles," he snorted.

Yes, I remembered. There it was. It was after I had arrived in the king's court. There was a party of Athenians, oligarchs who had been run out of Attica, and like the former Athenian tyrant Hippias before them, had come to the Great king seeking vengeance. Darius, always the diplomat, had set them up, as he did me, biding his time and waiting for the right moment to strike the Greek homeland and add another nation to the empire.

Darius' expedition, launched ten years earlier, had failed when the Athenians routed us on the field of Marathon. We exiles have had to wait until now to regain Greek soil. Yes, I remembered Androcles. A handsome man, proud of bearing. A natural leader. If Lysis was his son, I could see the resemblance. "I remember, Medarnes, but why should I know better than anyone?"

"Because you are Greek as well!" he exclaims. "And because it was your land for which they killed my father!"

I was still not seeing his mind. "My land? What say you?"

Medarnes looked exasperated, his pushed-in face grew darker. "It was Androcles the Athenian who claimed rights to hectares of my father's land. Land Androcles swore the Great king had given him," Medarnes raged. "My father had been told by the king to give that land to you, another Greek! And so, to defend his honor and that of his family crest, my father went to visit this Androcles. He never came back. We found him in a ditch near the home of the Athenian." Medarnes became incoherent with remembered grief and anger. "When we went for … looking for… the Greek dog, the bastard spawn of Angra Mainyu… I would have sliced his throat with my knife…but he was nowhere to be found, such a coward of the dark."

"Are you sure Androcles killed him?" I ask.

"Yes!" Medarnes cried. "Who else had reason? And if he did not, why did he seek refuge in hiding?"

He had insight I agree, but I resent his suggestion that all Greeks were somehow related and culpable. Besides, I had no memory of a land deal, and up until that moment, no memory of Androcles. Lysis had proven useful to me thus far, and I am, loathe to give up a useful person.

"Medarnes," I offered, "if the stars have spoken to you of this, bring it to the king. I'm sure he will have his court hear you."

"The king is busy, and not to be disturbed," he retorted.

I decided this discussion had to end. "Medarnes, I know nothing more of this son of Androcles, and the issue is not mine. Save your personal quarrels for better times."

I left Medarnes fulminating in my wake, I made my way back to the tent, where I found Lysis waiting, guarded by two warriors bearing the mark of the king's secret sentries.

Lysis

Scarface's revelations concerning my father are spinning in my brain as Demaratus approaches his tent. Persian guards had escorted and held me there since leaving Scarface's presence. They seem a tough lot, their apparel coarser than the king's guard and their manners thuggish. They have said nothing to me, even ignoring my periodic questions.

All through the day, I wait in the shade of the Spartan's awning and keep a wary eye out for Medarnes, who seems to have reason to kill me. I can not understand why, which makes my situation even more precarious. Demaratus, it appears, was all over the encampment and does not return until nightfall.

With the incredible carnage of the battle mere yards away, it is enough for me to avoid the troops moving toward it and the screaming wounded carried away from it. From the Spartan's tent, I can see much, but not all, of what has transpired.

The Spartans and allied soldiers in the pass have made me proud. I remember Leonidas' spoken truth. One solid unit, undeterred by the Persian masses, stood united in their clear vision to keep Xerxes out of the pass and out of Greece. I wait for word of the triumph over the enemy, or of King Leonidas' men falling. But none comes. It is excruciating to wait, and again, my memory is carried to faraway Olympia.

I had gone there with Hippocrotes four years before, as part of a troop of Kynosarges boys intent on experiencing for ourselves the wonder of the greatest athletic and religious festival in the Greek world. The experience had been awe inspiring. Olympia itself is a sanctuary, not a town. The town of Elis administers it, and the Eleans maintain a jealous control. When we arrived, after the games opened, the place was a madhouse. Tens of thousands inundated the countryside, camping in the open, filling the local inns, denuding the area of food and water, soiling the streams, and pouring into the arena daily. We followed the crowds and let ourselves get jostled, pushed, and shoved, lost in the excitement of the multitudes. They came from all over the world, these visitors to the Olympic games. They dressed as pilgrims and sporting fanatics—some arrived to worship Zeus in the sanctuary of the Altis; some intended to witness feats of athletic prowess.

It was intoxicating. On the first day, we swept by the Altis and past the sacred altar, lost in the press of the crowd. The smells of roasting meat, of horses, of men—the perfumed and the unwashed—overcame me. Flies, insects, and all manner of biting creatures filled the air, swarming around the open cesspits and driving the meat vendors to distraction. With little water to bathe and the hot sun burning overhead, dirt, sweat, and grime accumulated in every one of my bodily crevices, soon emitting a reek more familiar in the lower reaches of Athens than in the sanctuary of the great god. Despite the discomfort, despite the noise, the dust, and the smell, the palpable spirit of excitement charged my senses of adventure, possibility, and life.

The athletes moved above all of this. We could see them through the crowd, gliding by in their fine-spun tunics, grasping their strigils, olive oil bottles, and sponges, and slipping into the changing areas erected near the rear of the stadium. They would emerge later, their naked bodies glistening, oiled and dusted, and they would stretch, bounce, and preen, focused on the contest to come. I remember seeing the legions of admirers crowding outside the changing area, some to catch a closer glimpse of a particular hero, some to admire every aspect of their naked forms, others to seek the strigil-scraped debris sometimes hawked by the athletes' trainers.

Menilus, our Kynosarges pedagogue, shoved us away from the fawning crowd and hustled us toward the finish area of the running races, near the Hellanodikai, the judges for the games. They sat in their high-backed chairs behind their wood and stone rail fence, separated by authority and position from the pressing horde. We perched a plethron or so behind them, straining to catch a glimpse through the masses that lined the grassy bowl of the arena.

We had arrived early for the heats of the stade, and I remembered watching the runners preparing themselves, sprinting by in their warm-up routines, yet showing breathtaking speed. A horn blared, and an official of the Hellanodikai stood and raised a red flag, ordering the runners to the start. They responded, moving to the far end two hundred paces away and lining up along the balbis. They swung their arms and sprinted in place until ordered to take their positions by an official who waved another flag on the near side of the balbis. Gripping the stone with their toes and leaning with eyes and heads forward, they focused on the finish. After a moment of silence, came the shrill cry from a trumpet signaling the starting command, and the drop of the flag. Runners fired from the start, hurling themselves down their lanes. The crowd rose as one, willing their favorites to victory, the noise of their encouragement deafening.

Yes, I remember that, and remember the thoughts that filled my head. I had the fervent desire to be one of them, to be a runner on that line attuned to the hope of victory and the adoration of the crowd. But I was not. I was a spectator, and a boy, far away from that Olympic dream.

That is how I feel now under Xerxes's charge, watching the Spartans and their allies battle the enemy. Helpless, proud, wishing I was part of Leonidas' troops and part of our land's defense. Toward evening, when the Persian attack wanes, Demaratus returns, looking harried and in ill-temper.

He seems surprised to find me there, or perhaps surprised to find the presence of Scarface's guards. Either way, he approaches me with a different attitude.

"Lysis, we will speak now."

He trods past me standing outside and goes into his tent, then lifts the flap and motions me inside. He gives a curious look at Scarface's guards but says nothing. It seems a year since we had last spoken, but it is only one day. His servants had lit oil lamps, and the tent glows with their soft, undulating light. Seating himself behind his fine rosewood camp desk, he eyes me.

"How did you come to be guarded by these men?" His voice has an edge to it— not fear, but concern. I tell him the tale of what had happened that day, including Scarface's knowledge of my father. He listens, never interrupting but nodding in several places. When I finish, he gets up and paces the tent floor.

"It seems, Lysis, you have become quite important." He pauses, stroking his full, graying beard. "To some interesting and well placed people." He faces me, clasps his hands behind his back, and fixes me with a penetrating stare.

"Do you know the name of the man you met today?"

"I do not. He never told me."

"His name is Phraortes," says the Spartan. "He is the commander of a division of the king's secret sentries and in charge of most of Egypt, as well as the subject cities in that region."

"He speaks almost like a native Athenian," I say.

"Yes, there are many rumors concerning Phraortes' origin," replies Demaratus. "The Egyptians have reason to speculate—"

"On what he is doing here," I interrupt.

Demaratus straightens, as if surprised once again at my boldness. "Xerxes has brought these men along to sniff out potential rebellion in the conquered areas. Harvest the grains before the beetles, as it were. We do the same in Sparta. We train our best to seek out and eliminate those among the Helots who might incite revolt."

"But why is he interested in me?" I ask, pressing.

"I do not know. Did he confirm how your father died?"

"No, he said they were farming partners."

The Spartan continues to pace, passing a wrought bronze breastplate that hung on a post by the main tent pole. He strokes the twin centaurs that graced its face. "Well, there is a mystery here. You seem to have made a powerful friend if that is what he is to you. It is not many who can say that of the 'Butcher of Egypt.'"

"The Butcher of Egypt?" I cry. "This man is *that* Phraortes?"

"Yes, the same," he confirmed. "The people of Egypt have every reason to fear him and every reason to want him dead."

I recall what I had heard about Persian dealings in Egypt and also in the Ionian cities under their control during the previous 15 years. When the Egyptians had revolted against their Persian masters, the punishment had been brutal and uncompromising. Thousands had been killed or sold into slavery. The name of Phraortes had been on everyone's lips. I feel sick inside. How could my father have been dealing with the likes of this man?

Demaratus notes my reaction. "You must be careful, Lysis. I can protect you because you are useful to me, but it bodes ill for you to be caught in this new web, whether large or small." He walks to the tent entrance. "I will dismiss your guards. You will stay by my tent tonight."

He moves to the tent entrance, opens the flap, and speaks to Scarface's guards. They withdraw, looking back. The Spartan returns.

"Demaratus," I say.

"Yes?"

"What of Medarnes?"

Demaratus moves to his chair, sitting down with a sigh. "Medarnes believes your father cheated his family of land and killed his own father while doing it."

"This makes no sense!" I say. "My father was never in Persia."

"Maybe he was, maybe he was not. Either way, it would be best to make the gods happy. I will try to do so. You keep away from him."

He takes me to the tent door and, calling his men, has me led away to an adjoining awning. I will at least sleep in relative comfort this night. As I leave, however, I feel sure the Spartan king is not telling me all he knows.

Demaratus

As I watched Lysis go, I thought how sad it is that the truth can often take second place to some quick potion for relief. I wonder what he would think of his father if my suspicions were confirmed. What worries me more than anything right now, however, is Phraortes' proximity.

After I dismissed Phraortes' guards, Phraortes himself appeared in the entryway. It is eerie, both the reputation and the reality of this man. I have seen many ugly men, but no one sends a chill up my spine like Phraortes. He is not everywhere, though he seems to be.

"Demaratus," he pronounced in a voice dripping with ill-disguised hostility that belied his words. "It is always my pleasure. I see you have been entertaining our Athenian prisoner." He strode around the tent, pausing to inspect my hoplite armor, the weaponry I always take with me on campaigns. I may be dressed as a Persian, but should the time come, I will fight as a Greek.

"What did he tell you?" he inquired, slipping my heavy stabbing sword from its scabbard, and swinging it back and forth like a veteran.

"Phraortes, you would be wise to leave that sword to abler hands than yours."

He replaced the weapon, turning to me with a sardonic grin on that scar-ravaged face.

"What did he tell you?" he asked again.

I did not like his questioning. But he holds the ear of the king, more than any others, more perhaps than even Mardonious, the king's brother-in-law. I had to be careful "The boy is young and naive. He told me all that happened between you and him today. Is that a problem?"

Phraortes' smile faded. "That depends."

"On what I told him?"

His silence was instructive.

"Fear not, Phraortes, the young Athenian has no need to know affairs of state. Whatever his suspicions may be, I did nothing to reinforce them." The dreaded head of the king's secret sentries seemed to relax some then. "As for me, I neither know nor care of your interest in this boy. It is enough that you see fit to protect him for the moment."

Phraortes moved to the tent entrance, lifted the tent flap and peered outside. "And what need do you have of him yourself?" He turned back to me. "It cannot be just as a messenger? Are there other uses you have for him? Other, perhaps less public, needs? There have been rumors—"

"Phraortes," I snapped, "if you wish to keep your tongue, you will hold it where it may do the most good. I will have no trouble feeding it to the wild boars."

Phraortes flushed. "You cannot threaten me! I will have the king dispose of you as you should have been years ago. I know your sympathies, and I know your desires! If I find one shred of evidence of your treason, it is not my tongue you will find hammered to a post, but yours!"

"You dog! First you impugn my honor, and now my loyalty! And what of yours? Are you so removed from your roots that you have forgotten what it means to care about the gods and not just your-self? What matter is this boy with whom you have nothing in com-mon but the dubious fact you are both humans? Take care! I may be an alien in this army, but others would find glory with a sword to you if they knew what I knew!"

He glared at me, stunned. But he recovered, letting out a snarl. "Let fly with what you know, Spartan. I have the king's full confi-dence, and I fear no man within this army."

We stood, rooted to our positions, slinging pure hatred across the space between us. I straightened, remembering I had been, at least at one time, a king. "Get out." I warned, "It is in both of our interests at this time to protect this boy. For that, I will let you live. Count yourself fortunate. Now leave."

He left with his ugly visage wearing a mask of anger, leaving me feeling every moment of my many years. What did I know of Phraortes anyway? Only suspicions, rumors. He does not know that. At some point, I will have to find out what he was hiding. At some point, the spy would have to feel the eye turned upon him. But was it worth it anymore? Why can I not accept my fate? Why can I not acknowledge that I will never go home? Because, of course, I can't. For me, at least, the world —my world—is at war. In this current chaos rests my final chance, and it may never come again.

I need to get another message to Leonidas. Not now, while the tides are in his favor. But at some point, soon, that will not be the case. He has tasted our mettle and knows at least that Xerxes will not cease his assault. Meanwhile, Phraortes' suspicions are aroused. I will not be able to send another open message as I did today. I will have to wait for my chance.

It will come.

CHAPTER 5

Lysis

It is the morning of the second day's fighting, three days since I have lost my friends and my freedom. Another hot dawn. Greek summers are like this, but the driving winds that also mark this time of year are absent, as if Aeolus, god of the winds, is holding his breath. Only a minimal sea breeze struggles to push away the heavy, clinging blanket of heat. Impossible to escape is the smell of blood and death permeating my senses. When a man dies, he releases everything in his body that was formerly held in by nature. When thousands die, the cumulative effect is putrid. And even though the Persians have cleared many of their dead from the previous day's battle, more than enough of their once proud, living bodies remain as carcasses giving foul scent to the air.

Xerxes it seems, has decided he must take the pass no matter the price. The valor of Leonidas and his men has not deterred the Persian tyrant in the least. I watch from Demaratus' tent as the vast army again makes preparations for a frontal attack. At the Phocian wall, the pass' defenders also stir. I wonder *would today be a repeat of yesterday? Would the Greeks have the courage and skill to stand up to repeated assaults? How many Greeks would be there to clash?*

I have not had a chance to assess my captor's strength during my brief confinement, and my time in the fleet has not given me access to any real intelligence on them. What I do know is that the Persian army is angry — angry at the incredible losses of the previous day, angry at the Greeks, and angry, it seems, at their king. I decide to stay close to Demaratus. It was bad enough I had one

Persian, Medarnes, out for my head; it would not do at all to have the entire army feel the same..

And something is wrong with the Medarnes situation. I keep reviewing in my mind what Phraortes had said about my father. Could my father have been in Persia? Could the cruel rumors I had heard as a child be true? Maybe my father was not lost at sea. Could he have chosen exile as a means to escape enemies at home? In that case, my whole world would be turned upside down. Perhaps Medarnes has reason to hate me. I do not know, and it does not help that Demaratus seems to be withholding answers from me.

But what do I expect? I am his prisoner. Demaratus has his reasons for using me. And that was what he was doing. Despite my best efforts at contempt, however, I have come to understand that he, too, has demons within that tear at his heart. Though a Spartan, he is a fellow Greek, and though I cannot forgive his counsel to the barbarians, I know Demaratus still feels for his homeland. And events for me could have been far worse. I could have died many times, if not used for far worse affairs than messenger duty.

Nevertheless, this day is not going to bring me any closer to my freedom. I wonder what is going on out in the fleet and in Athens. For perhaps weeks, word will not get back to Andronica or my family that we have lost our ship. In two weeks, I could join others in the journey to Hades. But whatever happens, I am determined to find the truth about my father. If it means confronting Medarnes, or Demaratus, or even the dreaded Phraortes, so be it. The more I dwell on the situation, the more my determination becomes a steady voice in my thoughts. In such a mood, I greet the new morning.

I have not been alone in my single-mindedness. As I stand under the awning muted in the long shadows of the rising sun, Medarnes approaches with murder in his mien. The guards take note as well. They spring to their feet and draw their swords, stepping in front of me, at the ready. Medarnes stops before them with malice filling his dark eyes. Trembling, he glares at my protectors.

"Step aside," he growls. "This Greek does not deserve your shields."

"The Spartan has ordered his protection," the one on my left replies. "Lord, do not force our will to obey."

"Your will is wrong!" Medarnes cries. "This man is Greek! He has no worth! Let me turn him to ashes!"

The guards remain silent, eyeing Medarnes.

"Medarnes," I ask, "what is it you want of me? I am a prisoner here, no more. What is your grievance against me?"

"You know my name?" he fulminates. "Who told you the name of a nobleman of Persia? Speak, cur! Who told you?"

"Demaratus told me."

"Another damned Greek! Another traitor! Are we now nothing but an army of inbreds?" He is prowling now, pacing back and forth in front of the two guards like a tiger stalking its prey. "Do you know why I hate you, Greek? Do you know why I yearn for your end?"

"No, "I do not."

He stops his pacing and draws his sword. "You hail from a family of murderers spawned from murdering ancestors," he says, advancing toward the guards. "Your father killed mine and left him in a ditch to rot like a spent ox," he continues, forcing the two sentries back into the awning. "And then he ran like the coward he was, knowing we would condemn him to the scorpions of Dahaka."

Medarnes crouches into a fighting position, sword inches from my defenders. "I cannot have him, but I will have his son."

"Medarnes! This man cannot have been my father. He died at sea twelve years ago!"

"That is a lie! Androcles the Athenian arrived in the royal court seeking favor twelve years ago! The Great king gave him what he asked for, gave him lands that belonged to my family, to my father! I remember this!"

The guards begin looking for more sentries to reinforce their stance.

Medarnes continues and points his sword directly at my heart, "My father told me Androcles asked for more land, prime land that was supposed to have gone to your Demaratus! My father refused, and Androcles killed him! You bear the guilt of your line. You deserve to die!"

Medarnes lunges forward, knocking to one side the guard to my left and making a sweeping cut that catches the other soldier full on the chest, dropping him like a sack of rocks. He comes for me then, slipping in the sand as I back up through the awning.

An outcry erupts behind as other soldiers respond to the fight and race to restrain Medarnes. He ignores them, lunging with a murderous thrust. I am still weak from my wounds suffered a few days before, and am slow in responding. I lose my footing as I retreat and fall to the sand. Medarnes rears above me to finish the kill. I have never seen such hatred in a man's eyes. I watch as the blade descends, oddly it seems so slow in its movement; slow like a blade of grass titling in the breeze. I try to move, try to twist away, but I know it will be too late. I brace for it, brace for the searing pain. But it never comes.

Instead, an avalanche of bodies deluge us. They sweep Medarnes away as a voice rises above the shouting.

"Keep him down! Bind him!"

The soldier who had fallen on top of me pushes himself off and goes to help the others, who are busy disarming Medarnes and tying his hands behind his back. I look up, and Demaratus is there, extending his hand.

"Get up," he says. "The gods seem to have a keen eye for fools."

I grasp his hand, and he pulls me up.

"What happened here?" he asks.

I explain while Medarnes struggles against his captors.

"Hmm," breathes Demaratus. "I will have to escort Medarnes to the king. This cannot be allowed to continue." He moves away, calling the guards and the pinioned Medarnes to follow.

"Wait! Demaratus! Why do you care so much to save me?"

As the guards drag Medarnes away, his face lined in vitriol,, Demaratus steps toward me. "I have a special mission for you," he whispers. "It may save all of Greece." He pauses, his lips twist with concealed meaning. "It may even save me."

Then he leaves me, standing there with a dumb look. I feel I am on a stage, in the middle of some god-envisioned play, a tragedy, perhaps, like those I had seen as a child in the shadow of the Acropolis. Or maybe it was a comedy, in which I could not understand the joke. Either way, I know I am but an actor in a tale already told.

Demaratus

I have retired to my tent to write. It is midday and there is a lull in the fighting. No, not a lull; an exhaustion. Both armies seem spent. We began the attack three hours after dawn, and it continued until noon. We did better today. Leonidas used tactics similar to yesterday's, gaining similar results for a while. Toward late morning, however, the relentless pace of our assaults began to make headway. The phalanx splintered many of their spears that could not be replaced, meaning when our men got closer we could inflict death.

Yet we do not seem able to break through this impasse. It is as I have feared, as I have warned the king. So long as Leonidas stands firm and the allied fleet remains on station, an imminent military victory seems hopeless. We can wear them down through attrition, no question. We have more men. But there must be another way. For me, I would prefer the Greeks abandon the pass and meet this army elsewhere. And I would prefer Leonidas to remain alive as it suits my purpose to have him so, though I believe we will have to force him out. There seems no other way.

We captured some prisoners today. They were hacked up, their linen armor a mess of sword cuts, their bronze greaves nicked and dented. They had been left for dead during a feigned retreat and our forces swarmed forward plucking up those who could not retreat. I had the chance to interrogate them before the guards dragged them off, I assume, to the tender mercies of Phraortes. These men gave me another glimpse into the mind of Leonidas. They were Thespians, not Spartans, yet they acknowledged Leonidas as their leader. I asked them if the king had addressed them before the battle.

"Yes," one replied. "Both yesterday and today."

"What did he say?" I asked.

The one who spoke looked at his fellow prisoners. "He made us feel we were not fighting for our separate states, but for all of Greece. He reminded us of why we were important to each as his own man in a larger journey of all men."

Another nodded his head. "Truly," he echoed, "he gave us a vision of the future, of what it would be like for us when we cast the Persians from our shores."

"I have never felt that the Spartans were above us," the first prisoner continued. "The king gives us the strength that he himself possesses, no matter the soldier's heritage."

I assume they were so forthcoming because I was a Spartan. But it was more evidence of the special gift, the charisma of this king. I remember it in him when I was still home. Such a thing can make an army out of a rabble and can make good men great.

The same is not true of our Great king. At the war council this morning, Xerxes was his usual self, berating his commanders for yesterday's failures and reminding them of the punishment for their lack of victory in today's fighting. They are used to it, and they take it manfully enough, I suppose. Still, it can crush a man's spirit, as a pestle does mustard seed.

After the council, I approached the king concerning the matter of Medarnes. I explained what had happened that morning, expecting the Great One to deal with Medarnes as he usually does others. But there was no imprisonment, no flogging, or quick execution. Yes, the king called Medarnes forward and shamed him. But then after ordering him to cease his vengeful pursuit of Lysis, he let him go, even reinstating him to his unit and sending him back into battle.

I am perplexed in this matter. It has always seemed to me that Medarnes was an unstable warrior, yet the king tolerates his outbursts. *What else is at heart?* I wonder. I saw Phraortes lurking about after Medarnes had departed. The look he gave the Persian cannot bode well for Medarnes. But I also have the distinct feeling

Phraortes is keeping a close eye on me. Well, that is of no matter at this point. Unless this tactical battle changes, I can do nothing, no matter my intentions.

I have taken a liking to this Lysis. He is an intelligent man, and his story grows more intriguing by the day. Plus, he kept his word the other day in returning to our lines, and he has shown courage against Medarnes. Besides, it may be that I will have to confide in him at some point. There may be no other option.

I must go now. The king has sent a messenger asking me to join the council. He may listen to me now.

Lysis

The second day's fighting goes much like the first. I am under heavy guard, but Demaratus allows me to move close enough to see the battle unfold. The frustration of the Persians grows in proportion to their casualties. And their casualties are horrific. Even from where I am standing, I can see the sand and dirt stained with puddles of Persian blood. Those with wounds are not likely to survive. As I have found, an eight-foot spear can tear open a man's guts or obliterate his face. I admit I feel stirrings of pity for them.

But it can have been no less awful for the Greeks. They appear to be under a constant hail of arrows, and when not, they are fending off the flight of thousands of javelin spears looking for entry into their flesh. It is a desperate game they play. The leather "skirts" under a hoplite's shield can protect against many of the projectiles, but with one moment of fatigue in which his shield wavers he will find himself impaled in the neck or shoulder. I am familiar with phalanx fighting, and I know how hot it can get under that armor, and how heavy the nearly one quarter talent shield can become. That is why Leonidas keeps trying to rotate the troops. Their weapons would be broken or destroyed, and their physical fatigue combined with the terror and strain on their clear thinking, wears men out.

Anticipating this need, the Persians seem to be giving them little rest. From my vantage point, I see a great many more Greeks go down than in the previous day's fighting. And the noise. I cannot describe the din of battle, the missiles clanging off bronze-faced shields and helmets, the clash of spear upon spear and javelin against shield, the crash of swordplay. The piercing screams of the wounded. Some lay between the lines and moan all day long. It is wretched to watch. Wretched. Yet I have never seen such bravery from both sides. The Persians are less impressed by my countrymen. As the day wears on, my guards' animosity towards me grows in intensity. They begin to cast dark looks my way, and I begin to look for solace from Demaratus.

He does not appear until late in the day after their final attacks have been launched and beaten back. Once more, as the sun dips behind the mountains, the scene on the field of battle looks as I had imagined when listening to Homer's account of our ancestors' assault on Troy. Across the plain from where we stand to the Phocian wall, against which the Greek line holds, the bodies of the dead cover the ground. The cries of the wounded and the next-to-be-dead smother any other sounds.

Demaratus motions to me as he approaches my vantage point. "Come, Lysis," he says. "You will see nothing more today."

I follow him, surrounded by my ever-present guards, back along the beach toward his tent. We walk in silence, the gentle rolling of the low surf on the beach the only noise.

When we are at the water's edge, he stops and stands looking out over the bay, his gaze fixed on the darkening horizon. "Why do we do what we do, Lysis?" he says, surprising me. "Why do you think men throw themselves at death, heedless of the end?"

I think he means it as a question with no answer, and certainly I do not know one.

He glances at me, though, as if expecting one, and then raises his eyes to the heavens, where a few stars glow against the dark blue of the twilit sky. "Look up," he says, "and all you see is the gods' domain— unchanging, always beautiful, never sullied." He turns to me. "And look there." He points to the battlefield. "All you see is man's domain— cruel, heartless, and brutal." Pausing for a moment, he closes his eyes. "Would that it were the other way around."

He grows silent then resumes his walk, his eyes still on the sea. "Xerxes drives this army," he says, "and men do his bidding, even unto death. He whips them, threatens them, and humiliates them. Yet still, they give to him. They are lashed by him but their fear takes them into the fire. It is amazing, but it is not loyalty. It is having no choice or power." By this time, we arrive at the tent, and Demaratus orders a soldier to bring him his camp chair. He seats himself, and his eyes cling to the blackness of night.

"Yet over there," he continues, "there is a different kind of leader. There is a leader who does not lash, a leader who awakens the character in each man, who does not lead his men into the fire but creates the fire within his men. And yet," he pauses again, "his men still die. They still suffer. Is there any difference?"

I am not sure of my thoughts, but I venture out. "Demaratus, there is a difference. You can die with fear, or you can die with hope. I would rather die with hope or fight to live because of that hope."

"Yes, hope," he says. "That is indeed the answer, is it not? We must always have hope."

He stands up then and turns to face me, a grimace that might have been a smile spreads across his worn face. "Thank you, Lysis. I had forgotten."

A messenger stumbles through the encampment, his lighted torch dispels the gathering gloom. He is looking for Demaratus.

Demaratus

The king's messenger found me in a somber mood. Another horrific day, another display of bravery beyond imagining, but tactics worthy of a lesser army. So many good men killed. This news that we have, though, could change everything.

I answered the king's summons and found the war council gathered. The lamps were many and bright in the Great king's tent, and the rugs under our feet were soft and full. A sumptuous dinner had been prepared, and the tables were stocked with both local fare and all the delicacies of the East. I realized I was hungry, although it is difficult to enjoy lamb and goat meat amidst the butchery of battle. But the king did not offer food. He was seated behind the map table, charts spread across it, with his captains arguing and pointing. Off to one side, a Greek farmer stood, gazing in awe.

When I entered, Hydarnes caught my eye. "Demaratus," he cried, "a gift from the gods! We may perhaps escape this hell after all."

"What is it?" I asked.

"An alternative route around the mountain! This local came to us not an hour ago claiming he knows of a path that skirts the mountain's fastness and comes down behind the Greek lines."

The king looked up. "Ah! Demaratus!" he beamed, in a good mood not common to him. "Question this man for us, if you would. Tell us if there is truth to his words."

The king seemed elated, almost giddy. I bow. "Yes, Your Highness."

The others were looking at me with excitement sparkling in their eyes. They were exhausted, most blood-soaked and dirty with their light armor and robes rent and torn, their beards matted, their hair disheveled. In this moment, I was not the hostile, never-quite-accepted Spartan alien; I was their savior. If I could confirm the truth of this possibility, they would have their way out. I made my way to the back of the tent, where the Greek farmer eyed the spread on the tables with ill-disguised lust.

"What is your name?" I asked.

He seemed surprised to hear my perfect Greek but answered, "Ephialtes, son of Eurydemus, from Malis."

"Malis," I answered. "You are from around here, then?"

"Yes, I live in the mountains about twenty stade from the sea."

"Well, Ephialtes, you have news for us?"

"And what is it you have for me?" he countered.

"Ephialtes," I said, "the Great king does not suffer fools or interruptions. Tell us what you know, or your life is worth less than that wild boar you see stuffed on the table."

His eyes grew wide and fearful, but he clutched his dirty, broad-brimmed hat closer to his frayed tunic and persisted. "It is true, I know what can happen if I mislead you, but with Zeus as my witness, what I have to say will be worth the price."

I explained to the king the demands.

"Continue, Demaratus," he said. "Give the man what he wants."

I turned back to Ephialtes. "You will be paid, in gold, for your information. Now, what is it you have to say?"

He smiled but still clung to his hat as he blurted out what he knew. "The path I spoke of is called the Anopaea. It follows the river for a while but then goes up into the mountains, ending at Alpeni in Locris. It will take you to the other side of the mountain and a few hours from the East Gate."

"How wide is this path?" I asked.

"Wide enough for four men to go side by side. At least for most of the way."

"And how long will it take to traverse?"

"Eight or ten hours, perhaps. Maybe more."

If it is eight or ten hours for a single man, it could be twice that for an army, I thought.

"Do you know of any defenders?"

He looked nervous at this question. "I do not *know* of any," he said. "I have not been through the pass in many months, but the path *is* there."

I held him with my gaze for a minute, what must have seemed an eternity to him, as he fidgeted, frightened, but did not back down.

"Fine," I said. "You will lead us then."

He nodded, relieved.

"And my pay?" he inquired.

"You will receive your pay when you have completed your task. I am sure you will not be disappointed. The king has a long history of rewarding traitors," I said. He did not seem offended.

"These Spartans are nothing to me," he said. "They are as foreign as you are. And besides, the Phocians have always hated us."

He cast his eye on the heaped table. "I beg for the king's mercy to allow me some food and wine."

Lysis

No sooner had Demaratus left, disappearing into the encampment and becoming one of thousands of waving torches, then another light morphs from the darkness, trailed by a cluster of hovering loyalists, a few soldiers, and the block-like form of Phraortes. It is almost as if he had been poised on the edge of sight like a clever fly always outside of view. He dismisses his entourage, comes toward me, and waves my guards aside. They obey eagerly, bowing as he passes. But I remain cautious, despite him having been friendly on our first meeting. I am beginning to trust Demaratus, though I also question how I can trust a traitor.

"Good evening, Lysis," he says. "You've had quite a day from what I've been told."

"Surely you are told everything sire, " I reply.

"Yes," he says, looking me over. "No injuries, I see."

"The gods have watched over me, yes that is true. You were right to warn me of Medarnes. He believes my father killed his and was of no mind to reason."

"It is the king's wish that he believe this."

"What do you mean, 'the king's wish'?"

"What I said. It is of no account now. The king has his reasons, and I am his humble servant. I am having Medarnes watched, as is the king. He will not attempt to harm you again."

Phraortes comes closer, the torchlight glowing off his twin scars. For the first time, I notice the simplicity of his dress: a dark wool robe, knotted around the waist with a braided rope belt. From his neck glints a silver amulet, in the middle of which is the etched Greek letter "Alpha." The pattern and design seem familiar to me, and an image flashes in my mind but then fades. The amulet dangles around his throat as he leans toward me.

"I have come to warn you on a different matter," Phraortes says. "A matter that can get you killed if you do not listen."

I pay attention, as the number of ways I can be killed is increasing beyond my ability to track them all.

"You must be careful of this Demaratus," he says. "He is a traitor, and not to be trusted."

"I am aware he is a traitor to his people. But he has given me no reason to distrust him."

"A traitor once is a traitor always," he answers. "I know of what I speak." His demeanor remains cold and impassive, but still, there is something in his eyes that betrays feeling. "Besides, I am not concerned with what he has done in the past. It is what he intends to do in the near future that has my ire."

"I do not know of what you speak," I say. "I am not privy to his councils, but it is he who has served your king well, not me. So perhaps sire, it is for you to not trust me."

"Perhaps, but if he asks you to do anything that would bring dishonor to our Great king, you will let me know."

"And by 'anything you mean?"

"Why," he continues, "I mean communicating with the enemy." He looks at me then, seeing my nervous reaction: "You know something of this already?" he inquires.

"I know nothing of this," I reply, regaining my clear mind. "But I will inform you if I do."

"Good!" he smiles, or gives what could appear as a smile, on his ravaged face. "I knew I could see the wheels of your mind." Startling me, he puts his hand on my shoulder, squeezes, and fixes me with a firm gaze. "You will survive this war," he says, "and unlike many of us, you will go home to a peaceful life. I will make sure of this." He releases his grip.

"Please, Phraortes! Where comes your vision?"

"It is a promise I made to your father," he says. "A promise I have sworn to keep." He turns to leave, waving his attendants forward.

"Wait! What do you know of my father? Please, tell me."

He half-turns, his eyes finding mine. "Your father is alive," he says, and hesitates. "He would want *you* to live."

Demaratus

Once the news of the pathway was confirmed, the king dispatched Hydarnes with orders to ready the Immortals for a march that night.

Hydarnes slapped me hard on the back as he exited the tent. "Let's see what your Leonidas does with this!" I could see him, robes swirling, as he barked orders to his aides. They dashed off in different directions, torches disappearing into the fire lit vastness of the dark. I turned back to the king. He was watching me.

"Demaratus, I want you to go with Hydarnes." Nodding to the back of the tent where the farmer Ephialtes was gnawing on a lamb shank, he added, "And take this farmer with you. Slit his throat if one word of what he claims is untrue."

"Yes, Your Highness," I said, and turned to go.

"Wait! king of Sparta! Your attention for a moment." Xerxes stood, and gathering his robes about him, walked over to me, his long black beard and braided hair trailing below his shoulders. "Walk with me. I wish to speak of other matters."

He shouted to his generals. "Make sure the army is ready to attack in the morning. We will pressure them from this side while Hydarnes comes upon them from the rear. I wish to destroy them in total." They bow their assent, and, one by one, exit the tent.

Xerxes took me by the arm, and we walked, leaving the plush, lamp-lit environs and moved through the royal enclosure, both led and trailed by a tight group of torch-bearing sentries.

"You have been closed to me of late," he said. "I have listened to your counsel, which, as usual, has been given in good faith. But," and he paused, "I have detected a certain reticence in your bearing. Now, I know we are going against your people," he continued, "and that may be difficult for you, but you swore to my service, and you must honor it."

"I understand, Majesty, I have tried to be as forthcoming as possible about the difficulties the army will face in conquering these Greeks."

"Yes, you have, but you did that from a distance. Now that we face your kinsman, perhaps you have doubts?"

"I have no doubts, Highness."

"Good," said Xerxes. "Because I have received reports..."

"Phraortes," I breathe.

"Yes, Phraortes," he replied, amused. "An interesting creature, don't you think?"

I hesitated. "He is your servant, Highness."

"He is that. In more ways than you know. There is an interesting history I must tell you sometime. I'm afraid Phraortes was not a willing convert to his present position, but he has done a marvelous job, has he not?"

I thought of the endless rows of dead Egyptians I had witnessed after arriving in the king's domain, the grieving women and children sold into slavery, the pitiless nature of the task, but swallowed my truth: "Yes, Highness. A wonderful job."

Xerxes smiled. "A worthy servant, indeed. But a traitor. Did you know that?"

I remain silent.

"Yes, a traitor to his people. Well, an exile anyway. Greek, as a matter of record, I think my father told me. You can never be sure about people like that, can you Demaratus?"

I walked on, stone-faced, my stomach tensing. "No, Majesty, you can never be sure."

"No," he said. "But I can be sure of you, my great Spartan king, can I not?"

By this time, we had arrived back at his tent entrance. I looked the Lord of Asia in the eye. "Of course, Highness," I replied. "You can always trust me."

The king's eyes fixed on me, hard as iron. "That is wonderful. Now, assist Hydarnes with the Immortals, and," he leaned closer, his expression fierce, "crush this Leonidas like a beetle."

CHAPTER 6

Demaratus

I am writing this before departing with Hydarnes and the Immortals on our march over the mountain. I left the king's tent with what felt like a rock in my stomach. His words were a not so subtle warning, but I still don't see another road. That damned Phraortes is like a snake. He must have an informer among my aides. I will deal with that later. For now, there is nothing in me to spend on it. Unless word is sent to Leonidas this night, we will take him by surprise in the morning and will annihilate his entire force. If that happens, I will never see Sparta again.

I dismissed my people and told them to send in Lysis. I then deliberated on the content of my message to my former countryman. Leonidas' rejection of my last offer was proof of where he stands, no question. However, that was before he knew his flank would be turned. The Ephors, the ruling body of elders that must have dispatched the king and his guard on this mission, have nothing to gain by allowing one of their kings and an entire force of Spartiates to be wiped out. Leonidas must see a clearer path.

Having determined my course, I rejected the mode of communication I had used to contact the Spartans in the past. My first warning to them had been when Xerxes was preparing this expedition, well over a year ago. It was dangerous, of course, but I felt letting them know the fate that awaited them would be worth the effort. I took a risk they would be wise and have clear eyes. But word came back to me that Gorgo, Leonidas' wife, had understood the real communication lay etched in the wood underneath the primary wax tablet. I had done the same with Lysis' message the other day, but I dare not do it now. I must ensure that if anyone catches Lysis, the message cannot be detected. It is no longer a case of sending him across an open field where I can see his every movement. This must be done with precision and utmost secrecy.

I took out a piece of the king's valuable papyrus and began to write. When Lysis entered, I was ready.

Lysis

Phraortes' news stuns me. My father, alive! I cannot reason with the torrent of emotions these words unleash. Where was he? What was he doing? Why had he not contacted me? I drop to the ground, my knees weak, and struggle to regain my composure. I attempt to calm my breathing and try to make sense of things. Phraortes knows my father, knows he is alive, and knows where he is. I have to get that information from him. But how? I have no freedom of movement, and Phraortes is the head of the king's secret sentries. For the first time, I want to stay in the Persian camp and find answers, any answers about my father, rather than escape back to my people with no more than before.

The battle, which had seemed so Homeric in intensity and meaning, now fades to insignificance. I cease to think of the great cause and now nurse my private hopes and fears. As the night deepens and I await Demaratus' return, I scheme possibilities. For some reason, Phraortes will not tell me any more of my father. Was there someone else in this camp who knows more, or who knows anything, for that matter? There is Medarnes, but I doubt a homicidal maniac like him will be helpful. I suppose if he knew where my father was, he would have killed him.

There was Demaratus. He has access to a host of people in this army and to the Persian court within which someone must have knowledge of my father. I will ask him. That was it then. This new quest fills me with a fiery new resolve to live, a determination to find out where I had come from, and who I was. With my mind racing in circles, I see the Spartan king appear from his tent and I rush toward him. But the guards make clear I am to remain outside. Even though I am exhausted from the long day, my scuffle with Medarnes, and my wounds, I am still full of nervous energy and excitement.

After a maddening wait, the guards motion for me to enter. I rush into the tent, my first question already poised on my lips. Demaratus looks up and holds his palm out for silence. He is seated on his camp chair by his table and has been doing a great deal of writing. He waves me closer and then stands up, putting his finger to his lips.

"We must be quiet," he whispers. "I have a final task for you."

I am confused. I am also too excited to be under control. "Demaratus!" I say, the agitation in my voice betrays my efforts to remain quiet, "Phraortes has told me my father is alive! Do you know anything about this? Can you find out?"

"When did you see Phraortes?" he asks in a sharp tone.

"After you left to see Xerxes."

"What else did he say?"

I have the sense I have stumbled into a battle that was well over my head.

"He told me to beware of you," I respond. "He said you were a traitor to your people, and you could be a traitor now."

"And?"

"He said he knew all about traitors."

"I'm sure he does," hisses Demaratus. "Listen to me son of Androcles. The time is short, and I have no leisure for your father. I will tell you this, though," and he lowers his tone even further. "This Phraortes is an evil man, dung on a boot. He knows about betrayal because he's made a life from it. If he knows your father's fate, it's because he's been involved with it. I can tell you that. It may even be—" and he stops, avoiding my gaze.

"It may even be what?" I challenge.

"There are more important matters we must address at this hour." He reaches back to the table and picks up a sheet of folded-over papyrus. "Carry this to Leonidas tonight. He must get this message."

"But what about my father?"

"Damn you Lysis! There is no time for that. Tomorrow, Hydarnes and the Immortals will come down upon the Greek's rear and destroy them. Do you understand? Your father may or may not be alive. It could be that you would not want to meet him even if he were. But your fate and the fate of Greece may rest with this message! You must wrest your mind from your problems and devote yourself to this."

The fierce intensity of his emotion stuns me. And then the import of his words land. Leonidas's army destroyed. I see then a vision of the Persian soldiers pouring through the gap and descending on Boetia and the central plain, swarming into Attica and inundating my beautiful Athens. I see Andronica, and I see my family— my mother, my uncle, friends, and family I hold dear murdered, abused and dragged through the mud of their homeland in torture. And then I see the father I never knew. What did Demaratus mean by saying I may not want to meet him even if he were alive? But even with my confused images, the meaning of why I am here has become apparent.

"You are a traitor!" I say. "A traitor now to the Persian cause!"

He smiles. "One man's traitor is another man's patriot. I do these things for my own reasons." He leans over the table, his eyes inches from mine. "You didn't think the message you carried to Leonidas the other day was telling him to go to Hades, did you?"

"I didn't know," I say. "What did you tell him?"

"You'll have to ask him."

My head is spinning. It wasn't that I had to pass unseen through the vast majority of the Persian army and into the Greek camp somehow without getting killed. I would also be leaving the one man who could help me find my father. What were the chances of ever learning that information? And yet, the message I carried, if true, could alter the course of the war.

Demaratus could see the interplay of emotions running rampant across my face. "Lysis, do this for yourself. Do this for your city." He pauses for an instant and clasps my arms with his gnarled and weathered hands. "Do this, and I promise you I will find your father, one way or the other. There is no telling the way of this war, and perhaps we shall meet again before too long, but I will honor my promise. I will give you the answers you seek, by the gods, I swear."

I can see the sincerity in his face, the raw strain of his situation evident. In the end, I accept that his word is his bond. "I will trust you. What do you wish of me?"

Demaratus

I have given Lysis the letter and now must prepare myself for the march. It is in his hands now. There is no doubt I have taken the greatest risk of my life. Should Lysis be stopped and the letter found, they will know I wrote it. The odds of discovery are also higher because Phraortes and his people are keeping a close eye on both Lysis and myself. And yet I have little alternative. The plan we came up with will work, I think. I will know soon.

I don't know why I didn't entrust the message to Lysis verbally. He would have delivered the right words. But certain things should pass king to king. And this is one of them. If there are any doubts in Leonidas' mind about my intentions and my reasons, there would be none now. Time is short. I hear the troops beginning to move.

Lysis

I can feel the thin papyrus sheet pressed against my back. Demaratus has sewn it into my tunic, and we are both marching along near the rear of the Persian column. The plan we formulated was better than none at all, but risky. The Spartan king left my guards back at the camp and has taken charge of me himself. As the ten thousand Immortals march away from the sea and into the steep foothills of the mountain, we drift farther and farther back in the column.

About a mile from the camp, the thick oak forests force the marching men to close up to four abreast. At that point, Demaratus stops us. We fall out of the column, and he begins to berate me. He slaps me hard across the face as the troops slog by, some laughing as the king pushes me back down toward the wooded slope. Appearing angry and exasperated, the king draws his sword and leads me into the forest. Once we are hidden from the ranks, he sheathes his weapon and gives me a rueful look.

"My apologies for the blow, Lysis." he says. "It was needed for our ruse."

My bloodied cheek bothers me not. I am about to escape back to my people. That I will do so with mixed feelings does nothing to take the edge of fear and excitement from my racing heart. "I understand. So long as you honor your promise and find my father, I will be grateful."

"I will," says the king. "Whatever happens, I will contact you." He smiles then and turns to rejoin the troops. "Travel with the gods," he whispers over his shoulder. "You have many more fates in your hands than your own."

As the Spartan disappears toward the sounds of tramping feet and clinking weapons, I feel an unexpected surge of affection. It was more than gratitude. Despite myself, I find that I like Demaratus, and wonder what it had been that drove him from Sparta. I had never asked, but doubt he would have told me if I had.

Demaratus has given me a helmet, a robe, and a bundle of other Persian gear that we hope will allay suspicion as I make my way toward the Greek line. I stop in the woods and put on the disguise, waiting until all signs of movement have faded from the slopes. When the last torchlight up the path disappears from sight, I make my way back down the track, keeping to the trees. Soon, the enormous camp of the enemy comes into view once again. I know if I keep to the trees and the eastern slopes of the mountain, I can remain hidden from their outlying guard posts until I come into the open ground between the two camps: the Persians to my back, the Greeks to my face.

The going is easy until I make the turn south and begin to skirt the edge of the foothills. I am primed up and on edge, jumping at any movement. The sounds of the creatures of the night, of owls, foxes, and even mice, are to me like the advance of a full phalanx.

I stop to listen, crouching down low in the underbrush, and stilling my breathing. At times I swear the echoes of my movements do not fade as they should. I am certain it is only my imagination conjuring sounds where there were none and movement that in the light of day would seem harmless, yet I slow my pace even more.

There is no moon, but the brilliant stars and the glow of campfires off to my left light the way. Less than half a stade away now, I can see the edge of the Persian camp. If I can get by the last of the outlying troops, I should be able to make the Phocian wall. Whether I will die attempting to get into the Greek camp was another matter.

The slope steepens as I approach the last few yards. Loose rocks and dirt replace the brush and larger vegetation. With the field of battle a few seconds brisk walk from where I stand, I pause, but cannot pass. Before me, a sharp cut in the hillside with a sheer drop of fifteen feet affords me little leeway to navigate it undetected; the nearest guard post is an easy stone's throw away, and they will hear me. But I must brave it out.

Creeping the last few yards, I enter the domain of the enemy position. There is a chance they will miss me. If I can keep to the edge...

"Stay!" I hear from the nearest soldier. I freeze. "Identify yourself!" I hear hasty movement and a moment later see a lit torch coming toward me. I step out into the light, surrounded by three soldiers, their swords drawn.

"Who are you?" a blunt, square-faced Persian demands.

Demaratus and I had talked about this possibility, but now that it is upon me, I feel my courage falter. I hesitate.

"He is a Greek!" I hear one of them hiss. "A spy!"

"No, No!" I blurt out. "I was sent from the Lord Hydarnes to report on the Greek position before tomorrow's attack. I became lost in the woods."

"Well, I know nothing of that," the square-faced one says. "I say we keep you here." He whips around and shouts to a tall, broad-shouldered warrior, "Syloson! Get the Captain."

This is not going well at all. There is still a chance I can bluff my way out of it if I keep under control. But there is also the temptation to make a dash into the woods. My odds of escaping will be even better in the dark. I stand there, waiting, mulling my options. When I see who is approaching me through the night, I feel a rush of fear. I should have run.

Demaratus

What a strange fate awaits us all. It is the end, yet the beginning with so many ends and beginnings on this fateful day. The oil in the lamps burns away to nothing, and still, I write. I am here, though, so many are not. I have much to say.

When I left Lysis in the woods—and that seems so long ago—I rejoined the column and made my way to the head of the army. Hydarnes had been expecting me, and as was his usual good humor, entertained me with various jokes and stories while we made our way along the path. The mountains of Oeta loomed on our right and the mountains of Trachis on our left, or so we were informed by Ephialtes, who walked alongside us. A strange man, this Ephialtes, a man who would betray his countrymen for money. That thought may seem odd, coming from me, but what I have done I did for honor, with never any expectation of material gain. Ephialtes seemed cheerful enough, though, and knowledgeable about the route.

The men trudged on behind us as we entered the woods, approaching the crest of the ridge leading up and over the pass. The leaves were many on the ground and dampened the noise of our march. It was colder up here, as was to be expected, a welcome relief from the heat of the lowlands. We had been marching for about ten hours, much slower, I think, than Ephialtes expected, when the pre-dawn light began to filter through the trees. Shapes became distinct, and the damp musty smell of the oak forest became more pronounced as our senses seemed to awaken.

From ahead, one of our scouts came barreling down the trail, out of breath and excited. "My Lord! The enemy is encamped in front of us!"

"The enemy!" exclaimed Hydarnes. "How many? Of what strength?"

"I am not sure, my Lord," said the scout. "Many hundreds, at least."

Hydarnes glared at Ephialtes. And then to me , "He said this pass was undefended!"

I repeated the accusation.

"I did not!" squeaked the farmer. "I said I didn't know of any!"

Hydarnes turned away, disgusted. "What say you Demaratus?" he said, looking at me. "Shall we take a look?"

We dragged Ephialtes and a strong escort and made our way forward. Someone in the Greek camp had sensed our presence, as we heard frantic movement before we saw anything. Shouted commands and the clink and clash of shields and armor echoed through the forest.

"Damn!" spat Hydarnes. "Who are these Greeks? Are they Spartans?" He grabbed Ephialtes by the scruff of the neck and drew him close. "All right, Greek, earn your pay or die. Tell us who these people are."

Motioning to Artaharnex, his second in command, Hydarnes thrust the quivering Ephialtes ahead. "Go with him," Hydarnes said, "And if he is false, kill him."

In a moment, Ephialtes and Artaharnex with his sword drawn, disappeared into the undergrowth.

The forest had been thinning out for some time, and as the light increased, I could see the edge of the trees less than a stade away.

"I don't like this," Hydarnes whispered to me so others would not hear. For nothing kills soldiers like suspicion of a worried commander. "We must have a sense of what is in our front and deploy on open ground."

I agreed, and we both waited for the return of Ephialtes. A few minutes later, pursued by Artaharnex, he bounded down the slope.

"They are Phocians!" Ephialtes said. "I know those shields."

"They have drawn themselves up on the hillside in a solid position," said Artaharnex, coming up alongside.

"Is there open ground for us?" I asked.

"Yes, My Lord."

"That is the course before us then," pronounced Hydarnes. He spun and barked orders to his staff, who raced back down the forest pathway and shouted for the various commanders. "We must advance and deploy into line as soon as we are through these trees," Hydarnes said. "Then we'll see if these Phocians will fight. We don't have time to delay here. We must get around the mountain."

With that, he ordered the column forward, and we broke through the trees and into the morning sunlight.

Lysis

It is Medarnes. I am not a coward, but I admit that I feel my knees turn to water. I tear my arms from the grip of my guards and try to run.

"Seize him!" cries Medarnes.

I am almost out of the camp when I feel myself tripped up from behind. I roll in the dust, and in an instant, several soldiers wrench me to my feet and hold me. Medarnes approaches his eyes wide and bright in the glow of the torches.

"Son of Androcles," he seethes. "Who would have known?" He paces around me, his hands twitching by his side. "How fortunate I was in the area. As you know, Greeks and spies have my special attention." He stops, and with a vicious leer, punches me hard in the face. The pain is blinding. I feel my brain throbbing in my skull. Again he hits me. And again. I feel the blood pour down my cheeks and taste it in my bleeding mouth.

Medarnes leans closer and whispers in my ear. "The king says I'm not to harm you while you're a prisoner." He pauses, and I can hear the malice gathering in his voice, "But if you're killed while trying to escape, who am I to blame?" He walks away then, and I slump against my captors' grip.

"Bind him," he says, "and bring him to me."

I feel my hands tied behind my back before the soldiers drag me to where Medarnes is camped.

"We'll walk for a bit, my Athenian friend," he says. "You want to get home? I'll get you home." He then seizes me by the front of my tunic and drags me out into the battlefield.

"Stay here," I hear him snarl to the guards.

I can see, even with my swollen eyes, the torches flickering from the Phocian wall. They are so close. I stumble along the uneven ground as the light from the Persian camp fades. Medarnes' grip is ferocious. We make our way to the side of the hill, about halfway between both armies, and he throws me down into the dirt.

"It's time to die, now, son of Androcles," he says, drawing his sword. "Take this as partial revenge for my father's death."

I roll over, trying to avoid the thrust, surging with that energy that springs from desperation and fear. He tries to adjust, but misses, driving the razor-sharp weapon deep into the dirt. He swears, wrenching at the sword and tearing it from the ground while I continue to roll away. I try to rise to my feet, hoping to make one last run toward the Greek encampment, but he has me, dead in his sights. He smiles then, his eyes halfway between euphoria and madness. And then he lunges. I try to avoid him, but I know it will be useless. I am too slow.

Demaratus

As we broke into the clearing, I assessed the situation. The Phocians were up in a line ahead and off to our left. They were eight deep and halfway up the side of a steep rise bounded by tall oaks, rocks, and rough terrain on either flank. Their phalanx curled around the slope and clung to the natural protection offered by their position. All in all, they were as a fortress. But, in their haste to secure their safety, they had left one path free. Hydarnes saw it at once.

"We have them, Demaratus!" he said. "We have to keep them pinned and continue the march."

"That's right," I agreed. "These men are not Spartiates."

"You mean Spartans would fight?" asked Hydarnes.

"To the death."

"The gods have blessed us!" laughed Hydarnes. He wheeled and directed the troops as they poured from the woods. It was too bad. The Phocians could have held us all day and inflicted significant loss had they shown real courage. But there they stood, expecting our attack, and neglecting their task. Leonidas had known of this path and had placed them there in the event we would have scouted it. That's the way allies think sometimes. It's a benefit to have others when your own ranks are short, but it's always best to do it yourself.

Every moment, more of our men swung into position. Hydarnes was directing archers within firing range of the massed Phocians even as the rest of the army marched behind their protection, continuing on the path. To our front, the way was clear. It traversed a plateau dotted with spruce and brush that receded into the distance. This was the pass.

As the Phocians raised their shields, our archers let fly. Another volley and the archers, too, began to shift by degrees to the right. The army continued to surge past, swinging through us eight abreast. It would be another half an hour before the last of the column had emerged from the woods and passed where we stood on a large section of outthrust granite overlooking the action.

"Artaharnex!" shouted Hydarnes to his splendidly dressed and long-faced second in command, "Keep them at bay and under fire until the army has passed by and is clear!"

"Yes, My Lord!" responded Artaharnex. "We'll turn the ground red from those who wish to spill their blood, and let live those who set down their arms."

"Well done!" said Hydarnes. "I leave you here as rear guard. We'll move forward and see if Leonidas has left us any other surprises."

With that, he called to me, and we closed up with the leading troops, who were hustling across the plain with Ephialtes as their guide. As we strode beside the tall, caparisoned Immortals, I noticed, not for the first time, their confident demeanor. Heads held high, they chanted marching songs in their native Persian. They were on the move, kicking up the dust, free from the restricted killing field in front of the Phocian wall. Even the weather was under the gods' smiles. It was so much cooler up here, and the fact that we had been marching for ten hours with brief rest didn't seem to bother our troops at all. I found myself admiring them. What fine Spartan warriors they would have made if they had undergone the agoge, the Spartan life training that initiated and indoctrinated all young men in the Spartan way of war.

It had been a long time since I experienced such a march myself, and an even longer time since I'd been in any kind of training. Thus, I was weary. My mind wandered back to the days of my youth when such a trek would have seemed easy. As heir to the kingship, I did not undergo the punishment of the agoge. But I did undertake much of their training as a way to test myself and to let every Spartan warrior know I was their equal or better.

As a child, I remembered going out into the fields at night, creeping through the tall grass, the coldness of late autumn chilling my bones. I remembered hugging my thin tunic to my chest, shivering as I plotted every move that would take me closer to my prize: an unsuspecting lamb, the stored wheat in the grain house or bread cooling on a table. The agoge forced those who partook of its rigors to steal from their neighbors, and indeed, from each other, to eat. This toughened us. It forced us to rely on ourselves, on our resourcefulness. I was not required to, yet still, I did. There were many things I did, many things I endured, that to others outside our Spartan homeland might seem barbarous. I endured the whippings, the mockery of failure, just as the others did. They knew I wanted to be there. They knew my desire to know myself and to lead others was more powerful than any admonitions against it. And they knew to avoid acknowledging my station in life.

I've always had something to prove. It wasn't just Cleomones and the Delphic oracle that disparaged my birth. Rumors were rife from the earliest time I could remember. Cleomones used those rumors for his own ends. He cast aspersions on my father, my mother, my house; anything to advance his power. Yet, it was amazing to me that the ephors did not see him as the snake I saw him to be; did not see through his pious whining about the Argive War.

When tasked to take the city of Argos, he had failed; though he did kill 6,000 of their hoplites. He then claimed a goddess told him to refrain from an assault on the town itself! What rubbish! I had expected the elders to be more offended that he attacked and destroyed the sanctuary of Argus. After all, we are surrounded by the gods. If the goddess did tell him to spare the town, I would have thought that leaving the sanctuary alone would have been a parcel in the bargain. But he had friends among the ephors, no doubt, who shielded him.

Well, he's gone now. He paid in blood for what he did, if not to me, then to the Argive god. The heavens were avenged. I wish I had been of his killing. As for his pig- dung-eating toddy Leotychidas, however, he has not yet fallen as I had hoped. But perhaps I can still slay him.

Leonidas, of course, is related to Cleomones; he married his sister, Gorgo. But they are as different as two kings could be. I was counting on that. Leonidas knew the history. He knew what happened. He knew what Cleomones said about my parentage was nothing more than a cruel lie designed to divest me of the kingship. Young as Leonidas was then, I knew he didn't approve of Cleomones' tactics or ambition any more than I did. I could see helping him. We could have battled Leotychides together then. But that will not be possible now. If we close this trap, we seal Leonidas' fate. The only way I will return to Sparta, in that case, is as a conqueror. Conquerors are never embraced. They are tolerated, hated, and cast aside at the first opportunity, but never embraced.

In any event, these Persians are good soldiers. They could be better. If I do see Sparta again, I can train some of their sons. Today the Persians trudged along in their trousers and long tunics with sleeves, with their boots and felt caps, and as usual, I couldn't help but marvel at the difference in our heritages. They are not free, yet they fight. Maybe they don't know the difference. But we Greeks do. I do. The results of the fighting to this point leave me no doubt as to which is better.

As we crossed the short plain and began our descent down the mountain, I kept expecting another force to bar our path. But there was none. The way was clear, all the way down to Alpeni, behind Leonidas' lines.

Lysis

I feel a rush of terror overwhelm me as Medarnes throws himself behind the weight of his blade, springing forward for my death. *Everything slows down in my mind as I prepare to die. What used to be so important a moment before now becomes nonsense. What I could control in life before, I can no longer control. Helplessness overwhelms me. This time, there will be no escape.* I live through all of this in the time it takes to say the word "father."

I brace myself for the pain I know will follow, and it comes. But it is not like I expect. It isn't bad at all. I feel my skin tear and the sharp sting of my stomach muscle ripping, but not the deep penetration into my gut I expect. Out of the corner of my eye, a form has hurtled against Medarnes' extended body, diverting his thrust. Medarnes sprawls to the ground, his sword thudding to the dirt. I stagger back, dropping to my knees, and wrench my hands free from my bonds. With my right hand, I feel blood oozing from a jagged cut in my Persian robe.

In the darkness, two men roll on the ground, saying nothing but heaving and gasping as each seeks the advantage. Holding the torn robe tight against my body, I attempt to staunch the flow of blood while groping in the blackness with my other hand for Medarnes' sword. Before I can find it, the fight is over. I feel, rather than see, the swift downward plunge of a dagger. Then comes a sharp, silenced scream, and nothing. I am desperate to resume my search, and crawl about on my knees, my hand scraping back and forth in the earth.

I hear the killer then rise from the corpse and make his way toward me. Bile rises in my throat as the combination of pain and fear threatens to overwhelm me. Then, there it is! Medarnes' sword. I grasp the handle and attempt to rise, but a heavy foot comes down on the blade, forcing it back to the ground. A hand grabs the back of my robe, and a voice whispers, "Come with me now if you want to live."

It isn't Medarnes, but the voice is familiar. I half-walk, half-stumble after him; a big man, hooded, and cloaked. Crouching, he drags me toward the hillside, closer to the Greek position as more voices rise behind us, calling out for Medarnes. In a few moments, we arrive at the base of the hill, and my savior pulls me up the incline and into the protective mass of brush. Through the tangled branches, I can see torches fluttering in the dark as a group of soldiers fan into the open, searching. Breathing hard, I realize the flow of blood from my wound has stopped or at least slowed. But I am lightheaded.

"Here," says the voice. "Let me have a look." Rough hands pull aside my robe and probe at the wound. "You will heal, but I must bind it for you or you will bleed to death." His hands work, his voice muffled, his face hidden by a hood, as I try to collect my thoughts.

"Who are you?" I ask.

"Best I ask the questions, not you. Why are you here? How did Medarnes find you?"

I hesitate, remembering the story Demaratus and I had crafted, but also was sure it wouldn't fool this man. Thus, I decide to tell the truth, or as much of the truth as I thought is needed. "I was trying to escape."

"Just you? Are you in the graces of Demaratus?"

"No. I escaped from him also."

Now the man throws back his hood. I draw in a deep breath. My stomach flames in agony as I study his features limned in the starlight against the midnight sky.

"I don't believe you, but that is not of importance now," he says. "The soldiers will find Medarnes in a moment, but they won't find you. You cannot go back."

"Phraortes?"

"Yes," he replies. "I've been tracking you since you left the column. I do not know what you and the Spartan have made plans for, but you must tell me."

"He wanted me to get back to my people," I say, the pain in my gut dulling to a rhythmic throbbing.

"Lysis!" he growls. "Demaratus does nothing without cause!"

"What does it matter to you? I only want to get home."

He stops bandaging me and sits back on his haunches, looking at me. "You want to get home?"

"Yes."

"And home is through that pass?"

"Yes, through that pass and back to Athens."

He pauses for what seems like an eternity. His eyes bore into mine. They gleam and glisten with reflections of starlight, while shadows gouge deadened and darkened valleys in his scar-ravaged face. In the plain, the calling voices from afar turn to alarm. The soldiers have found Medarnes.

"We must move in haste," he says. "They will find us here." He hesitates again. "Lysis, we all have homes we wish to find again. In a way, yours and mine are the same."

"What do you mean?"

"I mean Athens was my home at one time."

"You were Athenian? That's how you knew my father?"

I can see him now, struggling to speak. He reaches for the amulet hanging from his neck. "Lysis, have you seen this before?"

I am confused, the picture again appearing in my mind, an image of the amulet, the "Alpha" etched in silver. "I have seen it before, but it was a long time ago."

"It was a long time ago." Grasping the amulet with a clenched fist, he lifts his chin, and in his eyes, I can see the glint of tears. "Your mother gave this to me."

"My mother?"

"Yes, Lysis, your mother." He looks at me again, the tears beginning to drip from his eyes and slide down his cheeks, pooling in the crevices of his face. "I am Androcles, son of Thraortis," he says, "and I am your father."

CHAPTER 7

Lysis

It feels as if I am somewhere else. I am detached, an observer of my own life. The physical wound I have sustained is nothing compared to the body blow this strange man has delivered. I cease breathing, and when I remember to do so, the sharp inhalation makes me gasp in pain.

"You are my father, That is impossible. My father was a patriot. He loved his city. He loved Athens. You are the Butcher of Egypt. You are not my father." I feel forlorn, distraught, and thinking in circles. My reasoning mind seems to have shut down.

"Lysis, please, it's not as you think."

"It is as I think" I stutter. "You are a murderer and a traitor. Why would you bother to torture me like this? Why don't you kill me instead?" My voice rises above a strained whisper.

"Stop it," he cautions and slaps me. "Stop." He holds me down and draws close to my ear. "I am your father. Now stop this. They will find us."

I struggle against his grip, but remain collapsed against the earth; my emotions crash down as well. He feels me relent.

"Listen to me," he says. "I was forced to do much."

"Like murder an entire city?"

His face seizes with pain. "I do not expect you to understand."

"I do not want to understand."

"So be it. But understand this, there is hope for you, though there may not be any for me. You have lived a different life than I. An honorable life. You must continue to live that life as you see fit."

"If you are my father," I spit, "what honor can there be for me?"

"You will find it within yourself, as I assume you always have."

We stare at each other, my heart a riot of emotions, my stomach torn on the outside and roiled and bound tight like a hawser cable on the inside. "What will you do with me now?"

"What can I do?" he replies. "I don't know of your mission, but I suspect you have one. I can't send you away for you'll be caught and killed. I must take a chance and let you take yours. I will help you these last few yards. My life is here now. I must repay loyalty with loyalty. Xerxes saved me once, a long time ago, against the father of this Medarnes, who now lies dead by my hand. Perhaps you will understand and think better of me when you are on the other side."

I am silent, though there are things I wish to say, many things I wish I could say. But I can not speak. I lift myself and rise to my feet, staggering as I feel the blood rush to my head. My father supports me.

"We must be quiet now," he says. "We need to get to the Greek pickets."

As we step from the shelter of the brush, I once again catch the glow of torches. A group of searchers is moving our way. We have to hurry. We make our way back to the plain, angling our descent toward the Phocian wall. We have not gone far when a voice from the dark commands: "Hail."

"Who is that?" comes the voice again, a firm, guttural, Greek one.

"A scout," says Androcles, "reporting back in."

"Move closer," says the voice.

We do, even as behind us the Persians have apparently heard our voices and move in our direction as the sharp twang of a bow-string pings the night air.

The Greek picket swears: "Down!"

Androcles and I fall to the ground. An arrow impales the dirt feet from where we lay.

"Go now," whispers Androcles. "Don't make me regret releasing you. And son—" he grips my arm, "I am sorry."

He releases me then, and I crawl toward the picket, choking back rage and joy and grief, feeling torn to pieces.

Demaratus

As soldiers, we knew the march down the mountain would be swifter than the way up. Ascending the other side, we had gone quite a ways northward and westward before turning south and east. We should be at the base near Alpeni by midday. We had not seen any Phocians attempting to pass by us to warn Leonidas, so Hydarnes and the rest of the column were confident of a surprise attack. Word from the rear guard was good. The Phocians had not strayed from their position, terrified lest the entire army be coming for them. I thanked the gods for their cowardice. For my sake, I also hoped Lysis had managed to get through.

I thought again of the Greek and his situation. I had promised to find out as much as I could for him, and during the march, I took advantage of the time and the open conversation with Hydarnes to pry for information. We had been walking for some time near the head of the army, and the path was still wide enough for four to six abreast as we traveled down the mountain face. I saw that Hydarnes was pleased.

"The men seem in high spirits," I said.

"Yes, my Spartan friend," he replied. "And well they should be. Running our heads into that wall time and again did not get us victory, and cost us many lives. They know the tablets of fate." He stopped for a moment and removed his felt cap, using it to wipe his brow. Already the air had heated up. The clatter of wicker shields and the tramp of thousands of feet echoed off the mountain walls.

"Hydarnes," I asked, "what do you know of this Phraortes?"

"The king's secret sentry?"

"Yes."

"More than I should." His voice became guarded. "Why do you ask?"

"The king has asked me to work with him to collect information on the matters in Boetia," I lied. "He seems a smarmy sort and I'd like to know if the man I must work with is of lower breed."

He relaxed a bit, but I could sense his hesitancy. "To most, the man is a bit of a mystery, but I met him after he first arrived to the king's court. He was—" and he paused, "different."

"My Lord, different?"

"He is said to have been quite a handsome man, before of course those scars that mar his face now. I'm not sure how he came to them," he shrugged. "No one is."

"You think not from honor in a battle?"

"Perhaps. He was an Athenian exile. I'm sure you've heard his accent."

I nodded.

"He was also a man of some influence in his country. When I first saw him though, he was not in our great king's service. However Xerxes had bestowed on him some land in the Troad region."

"Near the Hellespont?"

"Yes."

"That's where I have my lands."

"That's right!" he laughed. "I'd forgotten you Greeks want to be closer to home!"

I grinned. "How did he end up as head of Xerxes's secret sentries?"

"I'm not sure, nor are others. He changed his name to Phraortes, or the king did, and many people do not recognize him to be the same man. His old name was Androcles, I think. He used to come to the court, which is why I knew him. Then he disappeared for quite a while. The next time I saw him, he was as you see him now."

So that was it. Androcles the Athenian was head of the king's secret sentries and father to Lysis. I'd never met a father and son more different. It was as I suspected, though, and I prayed Lysis would never find out the truth. It would be better if he continued to believe his father was dead.

"What is it, Demaratus?" Hydarnes asked, looking at me. "You have other reasons for this information?"

"No, no," I said. "I only wonder what a man must do to warrant the gods' wrath."

"Believe me, my friend, whatever the gods have meted out to Phraortes, he has more than made up for in cruelty to others."

"I understand."

We walked along in silence for a while. *Better to be a soldier,* I thought. *Or a king. No, not a king, for I had been one.* Sometimes the things I did as a king chilled my soul. But it takes a special kind of man, or some extraordinary circumstances, to do what this Phraortes had done. There had to be a reason and I thought I owed it to Lysis to find out.

Lysis

I hear Androcles crawl away and the sharp ping and hum of a few more arrows slicing through the night. They fall to my left as I crawl the last few feet into the Greek lines, my face presses close to the dirt. My nose is assailed by the scent of death all around me, remnants of the last two days of bloodshed. There is no wind and though the midnight air is warm, I am cold as my wound seeps blood through the rough bandages with which Androcles has wrapped me, wetting my wool robe and tunic.

The picket is there to greet me. I can feel his surprise as he grasps the Persian robe and pulls me behind the low earthen wall of his post. "Who are you?" he asks, with his sword at my throat. "Where is the other?"

"I was a prisoner of the enemy," I gasp. "The other man helped me escape. Please, I have a message for the king."

I can feel his grip loosen. He turns and gives a low call to the rear. In a moment, the scrape of sandaled feet on the rough soil heralds the approach of another soldier.

"Take him through the wall," says the picket. "He says he has news for the king."

The man waves for me to follow him but at first I can only stagger to my feet. Trying to get my bearings, I see the Phocian wall outlined against the dim starlight a few plethron distant. That sight gives me strength to follow my guide, stepping over bodies whose spirits have left them, and stumbling on shattered spears and other weapons. We move along the wall to the gate, guarded by battered and weary hoplites. The bronze fittings on their scarred shields glint in the flickering luminescence of a single torch.

Here, where the actual wall is, the gap between mountain and sea is no more than a single plethron, and I can smell the marshland that runs to open water. When the soldiers open the gate for me, I slip inside, following my guide, but am unable to keep up. The guide stops. "You are hurt?"

"Yes, a bit, while trying to escape."

"The king will not appreciate a wounded man in his presence. We'll first visit disciples of the god Asclepius who will cleanse your wounds."

"No!" I say. "There is no time! The king needs this information!"

"There are a few hours yet till daylight," replies my guide. "The enemy won't move until then. And, mind you, it is the king's court you are to enter."

I give no resistance as I can no longer think with clear vision. The shock of my physical wound, combined with the realization of my father's identity, has overwhelmed me.

"What is your name?" he asks.

"I am Lysis, son of..." I begin to answer but cannot finish. Son of whom? That man back there? Who was he? I begin to feel an all-consuming wave of despair roll over me, like a mountain stream swollen with the winter's melted snow, cold and bitter. Who am I now, having lived my entire life in the shadow of a lie? What would be my tomorrow? How could I expiate this sin?

"Well, Lysis, I am Hippocrotes, son of Xaneander. You need to be nourished, if only for a while."

Hippocrotes? My boyhood friend? No, my Hippocrotes is dead, hacked into a dozen pieces, and ripped beyond recognition. This Hippocrotes is not the same. He is a Thespian, or a Theban, or somebody else. But he is not part of my world. My world turned upside down.

He leads me through the camp amidst a nest of sleeping men, their heads cradled on upturned shields or tough leather packs, eyes closed tight, sunken in an ocean of exhaustion. We pick our way through to a large, dimly-lit tent, filled with the soft moans of wounded men.

"Healer," my guide calls out as we emerge from the shadows. "I have a patient who needs to speak to the king. Can you make him more presentable."

"No room for 'presentable' here," answers a weary voice. "At least not in this world." He approaches from the entrance, his white beard and rheumy eyes keeping time with his deliberate movements. He wipes his bloodied hands on his tunic and looks me over, eyeing my Persian garb.

"What have you brought me?"

My guide says, "He is Greek. Escaped from the enemy."

"My wound is not bad," I answer. "And I must see the king."

"I'm sure you must. Sit down and let me see that." He opens the robe and examines the wrappings. "Bad, but not too bad. These cloths were bound well and may have even saved your life. I'll clean the wound and replace them, though. The bleeding's stopped."

He bustles about, washing, and dabbing at the wound. He applies a new set of dressings about my abdomen and around my lower back, then secures them. "You are cut deeply, but it could have been much worse. Another finger's width deeper, and you'd have spilled your guts."

He pats me on the back. "Get up now, and on your way. You've lost some blood, and the wound will sting, but you should be alright. More than I can say for most of these men." The healer is rueful, glancing back into the tent. "If only I could send everyone on so. Well, pray to Asclepius, I suppose. What else can one do?" He shuffles back into the tent.

The guide grips my arm. "The old man's spirit has been robbed from seeing too much death, but he knows what he's doing. Come with me now."

As we continue through the camp, the night rules over the stars holding court. Ahead of us a fire glows, its embers smoldering.

"I sent word to the king you were arriving with some information. He should be awake," says the guide. "I hope what you have to say will be of importance to him."

"It will."

We enter the circle of shadowy light. A warrior rises in front of us. I know him. It is Dieneces, he of the "We'll fight better in the shade" remark. He recognizes me also.

"Ah! Our Athenian messenger!" he says. "Is the Great king requesting we move again? I hope he has remembered to say 'please' this time!" He gives a hearty laugh, though grimaces with the effort, and I note his bandaged head.

"No," I reply. "I bear no messages from Xerxes this time."

"Well then, what have you to say?" asks Leonidas, appearing from the other side of Dieneces. "Lysis, isn't it?"

"Yes, Highness."

He moves to me, extending his hand in peace. "What is your message?"

"I bring further word from Demaratus."

"He wishes regular correspondence!" the king replies with amusement, looking around. "What could have changed that he comes back to me again?"

"Your Highness," I say, "the enemy is positioning to attack the rear guard."

"What? How do you know this?"

I reach around to my back, feeling the papyrus still safe. "I believe the details are in a letter sewn into my tunic. If one of your men could remove it for me, you will see, I am sure."

The king motions for Dieneces to do so. As he cuts the papyrus sheet out and hands it to the king, I continue. "I marched for a while with the Immortals, ten thousand strong, up a mountain path to the north of here. They seemed filled with the gods' will."

Leonidas strides to the fire and scans the letter in the glow of the embers. "He does not understand," he mutters, and lifts his head. "This is grim news indeed. Dieneces! Call the captains of our allied contingents. We must gather here immediately."

"Yes, Great One, at once," answers the Spartan. He bolts away, taking three other Spartans with him. In a few moments, I hear the stirring of men in their sleep, waking to the sound of raised voices. Leonidas crumbles the letter and throws it into the fire, where for an instant, it catches and casts a bright yellow light. Then the king rises and crosses to where I stand.

"Lysis, I dreamed you would have some part in this drama before it was over, but the gods have acted sooner than I imagined." He studies me for a moment. His brows furrow. "Something else is wrong...you look desolate, as if the gods have abandoned you."

I feel it then, another surge of emotion that roars from my aching gut but dashes against the shores of my inadequacy of expression. I feel tears form in my eyes.

"It is too small for your concern Great king," I say, tight-lipped but quivering. "I must address it myself."

He nods, but in his own eyes, I read concern. How was it, this king, in the middle of a battle, with all the worries of command, could somehow communicate the fact that he cared?

"Lysis, I feel sure you will come to me with this other matter you hide now, when it suits you." He pauses. "You have been a noble courier, I can use you tomorrow for the same task."

"No, Your Highness!" I blurt out. "I want to stay here and fight with you."

"My good Athenian," replies the king, " The fleet will need to know of our siege here. They cannot remain blind. You are wounded, that is obvious. But you must deliver my message to the Greeks at sea."

I stare at him, wrestling with my emotions. Bitterness and anger clash in my heart alongside despair while soldiers heap wood on the fire, and it crackles once again.

The king sighs, hesitating. "Lysis, I will give you the arms you need to fight, but you must take leave when I call."

I nod, sure that when the king calls, I will already be dead. It will be better that way. Honor will be served. The debt to my country owed by my family will be paid.

The king puts his hand on my shoulder. "That is good," he says. "Greece will need good men, long after this day." The king looks up as the other Greek commanders enter the circle. "Stay Lysis, and listen to what is said. The fleet must know the entire truth." He turns to another aide. "Tyrtaeus, get this man fitted for battle."

I nod my appreciation, and looking for a rock, sit down to await the proceedings. The other captains gather around Leonidas as he addresses them. He hesitates, studying their faces.

"My friends, we have been betrayed. The enemy has discovered the Anopaea and is marching Xerxes' Immortals around to our rear guard."

There is immediate consternation in a babble of voices with more than a measure of fear and uncertainty. "What of the Phocians?" a commander cries out. "Have they been routed?"

Leonidas is silent. Then he continues, "The enemy is still many hours away. We cannot count on the Phocians to hold, but we still have choices."

"What choices do we have?" asks one of the captains. "The Persians will attack in front and rear. We will be caught and slaughtered!"

"True!" says another. "We must abandon the pass now and retreat while there is time!" A chorus of agreement arises from the others, but Leonidas raises his hand, palm out.

"Men! I will not hold you against your will." The murmurs quiet. "But for my account, the Spartans will stay and defend the pass."

"What madness is this?" exclaims a tall, gnarled-faced commander. "There is no logic in certain death!"

"There is no honor in retreat either!" retorts a younger captain, moving forward in the circle.

"Are you impugning my honor?" snaps the tall one.

"You need not my help for that. You have sacrificed your honor on your own," replies the younger. And with that, he jumps across the circle, his hand on his sheathed sword hilt, as the taller man stands at the ready.

Leonidas steps in between them. "Leontiadas! Eurycles! Would you do the enemy's work for him?"

The two stare at each other, moving back a few paces.

"Men," says Leonidas, his tone conveying the urgency thick in the air, "we will stay and defend because that is what the Ephors of our country desire. Yet, you may leave if that is your wish. I pray to the gods that the majority of you and our other defenders live to fight again, but I know as you do that the Persians have bathed in pools of their own blood these last days of battle. The outcome of this war is far from certain. These so-called Immortals have attacked us in waves and still fallen in death each time. In our front, will the battle be any different tomorrow? It's true they have outflanked us, but they still have no cavalry. They still have to meet us line to line. They cannot defeat us in that way."

"They don't need cavalry," says the man Leonidas identified as Leontidadas. "The ground is open behind us. They will overwhelm us with their numbers. Their supply of men and weapons is the reason we took hold of the pass in the first place."

There is silence. All listen to what Leonidas will have to say.

"You are correct, Leontidadas," replies the king, after a moment. He draws himself up, his demeanor radiating power and quiet confidence. "We are at the bidding of the fates. But there is no certainty in life, other than death. We are to hold this pass and hold this pass we will. The honor you have gained in these last few days will never dissipate, even should you turn and leave this night." He casts his gaze around the gathering, taking in the measure of each man, their eyes glued to him.

"We have been a rock against the flood, and though battered and scarred, we have held their forces back with nothing but our Greek courage and the power of free men. And though you may live on this for the rest of your lives, as the sun outshines the moon, the glory we gather tomorrow will outstrip what we've done to this day. We have willed it so because we have stood together. If we are to make a stand here till death, the Persians will see what awaits them in the rest of our country, and that will give them pause, perhaps, and still their assault. I will not keep you here. The choice of free men is freedom. We Spartans, how ever many remain, will hold the pass."

The air is still, and in the hush punctuated by the snap of the fire, a pent-up flood of feeling emanates from the group and reaches out to the king and embraces him. A dark-bearded and powerful-looking man steps forward, his sandals crunching the dirt. He looks around at the other captains and turns to Leonidas. "I am Demophilus, son of Diadromes, of Thespia, and we will stay and fight beside the king's guard."

"Thank you, Demophilus," the king responds. "But you are free to take leave and know that you will see light after the rest of us have gone to rest in the dark. Perhaps Thespia will have more need of you than we will."

"Thespia needs glory, Leonidas. I do not wish to deny what is hers. We cannot have you Spartans keep the victory all to yourselves!"

The king smiles. "That is good then." He turns to Leontidadas: "I know your Thebans well. They have fought with vigor and passion these last few days and have honored themselves in the doing. I know they will feel, as I'm sure you do now, they can best protect Thebes in this faraway country. May the gods shine on you for deciding to stay."

Leontidadas gapes but he wilts under Leonidas' gaze and says nothing. The king then addresses the others. "Commanders, from the information we have received, I do not believe the enemy will clear the mountain before midday. You have time to ready your men. You will march south, alert the settlements in your path, and send messengers to Athens and the allied council. I will get word to the fleet, when appropriate. Now, be on your way, and may the will of the gods guide you."

They nod, bow, and then each commander comes up to the king, clasping him by the arm in solidarity, some embrace him as they take their leave. Some, with tears in their eyes, can say nothing; they only kneel before the king and leave. Leonidas watches them go, his expression hidden. He stands cast against the firelight, an immortal Olympian at that moment, regal and certain. Then he turns and walks toward me, his face betraying the weariness that crowds his features.

"Lysis, now you will be able to tell the full tale. Dawn is upon us." He wheels and strides away, heading for his tent, which now appears white in the lightening morning.

While we had been talking, the king's aide, Tyrtaeus, had arrived with an armful of armor and draped in weapons. "This is what I have collected for you, Lysis," he says. "Their last owners, riding on chariots in the heavens now, would appreciate them being used."

I stand and take the paraphernalia from Tyrtaeus, and lay it at my feet. I have nowhere to go, and my bone-deep fatigue rolls over me like a river. I thank Tyrtaeus and lay my head down on a dented and slashed shield, and a punctured linen breastplate and fade into slumber.

I dream of the gods afflicting me with a confusing panoply of images, some dark and dangerous, some of times gone by, all beyond my understanding to interpret.

I dream of the ships, the mighty ships, the flashing oars, the deadly rams. I dream of Hippocrotes slashing away, through the middle of a storm-tossed sea, tall and immovable as the vessel fills with water; then, of all the ships sinking, sinking to the ocean floor, as the storm rages. The water flows all around me until I am drowning in it. There is no escape, no relief. Panic descends upon me, and I claw to the surface, but I can not break free. I will die. Die before I can do anything, before I can seize hold of a fate that would make a difference in the world. Then all of it is gone, and I am with Andronica in the agora, the crowds all around us, pressing us together. I need to tell her something, but she won't listen. She is watching her servant buy the evening meal. She seems so sure of herself, so sure of me. That I can not talk to her makes me sad. She is so distant, like another person.

Dieneces shakes me awake. It seems I have come back to life from a great distance, swimming to awareness, through a heavy sea of dreams. When I pry open my eyes, it is mid-morning, brightness and heat once again infuse the fitful scene of the awaiting battle. I can taste blood. My own? No, my lips had rested on the linen breast-plate. It is the blood of our dead.

I push myself up, feeling my abdomen ache and my other wounds protest as they strain against the break of their angry red scars. Then the full impact of the moment hits me. I remember the night before. My escape. My father. The king. And once again feel the weight of anguish descend.

Dieneces remains standing above me, grinning. "So eager to fight, yet more eager to slumber! Wake now, time to meet the day!"

I rise to my feet, grasping the breastplate.

"I will help you with that," says Dieneces. "The king has com-manded me to stay with you as long as is necessary."

"Thank you," I mutter, blinking sleep from my eyes. I look around the encampment, now a riot of movement in the long shadows of the day. Off to my left, the short stretch of marshland dominated by tall reeds and green swamp plants merge with the sea. Rippling along its surface, a slight onshore breeze creates thou-sands of sparkles like miniature stars across the water, all the way east to the haze off the island of Euboea.

To my right, the mountain recedes from the shore plain, open-ing back at least twenty times the width of the pass at the Phocian wall. Straight south, along the shoreline, a hillock rises as an off-shoot of the mountain, sloping on all sides. Beyond that, the road, no more than a cart trail, stretches away in the distance and skirts the edge of the foothills. Wisps of smoke curl up through the air past the next rise and dissipate in the breeze.

All around me, hoplites arm themselves. Servants assist the non-Spartans, Helots assist the Spartans. They busy themselves adjusting armor, shining shields, polishing swords, bronze breast-plates, and helmets. A column of men marches away down the path with shields slung over their shoulders. I can see another column disappearing around the first bend. Dieneces notes the direction of my gaze.

"Our Peloponnesian allies, Mantineans, Tegeans, Orchomenians, Corinthians..." His cheerful expression dims for a moment. "All taking leave from battle." I look at him, so stolid and dependable. It must have pained him to see them depart.

"How many choose to stay and fight?"

"Enough for victory" he replies, his mood restored. "Two hundred of us Spartans, about the same number of Helots. Four or five hundred Thespians and three hundred Thebans. A veritable ocean of men."

"Those Thebans, why did they stay? Last night they told a different tale."

Dieneces smirks. "The king has a mind to ensure their loyalty. Thebes, I believe, has been teetering on the edge of collaboration with those barbarians. The king would rather they join us than spread ill-feeling in Thebes."

I can see that. But there is so much uncertainty, fear, and betrayal. Would whole cities in the heartland of Greece allow themselves to succumb to it?

"Dieneces, why do you stay?"

"Because the king stays."

"And why does king Leonidas stay?"

"Because he must," Dieneces looks again toward the retreating men. "The Delphic Oracle told us the Persians would overwhelm us. Well," and he pauses, "it said either Sparta would be defeated and occupied, or a king would die."

"And so Leonidas gives his own life so Sparta can live?"

"If you believe in the oracle, then yes."

"But there are two Spartan kings," I said. "What of Leotychidas?"

Dieneces grunts. "Leotychidas is not fit to stand in the same rank as Leonidas. That is my judgment. And I am not alone."

I am quiet, thinking of how opposite my father and this king Leonidas of the Spartans are. How different, indeed, is Demaratus, than is this king? How would he have behaved? I wonder more about what was in the message he had me deliver to Leonidas. What could have passed between them, now and in the past?

I nod, again looking southward. "And those pillars of smoke?"

"Ah yes! The hot springs. It's where our encampment gets its name, the hot gates. Those are healing pools dedicated to Heracles.

People come from all over to try the gods soothing hands." He grabs the breastplate from my hand and slips it over my head. "You will need to get beyond them once you leave. Alpeni and the terminus of the Anopaea are near there. The enemy will disgorge upon our rear between those hills."

He tightens the connecting straps of the cuirass down my left side and pulls the two shoulder straps down, tying them off on the chest plate. The linen breastplate, though less than a finger's width thick, is tough and resilient. He stands back. "Not bad, it fits you well. Now, your helmet."

I heft the helmet. It is Corinthian, but not like my old one; my father's that I had lost in the sea. But it has ear openings and long cheek-guards with a narrow nose piece. I like my eyes and ears clear. How can one hear with the ears covered? The helmet has a long and brilliant horsehair plume, black and red that stands straight up along the crest of the helmet, front to rear. I am not a man for gaudy display, but it is good enough to die in, I suppose. I pull the helmet on over my head and feel the smooth lining set itself against my scalp. Dieneces approves with a nod.

"Now, I think these greaves will fit fine," he says, slipping the leather-lined, bronze shin guards over my legs. "You will find these to be a gift from the gods. The Persian archers have much anger going against our shields, and now take to lower aim."

He stands back, surveying his work. "Good. Now, the sword bestowed upon you by Trytaeus. It is a fine weapon. I knew its former master. I am sure you will bring honor to it as it's next master." He hands me the sword, seated in a beautiful, bronze-buttressed leather scabbard. I pull it out, hefting it's weight in my hand, it's bright iron with a polished bronze handle, and a leaf-shaped blade. I sling it over my shoulder and feel it slap against my left side.

I bend to gather the shield. Reaching over, I feel my cuirass bend, and slip my left arm through the leather straps on the inside of the shield. No different than mine lost in battle. Four feet in diameter, this one will cover me from shoulder to knee and cross the front of my body to protect my left side. Its bronze face bears a large painted symbol of the Spartan warrior, the Lambda:

"Yes, I knew the warrior," Dieneces stares away, "who carried this before you."

I tuck my left elbow into my body and feel the shield fit over my left shoulder. It will rest there while I wield my spear with my right. Though the cuirass and helmet are light, the combined weight of armor and shield will test my strength.

Dieneces tosses me my spear, eight feet from tip to tip. Its shaft is sturdy cornel wood and its iron spearhead broad and sharp. The butt end holds a long spike, used when an enemy falls in front. I would not have to spin the weapon to deliver a killing blow since a swift downward thrust will do.

"We will fight like Cerberus," says Dieneces, "but you must care for that spear. We lost many in the last few days. Supplies are tight. You only have this one."

"So be it. I choose the sword over spear for killing anyway."

"Fortune fall on you then. But the spear, and less, may save you." He turns and looks toward the Phocian wall and the enemy. "They have made no move, as yet. I believe we will soon march out to attack them."

I spin and rest my gaze upon the pass. Above the repaired and rough-hewn barrier, a smoky haze rises and obscures the brilliant sky. The wall itself is ten feet high and lined with soldiery that stand on a wooden platform halfway up the inside surface of the rough rock. The parapet is crenelated, and from each embrasure, archers' arrows point. The defense runs up the ridge of the mountain until the wall reaches the cliff side where a short and stubby, square-faced tower stands. Beyond it, the wall plunges into the marsh and ends in another small tower. The marsh water laps at the base, cutting off all hope of a flank assault. Several small gates scatter along its length, allowing easy egress for our warriors.

Between Dieneces and myself, troops gather, completing their preparations, and organizing themselves under the barked commands of their officers.

"Come now, Athenian!" says Dieneces.

As we walk toward the others, I hear it: a distant murmuring sound like waves upon the shore, constant and sonorous. For a moment, in my stupor, I can not place it. Then it comes to me. It is the enemy. From past the wall, the sound of their multitudes reverberate in the narrow pass and roll over our encampment like a thick blanket of enormity. The smoky haze, too heavy for the breeze to penetrate, is the detritus from thousands and thousands of their encampment fires.

Though I had been in the Persian camp and had seen their numbers stretching to the horizon, I have never felt before the sheer size of their army. Though resolved to die, I am still intimidated beyond measure. The courage of these men who have for the last three days held that wall against such a host is unimaginable. And I am now among them.

Dieneces leads me to where Leonidas stands by a makeshift altar, close to the joining of the wall with the sheer cliff that ends the mountain's thrust to the sea. The altar is a hip-high mound of piled and blackened stones that has seen much use already in these narrow quarters. A priest and diviner appear, leading a leashed young ewe, pure white and docile. We gravitate to the circle of armored men who surround the altar.

Dieneces nudges me with his elbow. "Megistias of Acarnania," he whispers. "Leonidas has great faith in him, though his readings last night were not, ah, favorable."

I lean on my shield and watch as the wiry old man brings the unsuspecting victim to the altar. Holding the tether in one hand, he raises the other to the heavens and intones his prayer.

"Zeus Thunderer," he cries, "hear the prayers of those gathered here. Show us the portents of victory and your divine will."

With that, he receives a cup of water from his servant and sprinkles it on the face of the sacrifice. The animal bows its head in acquiescence to its fate. Megistias then draws a short, curved knife from his belt and in one motion, slashes across the throat of the startled sheep. Blood spurts from the severed neck, and the animal drops to it's knees, rolling over to the dirt. As it's lifeblood drains into the earth, the priest slices into it's belly, laying bare the steaming entrails, which tumble out in a rush.

Other men press in close obscuring my view. I can see the priest's head as it bobs above the sheep's remains. There is a hush, as Leonidas stands unmoving. Megistias raises himself to his feet and addresses the king.

"Your Majesty, the gods are pleased with the efforts of his servants." He pauses, "but there is death in these signs for all those here today."

Leonidas nods his head. "Thank you, Megistias, the gods' words have been heard. I now release you from your obligation to this army. You and your son may go."

"My Lord," replies the priest, "I will indeed send my boy away, but I will remain here with the sons of Lacedaemon."

"As you wish," says the king, who turns to the men standing by, their faces reflecting the impact of this news. "Warriors," he says, his deep and powerful voice echoing off the mountain side, "the gods have spoken, yet we can choose the manner of our end. It is to this choice we have committed ourselves, to fight to the last of our mortal selves. We fight for Greece, we fight for our homes, but most of all, we fight for each other. I have never been more proud of any other army I have been privileged to lead than I am of you from Spartan bloodlines and you from our ally states. What we do here today will be remembered in everlasting glory in the hearts of all Greece, for as long as there is memory."

He stops, as all strain to hear, every eye focused. "I know you will earn that glory with me today, and I trust I will earn the honor of your company from this moment and for all eternity."

I feel the tears well in my eyes as I sense all around me the gathering of soul filled power in this passionate communion. Leonidas continues.

"Soldiers of Greece, we will march out to meet the enemy. We will not let him come to us. Take your final sustenance now, for tonight we dine with Zeus in the heavens."

There is, then, a most extraordinary thing. A low growl begins to build among the men, and as it grows and expands, we move to the center toward the king. The noise is throaty but muted at first, swelling like the howl of the wind on a stormy night and growing to a roaring cacophony as we close in on the king, raising our spears and slamming them to the earth in a rhythmic hammer of agreement. We embrace him then, as he has embraced us, a final melding of power, a final rage against the rush of darkness.

It lasts for what seems a long time but can not have been. The king moves through the midst of our ranks as the troops begin to disperse, heading for their gathering places, fortifying themselves with bread, or wine, or what suits them. Leonidas walks right by me, but in his eyes, there is no recognition; in them is an expression, committed, and at peace. As he strides past, Dieneces touches him on the arm. He stops and turns.

"Ah, yes, Dieneces, are you ready?"

"Never more so, my king. But My Lord, we have Lysis here. What do you wish for him?"

The king notices me then, a slow smile creasing his worn features. "Of course, my messenger." He seems to come back to himself then and claps his hand on my shoulder. "I see you are armed and ready for battle. You will stay with Dieneces. When the scouts have reported the enemy is making its final approach, I will release you. You are to make your way along the coast beyond the hot springs. A boat and men await you there. Tell them all you have seen. Do you understand?"

"Yes Your Highness, but I wish this mission to be given to another so I can fight and die with you."

"Is the king's courier not honor enough for you?"

"There is no honor I could gain, other than through death for my country, that would restore to my house the honor it has lost."

"Lysis! There is no time for this. This task I give you is worthy of any warrior."

"Then, My Lord, I beg you give it to another warrior for whom honor will be more easily earned. Giving honor to me is but a waste as the spawn of Androcles, a traitor to his city and his family!" The grief and rage I have suppressed release in a torrent. "He heads Xerxes' secret sentries under the name Phraortes. He has killed thousands of people— men, women, and children in Egypt. I can do nothing to restore my family's honor. My Lord, I am ready to die as my last attempt at contrition for my father's sins."

A stunned silence hangs over Leonidas and Dieneces.

"So that is it, then," Leonidas remarks. "I can see the source of your pain, Lysis." He stands back, searching my eyes. "But I can see this also, you are not your father. There is nothing in you that speaks to this. You are your own man. You are now, you will always be. I ask you not to burn yourself in a pyre for the sins of your father."

I stare at him, my whole body taut with anger and despondence.

"We need you, Lysis," he says. "I need you. Please, do this, if not for yourself, then for me."

Even in my agitation, I regret my outburst. It is not right to further burden the king with my troubles. Not now, not ever. So I nod. I do not trust myself to speak. In my mind, however, my resolve has not changed.

Leonidas continues to search my eyes, allowing a rueful smile to play on his lips. He is unconvinced. "Very well then, let the final test begin. Your destiny is in your own heart, as it is with each of us." And he walks away, leaving Dieneces and me to stare at one another.

"Let us go," Dieneces says, "eat and drink, for without sustenance you are but a man, but with it you are warrior." He calls to his Helot, who comes to us with bread and a leather wineskin. We sit down on a rock near the altar. "This will hold you. I don't know what they serve at Zeus's table, but it is surely better than that of a Spartan." He grins.

I say nothing, gnawing on the dried bread and swilling the wine—the wine is almost undiluted and strong. I feel it warm my insides and ease the ache of my wounds. But I have to be careful. Whereas some warriors liked to go into battle drunk, I am determined to fight with a clear head. Only I can cleanse my house. And only I will know if I succeed, and that is all that matters.

A horn blares, and then another. Dieneces rises to his feet. "Time to march. We form on the king's right."

He gathers his shield and weapons, puts on his helmet, green horsehair plume waving in the diminishing breeze, and strides toward the king's position, inside the narrow gate. I follow, feeling my fatigue and the weight of my armor. I see Hippocrates forming with his Thebans to the gate's right, near the sea. He sees me.

"Put on your helmet, Athenian!"

I look at him and does what he suggests, slipping the bronze over my head. I have no other response.

"Open the gates!" commands Leonidas.

The reinforced wooden portals swing open, and the king leads the exit. Dieneces and I are right behind, debouching into the narrow battleground in front of the contested wall. With the army spilling out at our backs, we advance farther into the field, forming up within an easy stone's throw of the gates and wall. It is when I see the Persian host spread out before us that I feel renewed pangs of fear. Through my tiredness, through my emotions, through my determination, a gnawing, dry-mouthed nauseating surge of terror makes its presence known. It always happens this way. But in the midst of battle, it is hard to remember. This is different, of course. Before now, my fear had been of pain, suffering, and death. Now I do not intend to survive. Yet fear is fear, no different in the end. I find that comforting.

The battleground is as it had been when I first traversed this bloodied field to deliver my message to Leonidas. It is, yet not. True, the ground is still flat, and the marsh and the sea still lap on my right. But unbelievable violence has scarred the land in the interval. Hundreds of bodies lay scattered before us. The dirt has been stirred up by thousands of feet, the thudding of uncounted arrows, and the rip and ruin of tumbling death, spilling its fruits upon the earth in untold gallons. We march straight through.

On my left the mountain rises, the oak and pine cling to its sides, covering in summer softness the granite of its ages. Spreading along the coast in layers of enmity remains the haze of the enemy, unwelcome visitor to the lands of my ancestors. The smell has changed, the noxious taint of corruption and bloated death from the previous evening smell even stronger now. It rolls off the hillside and doubles back upon itself, settling again on the place of its creation.

Our line spreads out on either side of me, with Dieneces in the front rank and me right behind. The king is to my left, three men to the left of Dieneces, swinging in cadence with us as the line expands. Leonidas has given orders to cover the open ground from sea to mountain, so we will advance along a broad area, increasing the size of the killing zone. As a result, the normal eight-rank depth was to be reduced by half. That is a sound formation so long as we are close enough to strike.

The Thespians march on the right of our Spartan line, the king's guard, the Thebans on the left, while we hold the center. These men, these Spartans, are different from any phalanx I have ever leveled a spear with. Their precision is extraordinary, their confidence and determination, an enfolding aura. I will match them. I will match their courage and skill. I will make myself worthy of this sacrifice. Is that what we are, a sacrifice? Is there to be no libation from the heavens, where we will nod our heads in quiet acceptance? No, we have made our choice. We will be cleansed in the sacrifice.

In front of us, the Persians form. Through the narrow eyeholes of my helmet, I can see their myriad of archers move into position behind the Medean spearmen. They seem hurried, surprised. They have not expected this bold assault. We continue to advance, passing the gorge that the night before had foiled my initial escape route.

Last night seems like another age. My father waits over there, on the other side of that line. What is he thinking now? Does he know his son is marching to his death? Would this seem like a waste to him? I hear the skirl of pipes as the Lacedaemonian musicians draw the men into the lockstep bond of the phalanx.

Sweat beads in my helmet and runs down my cheeks, the salt stinging my eyes. As we close with the enemy, I hear the order, "Up, spears!" I shift my grip and raise my weapon shoulder high in my right hand, ready for the plunging thrusts that will follow. "Arrows!" comes a new cry, and then the thrum of thousands of bowstrings and the whoosh and whine of legions of tipped missiles hurtling death from the sky.

"Shields!" yell the officers, and I raise mine in rhythm with the ranks in front. The instant before impact, I feel the urge to move right into the protection of the shield wielded by the warrior beside me. I resist, sensing no similar movement from the man to my left. These disciplined Spartans hold their position as a rain of arrows descends on our upraised shields.

A sharp blow hits my shield, a glancing impact that skitters off the edge. Above the roaring in my ears, I hear the clatter of the Persians' iron-tipped cane arrows bounce like hail off our protection, then the screams of those who have not been so quick or have made a pact with Thanatos, the god of death. We are closer now. The pipes resume their call, and from the throats of our charging mass, primal cries erupt. Gone is my fear, banished in the melding of the whole. I am not on an island, assailed by my doubts and limitations. I am connected with my brethren, living in the moment, and drawing strength from the common strength, courage from the common courage.

Over the shoulder of Dieneces, I can see the enemy spearmen brace for the impact. "On the attack!" scream the captains, and we run the last few yards, shields down, helmets pressed against the edge, spears held high. The impact, when it comes, is thunderous. All along the line, our outthrust shields smash into the wicker protection of the Medes and drive them back. Dieneces pushes as his spear arcs up and down, reaching back into the line and dealing death. I press up close behind, raising myself up on my toes and driving my iron blade into the mass of men to my front. I feel the tip tear and rend flesh and hear an unbridled scream of pain. Around

He raised the 8 footer to strike, even as the battle raged around him

me, arrows ping off of armor plating, javelins appear in the gaps between our ranks, and the spears do their deadly work.

My sandals dig into the dirt as we push, tearing up the soil in my confined space. With the vicious pace of our attack, our line moves forward in moments. I step over the shattered bodies of two Median spearmen and see their blood still pumping in diminishing bursts, beginning to drown the earth as it reddens the mud beneath our feet.

The scent of decay mixed with the foul aroma of hundreds of men releasing their bodily fluids in death swirls around me. Despite the rush of energy generated by fear and excitement, I am exhausted. I don't have the strength or endurance of a few days before. In the fierce striving of the phalanx, I feel my wounds leaking blood as the tentative healing they have managed is undone. And yet, my spear never wavers.

I stumble over a crushed wicker shield with its owner's severed arm still attached. Behind me in the rank, a Spartan cries, "Roll back! Roll!" It is a dangerous maneuver, for myself and for the man to my left. My fatigue is hurting the efficiency of the line. I fall back, allowing the man to my rear to take my place. I am now in the third rank, my spear unable to reach the enemy, but I can lean against the back of the man in front, keeping the pressure on with the face of my shield.

An arrow thuds off my helmet, stunning me. The line continues to push forward. To my left, the king fights, his spear a blur of motion. But as I watch, the hoplite on his right goes down, pierced through the neck by an arrow. He falls like a sack, and before the next rank can close the gap, two Medes wade into the line. Stabbing left and right with their short, sharp javelins, they manage to bring another man down. The next ranker, however, steps over his fallen mate and dispatches both of the enemies. The world closes in around me. There is nowhere else on earth, but the few square feet of tumult I occupy; there is no other force but what presses upon my back. Then comes the order: "Retreat! Retreat!"

I panic. Were we to flee and expose our vulnerable backs? How can we run when we are here to fight to the last? As the ranks in front begin to half turn and move to the rear, I remember what Demaratus has said about Leonidas' tactics: Ours is a feigned retreat. There is no panic in this army. The phalanx steps back over the carnage it had wrought, all the while keeping shields high, deflecting the renewed hail of projectiles. The Medes, enraged with their losses and forgetting the lessons of the past two days, launch themselves in an undisciplined pursuit. Our line continues to retreat ten paces, then twenty pulling the enemy into the open. Then, the command.

"Stand!" yells the king.

"Stand!" echo the commanders.

The entire phalanx halts and, in perfect alignment, turns to face our pursuers, our eight-foot, iron-headed monsters scythe down in a catastrophic sweep. The destruction is instantaneous and awful to behold. The phalanx's wings curl in toward the center, compressing the Persian mob, forcing the enemy to trip and stumble, and become ready targets for butt spikes in the formation's rear ranks. Hundreds fall. The rest reverse headlong in retreat as the phalanx advances farther without mercy.

I sense fear turning to panic in the enemy. I hear them crying to each other, see them turning and attempting to push back against the endless ranks behind them, only to find the trap unyielding. The Persians to the rear can not know what is happening upfront. And they are more afraid of Xerxes, who undoubtedly has his officers scourging the trailing ranks, driving them into the fight as he had the two days previous. But Persian pressure on the front forces the unwilling into our spear points. We do not miss the opportunity.

Yet we can not go on like this forever. The enemy archers find holes in our armor, find spots that can kill. Hurled javelins at close range find their marks. Our spears shatter against shield and ground or are pried from stolid grips by the frantic massing of many hands. Soon the supply of spears the Helots had brought into battle disappear. On both my sides, the flashing of swords replace the up-and-down terror of the spears.

My muscles scream in pain, my breath comes in heaving gasps; I can not lift my arm or deliver another blow. My hands are raw and bloody, splinter-filled, and torn. But there is no surrender in me or in any of Leonidas' warriors. The men fight with fanatical urgency, with an outpouring of cold, hard, focused rage, like the promised depths of the underworld. When their spears break, they draw their swords and slash at the bodies in front, driving ever forward, pushing with their shields. Another feigned retreat, another turn and slaughter, but less of the enemy fall this time and they regroup.

Our solid line still extends, but our ranks are reduced to three deep now, sometimes two. This time the enemy comes at us, their eyes filled with fear and despair, torn between two unacceptable outcomes. We meet their charge. In that moment, I am behind the king, and Dieneces beside him. When we close, I catch out of the corner of my eye the flash of a javelin's tip gleaming in the sunlight. Before I can react, the javelin strikes Dieneces full in the side, threading its way through his shield wall to find its target.

The Spartan warrior drops his shield and falls to his knees, keeling over and collapsing to the ground. The line closes around him, with the king angling to take his place. There is neither time nor opportunity to do anything other than note the casualty. Men are falling on all sides, the line beginning to thin. Leonidas limps now. An arrow protrudes from his thigh, and one arm is hacked to pieces and spews blood behind his shield. Still, his long salt-and-pepper hair flows about him, and he continues, exhorting all of us to greater effort, calling on the gods for vengeance. But the enemy pushes us back, the weight of their numbers and the accumulated hammering begin to take hold.

A Helot weaves his way through the ranks shouting for the king. "Great One! They are in the pass! The enemy is in sight!"

Leonidas turns, ducking behind his raised shield. "Have they reached the plain?"

"No, Your Majesty! They will be at our rear guard in minutes!"

"Stay strong warrior," responds the king, "and tell the other commanders of your news."

He sees me then, right by his side. Turning back to the fighting, he speaks over his shoulder. "Lysis, you must leave now. Hesitate, and you will not get through!"

"Great king, I cannot!" I yell.

"You must! Will you let all this be in vain?"

"I will not abandon or betray you!"

"You betray me by your stay! Now go!"

The Medes come with another rush as he speaks these words, and then a broad-faced, bull-like spearman, eyes blazing with fury, crashes into the King, knocking him to the ground. Behind him, a flood of the enemy inundates our position. We close in, hacking our way through and moving them back while Leonidas staggers to his feet.

"Withdraw," he gasps, blood pouring from his mouth. "Make for the hills to the rear of the wall. There we will regroup." Before he has time to utter another sound, an arrow hums past my head and buries itself in his exposed neck. Leonidas' eyes fly open, wide in surprise, and then his head lolls over, his now sightless orbs stare at me.

The enemy see his demise and, with a cry, renew their attack with redoubled vigor. I am thrust backward and land on the ground, avoiding a javelin throw. Above me, the line closes about the body of the king. There the battle explodes with unabashed desperation. While my fellow Greeks break their swords over our leader's mortal remains, I begin to crawl away. Something inside me has broken.

Having wished and prayed for death to end my pain, I have been blind to the selfishness of my desire. Far from expiating the sin of my house and atoning for my father, I will add to his disgrace. I have been given the chance to perform a significant service for a great man and a great cause, and I have nearly laid it low, preferring my own misguided and useless quest for redemption for a crime I did not commit.

Now the king and leader who epitomized true loyalty and honor lies dead, fought over like a trophy by the lions of his pride and the hyenas of his predators. It is more than I can bear.

At last, my thoughts turn to escape. The urgency I have felt to acquit myself honorably in my destruction metamorphize into the frantic necessity of flight. I owe the king the telling of this tale. I struggle to my feet, abandoning my shield, pull off my helmet, and stumble back across the battered landscape, reeling from side to side toward the wall. Spent arrows scatter themselves about me, while the archers aim at a distant but easy target. None have the requisite skill to bring me to my end. I glance back once, taking in the whirling arms and weapons that slice the air around Leonidas. The entire line is close to breaking, close to collapse.

Embodying that thought, I break into a labored run, stumbling at times, but quickly getting back up. There isn't far to go until the wall, and the gates are all open, yawning wide, inviting my entry. In a moment, I am through. Then from somewhere, I find the strength to run faster. I hold my hand on my stomach to stem the ooze of blood, and though I can feel my body fall in on itself and the pain assaulting me in waves, I feel a raw surge of energy, a new outpouring of fear. I don't want to die. I cross the abandoned Greek camp, not seeing the strewn refuse of my army's final death. As I cover the ground, the air becomes cleaner, the sun nearer midday. *Has it been that long since we marched out to battle?* I ask myself. It seems a lifetime.

Ahead I can see the rising plumes of the hot springs. Dieneces had said I needed to get beyond them. The boat would be waiting there. But there is other smoke as well. The air has been sullied by the swirling dust of a horde of men, marching to seal our destruction. The Immortals have arrived.

CHAPTER 8

Demaratus

At four and sometimes six abreast, we marched through forested terrain, the oak and spruce about us framing a clear path for the army. We broke into the open, and the mountains reared above us, rocky crags and bare granite thrusting through a forest canopy of deep green leaves. Off to the west, more mountains fell away in a series of high ridges, some barebacked, others verdant with foliage as they receded toward the central plain of mainland Greece. Mountain goats clambered over the steep rocks, alarmed by the echoing tread of twenty thousand feet. Great crows and soaring hawks kept their distance high above us, witness to our unending and unfamiliar disturbance.

Ephialtes was confident as he led us onward. "Not too long now," he said, to no one in particular. "When the sun reaches midday, we will reach the coast."

That was good. The men, though enthusiastic, were tiring. Their chattering, so effusive after we crested the pass and began our descent, had tailed off to an occasional remark or irritated complaint. We had stopped twice since the crest of the mountain. Hydarnes had sent scouts forward, and none had reported back yet. There was no sign of Leonidas' pickets. Perhaps the Phocians, in their native land, scouted along this path. That was unlike Leonidas, however. He would get warning before we arrived. The question remained. What would he do with that information?

As if reading my thoughts, Hydarnes turned a wry glance my way. "Spartan, what do you think? Will our quarry be there when we arrive, or will he have slipped the trap?"

"I do not know. Though if they have word of our attack they must take leave or face certain death."

Another interval of trudging silence came and went. "Is it hard on you?" the Persian commander asked. "I mean, to see your countrymen killed?"

I had thought long and hard on that these last few months, never wishing this situation. I would have rather come into my own again, in a Sparta I could recognize. I wanted my country back, a country where the truth meant something, and principles would be honored as they had been in the time of Lycurgus. But I should have known that of course they would fight, and likely die, just as I would were I in their ranks. Besides, Leonidas believed in those things that had made our state the military and political force it was. I did not wish for his death.

"I would prefer it was not so. But they have made their choice, as I have mine."

Hydarnes nodded. The long march had dulled even his natural exuberance. Still my thoughts continued to race. I harbored the hope that Leonidas had heeded my last warning and the message that accompanied it. I had given him the chance to escape. To live to fight again, and to be delivered from this Persian army, as I had promised, if he would support my return to the throne. I could do it. Xerxes would listen to my counsel even more as we traveled deeper into Greece. I had been proven correct here concerning the fighting prowess of the Greek soldier. There was no reason why further intelligence from me to Leonidas and the right emphasis to the king would not give the allies a decisive victory over Xerxes' army. I needed Leonidas to lead that victory, and to acknowledge my part in it. We could take care of Leotychidas together.

I remembered then, with renewed bitterness, my final days in my native land when Leotychidas, my usurper, had mocked my downfall. Though I had taken my changed circumstances with the humility expected of all Spartans, his vitriol was excessive. Did he need to shame me in front of the peers, too? Those final insults led to my self-imposed exile. He then succeeded to the kingship in my place.

But I knew it was Leotychidas, in alliance with Cleomones, a traitor I shared the kingship with for fifteen years who had engineered my overthrow. Cleomones, that pig, paid off the oracle at Delphi, I am convinced of it, to issue a pronouncement that I was illegitimate, that my father, Ariston, was not my true father.

The ephors believed him. The fact that my mother testified to the contrary was not a strong enough reply to the oracle. I was early, they said, by a full two months. I could not have survived such a treacherous beginning. But they were wrong. I did survive, and thrive, and sat on the throne before them.

Cleomones suffered his punishment for the betrayal. The gods may delay retribution, but it always arrives. He died in the city stocks, they said, crazy in the head and trying to cut off his limbs to escape his fate. He was always a dishonorable man. I wished at least the same misery for Leotychidas, who now shared the unique Greek dual kingship with Leonidas. With Leotychidas gone, I could go home. I knew that. But not without Leonidas. He was an honorable man. He would help me persuade the people.

With these thoughts filling my head, my mind grew weary with worry: Did Lysis get through? What would we find when our army reached Alpeni? Would we see the tail end of the Greek army in retreat? Or would we find we had become the cap to the amphorae? If we managed to trap Leonidas, could we still negotiate his surrender? He would have no reason to fight to the death in a hopeless battle. The knot in my stomach loosened as I thought *yes, either way, the king will live.* Perhaps it was better then if we caught them. Maybe then I could speak to him alone. We could make a common cause against Leotychidas with this massive Persian army behind us. But then we would have to tolerate the Persians as occupiers and that would make it hard to rule my people. Well, there was no good in worrying. The end would be as the gods ordained.

The cry of one of the column's advanced scouts coming at the run interrupted my musings. He panted as he came to a stop in front of Hydarnes. "Commander, there were lookouts in the hills to our front. They have seen us and fled their posts."

Hydarnes turned to his aides, who had kept their respectful distance during the trek. "On the quick march, now, men. We must spring the trap!"

We picked up the pace. Surely we were getting close. The path flattened as we descended, and now, even through the pine sap and dampness of the forest, I could catch once again the distant smell of the sea.

The trees thinned and gave way to sea level vegetation: large shrubs and bushes interspersed with clumps of boulders and tall grass lining the path that exited the hills and led to the final approach to Alpeni and the narrow coastal plain. We quickened our pace more. I looked back at the Immortals. Tall and strong, they had been chosen for their pure Persian ancestry, their size, and their warrior prowess. Now that they were once again near their foe, their heads came up, their eyes reignited with desire for battle. And they showed why all Asia feared their approach.

Soon the sea drew in sight. At midday we found ourselves emerging onto the strip of coastland bordering the Malian Gulf before arriving at Alpeni, the so-called "East Gate" of the pass. The village, a miserable collection of mud huts and fishing cottages, was not our concern. We turned to the west and marched straight along the water's edge to Thermopylae.

"How long until we reach the Greek position?" Hydarnes asked Ephialtes.

"It is about fourteen stade," replied the guide. "Perhaps an hour."

"Excellent." He ordered scouts to advance along the coastline both in front and to our rear. Perhaps Leonidas and his men had escaped? We would soon know. As we marched toward the hot gates, I noticed the imprint of many feet heading the other way in the sand. They were fresh tracks. Pieces of equipment, broken carts, and other discarded implements of war appeared by the roadside. Hydarnes noticed also.

"Close up, men!" he shouted. "Be at the ready!"

The breeze had died, and the late summer sun was hot, baking the men in their war gear, in their long tunics and bronze helmets. The air was still, and the gulf was quiet with only the slightest of sea waves timidly moistening the shoreline on this oppressive day.

Through the thick air, I heard the sound of battle. The clash of weaponry and the roar of wounded, dying, and desperate men permeated the atmosphere and came to our ears like the distant rumble of thunder over the mountains. My heart sank. The Greeks had not escaped. They were still there. And they were fighting.

Hydarnes turned to me and saw I had heard the roar too. "We have them, Spartan. They cannot escape."

Lysis

The enemy stands between me and the boat. I am too late. Is every choice I make wrong? I begin to angle my path toward the hills, though there is slight chance, in my present condition, I can survive a mountain trek. I can try to find a hiding place until the Persians pass. There is time for that. So determined, I try to go far east as fast as possible, as close to the covering vegetation dotting the rise as I can . I have to put distance between myself and the Greek position. I am nearly prostrate with exhaustion.

My head spins, and I feel the onset of delirium as the blazing sun cooks me, so I seek a shaded place where the Persians will not pass. As the dust cloud comes closer, and I can make out the forms of individual faces of the enemy, I find my spot. Tight onto the hillside, a single gnarled oak clings to its perch amidst scrub brush and rock. I head for that, collapsing under its welcoming branches. I doubt I have been seen. In any case, my fatigue has turned into surrender. I wonder why I had left the battle and why I am here in the shade.

But the rushed passage of the nearby Immortals reminds me soon enough. They march past by the thousands, and begin to position themselves even as they hurry by my hiding place. The sound of battle becomes engulfed by the growling of the Persian host. If the remaining men of Leonidas' command still stand, these troops will see to their annihilation.

This is my chance. I see no trailing pickets. The way is clear. I push out from my refuge and, staying to the hillside, ignore my pain to make my way east. Behind me, the noise intensifies, however I have no time to grieve. I do have in my mind though to make it to the boat, to carry word to the fleet, to fulfill, once and for all, a dying king's last wishes.

Demaratus

We swept by the hot springs, their steaming, bubbling waters sending vapor trails into the deadened air. Hydarnes ordered the men to divide into lines from their column formation as we neared the Greek encampment. The battle sounded sharp and desperate. The Greeks appeared ahead, pouring through every open gate in the Phocian wall. I watched the red-robed Spartans reforming in a disciplined set, rallying the others around as they streamed through the wall. They moved toward us, setting a course to our left toward a small rise that marked the last undulation of the foothills falling to the sea. Most of the Spartans that is. A group had broken off to the right and distanced itself from the others.

Hydarnes had noticed this as well. "Ithayantes!" he commanded. "Take your section and cut off those insurgents. Do not let them pass to the shore side! We will hold back the rest!"

"Yes, sir!" replied the Persian captain, racing off to snap out orders. Our right wing peeled toward the gulf and marched toward the small, packed splinter group of insurgents. The rest of the army swung toward the Spartan survivors and their allies, who had reached the rise. Behind them, Xerxes' Medes roared through the open gates and followed in close pursuit. It was only a matter of time...I looked for Leonidas. Was he still alive?

We came to the base of the hill as the Greeks formed a circle, shields facing outward, and prepared to receive our attack. Perhaps

'Back on the Hill, the ferocious fight raged'

three hundred remained, all in appalling shape. Their armor and shields had been hacked and battered to pieces, and their spears remained few. Most had swords drawn. Some had no weapons at all.

Hydarnes hesitated, and the Immortals halted, lapping around the hillock like spilled red wine around the base of a cup. As they completed the circle, their bows pointed at the enemy, their faces expectant, there fell a pause on the battlefield. We waited, in that silence, as a rider on horseback approached. It was Mardonious. He halted right before us, his handsome face constricted in rage. His long silky beard, usually the envy of all the court, was matted and flecked with blood. "What are you waiting for, Hydarnes? Finish them!"

"Will there be no surrender demand, my Lord?"

Mardonious looked at him as if he had swallowed a pomegranate whole. "Surrender? There will be no surrender. Leave not one alive!" He spurred his horse, then racing around the hillock shook his javelin in the air and cursed commands: "Attack!" he cried. "Attack!"

Hydarnes looked to the captains of the Immortals. "Finish them."

So ordered, the Persian soldiery let loose a massive volley of arrows and surged forward up the steep rise. The two sides met around the edge of the ring, but it wasn't the Greeks who were driven back. Possessed of some otherworldly strength, they fought with fury, their weapons a blur of motion, their desperation to kill or be killed filling them with volcanic energy. I would not believe a story such as this were I not to have witnessed it with my own eyes. It was inspiring. It was heartbreaking. These were my people, and my pride in them overwhelmed me. Tears sprung to my eyes, and I had to turn away.

When I did so, I looked to the sea. There, a different scene played out. Ithayantes' men had surrounded the insurgents, who had split off from the main group. These Greeks had thrown down their weapons and were huddled together under the watch of Persian troops. Mardonious had not seen this. I prayed he remained distracted until his blood lust abated.

Back on the hill, the ferocious fight raged. I saw my Spartan kin fall, their scarlet cloaks shredded, their helmets leaking blood, and their swords broken. The few Helots alive stood behind the protection of the hoplite shields and did their best to counter the avalanche of missiles hurled their way, replying with their own slung stones and well-aimed arrows. But it seemed a futile response, a leaf against a maelstrom.

The allies, fighting side by side with the Spartiates, were inspired to their true glory by the example of their betters. But they fell, too, clubbed to the ground and deluged by the enemy's sheer numbers. Their circle shrank, the survivors withdrawing into themselves. The Immortals continued to press, piling themselves in heaps in front of the circle, spilling their life force in rivers on the sodden earth. Yet the Greeks continued to resist with their shattered spear shafts, broken swords, shield edges, hands, fists, feet, and teeth.

Hydarnes worried for his losses on this battle front. "Withdraw! Withdraw!" he shouted to his commanders, and to any who might hear.

They did hear. The attacking wave receded with the Persian warriors backing down the hill, shaking their fists, shouting curses and jeering the Greeks, under fifty men at most still alive, raised their shields and prepared for the next assault..

"Arrows!" commanded Hydarnes. "Continuous fire!"

The archers, bunched together all around the circle, opened a fusillade that descended on the doomed Greeks like a torrent of molten rock. The outnumbered raised their shields in an attempt to stave off the inevitable, but there were too many missiles, too much unprotected flesh. Moments separated the men from their ends, but the fight was not easy for the Persians even then. The outline of the compressed ring still showed movement after they released ten, then twenty volleys. Then, it was done. Hydarnes ordered a halt. At last, silence descended upon the battlefield.

The Immortals approached the circle, stabbing every mound of remains that evinced any shred of movement, any heaving chest of a last gasp, any moan for relief. Like ants too long denied their picnic, the Immortals crawled over the face of the rise.

Hydarnes approached me, his face an unreadable mask. "Come with me, Demaratus, I'm sure the king would wish to know if Leonidas is here."

I nodded my head, surprised to find I had become numb to my surroundings. I had floated above myself and looked down at the man I had become. This slaughter of my countrymen shook me like no single event in my long life. Their courage and willingness to die left me bereft of hatred for the petty quarrels that exiled me to this place, on this side of the line. There was no room for this any longer in my heart. There was a profound and canyon-deep sadness that reached the corners of my soul. I knew many of those men who had stayed true to their native land and died for it. Now they were gone. So many good men. What was I but a vessel for minuscule and unimportant personal vendettas, for principles that, at this moment, meant nothing? Was assuaging my wounded pride worth this?

They had died for the only principle worth having. They had been loyal to each other, loyal to a bond and connection that could not be physically seen. I had left that connection, and could never, ever have it again. Even if Leonidas, by some miracle, still lived, it was clear I did not belong among these men. No, I realized now, as if for the first time, I was an exile from all worth living for.

With a hole in my heart that could be filled with naught but dark and bitter thoughts, I ascended the hill. This hole was a chasm, the end of real hope. I stepped over and around the piles of bodies stacked two and three deep on the outside of the main ring. Inside, where the final circle had formed, the feathered arrows were so thick on the ground, walking around them was impossible. Hydarnes and I pulled them out by their barbs. The bodies here, stuck like porcupines, bristled with death.

I searched for Leonidas.

I found him. He lay on his back, his torso covered by a shield, his long scarlet cloak wrapped around his body. Arrows protruded from his exposed limbs, but none had pierced his face. His eyes lay open, staring into nothingness. He had not died here. He must have been killed earlier and dragged to this spot in the final siege.

So many slain, so many bodies, on to their next stations as the gods saw fit, covered the earth. Leonidas was one more. The kings of Sparta, one now a corpse, another a liar, and still another a traitor. I stood atop his torn body, bitterness filling my heart. He could have helped me return to where I belonged in a manner all would have found honorable. He could have chosen to survive, but he did not. He had made another choice, a final choice.

Hydarnes had been watching me. "Is this the king? Is this Leonidas?"

"Yes, this is the king."

We stood in the middle of the hillock, Persian soldiers already looting the dead. It was mid-afternoon. "Xerxes will be pleased," Hydarnes said. "I'm sure he will honor such a brave soldier as this."

"Yes, I'm sure he will. You Persians have always respected your foes." I turned and made my way down the hill, leaving Hydarnes staring after me. I was a man without a heritage. I was no Persian. I was no Spartan. The fiction of my return had fallen to ashes in my heart. I was now for certain a man adrift, belonging to no one but myself. Alone.

Lysis

I arrive at the village at the absolute limits of myself. I have faced none of the enemy on this journey, and the town seems deserted. Alpeni is a tiny settlement, a dozen or so single-story mud, brick, and stone houses dotted around a central courtyard abutting the hillside. Goat paths wind up into the mountain, but otherwise no sign of life. The one main road twists through the center, following the shoreline, and disappears into the distance, bisecting the plain between mountains and sea. I stagger through the village. My path has ended, my delirium returns, and the boundary between my dreams and my reality has ceased to hold. I come to the last house and support myself against the roughened darkness of the mud-brick wall.

When I hear the muted and stealthy crunch of sand around the corner, I stop. With my heart racing I croak, "I bring no harm."

A short, thin, older man appears from behind the wall. Barefoot and dressed in a dirty red tunic, his rope belt stained and frayed, he brandishes an ancient rusty sword and looks as fearful as I feel. The gaps show large in his yellowed teeth as he grimaces and takes in my condition, hopping from foot to foot with his eyes darting back and forth.

"Have you come from the battle?" his words tumble out staccato.

"Yes."

"Are you all there is?"

I nod.

He lowers his sword and hops forward. "I was told to wait here for any who came bearing messages from the Spartan king. Do you bear a message?"

Once again, I nod yes.

"We must hurry then," he says, assuming an important air. "The others fled with the approach of the barbarians."

"Others?"

"Yes, from the fleet. They were too afraid. But I am not," he cackles. "I am not afraid of any Persian fools."

I try to smile, but instead begin to keel over.

"Ah," he says. "Don't fret. I will row you out to them. You are safe now."

For such a fragile-looking soul, he is strong and wiry. He hoists me up by lifting underneath my shoulders, and half drags me around the house where a small boat sits, not much bigger than the rafts I used for fishing when I was a boy. The man skitters back and pulls it through the sand to the water's edge. He pushes it into the gentle surf, and I follow, almost rolling into the bottom. My head rests on the thwart. Slipping the leather oar thongs around the thole pin, he reaches forward with a jolt and begins to lever the boat forward. We are on our way, rocking with the motions of the bay, surging with every determined stroke farther away from the shores where Thermopylae lay. My head lolls against the dampened hull.

"Rest now," he says. "I will get you there, but it will take me a while. I am strong, you will see, but we have a long journey."

I can no longer listen. My eyes close, my hand, it seems, locked in a permanent push against my gut, as I slip into unconsciousness.

Demaratus

Xerxes had not come. He would not come, in fact, until the danger passed. I strode from the tiny hillock toward the shore. There, Ithayantes had gathered the new prisoners. They were Thebans. The Persian commander moved to meet me. His hard and chiseled face seemed not to fit his spotty beard. His dark eyes hooded and perpetually sad, he presented a fitting contrast to his upbeat superior, Hydarnes. Ithayantes was reputed to be a great swordsman and a brilliant man, though this day's circumstances and his dour disposition had left few chances to show it.

"Demaratus," he said. "These men claim they were coerced into fighting here. They say that their country of Thebes has already offered its help to our cause."

"Let me speak to them," I replied, my heart like a shard of ice.

"Of course."

One of the Persians dragged an exhausted hoplite in front of me.

"Who are you?" I demanded.

"I am Leontidadas of Thebes."

"So I see. Why have you survived while the Spartan king has fallen?"

"We were forced to stay," said the Theban. "We were hostages against the guarantee of our city's loyalty."

"Is there proof of this?"

"Xerxes knows. He has received our embassy." I paused, my gaze hard upon his eyes.

"You are saying Leonidas had reason to doubt your courage?"

There was a hesitation. "We did as we were told," he sulked.

"Humph." I was disgusted. "Why didn't the other troops stay? We saw their tracks this morning."

"Leonidas gave them the choice to leave when he heard you would come down on our rear guard." I stared at him. So, they had heard.

I grabbed him by the arm and dragged him away from Ithayantes. "How did you know?"

"We were warned before dawn by Hippocrotes that a scout had come in from the Persian camp."

"Is this man Hippocrotes here?"

"Yes." He turned and shouted, and another Theban stepped forward. Tall and slender, built like a pentathlete, he walked with what appeared to be great pain, his many wounds oozing blood.

"What do you know of the man who warned you of our assault?"

"He was Athenian," replied Hippocrates, his breath coming in short gasps. "Lysis, he said, though he didn't name his father."

I felt a thrill of fear. Had Lysis indeed made it? If so, where was he now? And where was my letter? I could not afford to have that found.

"Where is he now?"

"I do not know. I left him with Leonidas this morning."

"Very well. Go back with the others." He limped away, collapsing amidst the two hundred or so Thebans who huddled together in the afternoon heat.

Ithayantes approached. "What have you?"

"They were warned. Persian deserters, probably."

"Oh. The king won't like that."

I looked at him. "Xerxes will not like any of this. This country will not be the easy conquest he has dreamed it to be."

"Be careful, Demaratus. The king has tolerated your counsel, as have we. It would bode ill for you to remind him of his displeasure."

"I will be silent Ithayantes." I resolved then to return to the hillock and search Leonidas' body before others did for there remained one other piece of information that I had to have. Leontidadas stood by, awaiting his dismissal. "Theban, why did the Spartans stay, though they knew we would defeat them?"

"Why, the oracle," he replied. "Didn't you know? The Spartans were told in order to save their kingdom, a king of theirs must die."

"The oracle?" I questioned. "The Delphic priestess?"

"Yes."

I was dumbfounded. We Spartans are a pious people, though I no longer was. Twice now, the oracle laid me low. Once with a lie about my birth, and now this. I could not imagine how the death of a king, of one who could lead men in battle, would help the Spartan cause. It was madness.

That explained why Leonidas held his ground. His duty was to the state, as was the duty of our entire people. He sacrificed himself so the state might live. My messages pleading with him to leave the pass for future victory were useless. I might as well have been dropping rocks in the ocean in hope of stemming the tides.

A cloud of grief rolled over me. So much accumulated hope over so many years, so foolish in the end. The best I could hope for was to ensure my position here and return by conquest. Would it be the same? No, it would not. I didn't even think it would be worth the gambit. But it was all I had. Now, I had to get that letter or make sure Leonidas had destroyed it. I let the Theban return to his men and set out for the rise.

Crossing the spit of land between gulf and mountain, I looked in the sand and chalk white dirt for the body of Lysis. Climbing the hill, I searched for any sign of him, lifeless or otherwise. Maybe he gave the word verbally? Or he had never delivered the letter? Hydarnes was no longer there. Individual soldiers pawed over the remains looking for whatever valuables they could find, the usual way of the victors in war. I came again to the body of Leonidas. He had not been disturbed. Throwing aside the shield, I slipped my hands inside his bloodied bronze breastplate and looked for any evidence of the letter. There was none. I hefted him over and drove my hands under his inert corpse, searching his back and the small leather camp sack he had slung on his right hip. Nothing. He may have given it to someone else, but that was unlikely. Either Lysis still had it, or it was gone, destroyed. I felt a surge of relief.

"Looking for something, Demaratus?" a voice rasped. "I did not think you had stooped to corpse robbing." I spun around, rising. Phraortes was there, an ugly yellow-green bruise on his neck. His eyes held the hard-edged look of a man who knew something unpleasant. "Whatever it is, better finish up. The king is on his way."

He moved beside me, fixing me with that uncomfortable stare, before looking down. "Is that he?"

I nodded. "Yes, that is he."

Phraortes glanced around, searching the battlefield. "They are not all here," he said. "Some must have escaped." He turned to me with malevolent eyes. "Now, how do you think that happened?"

Chapter 9

Lysis

I awake to the sound of waves lapping against a wooden hull. The rays of the setting sun paint the evening sky brilliant shades of crimson and gold and caress my face, encouraging my rise to consciousness. I am alone, lying on my back on a cushion of cloaks. Above me looms the ornate sternpost of a trireme, its gilded lion's head snarling with determination. I stir, trying to feel my limbs, trying to get a sense of myself.

"Captain! He awakes!" shouts a voice.

The hammering of sandaled feet echoes off the woodwork of the battleship. I feel a hand slip under my neck. "Here, drink this."

Sweet, cool water brushes my lips. I sit up further, welcoming relief to my parched mouth and throat. I feel so weak. Even as the water fills my insides, bringing life to my deadened extremities, I can feel the stinging pain and dull aches of my various wounds. I gulp the liquid.

"You'll live another day, thati s for certain," I hear the cupbearer say.

I nod, continuing to guzzle.

"That's enough, you will drown him," says a stern voice. "Give him room there."

Men shuffle away as I widen my eyes and see the world come into sharper focus. The man with the stern voice takes a knee beside me, pulling the cup from my mouth. It was Themistocles.

He seems shorter than I remembered, but then again, I had never been this close to him before. His eyes are the color of the sea, slate grey and deep. Gray flecks his dark brown beard against his face, chiseled like the statues in the Temple of the Earth Born on the Acropolis. Themistocles wears a loose-fitting, off-white tunic edged in brown and red. From his sharp-fitting leather belt, a long dagger hangs.

"What's your name, son?"

"Lysis."

"Your father?"

I hesitate, staring up at him, saying nothing, listening to an uncomfortable moment of silence.

"Perhaps he has no father!" says another man.

"Maybe he's a god!" yells another.

"Silence!" says Themistocles. "Let him speak."

"My father is dead to me," I say.

"Very well. I am Themistocles, son of Neocles and captain of the fleet." He pauses, looking around, "Or at least the Athenian part!"

The crew laughs.

"The real fleet!" someone shouts, followed by more laughter.

"Yes sir, I know who you are. I was on *Winds of the Gods* when she was taken."

"Ah!" he exclaims. "Miretus was tetrarch of *Winds*."

"Yes sir, he was."

"Sorrows befall us from the gods though we mortals know not why. He was a good man and a good captain. Too many good men lost." He pauses again, examining my appearance. "You are in Spartan armor. How did you come to Leonidas? The man who brought you said you had come from Thermopylae?"

"Yes sir. The Persians captured me in the assault on the *Winds*. Though I had wanted to die in battle, I escaped and came to Leonidas."

"Escaped? Eh?"

"Yes sire."

"We have had no word since early today," he says, gazing at me with a keen appreciation. "Some of the army retreated southward?"

"Yes sir, Leonidas sent them away."

"And he stayed?"

"Yes."

Themistocles hesitates. "And what has happened?"

I think of the battlefield and of the king. It seems so long ago, and so distant, though it had been only hours. I tell of the fight, Leonidas' words to me, the coming of the Immortals, my duty to carry forward the Spartan message.

Themistocles and the others listen in silence.

"They could not have gotten away," I conclude. "They were trapped front and rear. I don't know if they're alive, but if so, only as prisoners. The pass has fallen."

There are a few low whistles, and then, a burst of excited conversation.

"Men!" Themistocles bellows, rising to his feet. The babble trails off. "We must verify if this report is true, though there is no reason to doubt it is not." He turns back to me. "You will need to be looked after. We have a healer on board. We are grateful for your report and for your courage. I'm sure Eurybiades, the fleet commander, will want to be briefed on this. I may have need of you later."

"Eurybiades is a Spartan?"

"Yes."

"I have news for him also. I met with Demaratus, son of Ariston, where I was held prisoner in the Persian camp. It was he who helped me escape." I make no mention of the role my father played, nor had I an understanding of who he was. I realize I might never understand. There was no reason to speak of my father.

"Demaratus!" exclaims Themistocles, letting out a sharp breath. "You bring many gifts, Lysis. Yes, I'm sure Eurybiades will be intrigued by what you have to say." He strides to the gunwale, placing his hobnailed sandal on the low rail that circled the trireme's main deck, and looked out to sea.

I turn my head to follow his gaze and can see a forest of masts filling the water on all sides, their long yards standing against the twilit sky, their well-used sails furled in the quiescent air. Oars were shipped, and the vast array of trireme warships lay like quiet sea birds on the water, wings tucked in, heads bowed, but ever-ready to lift into flight.

Themistocles glances once again at me and sees the direction of my gaze. "Yes, the fleet will need to know also. We will do nothing tonight, except beach, of course. If this news is correct, we will get underway in the morning down the channel toward Athens." The allied fleet had been in action that day. Though the ships bore no noticeable damage, talk all around me indicated they had given the Persians another defeat and driven them back in retreat. Our fleet had received orders to stay at sea until nightfall in case the enemy had a mind to attack again. It had not. Swinging his leg off the rail, he begins barking instructions. "Order the fleet ashore! Assemble the captains to me as soon as their ships are secured."

The stamp of feet thudding against the tough oaken deck follows his commands. A horn sounds, and I can feel the unshipping of 170 oars under my prone body. The timbers vibrate and shake as the call "Up anchor!" reverberates through the gathering night. The oars plunge into the sea, and as the anchor rises and clears the sandy bottom, the ship masters' shouts echo across the water, joining his fellow sailors in their much-rehearsed refrain: "Sit Forward! At the catch now! And... row!" The great warship shudders and shakes as the oarsmen swing their torsos forward and dip the long wooden shafts into the ocean, throwing themselves toward the bow and hurling their weight on the ends of the handles. She is underway, the stroke setting a rhythmic cadence that pushes the ship toward the shoreline of Euboea.

A healer comes to me, clucking over my various injuries, redressing my wounds, cleaning away the dried blood and grime, and salving the cuts with diverse unguents he pours from a mess of clay jars collected in his leather sack. I settle back against the sternpost, pain and fatigue ravaging every inch of my body, but enjoy the feel of a trireme under oars. She glides through the darkening waters of the Gulf, the magnificent crew catching and picking up the 50-ton craft with almost no discernible check. The smooth lock and pry of each stroke, along with the drink the healer has given me, threatens to put me to sleep once more.

With the beach now upon us, I watch as Themistocles orders a well-executed hold water that stops the vessel within the space of its length. Like the beating of a hummingbird's wings, the oars on either side alternately back and row the ship around. In a moment we are stern to.

The deck hands hop to the soft sand and use the lines from the main deck to drag the flagship of the Athenian fleet farther onto the beach. We are secure for the night. In the morning, reversing the process will be easy. I know that a crew on alert can prepare for sea, and battle, in minutes. Even in the state I was in, being on the deck feels so natural. The terrors of Thermopylae seem far away.

The men come pouring up from their positions below decks, three levels of rowers —thranites, zygites, and thalamites— each shipping their oar and most carrying their seat cushion as they leave the ship. They swarm past me and jump onto the beach, making their way toward a huge campsite that sprawls down the coastline wherever the shore is flat and able to receive our ships. The smoke of hundreds of fires spring up as those left on shore prepare the evening meal.

On either side of us, other Athenian ships have beached or are beaching, the rest of the fleet following Themistocles' example. As I watch this graceful activity, I feel an overpowering urge to sleep. It is hard to believe I am safe, hard to believe I am back among my own. Whatever had happened is gone, whatever is to happen would be shared with those of my bloodline. Despite the debilitating shocks of the last few days, I am young and I will survive.

Again I think of my father, and my stomach twists in pain and grief. He was alive. But for what? I can not find peace in my mind thinking of him, much less ease the ache in my heart. There is much I do not know. Perhaps later I can think it through.

I thank the gods for Leonidas and his wisdom. Blinded by my grief, I could have been killed, but he had reminded me of myself. I owed him that and would be indebted forever. Demaratus, too, had done his part. I do not understand the motivations that drove him to use me, nor the plan the gods had for either one of us, but I am grateful. I think how odd it is that Spartans, whom I learned to fear my whole life, are so much a part of it now. But that is in the past. I am once again in the service of my city, and as I drift off, it is a most comforting thought.

Demaratus

I stood up, wiping my hands on my robe to cleanse them of Leonidas' blood, and returned Phraortes' piercing glare. "Deserters," I said. "How else would this information arrive?"

His face reddened, his scars deepening. "Where is Lysis, the Athenian?" he asked.

"Dead," I replied.

He started. "Dead? Where is his carcass?"

"Of what concern is he to you? He was a Greek prisoner who displeased me. I killed him during the march up the mountain last night."

"You have not found him here?"

"I have not looked for him here!" I said, acting irritated. "He is dead!"

Even though he appeared to relax when I told him this, I admit, I enjoyed bearing weight on him. I knew him to be Lysis' father, while he only suspected me of collaboration with the enemy. If the letter never appeared, nothing would be confirmed. I wondered as I looked at him, where he had learned to hate so. Why, indeed, had he taken an instant dislike of me? He would demand my close watch.

"The king may trust you, Spartan, but I do not," he threatened. "I had my own reasons for contacting this Lysis."

"Ah, I suppose you'll have to find another," I mocked. This time, he reached for his dagger, but the approach of the king stilled his anger. Shouts of the king's guard interrupted us. I smiled. Xerxes had come through the gates of the Phocian wall. Surrounded by his royal retinue and accompanied by Mardonious and Hydarnes, he picked his way through the battlefield.

Xerxes and his generals mounted the rise, bathed as it was in the still oppressive heat of the late afternoon. The king stopped a few yards from me near the crest of the hill and cast his gaze across the battlefield. On this mound overlooking the strait, a whisper of a sea breeze caressed the hundreds of forms lying bunched together as if asleep after a long night's carousing.

On the beach, work parties moved, some stumbling about, exhausted, and numb, yet all, it seemed, inured to their ghoulish task. Gulls screeched and whirled overhead as large black crows began to appear from the landward side, hopping and gliding to rest all about the mound, the wall, the stained and trampled earth.

They trod avoiding the pointed hazards which lay by the thousands all about them: iron arrowheads, broken swords, shattered spears, crushed and splintered wicker and bronze shields. Cawing, birds landed on linen breast plates and aimed their sharp beaks at the sightless eyes of the slain—windows to souls now fled from their physical moorings, witnesses no more to the painted clouds of evening—for a scavenger's meal. In the air hung the putrefying scent of death.

Striding up to me, his face a mask of concealed rage, Xerxes pointed about the hill. "Where is he?" he asked, his voice quivering. "Where is this king of the Spartans?"

I bowed and pointed. "This is Leonidas, son of Anaxandridas. It is he who commanded this army."

Xerxes loomed over the body, his anger now informing his voice. "Take this man and behead him. Stick his head on a pike and mount it in front of the wall for all the army to see."

I was stunned. The Persians never treated enemies who had fought with honor in this way. It was barbaric.

"Sire! This is not the Persian custom. Leonidas fought here with great bravery. You do your people a grave injustice!"

"What do you know of Persian customs, son of Lacedaemon?" he said, infuriated. "I will do as I please. This man killed my people and would not see reason. His name will be one of infamy!" And then, turning to Mardonious, "Do as I say!"

"Yes, Highness," said the general. "I will do it myself."

"No," said Hydarnes, gripping him. "Use one of lower rank."

The commander of the Immortals hesitated, glanced at the king, and then called out to the guard. They came to the body and, drawing their swords, hacked at the corpse until the severed head rolled off the torso, trailing blood, and matter. I could not watch and turned away, sick.

Xerxes did watch, however, and as the soldiers took the head to affix it to a pike, he turned to all of us. "Generals, take our march to more victory." He glanced around, fixing me with his angry stare. "There will be no quarter given to those who oppose us. They must learn to fear the power of my throne. They can have none other than me to lead them."

He strode off the mound, heading for the sea, and his commanders followed, including Phraortes. But a few paces on, Xerxes turned, again looking at me.

"Demaratus, I have given orders to bury our dead, as is our custom. Since you are so fond of these Greeks, you will look at them a while longer. They will not be buried. I want you to gather and pile their bodies. Their allies, locals, and those in their fleet who have not seen this site will be allowed to do so. That will make them understand, make them all understand," he said, raising his voice, "the price of opposition."

I watched him take leave, making his way to the Theban prisoners. Would he kill them? I had not seen the king so angry in my twelve years of service to the Persian court. He was of foul spirit and mind. This did not bode well for the rest of the invasion, yet it also made clear that opposition would not be wise. I was now out of favor. Phraortes could use that to his advantage if he chose. I had to be more careful.

But now what a sad task I received. The redeeming element was that I could search for Lysis, and if here, retrieve my letter. I did so, scouring the battlefield, but he was not here. He had escaped the fate of these other poor souls ferried across the Styx into the darkness and mystery of the afterworld. In my heart, I wished him well. Perhaps we would meet again. Perhaps, in the end, some good would come of all this. I doubted any good would come of his father.

With a heavy heart I ordered my soldiers to do as the king had ordered, though I neglected to oversee their duty and retired to my tent. For the remainder of the long summer's day they labored, collecting the Greeks who had fallen on the hillock or during the race to their last stand in front of the wall or in the sea-girt field in front of our encampment. By nightfall, they had finished. Bodies lay in heaps, piled high in front of the wall with the head of Leonidas propped on a long pike as if overseeing his dead followers. As I stood beholding the scene, forced by authority to do so, I hated Xerxes. I hated my situation. I hated myself. But there was nothing I could do. If good were to come from this, it would be a gift from the gods, for it was more than mere men could give.

Lysis

At sea again, the air is crisp and clean, with the wind fresh on the head but not excessive. It raises the water in the channel to a light chop that the low freeboard of our ships had little trouble navigating, and it smells of the ocean, the salty, almost musty scent rolling off the land on either side of us, sweeping and swirling its way through the vast fleet.

With sails furled in the headwind, we are under oars and rotating the crew through in shifts, making sure only two-thirds of the oarsmen were working at any one time. Journeying down the Euboean Channel, soon we will see the town of Styra off to our left, and then, the plain of Marathon and our home country of Attica on our right. I am beginning to feel better. The calming nature of the voyage and the healer's care has combined to speed my strengthening.

I was brought in front of Eurybiades, the fleet commander, on the night of my arrival. A massive, muscled man, Eurybiades had the characteristic long dark hair of the Spartan warrior. Reticent, like most of his kind, but direct when he spoke. His bright eyes searched mine as I entered his tent, and he proceeded to interrogate me at length about the battle at Thermopylae, Leonidas' actions, and what had transpired with Demaratus. He seemed interested in the nature of the messages Demaratus wanted passed to Leonidas. On that issue,

I could only hazard a guess, but I told him all I knew. He thanked me and then joined Themistocles in calling for a meeting of the fleet's commanders. I took leave and collapsed once again, this time for a long sleep on the deck of Themistocles' flagship, *Athena's Victory*.

In my exhaustion, I awake as the fleet puts to sea the next morning, heading west and then south down the Euboean Channel. In the early morning, we pass Thermopylae, rounding the cape opposite, and continuing on our way. The Persian navy does not pursue, maybe too exhausted. I do not come to full consciousness again until the night of the first day at sea when I stir to the further ministrations of the ship's healer.

"Themistocles says to take care of you," he rasps. "Says you're some kind of hero," he continues, washing my injuries. "Don't know if you are or not. There's enough heroes these days, and I imagine the gods have plenty more coming."

I silently agree. The Persians are on their way, and there will be plenty of time and opportunity for Greek heroics. I want to get home again, to see my mother, my sisters, and my uncle. To see Andronica.

We travel down the channel, using sails when the wind favors us and going ashore at night. As we come upon Marathon, I stand at the bow rail, feeling the rhythmic motion of the oarsmen and the wind in my face. The steersmen on the stern look alert, guiding their twin rudders as the vessel swings a few points to starboard and leads the fleet closer inshore.

Our arrival reminds me of the great battle fought here ten years before. I was no more than a boy, but I remember the paroxysm of fear that seized the city as word of the approach of the Persian fleet spread. Rumors of their coming had been rife for years. Around the time of my birth, Athens had voted to send aid to the Ionian cities, particularly Miletus, which were revolting against Darius, father of Xerxes, and against the Persian Empire.

We had done so, marching inland and burning Sardis, the Persian provincial capital. Darius never forgave us for that transgression, but he bided his time. He had other revolts to put down before launching an attack on us. That was after my father disappeared.

My mother had told me that my father was lost at sea, in a storm, never to return and never to be heard from again. My insides twist as I remember that night. My mother was in agony, my uncle stoic, and I—I did not understand then what it meant to be fatherless. I learned in the years that followed, with constant taunts from other children my age and our slide into poverty, saved by my uncle's largesse and, later, adoption.

My mother had told me my father was a patriot, loyal to his city. He had been on the expedition to Sardis, had fought against the Persians. What had happened to him? How had he ended up with Xerxes? What could have made him turn against his city? There were Athenians, oligarchs, and men of wealth who, like my father, hated the democracy we in Athens had become, which was so different from the Spartan system of kings. Many of them had gone over to the Persian side both before and after Marathon, but most had only been outspoken in their opposition to the new ways. My father had never been outspoken, at least not publicly. And I cannot remember his private musings. Mother and uncle never talked about the matter.

There were dark hints from my friends about my father's loyalty as I was growing up. But reacting to them got me in trouble, as I had always assumed they were false stories. People were jealous of my father's previous status, I think. Jealous of his heroic deeds in front of Sardis. There is much I do not know. I think again of that battle ten years before. Were there more clues about him?

The enemy had landed on our shores, right on the plain of Marathon, confident of victory. We called for help from all of Greece, but primarily from Sparta. They agreed to come, but not before the full moon would their army set out. The Persians were not bound by Sparta's religious vows and came ready to fight. Our army, joined by our loyal Plataean allies, formed on the high ridge surrounding the plain and waited for the right signs from the gods. Under the command of the strategos Miltiades, we attacked, charging across the wide flat plain for over a mile, unsupported by cavalry, weak in archers and light troops, but armed mightily with hoplite-heavy foot soldiers.

I remember the talk in the streets afterwards about how the Persians were surprised, having formed up expecting easy victory as they had so often before in their conquests of Asia and Egypt. We were weak in the center, my uncle told me, but strong on the wings. The Persians drove through our center, and we were close to breaking, but the wings were so powerful, they crushed all before them and enveloped the enemy on both sides. It was a resounding victory. We chased them back to their ships, capturing and burning some but driving the rest into the sea. They lost ten thousand. We suffered one hundred ninety-two deaths. The magnitude of the triumph was overwhelming.

But the enemy was not finished. And that was most significant, at least for me. They had suffered so much, but their casualties were still only a portion of their strength. They attempted to sail around the cape at Sunium, trying to get to our port of Phalerum and Athens before our army could make it back to defend the city. Rumors spread they had help from some of our citizens, some of those oligarchs who had no love for our democracy. People said the traitors communicated with the Persian fleet through a series of signals transmitted by flashing shields from the walls of the city. How had these contacts been arranged? Could my father have had something to do with them? The thought drives a pain in my chest. And could it be even worse?

Later, after the battle at Marathon and after the Persians had been foiled by the arrival of our army outside the walls of the city and close onto Phalerum, the Spartans arrived. They asked to go to the battlefield. They wanted to see for themselves the work of our Athenian spears. They wanted to see the Persian dead. I remember them marching through the streets of the city. Their scarlet cloaks hung from their shoulders, their burnished shields shone like the sun; their demeanor and discipline inspired awe. I had never seen anyone like these warriors. I was so proud of our soldiery—friends of my father, all the important and landed men of the city—but even so, I recognized the difference between the Spartans and our Athenians.

Still, we had been the ones to triumph. Not the Spartans. I had no doubt they would have as well, but it was our spirit that took the day.

We were fired by a different kind of motivation. And yet, as I had seen at Thermopylae, we achieved the same result. We are a fractious people given to passionate expressions of who we are. Sometimes, there appears to be as many opinions and ways as there are people. But it is the strength of each individual that makes us who we are. We are part of something bigger, for certain, but the whole of us is never more important than what each of us brings.

And we love our city. We love our country. We love it with a determination and a commitment that is the envy of all others under the heavens. We are free to do what we desire, as constructed by ourselves. We abide by the will of the majority, a will debated and protected.

The Spartans, I have learned, are committed to the survival of the state before themselves. I saw that. What they did at Thermopylae was for the state. They died for it. We died at Thermopylae too, but it wasn't for the state. It was for us, as individuals, within the state. We were different, yet we were the same.

In our city, an aura of energy, of possibility, and of hope abounds. I feel it every day. Even after my father didn't return, I could feel it in myself. His disappearance didn't mean the end. No one said I could not or would not do what he had done to be honored. They still did not. Though he spoke from a different perspective, Leonidas was right. I am not my father, I am myself. I can do what I want. I can make my own future. The ancestral fiction under which I have lived is dead to me, gone. I can create my own future.

And yet, my family does not begin with me. Though I am not my father, my true ancestors still possess me here in Attica, as do all true Greek ancestors for each of us. I must find out what happened, and I will. I can always create new jars to carry my water, but still the shattered jar in the corner needs piecing together. I need to know.

It occurs to me, even as my legs weaken and I can feel the rush of blood to my head, there is one man who might be able to help. Leaning against the rail, I sit down and search the long main deck of the ship for him. There, emerging from below decks and bounding up to the steersmen with his customary energy, is Themistocles. He looks buoyant as he engages in discussion with the ship's master.

I get up and make my way the length of the vessel, noting, as I always do, the coiled lines, the taut stays on the fore and main mast, the general air of seaworthiness of this ship. That is not always the case. Each tetrarch is responsible for his vessel, and standards vary. But Themistocles was the motivating force behind the development of our Athenian navy these past ten years, ever since Marathon, and his focus and vision had seen us build the largest and most powerful fleet in all of Greece. With two hundred triremes fitting out and sailing from Phalerum and the Piraeus, Athens had become the premier naval power in the Aegean— outside of the Persians. His ship would reflect his personality, as most ships did of their officers. I reach the stern and wait until the commander finishes. After pointing out the hazards that lined the shore and directing the steersmen on a suitable course to avoid them, he speaks to the ship's master. "Nicias, we need to adjust both hypozomata in this moist air. I can feel the slack. See to it!"

"Yes sir."

The hypozomata are the lines that gird the ship. They run fore and aft about the level of the lower level of oarsmen, the thalamites. Made of wound hemp, they keep the keel from bowing upward amidships, or "hogbacking." They also increase the stiffness of the hull, important for speed and stability. Too little tension in the line, and the bow and stern carry more water, reducing speed. And in a trireme, all is for speed. The ship is a living body, responding to the elements in every way, and the lines need to be adjusted. If they break or snap under pressure, they cause havoc below decks, and the ship feels the results. Themistocles is a first-rate commander, that was obvious, attuned to his vessel. It is his meticulous nature that keeps *Athena's Victory* prepared.

He notices me as I lower myself to a seat on the planking that covers the top tier of the thranites and dangle my legs over the edge into the hold. Taking leave of Nicias, who then goes below to check on the hypozamata, he sits down beside me. "Getting better?"

"Yes sir, but it will be a while."

"Well, you will have time once we make home port."

"How much time?" I ask. "When do you think the Persians will attack?"

He purses his lips and leans back, bracing his palms on the deck. "Depends on the gods. The enemy has to go through Boetia. They may be resisted, though I doubt it. The Persian army does not move fast. It is fearsome but too large." He pauses. "They will be here in due time."

I nod, imagining that monstrous mass descending on my Attica. They would fill the plain in front of the city. They would wreak ruin on the entire country. No forces there to resist, unless the Spartans led the main Peloponnesian forces out to do battle. Thinking of my family fills me with worry. The men would face danger, as expected, but what of my mother and sisters? What of all the women and children?

As if reading my thoughts, Themistocles continues. "When they reach Attica, it will be hard to defend the city. We will have to evacuate our citizens to one of the islands and then the burden will be upon the fleet to keep them safe."

"But what of the Spartans? Will they not fight with us as they did at Thermopylae?"

"I know not of their plans. They may think it wiser to hold the Isthmus of Corinth. They've been building a wall across it, trying to prevent the enemy army from advancing. They feel Attica is too open to defend."

Yes, the isthmus. To attack the Peloponnese, where Sparta and most of her allies reside, the enemy will have to go through the narrow strip of land between the Aegean and the Corinthian Gulf. With a wall straddling the isthmus and men to defend it, the Persians will find that hard-going indeed.

Themistocles continues, "Thus, unless we defeat the Persian fleet, they must only sail around the Spartan's barricades at the isthmus and come ashore anywhere on the Peloponnese." He gives me a wry smile. "It is going to be tough to get the Spartans to see that though. They think land based first, last and always. They are just now realizing the power of a fleet."

We sit in silence, listening to the creak of the timbers and hum of the wind in the rigging.

"Sir," I ask, hesitant.

"Yes?"

"My father was Androcles, son of Thaortis."

His eyebrows raise, and he studies me. "Androcles?"

"Yes sir. Did you know him?"

He turns away, raising his chin to catch the wind on his cheek. He says nothing for a long while, before slowly beginning. "Yes, I knew the man you call your father." He gazes upward through the rigging, searching the clear powder blue sky. "We were on the expedition to Sardis, among other duties in service to our motherland. I rarely saw him outside of our military duties though. After Sardis, he seldom attended the assemblies."

I see his reluctance to speak, but press him, determined to learn the truth. "And you know something else, sir?"

He searches my eyes. "Androcles fought well at Sardis. But there was talk that he had made...other contacts while there."

"Other contacts?"

"With...with the enemy. I am told it was only after he returned from the Sardis expedition that he became a wealthy man." Drawing his hands closer, he grips the edge of the plank. "This was from idle talk in the ranks that then spread through the market where he was known to buy the finest wool and baskets of dates, though no one knew from where he had the coins for such pleasure. His shipping trade was not profitable, or so it was said." He looks at me again, seeming uncomfortable. "And then he disappeared from our lives before the Persians attacked us the first time."

"Sir, where do you think he took leave?"

He continues looking me straight in the eye. "I think your father went to the Persians. I think he made some kind of barter. I don't have a clear vision, but that's what I think."

"But you don't know why?"

He draws a breath, expecting a different reaction from me. Furrowing his brow, he adds, "No, why does any man of honor bring shame to himself? Perhaps he was in need of coins. Perhaps he thought his actions to be innocent. Who would know? Those were tumultuous times. Our democracy was young and many opposed it." The steady sound of oars ripping through the sea fills the silence between us, until I break in.

"I saw my father when I was captive in the Persian camp."

Surprised, "You say that upon the god's word?" He sits up. "For what cause would he be so treacherous?"

I explain, leaving out my father's exact position, that he gathered information for Xerxes. When I finish, Themistocles drops his chin, deep in thought. "You say your father saved you?"

"Yes, he even seemed joyous to find me alive and looked after me from then on. Surely he faced death had he been caught."

"Then you do have a bond with him?"

"Not a bond, sir. I do not know what it is. I do not have in my belly what sons feel towards fathers."

"I can see that. But there may be a time, if I may be so bold as to suggest it, when contact with your father may prove useful to the land of Greece as much as to yourself."

I can not see that event, but I also do not argue the point. Themistocles sees I am tired and is also willing to let the matter drop.

"Lysis, my heart is heavy with this news about your father, but answers will come to you. Only the gods know why they do what they do. No one can see the ending. For now, though," and he stands up on the solid oak, sniffing the wind, "rest. We will be in Pharlerum by nightfall." He offers his hand.

Grasping his firm calloused grip, I raise myself to make my way back along the rail toward my perch on the bow. During our talk, the plain of Marathon had faded from view. Behind us, the powerful fleet labors against the wind, proceeding home, for however long it would remain so.

CHAPTER 10

Demaratus

The invasion proceeds apace, however, I have never felt so low. Three days after the battle of Thermopylae, the king got the army moving, and we journeyed through the pass into Phocis, where we laid waste to the country and then marched into the Boetian countryside. The Boetians submitted to Xerxes, offering earth and water. But the king's anger over his losses at the pass manifested itself in brutal treatment of those who resist us and those who assisted in the defense of Thermopylae, such as the poor Phocians. We chased them into the mountains and hunted them down, killing all the men we could and ravaging their women. I'm not sure Phraortes was behind it, but I would not wager against it. I always feel him watching.

For those who joined us, such as the farmer Ephialtes, life is better. The king rewarded him in gold. May the gods help him if we lose this war, which at this point, does not seem likely. Our army is too strong. If Xerxes takes my advice, the campaign will be over by fall. We hear the Spartans are supervising the building of a wall at the Isthmus of Corinth, which is both predictable, and stupid.

Much as I hate to admit, the sea is the key here. If our ships can destroy the Greek fleet, the wall at the isthmus will be turned. But I have fallen out of favor since the pass, so there's no telling what the king will do. He has to be pleased so far. We are close to Attica, the birthplace of dissent against the empire. There is no army to oppose us—any would be foolish to do so. Our cavalry and superior numbers are perfect for these open plains. No opposing force in the open can survive against us. In a few days, we will be at the gates of Athens.

Lysis

The city is in an uproar. Word that the Persian army has made its way into Boeotia unopposed and is headed for Attica sends waves of panic through the populace. Citizens pack up, ready to flee. Some leave without waiting for the assembly to meet and decide on a course of action. These early departing souls rely on the safety of the isthmus before anything else, and head for Corinth through Eleusis and Megara.

Those remaining learn the assembly's decision to evacuate all who wished to Troezen on the northeast corner of the Peloponnese and to the islands of Salamis and Aegina. The fleet, and all available load-carrying vessels that can be pressed into service, will transport the citizens. At Phalerum ships load panicked families, and triremes ready to join the main Greek fleet positioned off of Salamis in the bay of Eleusis.

Ten days have passed since I arrived home, but I am healing well. Assigned to Themistocles' ship, *Athena's Victory*, I busy myself assisting in the evacuation. It has been a fear-filled time in my home city ever since we brought news of Thermopylae, Artemisium, and the enormity of the enemy's invading force.

When our ship first beached at Phalerum, I was too weak to travel unassisted. Although eager to get home, I waited until the following morning to depart. I had hoped Andronica would greet me, perhaps having heard of our arrival by one of the advance ships, but she was not there. Nor was anyone from my family.

I considered going to Andronica's home in the city — Hippocrotes' home— but decided I did not yet feel up to facing her family's worries. I would send word to Andronica, and she would come to me. But first I would make my way home.

Two marines with homes nearby my mother's farm helped me get there. They hired a cart, and we wound our way through the throngs of wives, maidens, and families crowding the beach searching for their loved ones. I looked for my mother, but I knew she would be searching for *Winds of the Gods*, which now lay broken and dashed on the rocks of Euboae. Limping in from the farmhouse gate, I surprised my two young sisters who had been busy preparing the midday meal. They leapt on me, driving me to the floor with their enthusiasm. At twelve and fourteen, they were almost ready to marry, and seeing me meant the return of their primary link to Attica's young male society. Or so my cynical heart told me.

"Wait until mother comes home and finds you here!" said the younger Androcla, sniffling as she cried, still hugging me. "She may become worried sick when she doesn't find you at the port!"

"We are glad you are back," said Cleiestha, wiping her face. "Everyone was so worried. We had not heard anything for such a long time! And Andronica—" she continued, giving me a sly look, "I'm sure she cannot wait to see you!"

She noticed my bandages. "You are hurt! Here, brother, sit down, what happened?"

I explained that my wounds were not bad, and that I would recover.

"You need to rest," said Cleiestha, now all serious. "Brother, we will take care of you."

I had no doubt they would but wished my mother and uncle had been home. I felt an urgency to learn more about my father, but that would have to wait until both returned from Phalerum.

They arrived past midday. I was lying in a bed my sisters had prepared, propped up in the main room where the afternoon sun warmed my face. My mother and uncle entered, pushing open the thick olive wood door looking defeated. When their eyes rose, adjusting to the darker interior, they saw me. My mother dissolved into tears. My uncle appeared relieved.

"Oh Lysis!" cried my mother, rushing to my bed and throwing her arms around me. "We were so worried! There was no news from the fleet. We found no one who knew of you. And your poor ship, lost!"

I hugged her back, feeling my own welling emotion but grunting in pain as her embrace stressed my new wounds. Reacting, she drew back, wiping her eyes. "Is it bad?"

"No, Mother," I assured her. "It could have been much worse. I will heal from this."

She seemed about to cry again but bit her lip and looked to my uncle, who stood by the door. "Please, Laertes, bring me a jar of water. I wish to have a look at these."

He nodded, eyebrows raised and a grin forming across his long narrow face. "Of course," he gave me a wink. "I'm sure you're in good hands now, Lysis." He exited, and I lay back again on my cot as my mother redressed the wounds, criticizing the work of the ship's healer, but not displeased at the results.

"You will have some scars, my dear son, but at least you have come back to us." She finished the last of the dressing and as the day crawled to evening, both she and Uncle sat close by my bedside, ready to hear my tale.

I knew what I wanted to say, but I felt the best way to broach the subject was to lead them through what had happened. I began with the sea battle off of Artemisium, the day my ship was rammed and sunk, the day Hippocrotes died. I left out what my friend uttered as he lay dying, which was still a mystery to me. Hippocrotes' death saddened them. I described my capture and the fate that delivered me to Demaratus.

"You will have to visit his family when you are able," said my mother. "We will get word to them, as they will have no other who can."

I nodded, pausing for a moment. "Mother, did you see Andronica by the shore? Does she know I am back?"

My mother glanced at my uncle, who shrugged.

"We did not see her or anyone from her family."

My heart sank. Another disappointment. Yet there had to be a reason. I continued my tale. Mention of Medarnes and his insistence that my father killed his father intrigued them. They stopped me, my mother puzzled.

"This man said your father committed a crime against his father?"

I nodded.

"That is impossible. Your father died at sea years ago."

"Mother," I said, taking a deep breath. "Father is alive."

They both gaped at me.

"What?" my mother asked in a whisper. "Androcles is alive?"

"Yes, I met him in the camp of the Persians." I paused again, feeling the enormity of what I was about to reveal. "He is in the pay of the enemy."

Stunned silence.

"How is that so?" cried my uncle. "How can you be sure it was he?"

I told them of the amulet and of all Phraortes had said. My mother gasped, her hand flying to her own throat where the twin of Androcles' keepsake swung by its own silver chain.

"Alive," she mumbled, and slumped on the couch, her head falling into her hands. "Alive." She seemed to withdraw then, unable to grasp what I was saying.

My uncle's face, however, became hard. "Sister, it sounds as if what Lysis says is true." He then searched deep into my eyes. "Of what measure is he to the barbarians?"

"He gathers information, I think." I did not wish to go any further into his history. There was no reason to add to my mother's pain. My uncle rose and paced.

"It troubles my heart to say this, Lysis, especially in front of you both, but your news is of no surprise to me. Your father was never…, was never a…moral man."

"Stop!" cried my mother. "I loved Androcles. Do not dwell in the past!"

"But he is not in the past!" retorted my uncle. "He is alive today and marching toward us in the ranks of our enemy!"

My mother burst into tears. My uncle, abashed, sat down by her side, hugging her as my sisters entered the house, brushing off chicken feathers and holding baskets full of eggs. Seeing our uncle rocking our mother back and forth startled them.

"Do not cry, sister. It will be alright. You do not know what to think right now, but I am sure there is more to this story." He looked at me.

My sisters hurried to my mother, and Cleiesetha asked, "What is wrong? What happened?"

"Nothing," my uncle snapped. "Look after your mother in the other room for a while. She's overcome by having Lysis home."

Cleiesetha looked unconvinced, but the two of them complied, guiding my mother into the back room. They tried to sooth her quiet sobs without knowing the reason.

Laertes watched them take leave and shifted a steady gaze to me. "Lysis, how much do you remember about your father?"

"Uncle, I was eight when he left and have only few memories to bind me to him." I had tried to form an image of an old life, tried to see my father as he was, but that was hard. "He was big, but I suppose to me, everyone was. Handsome, yes. And strong. He was good to me. I do remember that."

"Yes, you were always his favorite," said my uncle.

"Beyond that," I continued, "I know what you and mother told me. He was a hero. He worked hard. He loved us. He loved the city."

My uncle leaned forward. "You are sure this was your father you saw with the Persians?"

"He knew things," I replied, but added hesitantly, "I...well, I felt it more than knew it."

"Hmm. Lysis, listen to me, you are a grown man and heir to this estate. There are things you must know about your father." My uncle's eyes were sad, and his hands gripped his knees. He drew a deep breath. "Your father, Lysis, was an ambitious man. When he took your mother as his wife, we were happy for the match. Your grandfather was a powerful man in the city and owned a number of estates with a thriving export commerce. Your father was as you remember big, brash, and handsome. Also a triumphant fighter. The city was in an uproar in those years, and when we became a democracy," he hesitated. "When we became a democracy, some had a difficult time adapting."

Uncle got up and went to the door overlooking the garden path. "Your grandfather never approved of the change, and he made some enemies, people who had personal stakes in his commerce. As long as he was alive though, and the good merchant of land and of crops, it was of little account.

He turned back to me again, "But when your father took over, the family's fortunes started falling. He had no knack for commerce. He wanted to be with the action, with the men of power; he felt a new way of moving about his affairs would benefit his personality. Thus, he had no patience for what needed to be done every day to keep the farm producing, to manage the other estates, or even to make the plans that could ship all he had to the far corners of the world."

Uncle paused for a long moment, his gaze far away.

"Soon, he found himself in trouble. He ran up obligations, your grandfather's enemies seized some of the estates, and things worsened from there. He took his grievances to the assembly, hoping his friends would cast aside his debts, but they were not sympathetic. They had all earned their money the same way your grandfather had, and, I am afraid, your father's sense of being in the same air as the gods did not endear him to many. His proceedings became so bad, at a point I remember a change in his presence. His rebuke in the assembly seemed to have turned him against his former friends.

"That is when the call for help came to us from Miletus, after you were born. As you know, the Milesians, like us, are Ionians, and their revolt against Darius and the Persians excited everyone. We responded, and your father was one of the most enthusiastic. I think he saw it as an opportunity to bring back some spoils from the expedition. I went along also, as did thousands of others. The city responded with confidence. Well, you know the story. We got to Miletus and joined together with the Milesians and some of the other rebel cities and marched on Sardis.

"Sardis was brutal, but we took it, sacked it, and burned it to the ground. We thought that would teach the Persians a lesson. I suppose it did, but not the one we wanted.

"Before the final assault, your father took leave to scout for food and supplies. We would take our provisions from the conquered, though I'm sure your father desired more than food. He returned two days later, alone, his entire group wiped out. He said a Persian force of cavalry had come upon them, and he, by the hands of the gods, was the sole survivor. We were relieved, and none questioned his tale.

"After Sardis, in which your father fought brilliantly, we returned home, leaving the Milesians to continue the revolt themselves. Your father changed though upon return. He became more secretive, less ebullient. He worked harder on the farm, going less and less to the city as if hiding. I thought that strange, seeing as he fought so well and received accolades from the Strategos in charge of the expedition.

"And another change in him happened that did not make sense—his debts seemed to have gone away, or at least lessen by a large amount, and he was flush with coin, though not able to recover lost lands. I think most, including me, pegged his new wealth to his increased attention to the farm. But his work was harder, not smarter. Indeed, he was almost frantic in his labors. This went on for several years and I lost sight of the man who had taken my sister in marriage.

"Rumors were plentiful about the King Darius and the Persians in those days. We had done more than twist his tail. Word was that Darius was ready to invade Greece. But right before they marched on us, and while we readied ourselves for war, your father spoke of a voyage he would take leave for. He said it would give us a great exchange of goods and coin with the city of Siracusa, in Sicily. I had never heard of this before, and it did not seem urgent given the impending Persian invasion, but he was insistent.

"So I saw him off from Pharlerum where I watched him take leave, though the winds he rode were contrary; he was not heading west. He was heading east. I said nothing of this to your mother, or to anyone. At the time, I thought it only a mariner's necessity that drove him in that direction; I was never a sailor to know of these matters. Besides, the arrival of the enemy thrust it from my mind. We never heard again from your father. Not a word of his fortunes. Until tonight."

My uncle stopped, then seeming worn, stood outlined against the open door. A gentle breeze had risen and stirred the air, slipping through the portal and drying the sweat on my forehead.

Looking up, I caught the last rays of the evening sun dancing on the rear wall, transfixing the dust of the day and illuminating the cracks in the sun-dried brick. Here, near the base of Mount Hymettus, the sun bathed the lands worked by my father, my grandfather, generations of my family, and my ancestors before them. It cast shadows on the olive groves and suffused the vines in a rich glow, warming the animals and the men who worked this farm in a final farewell to another day, like thousands of days before it, in the long memory of Greece.

I remembered my father then, in another way, a man coming home at night from the fields, tired and dirty, beaten, it seemed, unhappy with his lot in life. A farmer, and yet not. Still, he made time for me, even then, even in the cool of evening with the few lamps we had burning. He used to call me his "little Achilles," his hope for the future. I remembered that. He would tell me stories, tales of faraway places and savage battles, filled with strange peoples, and alien gods. He would talk of the city, of our fathers, and of the many generations which served Athens by fighting in the wars, watching her grow, feeling her life pulse in the ground beneath our feet. He promised me many times how he would forever be with me, to help me to manhood, to assume my rightful place. I remembered his words, and my stomach spasmed.

He would send me to bed and remain on his stool, and sometimes I would peek from behind the curtain and watch the sadness falling like a pall over his face, his eyes losing focus as the lamps burnt low. I knew he was sad, but I did not know why. I had wanted to make him happy. He was my hero, and I adored him.

When he took leave to never return, I could not understand. The days passed into weeks, and then months, and I kept alive the hope he would come back. Every day, I would pass his great shield hanging on the wall, the wall I gazed at now, and wonder when he would again sling it over his muscled back and show me the warrior I knew him to be. I would open the huge oaken trunk and touch the sword and corselet, the bronze greaves and crafted bronze helmet, hefting it onto my growing head and feeling the echo in my ears as the weight bowed my boyish neck. But he was not to return. The years passed, and my hopes for tomorrow retreated to memories of yesterday, ones in which I reflected from him what I wanted in myself. I longed to grow into what I thought he had been—the defender of his family, his city, and the hero of my life.

I practiced with that armor, that huge shield, and that long, sharp sword, until I did grow into it. I practiced until my city called me to service, until I became old enough to join the world of men, old enough to take my place in the ranks of Athenians sworn to protect the life we loved. For two years, I trained with my boyhood friend Hippocrotes. I trained with the others as an ephebe, honing my skills and becoming worthy of the phalanx. Yet my heart drew me to the sea, to the great navy Themistocles was helping amass to guard against the inevitable Persian return, to the city's new course. It could have been because my father had disappeared into the mist, or because it would give me the glory I desired. I was not sure. But I joined, and I sailed.

When the time came, I fought in that armor. With every thrust of my spear, every slash of that sword, I cherished the image of my father and strove to live up to it, strove to live up to the legend in my heart. When I lost it all in the fight on the *Winds of the Gods*, when it was stripped from me, piece by piece, and hurled overboard or in the bowels of the ship where I could not retrieve it, I thought how little I had done to bring the memory of my father to life. I thought of my failure as I watched my friends die, of how unworthy of his memory I had been.

As I listened to my uncle and I remembered, I felt the rush of despair I struggled to resist roll over me like a tide. My father was not my hero. My father was a man, like any other man, strong and weak, hero and failure. But his path had gone wrong for him, a path I could never know or understand and maybe never would. The man I had seen in the enemy's camp was my father, just not the one I had known; I could not reconcile the two. It was a battle I could not be victorious in.

I let my head drop onto my chest, and the weakness of my body overcame the strength of my will. I felt my uncle's pitying gaze upon me, as the last light of day fled the house, and I fell to sleep, no longer caring.

The days passed by like this. I regained my strength while news of the Persian advance spread through the city like a stampede of wild horses. Daily, my uncle came to me from the Pnyx where the assembly had met with reports of the latest preparations for resistance. Debates raged over the Delphic prophecy being bandied about the city.

When news of Xerxes' armies had first terrified Athens, the Delphic oracle, or the "Pythia," had been asked for pronouncements about our fate. He had responded with the assertion that a "wall of wood" would help us against the Persians. We should not stand and resist the huge armies descending upon us but should flee the city.

Some priests of the temples and others insisted the "wall of wood" was a wooden barricade they would construct guarding the Acropolis itself. Others, more level-headed, it seemed to me, and led by Themistocles, ridiculed that interpretation of the Pythia and said the "wall of wood" referred to our ships. They voiced we should indeed flee, as the oracle had advised, and rely on our fleet of over two hundred triremes, allied with the other Greek allies, to bring us victory. Either way, most of the populace had agreed to evacuate. The assembly agreed as well, and preparations began for the movement of the women, children, and elderly to safety.

We all knew, especially men like me who had seen the spoils of war pass to the victor, that abandoning our lands, fields, and crops meant their destruction. After all, Athens was the primary target of the invaders. We knew the enemy would ravage our dear city end to end, and that anyone caught within its environs could expect no quarter.

I healed, my young body eager to restore its strength, and I told my mother and uncle more of what had happened to me, and more of my father. I urged them to take leave for safety, to waste no time. My heartbroken mother was determined to take as much as she could, lest it pass to the enemies of our gods.

On the day after I had arrived, my uncle went to see Hippocrotes' family in the city to tell them of their son's death. He came back later in the day, again mournful. "They want to see you Lysis. I think they want to hear from you how he battled to the end and brought honor to his family and to all of Athens."

"And Andronica?"

"Her father has sent her to Eleusis, to some friends there. She's to remain there until the city is once again safe."

I was stricken with anger. What was the meaning of this? The Persian army was marching on us! The safest place was in Athens, not an outlying city like Eleusis! Of what mind was her father? I was hoping she would see me, but with this news thought it unlikely. Her father's edict was immovable but I wanted to see them, and ask permission to visit Andronica.

I nodded to my uncle. Seeing her parents would be hard. They would want to hear of Hippocrotes' death. So much had happened over the last few weeks, it was hard to tell how and when the death of my best friend has added to my numbness. This is a matter I had not acknowledged, unable to separate it from so many others killed. In the terror and blood of war, where had my heart gone? I needed to understand, and stay connected to what was my old life. And there was that cryptic remark Hippocrotes had made while his life ebbed away. As soon as I was able, I left for the city.

Andronica and her brother Hippocrotes live in the city near the Dipylon Gate. I had met him in the Kynosarges gymnasium a year after my father set sail to never return. He was a metic, an alien, his family having immigrated from the East only a short time before we met. Metics were not allowed full citizenship, but he was allowed into the gymnasium. I met him on his first day there. Hippocrotes was as loud and confident as I was not. But for reasons unknown, we became fast friends. On days when my uncle would take me into the market, we would run through the Agora spreading havoc and spy on the assembly when they met in the Pynx; hanging from the trees, and joining in the jeering that greeted a bad speaker.

Hippocrotes was always at the ready to spread mischief, and I was more than willing to oblige. As we grew, he would come to our farm where I showed him my father's sword and armor. We'd enjoy long explorations on the slopes of Hymettus, searching for tracks of wild boars while terrified at the prospect of meeting one. And we would earn my uncle's wrath by cutting long saplings from the olive trees and fashioning bows and arrows, swords and spears.

In the gymnasium, we competed in boxing, wrestling, the pankration, sprinting, and the broad jump. He was always bigger and stronger, a specialist in wrestling and an absolute god in the pankration, knocking opponents flat with one sweeping blow. I was more like my mother, lean and quick. I loved the pentathlon, preferring the mastery of many. But as words in poems, Hippocrotes and I complemented each other. We dreamed of Olympic glory, planned our assault on Olympia, envisioned the laurel wreaths, the staggering prizes, the everlasting renown. But there were others who were better, and others who could afford to train. I was not among them. And even though Hippocrotes never was in lack of coin, in the end, he followed my lead, not the other way around.

His family was made of merchants without land, but they had done well from the vessels they owned, ships they had brought with them from the East. As I approached their house along the narrow street that paralleled the city wall inside the gate, I remembered again how mysterious it was that Hippocrotes, a metic, had been allowed to join me in the military training that only full citizens can do. Yet, as at the Kynosarges, Hippocrotes was able to circumvent the rules.

His house is like many others along the twisted road, and speaks of wealth; its mud brick and stone walls are stuccoed and painted red, though without roadside windows. Clay tiles make up the roof, and a heavy oak door was bolted and locked from the inside.

I made my way through the rutted, graveled, and dusty lane, lined with the night's refuse. The slaves had not been by to sweep, and maybe would not anymore. Garbage accumulated in the meandering drainage ditch abutting the houses.

Citizens hurried by in both directions, many carrying bundles slung over their backs or leading donkeys that pulled narrow carts filled with belongings. The city emptied. I knocked on the door. It cracked open, and out peered the frightened face of a young girl. I was startled for a moment as she looked much like Andronica. But she was not. She was a slave girl, I suppose, one who had not been with the family long. She seemed to know I had an appointment with the family and swung the door on its post, allowing me to enter.

Without a word, she hurried off to inform the master of the house. I looked around the familiar haunt. Wooden pillars lined the entrance hall and stretched back into the house, opening into a stone-floored courtyard. Next to the hearth occupying the far-right corner of the courtyard was a large cistern half full of rainwater caught from the roof drains. Sunlight came from the open yard, and several stations in the walls had space for lamps when darkness fell.

Hippocrotes' parents came from the back of the house looking old and stooped, though his father could not be more than forty. "Lysis," his father remarked. "Do enter. Blessings to you for making this journey."

I nodded, unsure of what to say, and followed them into the house. They led me to the dining room and bade me sit on a carved high-back wooden chair by the doorway. Hippocrotes' mother did the same, while his father sat on the long dining couch.

In the quiet, they both looked at me in what seemed to be gazes of resentment, or anger, or some spite I did not expect. There was grief, yes, but, more too. It took me aback. "I came to tell you of your son, to tell you of his death."

I saw the tears beginning to pool in their eyes, but they remained stoic.

"Tell us," said his father.

And so I did. I recounted the last fight, focusing on Hippocrotes' astonishing strength, his battering of the enemy as they swarmed over the ship, the final push that funneled us to the stern and, at the last, the axe from the enraged Cypriot that laid him low. I told of his final words, or at least most of them. Something in the spirit of his parents told me not to reveal all. "He was magnificent, a true hero worthy of his name and yours."

Their heads bowrd when I finished. His father looked up, and with a bitter tinge to his voice, asked, "And how is it that you return to your mother,"— Hippocrotes' mother wept loudly—"yet he does not return to his."

"I was forced into the sea and did not expect to survive. Believe me, there are times when I longed for your son to have lived and for I to have been the one taken by the gods."

"Did he say nothing else, nothing at all?"

"No sir."

He locked his eyes on mine, and I saw a look I had never seen from this old merchant, and one I had never expected from him. His eyes were full of hate.

I clenched my spirit tight trying to hide my reaction, and I stood to take leave. I wanted to inquire about Andronica, but again my spirit warned me off. I would find another way. "There is much to do before the enemy arrives. What will you do?"

"We will take care of ourselves as we always have." Hippocrates' father reached over to his wife, enfolding her, and then said to me, "You may take leave." There were no further words.

I stepped out into the hall and into the courtyard. Across the flagstones stood the entrance to Hippocrotes 'private chamber. I glanced behind me and heard crying but saw no movement. The slave girl was in the kitchen off the courtyard. The way was clear. I scurried into his chamber and swept my eyes across the few pieces of furniture, the small table, the tall cupboard, the chairs, and the stout oak chest.

Hippocrotes' parents had made me cautious and also determined to find the answer to the mystery of his final words. He told me to look in the chest for the answer. The answer to what? Once more, I searched behind me and moved to the carved lions on the lid of my friend's chest, the one, where, in the past, Hippocrotes had kept all of his most prized possessions. I lifted it open and peered inside. It was empty, but for a single half-size papyrus roll in a goatskin case. I took it, holding it tight to my side, and close to the chest. When I entered the courtyard it was empty and cautiously I took leave into the tumult of the road. I was afraid his father would pursue me, but he did not—only the ghost of Hippocrotes now walked beside me.

I felt terrible for taking what could be of no import from these parents who have lost their son, but I was also of one mind to find truth. Hippocrotes' parents were hiding something. If the papyrus roll had no answers, I would arrange for its return. I vowed to go to Eleusis to search for Andronica.

It was not until I was through the Dipylon Gate, on the western road, past the cemetery, past the river, and under a grove of willows that I sat down to see what mystery my friend had yielded to me. I pulled the roll from the bag and spread it across the ground, unrolling the first page and beginning to read. As I read, even under the hot late morning sun, I could feel the blood chill my veins.

CHAPTER 11

Demaratus

We had camped in the open stretches of the Boetian plain a few marches from Attica, and the army was spread to all points of the horizon. It was raining, a vicious thunderstorm, and I was sitting in my tent, listening to the battering of the water on the tent tarp and writing what I could in my journal under the dim light of the olive oil lamps.

Hydarnes flung open the tent flap and entered, soaking wet but cheerful, lifting my spirits as usual. "Demaratus! The king would like to see you. I'm to bring you to him."

"Very well." I secured the papyrus roll in my camp chest and flung a cloak over my shoulders. I had no knowledge of how the king wanted me to serve him, but perhaps I am back in good fortune. We moved in the pouring rain, trudged through the thickening mud toward the royal headquarters and finally ducked under the flap of the royal enclosure and into the king's tent.

Xerxes was lying on his couch surrounded by lit torches in the rear of his abode. The floor was covered in rugs and skins and it was only Mardonious, Hydarnes, and myself. No slaves were present.

Xerxes motioned me forward. "Come, Demaratus. Sit."

I felt stiffness in the air and worried as I came forward and sat bolt upright on the couch next to his. Hydarnes continued to stand.

"My dear Spartan," said the Great King Xerxes. "Have you had any messages from the gods?"

"No, Your Highness."

He stroked his beard, oiled, and curled and smelling, as all Persian beards of the blessed rulers and the rich did, of incense and myrrh. "That is strange, I think. You seem to be in the god's favor for sending and receiving messages."

"Sire?"

"Oh come now, Demaratus, let's not be coy," he said, swinging his legs onto the lush floor coverings. "Phraortes has been more than forthcoming about your activities."

"I don't know what you mean, sire," I answered, keeping calm.

"Then, let's try another tack. What do you know of Medarnes?"

"Nothing sire. I have not seen him since the last battle. I believe him to have passed through the dark valley of death."

"Indeed!" cried Xerxes, springing to his feet, on the verge of one of his well known fits of rage. "As well as two of my brothers, and uncounted others!" He took a step forward but seemed to gather himself in, retreating from the edge of eruption. He took a deep breath. "Demaratus, you have been a true advisor for the length of my reign. It was you who counseled me on the matter of my succession, reminding my father Darius that I was the firstborn of his sons produced while he was king, thus negating the claim of my older half-brother Artobazanes. I have never forgotten that. It was you also who warned us of the prowess of these Greeks, and I acknowledge that as well."

He paused, his brows furrowing as he struggled to control his anger. "But, according to Phraortes, you have been consorting with the enemy. You warned the Spartan king of our attack, and your messenger killed Medarnes!"

"That is not true, my Lord! I know not of Medarnes' death."

"Then where is your prisoner, this Lysis of Athens?"

"I killed him when he displeased me. His bones scatter the woods on the slopes of Callidromus."

The king retreated, lowering himself to the settee. "So Phraortes said. You know who this Lysis was, don't you?"

"He was an Athenian marine."

Xerxes let out a stifled laugh, and glanced to Mardonious, who grinned. "He was Phraortes' son!"

"Sire?" I said, feigning surprise.

"Yes! The spawn of my sentries commander!"

I did not respond.

"No wonder Phraortes calls for your head on a pike!" And he laughed again, looking at Mardonious. "Well, that, and for other reasons."

"Sire?" I said, no longer feigning surprise, but of a deep worry.

"He thinks you had a hand in turning his heavenly face into a hellish one, and doing the same to the parts on his scarred body not seen by men." Again that knowing grin.

"Of what mind is he to think such lies. I did not even know him until this expedition. What harm could I have brought him?"

"I know, he is of many minds, but with what he has done that is to be expected. He believes you were conspiring with Medarnes' father, Hystaspes, to steal the lands I had given him in the Troad region, which is where your lands are."

"Who would tell him these lies?"

"I have no answers to that. Though you understand how these words pass from one to another so you should ask him!"

I sat stone-faced.

The king rose and paced to the opposite side of the tent, gazing out on the pounding rain and silhouetted against the lightning that blazed across the night sky. He turned. "Demaratus, I know you would not betray me. I believe you. It is this Phraortes we must keep watch on. He is accustomed to mystery and betrayal. It is his occupation, is it not?"

I nodded in agreement.

"Yes, I see that." He came back toward me with his arms open in acceptance. You will hear nothing more of this. The matter of Thermopylae is forgotten. Serve me well henceforth."

I stood to take leave, feeling sick to my stomach. It was not the fear of my king that left me so. It was the clear sense the king was rotten to his core—manipulative and uncaring in a way I had never experienced before. Why did I serve this man?

I thought of Phraortes and his hatred for me. Who was doing the lying here? I felt the need to know this man Phraortes, not for the sake of Lysis, whom I would probably never see again, but for my own sake and to learn the depths of the king I served, and had served, for the last ten years. If indeed Sparta was now closed to me, except by conquest, how could I continue here with what I was learning about Xerxes?

"Thank you, Your Highness, I beseech you to ask my counsel and I will give it, as I always have, honest and for Your Majesty's eternal reign."

"That is good, my Demaratus. Go, and we will meet in council in the morning. We must plan our moves after Athens."

I bowed and took leave, trailed by Hydarnes, and feeling the weight of the king's stare on my back.

Lysis

My fingers trembled as I read. I felt lightheaded by the moderate heat of the morning. The whispering breeze that swayed the willows was noiseless, drowned out by the thumping of my heart. The papyrus roll that lay open at my feet was covered in writing, big and bold, arranged in columns. It opened with a letter, or a commission, and was then followed by a listing of numbers that looked like payments received, or accounted for over years.

The letter was addressed to Hippocrotes and Andronica's father. It named him as "friend of the court" and "protector of the royal interest," and read:

> You have been charged to this task by authority of Mardonious, son of Gobryas for the purpose, as enumerated in our discussions, of close surveillance of the family of Androcles, son of Thraortis, of Athens in the Greek states. You will continue with this service until you receive

instructions otherwise. You will be prepared to eliminate the family of Androcles, should you receive orders to do so. This will be based on his continued loyalty to our common master, until the time when such will cease, or our master will decide otherwise. Payment for your service is as agreed and will be delivered yearly.

It was signed by Mardonious, son of Gobryas. I felt weak, almost unable to hold the papyrus steady. Yet I felt compelled to continue. The next sheet detailed annual payments, dates received, and amounts for the previous ten years, the years that spanned my childhood and young manhood. The years when Hippocrotes and I had solidified our friendship, grown up together, trained, marched, and fought together. I thought of Andronica, as I had so often these last weeks. Did she know? Was she a part of this? Nothing seemed impossible. Though my gut wrenched, I unrolled the book further and found a journal of betrayal dating back to when this commission had first been issued.

It was in a strange hand, not Hippocrotes'. It must have been his father's. It spoke of his arrival in the city from the East, his loathing of my countrymen, and his longing for his home city of Halicarnassus. It was an intermittent account but was damning enough. I saw the entry where Hippocrotes and I had first met, read how well my boyhood friend had followed instructions, even to the point of pretending to like me. There was no mention of Andronica, but the scroll was long, and how could I ever know?

I could read no more. I dragged myself to the base of the tree, pulling the roll after me, and collapsed, my back against the rutted bark. My heart was a void, an empty shell from which all life had been sucked. It didn't seem I could sink any lower. All the illusions of my life felt shattered, like a lance impacting pottery. I stared into nothingness, feeling nothing, seeing nothing, hearing nothing. The sun came to midday, people hurried by, bowed under their burdens, and I sat. The wind died and rose in fits and starts, insects obeyed their urges and explored my flesh, and I sat.

I recalled my friendship with Hippocrotes and looked for signs, clues to this betrayal. But could find none. He had been my strongest ally. Our bouts in the gym had been ferocious. He had stunned me more than once with the violence of his blows in the pankration. But had I not done the same when given the chance?

I remembered with a pang then, the time we spent in the frontier forts on the Megarian border, after our training as ephebes had begun in earnest. We had stood on the crumbling ramparts, gazing eastward as the night descended, silent as our long day's watch drew to an end. We began to talk. Or, he began to talk. Hippocrotes, confident but never deep, spoke of his parents, of their aloofness, their coldness toward their adopted home. And he spoke of that home, the city in which he had grown from boyhood to manhood, and what it meant to him. And he spoke of the future.

"What do you think will happen, Lysis, when the Persians come again?"

I was surprised. "Come again? Why would they return?"

His dark eyes serious for once, he said, "They will come. What do you think your father would do, my friend, if he were here, and the Persians came again?"

I stared at him, slack-jawed. He had never asked of my father before, but only of my stories, of my pain.

But there he was, looking at me, expecting an answer.

"He would fight. He would fight like Aries himself, and so would I."

Hippocrates said nothing, his face remained covered in an uncharacteristic cloak of heaviness. Then, as if a dark cloud that obscures the sun passes, his good humor returned. He laughed. "So would we all! And with the gods behind us!"

This was all I could retrieve from my memory. If Hippocrotes had betrayed me, he had hidden it well. Now, there could be little doubt he had; I could see no other reality since the scroll did not lie.

I moved because I had to. At Thermopylae, I had forsaken the thought of death as a solution to my pain. I relived in my mind the tale of infamy I had called my best friend and then wished to delve no further into its depths. Unable to think of a better course, I carried it with me and set off for home. My plan for making my way to Eleusis died in a welter of confusion. What if she knew? What if Andronica, too, had betrayed me? Were her professions of love the words of a courtesan?

When I arrived, soul sore and weary, there was no quiet to greet me. My uncle met me at the gate, frantic and worried. "Lysis! Where have you been? A rider came by from the assembly. He is alerting all of the western farms. The Persians are within a day's march. We are to journey to Phalerum and Piraeus for evacuation. We must take leave now! They are saying even the sacred snake has taken leave of Athena's temple. There are none who wish to stay now!"

I nodded and walked by him, saying nothing.

"What is it, son? What has happened?"

I shook my head, gripping the damming documents viselike and hurrying past. Inside the house, my mother and sisters were gathering our belongings, completing their frenzied move. They carried all they could, knowing the ships would be crowded, and took nothing of luxury, only those of necessity. I helped, moving like the steady turning of a wheel, knowing what I had to do, but uncaring. Before long, we were ready to set out, leaving the farm and its livestock in the hands of the few slaves we possessed, hoping the scourge would pass by, or in passing, would spare their lives, both livestock and slaves.

I knew I would not take leave with them. Though not healed, I knew my path lay with the fleet in defense of my city, even if in the end the city fell to the enemy. The strength and blood of the polis lay with its people, not in the stone, wood, brick, and dirt that made up its physical form. My uncle would need his own armor and weapons should we fail in our defense or should the future of those fleeing our shores include further wanderings on a sea of despair. I would find my own armor and weapons to guard my body, though knew not of what would guard my ravaged soul.

I looked again at the rolled papyrus and had a thought. I reentered the house for the last time and found in the corner my father's old chest, once holder of his armor and his honor, now empty of both. Although my heart had struggled to renounce him, and a veil of black spirit threatened to envelop me, hope flickered in my heart. I unrolled the papyrus and tore the first two sheets off, dropping them into the chest.

We loaded all we had onto the donkey cart, and allowing my mother's servant to drive, hustled back toward the city as fast as our spry animal would carry us. We arrived amidst a scene of mayhem straight from the tales of Homer. The air was full of tempers and shouts, wails and tears, children calling for their mothers, mothers calling for their children. Old men shuffled along, and harried officials tried to keep calm; directing all to gathering points where some semblance of order might be maintained. The transport ships, mostly private merchant vessels but also some provided by the city treasury, hauled families aboard in disciplined haste. Even many of the battleships, half-crewed for more space, had been designated to help.

I helped lift my family and our belongings up the rickety ladder to the single deck of a transport not yet full. The captain was a grizzled old man, fat and bald. "Come one, come all! We are off with the tide, and she waits for no one. There is plenty of room on board the old *Eros*, so step up there!"

She was a stout ship, the *Eros*, with enough oars for steerage and a large, much-used sail partially reefed and flapping with the onshore breeze, seemingly separate from the human energy pulsing around it. I kissed my mother and sisters goodbye; my uncle followed, embracing me.

"Come Lysis!" Cleisestha cried. "We are the last of them! The captain readies the ship!"

"He is not coming, Cleisestha," I heard my uncle say. "He must stay and fight."

"But you are not healed!" shouted my sister. "You are not ready!" She burst into tears as my mother hugged her, looking at me over Cleisestha's sobbing form.

"Son, may the gods protect you and bring you home again."

I waved but could say nothing. As the *Eros* gripped the ocean, floating into the tide, the crew settled to their oars and began to pull away against both wind and water, edging from the shore, leaving the land of our ancestors and flowing into the motley fleet that already stretched out to sea toward the isle of Salamis.

I sought Themistocles' ship, *Athena's Victory*, for I knew the Navarch would be in the midst of this great movement, making sure it went to the credit of the navy. The flagship was drawn up on the crowded sand halfway down the strand, its red-painted gunwales and sternpost welcoming me back into the fray. A group of captains stood in the shadow of the hull near the rising waters of the sea. I could see Themistocles among them, gesturing up and down the beach, issuing commands, strong and sure. None were dressed for battle, but all already carried with them the worry. They listened, and then headed for their own individual ships or sections. I came up on the stern as the last were departing.

Striding into the middle of the beach, casting his eyes left and right to assess the strength of approaching warriors offering their deaths so Athens might live, the Navarch spotted me.

"Ah! Lysis, you've returned!"

"Yes, sir. Can you use another marine on *Athena's Victory*?"

"We can always use another good man." He looked me over, noting the sack I carried slung over my shoulder and the roll I still held in my hand. "But where is your sword? Your shield? A marine can not fight with his bare hands."

"I lost it all at Artemisium, and then lost replacements at Thermopylae."

"Ah, do not worry. We'll fit you with the finest. For now, join the crew. The rowers will like an extra body and it looks like you could use some strengthening."

That was true. My convalescence had cost me strength. I felt tired and weak from the short journey to Phalerum, but knew a few days on the oars would restore my vigor.

He looked then at the roll I carried. "Do you read and write?"

"I do, but I did not write this."

Themistocles sensed my change in mood. "Lysis, you are a man of many secrets. Ones which I wish to know of one day."

"Yes, one day sir."

"Take leave then!" he said, his boundless commander's energy refocused. "The trierarch will assign your duties. Welcome aboard!"

"Yes sir," I said, and watched him sprint away, bellowing instructions and injecting the entire port with purpose and direction. *This man is of gold and jewels* I thought, sweeping my gaze over the beach. How lucky we were to have men such as him among our people. How lucky we were to have men like Leonidas as well, leaders who knew what it was to reach into the souls of men and remind them of who they are.

And yet, on the dangerous emotional road I trod at that moment, there was little difference between the urge to commit to another man I admired and could trust to stand by my side, and the bitterness and cynicism rising in my young heart that had built walls as high as the Acropolis itself, protecting against yet another disaster. I could not trust my feelings, so I decided I would not feel. I would work. I would fight. I would survive, but I would not feel. It was safer that way.

I ascended the ladder to the main deck of the trireme, standing once more by the stern and looked out to sea. *Athena's Victory* was a warship and would remain so, taking no passengers. The deck swarmed with men splicing lines, painting, passing supplies into the hold, and doing a myriad of duties to ready us for battle. Out to sea, the evacuation fleet made slow progress, their hulls filling the horizon, being joined by others in a mass exodus with no end in sight.

In the distance, the walls of the Acropolis rose high above the mud brick houses and walls, the narrow winding streets, the temples, markets, and public places of our sacred home, now empty. I thought of Hippocrotes' parents. Would they flee the city also, or would they stay and announce their continued allegiance to the conqueror? Were there others like him, others who had been watching my family? And my own father, what part would he play in the destruction of his homeland? And when they were all through, what would be left of all we had known? What would we return to if we ever returned at all?

It was out of our hands now. The gods would determine the final outcome of this drama. I had nothing left to give but myself, and perhaps that would be sufficient. Almost the entire population of our country moved away under the flags of two hundred warships of the fleet in which thirty-four thousand rowers toiled, four thousand marines and archers rode, and thousands of sailors commanded, rigged, and maintained these beasts of war. It was staggering. It was magnificent. It was sad. We were all now souls without a country, exiles en masse.

And now, as I stand remembering all that has happened in these last ten days, I feel so strongly the winds of another feeling. Those of us who will now fight together are more united in our scattering than we have ever been in our gathered security. We will soon see if this wind shall hold. Alas, the enemy is upon us.

Demaratus

We invaded Attica on the heels of the enemy's retreat. Xerxes was in a foul mood. We ravaged the land, stripping it of livestock and foodstuffs, burning farms and estates, killing all who resisted. The army did not intend to stay long—only enough to punish the Athenians, to state the price of continued resistance. This morning we would enter Athens itself.

At our last council of war, the king announced his intention of pressing further into Greece, of meting out vengeance to all who had fought at Thermopylae, the Spartans chief among them. To do so, of course, he would have to either defeat the enemy on the isthmus or go around and land on the Peloponnese in force. We had learned the cost of attacking a well-fortified position, and Xerxes was loathe to repeat the mistake. An attack on the isthmus could lead to a bloody repulse. He could not afford such a reverse. That left the sea option, and that meant defeating the Greek fleet once and for all.

The king asked my opinion, even as the other generals, with the exception of Hydarnes, sneered as I rose to speak. I ignored them, though their gibes seemed worse now. Before, they had been jealous of the king's favor. Now, their evident distrust charged the air as word of my supposed treachery had spread.

I said, "Your Lordship, the situation remains the same as before Thermopylae. True, we have entered the lands of the Athenians and will wreak the havoc they have brought upon themselves. But, to carry out your wishes of further conquest, we must scatter the enemy's naval forces. It does no good to repeat the losses we had in front of the Phocian wall. Threaten the Peloponnese, and the Spartans will run home to protect their own. When they do that, the other cities will fall without a fight."

"Your Highness," said Mardonious, casting me a malignant stare, "We can defeat these sons of whores on land. We have learned the enemy's tactics. My men will do what is necessary."

The king listened to both of us, then waved his hands at Mardonious. "My good brother, Demaratus has a point. Let us test our strength on the sea first. I have been assured by the captains of the fleet the Greeks cannot stand against us when we are united." He glanced at a tall, regal Persian—Megabazus, son of Megabates—who commanded the Phoenician contingent: "Is that not so, Megabazus? Is it not true that the Phoenicians are renowned for their ship handling?"

"That is so, my master," bowed Megabazus. "Our ships are lighter and faster. If we engage them in the open sea, we will destroy them."

Xerxes looked satisfied. "It is agreed then. We will occupy Athens and wait for the enemy's capitulation. If they do not comply, we will destroy their fleet and move further into Greece."

Mardonious gave me a poisonous stare as we exited the tent, but it mattered not to me. He was wrong, and I was right. What concerned me more was the king's position. I had served him for many years and known of his capriciousness. But I had felt certain of his basic sense of loyalty to his retainers and statesmanship when commanding over his holdings. Now, I questioned both.

I needed to explore a new path. Conquest of Sparta could allow me to return home, but not with honor. I could return to the Persian court, but my distaste for the king's manipulations had morphed into disgust, and that was a dangerous emotion in the lair of a tyrant. Perhaps I could arrange lordship over a conquered province, far away from the intrigue of Susa. There were few other options. Either way, my continued position depended on my show of loyalty, which once again brought me back to Phraortes.

He hated me and was out to destroy me, or so it seemed, and yet he had been wronged himself, that was clear. Wronged by Xerxes? I needed to find out. I could turn Phraortes to my side if I could find the truth of his own lot and convince him it would be wise to work together, not against one another. He could be a powerful ally.

But how? Who knew of the depth of Xerxes' machinations? Hydarnes was a good man and trusted by the king. But to what extent? That was worth pursuing. Otherwise, I knew not what to do. I had not seen Phraortes at the council. He might have been in Attica on the ready to attack. Perhaps it is best to confront him directly.

As I sat with these ponderings, Hydarnes entered my tent. Ever since Thermopylae, he had been a frequent visitor. He was an empathetic man, loved by his troops and the best commander in all of the Persian army. He respected me, had seen with his own eyes what my Spartans could do, and understood in some measure of mind the division in my heart.

"Today, we will march into Athens. Will you ride with me?"

"Of course!" I replied. "I would be honored."

"That is good then," he said, taking his seat on a camp stool. He arranged his robes about him, looking down. "Demaratus, the other night, I—" He hesitated to gather his thoughts, then began again. "I was sorry the king spoke to you as he did. There is no truth to what he said. You are an honorable man."

I nodded.

"The king has a sharp tongue on his subjects like a hawk on a rabbit. People have been beheaded following his rages. I was worried for you."

After all these years among the Persians, he was the closest I had to a friend. "The king is the king because he is always suspicious," I replied.

He pursed his lips, again hesitating. "There is more to this story than that. I have done a great deal of thinking, pondering on the significance of his words to you. As I'm sure you have."

I nodded again.

"His Highness does not always respect his people."

"He finds uses for them and when they are not longer of use—" I made a slashing motion across my throat.

"You could say that."

His admission was surprising, even though I and most others had seen evidence of this from the Xerxes, it was not spoken of. It was one matter to throw common soldiers into the maw of combat, even under hopeless conditions. It was quite another to twist the men closest to him. That could be dangerous indeed.

"The king will do what he must to ensure the loyalty of all he rules over, especially if he is not a Persian."

"So you're saying—"

"I'm saying I believe Phraortes involved himself in matters without knowing he had been tricked to be but a mouse in a den of snakes."

"Hydarnes, of what snakes do you speak?" I asked.

"Do you remember before Xerxes came to the throne, right after you arrived at Susa?"

"Yes, he was locked in a bitter struggle with his half-brother over which of them would succeed their father to the throne." The image flashed in my mind of my own kingship, of Cleomones and the hatred he had felt for me because I disagreed with him about invading Attica; ironic now that debate. Cleomones, who had wanted to invade, was dead, and I, who never did invade, was in the midst of planning to.

"Yes, bitterness and intrigue. People fell whether they supported one side or the other. Darius tried to control it, but the time was tense for years before he died." Hydarnes shifted in his seat, leaned forward, and spoke in a low voice. "Hystaspes, the father of Medarnes, was a close supporter of Xerxes' half-brother, Artobazanes. He commanded many secret duties for him. People in Xerxes' camp were scared away, or were but tinder for Hades' fiery pits. Hystaspes lived near you in the Troad."

"As did Androcles, or as we know him by today 'Phraortes'."

"Yes."

"What then was to become of Hystaspes?"

Hydarnes shrugged. "Fallen. But his murder was blamed on Androcles."

"Who blamed Androcles?"

"I know not. These words came from the mouth of Artobazanes, but who told him I again know not."

"But you think it may have been Xerxes?"

He shrugged. "I only know Hystaspes did secret deeds for Artobazanes, and I believe to have Hystaspes perish would please Xerxes."

"If this is true, Xerxes used him as a scapegoat."

"And Androcles, who lived near to him in the Troad, was the man to satisfy the king's pleasure."

"But Phraortes now serves the king like a dog its master. Of what mind is he?"

"Androcles does not know what you and I know. But perhaps if the king told him that you conspired with Hystaspes to steal his lands and change his fate, surely he would be filled with hate for you. I know not of their counsels beyond what I told you on the mountain path: Androcles fell and rose as Phraortes."

We sat in silence, my head full of possibilities; yet none were of one mind. Except one: giving this information to Phraortes could be helpful. I looked up at Hydarnes. "How have you served this man with your loyalty as you have, for these many years?"

"He is a kinsman. But that he is of my blood, does not make me his slave." He got up, stretching his cramped muscles, and turned to take leave. "Besides, I supported Artobazanes." He moved to the tent opening, cast a glance over his shoulder, and said, "Of this do as you wish Demaratus. You can trust me to keep my silence, and to be with your side if you wish that too."

"Thank you," I replied.

It was time to meet Phraortes.

Lysis

Warships pack the beaches and waters around Paloukia Bay on the Isle of Salamis. The entire Greek fleet lay either at anchor or drawn up on shore awaiting the next messenger. The water is calm now, and the air hot, even in the waning days of summer. Eurybiades and Themistocles have brought us, the survivors from Artemisium, to this isle, distant from the enemy yet close enough to defend our homeland. The cities not originally present at the northern battle have now sent reinforcing warriors from where they had been gathered in the harbor of Troezen. In all, we have upwards of three hundred and eighty triremes, plus several single-decked fifty-oared penteconters which are almost useless but for boarding and claiming already damaged enemy ships. Nevertheless, the help is much appreciated.

Our armada hails from Sparta, Corinth, Sicyonia, Epidaurus, Troezen Hermione, Athens, Megara, Aegina, Ceos, Eretria, Naxos and Styra, among others. We even had a single ship join us from far off Croton, on Italy. As grateful as we are though, many allies did not, or could not, send ships and warriors. Much of the Peloponnese lay idle, Argos was silent; and rumors flew that special barters had been struck with Xerxes. All of northern Greece has fallen to the barbarians, and the help the northerners had provided landed in the camp of the enemy. So too with Ionia, the original reason for the enmity between Persia and Greece. They are under occupation, and their ships and their men now fight under the Persian flag.

Right after Thermopylae, while I lay in a stupor off of Euboea, Themistocles had sailed his fastest ships to scout all the watering holes the Persian fleet would use on the island. At each one, he had messages cut in stone asking the Ionians to remember their Greek origins—for many of their cities, that meant Athenian origins—and either refuse to fight with the enemy or, barring that, at least to fight without vigor. I had seen Xerxes' anger firsthand, and I can imagine the fate of the Ionians if they follow Themistocles's plea. I am not hopeful of the outcome.

Farther from our shores, to the west, we had hoped for succor from those states and colonies that were offshoots of the Greek homeland, but we receive little aid.

Our appeals to Dionysus of Siracusa fall to silence, and that city sends nothing. The city's tyrant remembered old wounds, of help he'd asked for but was never received. It is also said he demanded full command of our forces. We were not of one mind, and so he refused our help. We had hoped Sicily and especially Siracusa would regret their intransigence, yet they did not.

Even with our numbers, our fleet's crews lack confidence. Our ships are heavier than the enemies and not as nimble, and those who had not fought at Artemisium do not believe our assertions that the enemy can be beaten. We recent warriors know in close battle, our superior size and weight will give us more favor from the gods if we maneuver our ships properly. Yet, convincing those yet to battle of this favor is a challenge. Alas, taking arms in war and killing forces a man's mind to change in ways peace cannot.

I remember the trepidation I felt when first glimpsing the vast array of vessels the enemy launched against us at Artemisium. I recall the knot in my stomach and the raw fear when they first ran upon us. But as I discovered, the Persian and Medean marines were not gods. They bled and died like other men, and their ships, while more craftily made, splintered when rammed, like any other. It was a source of surprise to all of us that our tactics were superior to those who we had thought would deliver us to death.

To the newcomers, we try to share our knowledge, passing on tales of the battles and discussing tactics until all hours of the night. They listen,and as the Persian horde descend on Attica and the immense Persian fleet fill up our abandoned roads at Phalerum, we gather around the beach fires and strategize. I, and the other bloodied "old" hands, try to overcome the doubts wavering in the air. Themistocles hails, "We are a fleet, the most powerful assemblage of war-fighting craft assembled in Greece since the invasion of Troy in the time of Achilles!"

The power we possess lay not in our strong timbers or bronze-beaked rams but in the steady nerve and resilience of the men who stride the decks and man the oars. These men will engage the enemy toe to toe, mixing sweat with sweat and blood with blood. It is this courage that determines the ultimate measure of our strength. As I had seen at Artemisium, and even more so at Thermopylae, our courage depends on our leader. From the leader springs a belief in self and belief in cause. As we gather around our food and fire, I realize how tenuous that belief is. We need leaders more than we need spears, oars, or bread. At Thermopylae, it was Leonidas who had supplied it. At Artemisium, it was Eurybiades, another Spartan warrior, and, it must be Themistocles in this battle before us.

Even in my numb state, reeling as I am from the blows of betrayal that flay my heart, I can still be of clear eye about my destiny. The iron walls I have erected around my feelings allow me that vision at least.

I've had no time to befriend anyone, especially Themistocles. Though in the depths of my soul I can sense the desire to do so, I will not allow myself and quash the urge at every fresh shoot. He is a dynamic man, a ball of energy that represents nature's core essences: fire, water, wind, and earth. In normal times, I, like every Athenian and every man Themistocles met, can not help but be drawn into his spell. He is a natural leader, a man in the mold of the great Leonidas, who now assumes the mantle of legend, god, and hero.

These are not normal circumstances. My most effective personal defense is an unwavering commitment to neutrality in my heart as I can not battle the enemy from a sense of attachment, obligation, or family. That will be too close, painful, and confusing. I can battle from habit, from circumstance, from situation. I can battle because I am an Athenian and am with my countrymen. I choose the latter.

When we had first landed on the island, Themistocles remembered enough of my condition to inquire as to the success of my search for arms. This when I had risen from the rower's benches, exhausted after one shift on the oars, my soft hands bloodied.

"I see you've thrown yourself into the oar, Lysis," he said.

"Yes sir, the time is short. I must be ready when they come."

"No doubt you will. But you'd do better with what you're used to. I'll see that you are with armor and weapons." He slapped me on the back, then proceeded onward, eyes dancing, and feet bouncing. He enjoyed his command, I realized— the thrill of authority, the power of our concentrated forces, even the approach of the enemy. Here was a man who lived to lead, who thrived on danger. I watched him race to the bow to look ahead at the fast-approaching island, sniff the salt-laden air, and take it in. Who would not want to serve this man? Who could resist?

The trireme trierarchs and men of our proud Athenian fleet worship him. Other contingents are less impressed, not having witnessed his persuasive and rhetorical skills firsthand though they will soon get the opportunity.

We received word Xerxes and the Persian land army had occupied the city, and were besieging the Acropolis where a group of priests and others stood behind their "wooden wall" of doors and planks. The enemy fleet was on our beaches, polluting our sea, rampaging through the Piraeus and through Athens itself, shaming and humiliating our country, ravaging and laying waste to our crops and fields, our homes, and estates. Despite my confusion, I fear for Andronica, not safe in Eleusis, not safe anywhere on the mainland.

Eurybiades calls a meeting of the fleet captains, representatives from the various contingents, to discuss our options. Themistocles readies himself, realizing he would be called upon to give his opinion of our city, since we existed now as an entity only through our fleet. I am on the beach, talking with a marine from another ship, hoping to begin collecting cast-off weapons and armor, when Themistocles strides by, dressed in his usual tunic but wearing a broad-brimmed straw hat that gives some protection against the noonday sun. He sees me and pauses.

"Lysis, come with me, if you will. I'd like to have you at this meeting. Remember what we talked about earlier. I may have need of you."

I take leave from bantering and come alongside the Navarch. "Sir?"

"Yes, I know this is an uncomfortable subject for you, but your father's," he hesitated, "your father's position could prove useful to our cause."

"Yes sir, as you wish."

We are walking along the beach, the ships drawn up to our right, the hills of Salamis rolling away to our left. The smell of the sea mixes with rotten fish that lay on the sand and contrasts with the scent of the wooden vessels, the cordage and sap, the canvas and leather, the overwhelming aroma of sweat soaked timbers and the tide of unwashed men who go about their routines preparing for war. Such an assault on my senses should have been second nature, but for some reason, I notice it as if for the first time, as if part of me is struggling to open up again. The mention of my father has not closed me off, nor caged my emotions, but rather has had the curious opposite effect.

"We are in a precarious position here, Lysis. We must fight the enemy now, in this place. To do otherwise would be foolish."

"Are you worried sir that the others might not have your vision?"

"Yes. Our alliance is a fragile one. It rests on threads of hope and despair. We must convince the others our best hope is here, not farther west."

"And how might the man I know prove to be useful?"

We are almost at the meeting now, a large gathering of a hundred armored men who sit on rocks or squat under a grove of trees off the beach.

"I'm not sure, but listen closely here for I'd like to have new paths to explore."

"New paths to explore." I had heard that before from another leader of men. I hope the end would be different this time. We approach the group, many of whom are now standing, shading their eyes against the blazing sun and shouting greetings to Themistocles. We are almost the last to arrive. Eurybiades stands amidst a circle of seated captains who offer up questions and comments. An air of nerves hangs over the meeting like a pack of starlings twittering in a tree. *Not a good sign*, I think.

Themistocles indicates I should stay outside the circle and walks right up to Eurybiades. I join the other gatherers who stand around the edges, their gazes fixed on the leadership. They are a distinguished group of men; trierarchs, captains, and leaders of their respective ships and naval forces. They are dressed in an assortment of arms and armor, some polished and cared for with the greatest attention, others showing much use and no inclination for ceremony. They are tanned and fit, with upright demeanor and presence that speak of their positions and importance.

Eurybiades breaks off his discussion with the inner circle of captains and addresses the gathering. "Captains of Greece, trierarchs and defenders of freedom, we meet here in a time of great danger for our cities and for all of Greece. I am a man of few words, and I will not disappoint you this time."

Muted laughter greets him.

"We come to it now, the great trial of our time. What we do here may decide the fate of all of us. We must choose well."

Attentive, some heads nod in agreement; others stay still.

"We will open our debate and discussion with Themistocles, son of Neocles, Navarch of Athens."

A murmuring arises from the group as Themistocles comes to his feet. "Warriors, as you are aware, Athens is besieged as we speak. We must decide a course of action that will ensure victory for our cause, and I say this knowing my city has already fallen and must be retaken." He pauses, casting his eyes north and east toward where the sacred Acropolis lay.

From the crowd, a harsh voice rings out. "Then why is it you speak? What has a stateless person to say to this gathering?"

"Who is that?" questions Eurybiades.

A tall and splendidly armored warrior steps from the far side of the circle. His jet-black hair matches his eyes, and his haughty mien fits with his arrogant tone. "You know me, Eurybiades, I am Adeimantus, son of Ocytus of Corinth, and it is I who still has a state, I who still has a voice."

Themistocles bristles. "Adeimantus, humble yourself before the gods; they gave you just as they gave an ass a jaw to close, and allow me to finish. We will have time to discuss the many contributions of the Corinthian fleet when I am done."

Adeimantus' face clouds, and he looks like he will strike Themistocles until Eurybiades intervenes. "Please sirs, we can ill afford such fighting. Allow the Navarch to continue."

Adeimantus growls but keeps silent.

Casting an equally contemptuous glance his way, Themistocles resumes. "We Athenians, provider of over one hundred-eighty triremes to the effort at Artemisium, had expected a land army to be encamped in Attica, ready to defend our city upon our return. We were disappointed."

He searches around him, seeking out the eyes of the Peloponnesian captains. None avoid his gaze. "Now, our city is taken, but though it is so, the battle is far from over. I believe we have the chance, here and now, to take on and defeat the Persian fleet. Here, where we can best apply the lessons we learned at Artemisium. Here, in waters of our own choosing. We are united here. We have the enemy here. It is here, at Salamis, we must strike."

There is a rising murmur of agreement from a good portion of the gathering, but the majority keep quiet.

Once again, Adeimantus speaks. "If he's done, Eurybiades, I have a few points to make."

The Spartan looks at Themistocles, who nods and steps aside, keeping his sea-grey eyes fixed on the Corinthian captain.

"Athens is lost. The Peloponnese, on the other hand, is whole and united. The army waits behind an impregnable wall at the isthmus. If we fight here, we risk being blockaded. The enemy can cut off both ends of the channel. If we leave, we live to fight another day, supported by the land army and in a much better position to defeat the enemy. Their army occupies the mainland. Should we wash ashore during the battle, there will be no hope for any of us. Themistocles is foolish, and his plan is that of a fool. We must acknowledge truth and take leave of this place."

This time, there is a much greater swell of agreement. Adeimantus takes a few steps back and looks with satisfaction upon the Athenian Navarch's now impassive features. Themistocles moves forward again.

"Captains," he begins, "Adeimantus does indeed have a point. But it is not an informed one."

Adeimantus leaps to his feet, his face reddening. Eurybiades restrains him with a look.

Themistocles continues. "To fight off of the isthmus means to fight in the open sea. This would be disastrous for us. The enemy ships are more maneuverable, and they outnumber us. We would be at a great disadvantage."

"Are you afraid to face the enemy?" shouts Adeimantus.

"Afraid?" Themistocles looks bemused. "Why were you not in battle at Artemisium? Were you suckling at your mother's bosom while others bled?"

This time the Corinthian has to be held back and a few fellow captains spring forward to prevent fists upon another.

Themistocles is angered now. "Afraid? I offer advice for victory, a plan that has a chance. I am afraid of nothing but stupidity, so in that way, I fear you Adeimantus."

a chorus of angry shouts from the other captains follows. I admit, Themistocles was usually more even-tempered. Before the tumult dies, a runner races across the beach and casts himself into the middle of the circle.

"A message" he cries. "A message for the fleet commander!"

"What is it?" asked Eurybiades.

"The Acropolis has fallen! The enemy is in the citadel!"

Even though this had been expected on the day our city had been taken by Persia, it still comes as a shock to all of us, and especially to us native Athenians. Everyone looks to the east, toward the city where smoke can be seen rising across the heavens, spreading like a dark stain black in the middle and edged in angry grey as it drifts seaward. Now, from order, comes pandemonium.

"That is of my own words!" shouts Adeimantus, through the din. "There is nothing left there to fight for! Athenians are truly stateless! We must go to the isthmus!"

Eurybiades tries to restore order among the loud yells and growls of assent. He raises both his arms high, his eyes blazing with fury. "Silence! Silence here!"

The confused and anxious babbling quiets as discipline reasserts itself. Eurybiades looks around him. "Captains! Is Themistocles with whom you will fell the enemy when the time comes to meet him?" There were shamed glances and bowed heads as Eurybiades continues,"The answer is clear! We must wage battle at the isthmus! We have no time to dither. The enemy could be at our throats in hours."

"We will take a count!" yells Eurybiades. "Those who wish to follow Themistocles and fight here at Salamis, stand to my right! Those with Adeimantus, to my left!"

There is a brief pause as the group sorts itself. An overwhelming majority move in a mass to Eurybiades' left. The council has decided. We will abandon Athens to its fate

CHAPTER 12

Demaratus

Hydarnes and I entered the deserted city through the Dipylon Gate, making our way to the Agora along the Panathenaic way. Refuse littered the streets, shattered pots and jars dropped from carts or nervous hands, pieces of clothing, implements and articles of all descriptions. The smell that arose from a modern city was muffled in the absence of its people, but it overwhelmed me. Urine and feces, dead animals, rotting vegetation, sweat, blood, and spilled wine—all blended together as one stench; an unforgettable record of a once-tight-knit human existence.

Solid bricks and stones paved the road through the Agora up a rise to the base of the citadel. We passed shrines to the gods erected here and there, in no apparent order, except for a larger altar near the entrance to the generous open square that defined the Agora. The Agora itself was lined with shuttered shops and abandoned market stalls, their soiled but colorful awnings hanging in the dead air. We walked along the silent street preceded by Hydarnes' Immortals, making little noise but gazing about with curiosity inside the house of the enemy, the object of the Persian's long march.

Ahead stood the Acropolis. I had been here more than once. I remembered it as a thriving place, full of rude and loud-mouthed citizens, for the most part, people who bore too much pride and not enough respect. It had been an exciting place to be, with contagious energy, but the Athenians absence now was a decided improvement.

The Acropolis marked the center of the city. It had been the original home of Athens, where the palace, temples, and homes of the population had stood. But it was not extensive, a stade or so square. Long ago it had outgrown its founders' use and was now home to the city's temples and the sacred heart of Attica. A solid mountain of rock thrusting from the surrounding countryside like a misshapen wart on a hand, the Acropolis was flat on top and surrounded by a stone and mud brick wall with crumbling façade yet it still rose above a few hundred feet. The wide and paved Panathenaic way ran to the base and then up the face of the citadel, angling back on itself as it climbed, entering the plateau through an arched gate protected by solid watch towers and crenelated battlements that frowned on the road beneath it.

The lead elements of Hydarnes' troops approached the gate when heads appeared above the wall and a volley of ill-aimed arrows followed. Most skittered and broke against the rock, but a few hit their marks. Hydarne' men backed down the road not having expected any resistance. The citadel was occupied, but by whom it was hard to tell. The enemy did not seem to be many or well-organized. Still, it was best to be cautious.

Hydarnes and I ran forward to receive the report of the column leader and assess the resistance. I knew from previous visits that the Acropolis was impossible to assault from any angle other than from where we stood. Its faces were sheer, and while some stubborn vegetation clung to its limestone and marble, there was little hope of concealment. If an enemy wanted to make a determined stand, little could dislodge him, save starvation or betrayal. That is the way of many sieges, and it would be no different here. I wondered who was encamped there. It was not the Athenian main force, or any of similar strength. Fanatics? Priests of the Temple? If so, what cause were they to die for?

Hydarnes shook his head. "Damn! Demaratus, what say you? You've seen this place? What plan do you advise?"

"Surround the rock, and rain arrows upon them from the Areopagus," I replied, pointing to a smaller hill that rose to our right on the far side of the Acropolis. "Or, a direct assault may carry you to victory as it appears they are only but a few."

"I will take that advice," he said, gesturing to his commanders. They came racing over and Hydarnes issued the necessary instructions. "We will go right at the dogs. They have no real gate to prevent us—only planks and boards, such a primitive barricade that we should be able to break down."

As they darted away, getting their troops ready, he said to me, "Best this be done before the king arrives. There is no reason to anger him any further."

I nodded, thinking of our last conversation. I had been trying to get a message to Phraortes for the past two days, but without success as his whereabouts were unknown. I knew he had entered Attica ahead of the main body of the army to scout out the land, and had not been heard from since. A plan had been forming in my mind, a plan that would involve Phraortes, if I could convince him I was to be trusted. A plan that could perhaps return me to Sparta with honor after all.

The plan depended on many things for which I did not hold much hope for success, but it was worth an effort. Though my confusion over where I belonged had increased, I continued to drift back to the place where I felt most comfortable.. I was certain of few matters in my life, and for someone like me, uncertainty was unfamiliar ground. I knew I could no longer trust Xerxes, and I knew I was an outcast from my own people. That was the extent of my certainty. Beyond that, I knew not where to journey. My plan could protect me from Xerxes, give me some power, and perhaps return me home. That was enough to hope for at this point. But I needed to find Phraortes first.

During my musings, the Immortals had been massing for an assault on the gate. Hydarnes gave the order, and the attack commenced, the men surging upwards, shields at the ready, spears leveled. They were within half a stade of the barricade when the defenders once more appeared above the walls and fired down into their midst, this time hurling boulders, too, atop Hydarnes' ranks. Then, from behind the barricade, another group emerged heaving several larger rocks to the edge and rolling them down on the chargers. The effect was instantaneous and catastrophic. The boulders rolled into the Immortals at breathtaking speed, crushing and maiming the lead elements and bouncing down the slope to leave havoc in their trail. Before the men could recover, the defenders had resupplied themselves with more boulders, and with loud cries they readied to crush any other invaders. A few of our troops had kept their wits about them and were clinging to the side of the road attempting to let fly arrows, but for the most part, the attack had failed, and Hydarnes' command came streaming back down the narrow path to protection.

Hydarnes himself raced to the bottom of the road with his features sculpted in consternation. "Reform! Move out from arrow range and reform!"

The men obeyed with alacrity, some wheeling and shaking their fists and shouting up at the defenders, who hooted. Hydarnes strode back to me angrily.

"They were ready for that!" he shouted.

"Yes," I said. "But I watched them. Not a trained hand among them. They're fanatics alright, but no real fighters in the group."

"That's not going to help us so long as they have rocks. And they're sitting on a mountain of rock. This could take some time."

"Sire, I advise the Areopagus. Perhaps fire arrows will help persuade them."

He smiled. "Demaratus, you have some real genius in you."

"It helps to know the land."

Hydarnes hurried off, once more all energy as he gestured, issued commands, and brought organization and purpose out of chaos. In minutes, groups of archers had detached and moved through the narrow streets of the town that ringed the Acropolis. They hurried toward the Areopagus and the high ground with flax dipped in olive oil wrapped around their arrow heads and torches prepared to rain fire on the wooden structures that dominated the summit.

Hydarnes had sent other men scurrying around the base of the fortress, searching for any other path up the escarpment. Others had fanned out through the city, rooting out the occasional beggar or even one or two sympathizers who still occupied the abandoned city. The main army was spread before the walls on the Attica plain, and messengers had reported the arrival of the fleet, with the king in procession, anchoring along the coast from Phalerum to the Piraeus.

Hydarnes was informed of Xerxes' approach and decided to expedite the attack. We'd made our way around to the Areopagus where the Athenian assembly met, and from that vantage point, we watched as the archers unleashed slews of flame-tipped arrows that slammed into the vulnerable timber roofs of temples and outbuildings. Some ignited the dried tinder, others burnt out in flight or missed the mark. Enough hit so that fires were set in all quarters of the sacred fortress. It was pitiful to watch the frantic efforts of the inhabitants trying to extinguish the flames. The Athenians crawled on top of the buildings wielding blankets and hauling buckets of precious water. They pounded at the ever-widening reach of the fires, all while under attack by our archers who skewered them without mercy. Stifling their agonized cries was the increasing roar of the flames that spread from roof top to roof top, igniting an inferno. On the strength of a slight sea breeze, the clouds of smoke that rose into the air now drifted inland. But there was no sign of surrender from the defenders. If they could somehow survive this firestorm, they might still be able to resist, hold out for days, if not weeks, or longer. Hydarnes looked like he was having the same thought.

"Demaratus, what will be needed for these Athenians to surrender?"

"Death, of course."

Hydarnes looked disgusted. "You Greeks are a stubborn people."

I was silent. As we stood there, a young Persian, barely bearded and with dark eyes shining, ran up to us. He bowed in front of Hydarnes.

"Sire," he said. "We have found a way up the mountain."

Hydarnes looked startled but pleased. I was surprised.

"Where is it?" asked the Persian commander.

"On the gate side, near the base over there," replied the messenger, pointing to our front.

"There is no path there!" said Hydarnes. "That looks as steep as the rest!"

"My apologies, master, but there is a series of handholds that go straight up the cliff's edge. We have some men who believe they can climb it."

Hydarnes looked again at the rock face, shaking his head in disbelief. "Very well, if they so choose, but tell them to turn back if they cannot go all the way."

"Yes sire!" snapped the young man, sprinting away back down the hill. We waited as he disappeared into the city streets, then watched the drama play itself out among the burning temples of the Acropolis.

We began to see a score or more of stripped-down warriors crawling up the sheer face of the escarpment. Searching for foot and toe holds, they clung to the hard rock and, foot by foot, made their way toward the summit. I found myself holding my breath, admiring their bravery but also seeing them from my Greek perspective as engaged in an athletic contest with great merit. What these men would win in the games, should they be allowed to attend!

No Athenians paid attention to these climbers, covered as they were by our own archers and by the chaos within the citadel. It was a slow and painful wait before the first of them had reached the bottom of the crumbling wall and leaned back over, helping the next to his feet. One by one, they arrived at the top, spread out along the base, and headed for a spot opposite from where we watched with fascination. The wall had collapsed in on itself at that point, and when the armed soldiers came to the break, they vaulted inside without hesitation.

Even above the roar of the flames, I could hear the terrified shrieks of the Athenians trapped inside. In moments, men appeared on the ramparts, looking backward and forward in terror. Many stepping to the edge chose the one fear over the other and threw themselves headlong off the cliff, their bodies colliding against the rocks two hundred feet below or smashing into the thatched or tiled roofs of the city. They had expected no quarter, and from what I could hear within, they were not getting any.

A large detachment of Immortals raced up the road, stepping over the bodies of their fallen comrades, and were now streaming to the gate undeterred. As they arrived, the climbers flung open the gates and the Immortals pushed their way past the barricade into the citadel.

Hydarnes said, "It is time we go. It will be over in a few minutes."

I nodded and followed him down the Areopagus. We were back at the base of the Panathenaic, winding our way up the road and toward the awaiting mayhem. We were not disappointed.

Soldiers guarded the barricade, its timbers blackened and charred by fire, its purpose dissolved. We strode past and into the Acropolis itself, now a sea of flickering flames, ruined temples and scattered bodies. Most dressed in paupers' clothes; torn and dirty tunics, pieced-together chitons and old weathered hats. But some were priests of the various temples. Their long robes and handcrafted sandals bespoke their rank. Some held tightly clutched in their bloodied hands the crude weapons they had died with. Their eyes had frozen wide-open in fear, while their bodies bled from every orifice, some natural, some battle-made. The Persian soldiery ran about the place dragging the gold, silver, and other items of value from the temples that had escaped the flames.

We walked to the center of the plateau where Erectheus, the temple of the earth-born, had stood. It was a shattered shell. Within its environs, the sacred olive tree of Athens lay shrouded in smoke, burned to its roots and tortured by tongues of flame that licked its charred trunk. A broad basin of water bubbled, hissed and steamed, boiling hot and absorbing the occasional bits of orphaned wood that fell into its shallow depths. This was the price of pride, I thought, the price of refusing the demands of earth and water delivered by the king of the Persians. Here the population of this once great city had given up all of its earth and all of its water to the enemy. It had, for all matters of everyday life, ceased to exist.

Traversing the circumference of the fortress, Hydarnes and I noted the piled bodies in an unburned temple, apparently where the last had gone to seek sanctuary in a final, desperate appeal to the gods who had failed them. It seemed that whenever I walked a battleground these days, it was as witness to self-sacrifice or immolation, to senseless acts of suicide, or hubris, or both. I admit, even I, who knew my people and something of Greece as a whole, had not been prepared for this. It was bad at Thermopylae, but the enemy knew well of our strength. Their sacrifice, while tragic, was at least understandable. But I was not prepared to give the same qualities to these Athenian corpses at my feet. If this is what they were capable of, the campaign was going to get worse for us before we saw greatness.

Lysis

"Themistocles!" shouts a voice behind us. "Wait!" Marching away from the meeting with me, the Navarch is trying to remain calm, but his creased brows and pursed lips can not suppress his fury. He spins around, hands on hips, glaring at a captain I had never seen before until he'd stood near me during the council. He is a squat, powerfully built sailor who has seen many storms. His beard is fleece white, and his dark eyes hold reservoirs of experience.

"Mnesiphilus," says Themistocles. "For what matter do you chase me?"

"Navarch, listen to me," says the fragile old man. "Has the council decided to abandon Athens then?"

"It seems so."

"Well, you must stop them!" Mnesiphilus cries, planting himself in front of us.

"The votes were cast! What do you wish me to do?" asks an exasperated Themistocles.

"What only you can do! Navarch, if the fleet leaves here, it will never remain as one. You know this. The various cities will lose their nerve and sail away to defend their own homes. The danger will seem less to them once they believe they are safe beyond the isthmus. You must turn them!"

Themistocles opens his mouth to speak but seems to be stricken mid-sentence, and stands in silence for a long moment. "Mnesiphilus, you're right. We must turn them. I must turn them. And there is only one way to do it." Clapping strong hands on the shoulders of the elderly captain, he says, "I must go see Eurybiades. Come with me, Lysis, we have work to do!"

He turns back toward the Spartan's ship and hurries off. "Lysis," he says, as I come up alongside, "Do you remember what we spoke of on the voyage here?"

"Sire?"

"About your father and the use we may have for him."

"Yes sire," I reply, a ball forming in my stomach.

"Would you contact him again if your city asked that of you?"

I can feel my insides churning, emotions rising from my gut, clamping onto my heart like an iron vise. I try to control myself, to keep my vow to remain frigid, aloof, unfeeling. I say nothing, but my face betrays the struggle. Themistocles glances across at me as we move along the shore, sensing my pain.

I resist the surge, pushing it back and bring myself under control. I am frightened by the power of the anger and humiliation that festers within me. I can make no sense of what rages like an uneasy volcano, mocking my vow, hammering against the new and feeble walls I have built. But I can not lose myself, so I tame the volcano and come to the present. I listen to Themistocles. I listen to myself.

"I serve the will of my fellow citizens and my country sir," I reply, looking at my commander.

"That is well. Then you must find him, find your father in the camp of the enemy, and tell him his old friend Themistocles has a proposition for him. I will send you with my servant under a truce. I am certain it will be honored." By this time, we have come to the Lacedaemonian trireme of the Spartan Eurybiades, and

Themistocles prepares to board. "Ready yourself Lysis. You must deliver my words to your father before sundown."

"Sir, " I am but a humble sailor in your presence, but will not your actions anger Eurybiades?"

"He can lead the rest of the fleet away from this place if he desires, but if he does, he goes without our city's two hundred ships." The Navarch of Athens climbs onto the Spartan vessel. "We stay and we fight!" I watch him disappear onto the deck and turn the other way, toward *Athena's Victory*.

Back to Athens he has commanded me, back to the lair of the enemy. What will I find there?

Night falls. I stand once again in the camp of the enemy, this time not a prisoner but a courier, under guarantee of safety. One of Themistocles' servants, a house slave named Sicinnus, has come to me with further instructions from the Navarch. We make our way to a small fishing vessel pulled up alongside a rough quay at the end of the long row of warships. Sicinnus briefs the small crew and we set sail, heading out with a fresh breeze toward Pharlerum and the newest conquest of the Persian fleet.

After leaving the channel, we are hailed and stopped. Enemy guard ships patrolled the area, keeping an eye on our own fleet. One of them, a Phoenician trireme, rows alongside us and asks of our journey.

"We bring a message to Xerxes!" I shout. "From Themistocles, commander of the Athenian fleet!"

"For the king?" asks the vessel's commander.

"Yes, for the Great King Xerxes!"

"Come aboard then. We will take you in. Your ship remains here with our men aboard. We will sink her if you betray my trust."

"My trust will hold sir."

"Then when you take leave from the king, I will allow you to return to your ship without harm."

They hoist Sicinnus and me aboard the battleship, leaving behind our erstwhile companions, who look up at us with anxious faces, more fearful for their safety than for ours, I wager. They show us to the stern while the ship turns. I look with interest upon their oarsmanship, noting the swift, sharp catches and the rhythmic swing of the bodies. These Phoenicians are like a field of wheat in the wind, waving to and fro as one. I can feel them advancing the vessel beneath me, and I sense the lighter nature of the ship. It seems to lift quicker and be nimbler than our heavier Athenian warships. No wonder Themistocles has been afraid of an open-sea battle. A tiny advantage in speed or maneuverability can be the difference between sailing on victoriously or sinking to the bottom of the sea.

No one speaks to us as we make our way to the harbor at the Piraeus. There the vessel's commander deposits us on a quay. There, we learn the king has left for the citadel a while before. As we trudge up the road from the port, we see the sky around the Acropolis darken with smoke and flames, the land burning and smoldering so that a black and depressing pall is cast over the entire city. The enemy laughs at us as we pass, pointing, and joking at the spectacle and smug in their victory. Once more, my anger awakens and I find it more and more difficult to stay neutral and unattached in what had been my city, my home, now brutalized and pillaged. It seems the land itself is quaking underneath with rage.

I look at Sicinnus. Though a slave, Athens had been his home, too, and he struggles to hide his emotions. The cavalier and taunting attitude of the enemy adds to our insult. We are told Xerxes has gone to see to the burning of the sacred temples, to bask in the revenge he had sought ever since the destruction of Sardis and the defeat at Marathon years before.

On my road, in my city, I feel alien. The land is deserted of citizens, filled with hordes of the enemy. These men I have seen before, these men I have fought, and my wounds ache with the memory. Now, here they are, soiling the earth of our home, ruining the shrines of our fathers. They are like locusts eating, destroying, and moving on. That my beautiful Attica now lay prostrate at their feet seems only a mirage, but I affix my eyes more clearly to see it is not.

As we move closer to the city, my anger grows, fueled by each fresh depredation, each new burst of flame from our city's citadel. Before, the fight against these people had never seemed so personal, even as we were hacking at each other at Artemisium and Thermopylae. Though terrifying, those conflicts were battles, of opposing forces and they were what I had been trained to do.

Even though the result could be wounds, dismemberment, or death, war was almost like athletics; it was competition. The rewards, we thought, were the glory of victory, the envy of the crowd, the joy of our own strength. Though once engaged in battle, my views have changed. I had made the decision at Thermopylae to live because life was good. To live was better than to die. Though battle was horrendous, we fought for our friends, for whom we were with, for being part of something noble. If I had not learned that with Leonidas, I never would. The whole vision of defending our homelands cannot be fully appreciated, however, when our cities are filled with happy families, still bursting with life. Now, with Athens depopulated, burning, and desecrated, the scope of what it means to have an enemy like this, comes into my heart.

Demaratus

Another weary end to a long day in which I witnessed much slaughter and destruction. The king arrived in the city long after the last temple had been looted and the final priest put to death. Accompanied by the usual faithful entourage and led by Mardonious, he arrived at the gates of the Acropolis and swept through the glowing embers of the barricaded gate bearing the icy appearance of a conqueror. It was an impressive entrance, save those of us choking on the smell of burning human flesh to take much notice. Xerxes approached Hydarnes and me where we stood surveying the city and harbor from the south wall.

Even obscured as it was by soot, the view was of a spectacular bronze sunset cast upon Attica, spread out for almost ten stade, ending at the walls and then picking up again in clusters of houses that led down to the harbors at the Piraeus and Phalerum. From our exalted perch, we took in the pageantry of the enormous Persian fleet arriving in droves and setting up camp on the beaches. Hundreds of vessels anchored off the surf, and others rowed across the face of the sea searching for suitable anchorages..

Tens of thousands of marching men emblazoned with color, weapons glinting and sparkling as they moved, filled the roads around the city. The tall slopes of Mount Hymettus overshadowed the plain to the east of the city and were settled by the army. Their tents and camp stations were abundant, like spring mushrooms after a rain. But there was no rain, no water to quench the coals or to wash away the blood. There was only the heat, the land, and the sea.

We turned and bowed as Xerxes came upon us.

"Hydarnes, Demaratus, was this burning necessary?"

"Necessary, sire?" asked Hydarnes.

"Yes, necessary!" yelled the king. "Did you have to burn their temples?"

"We thought it best rather than spoil our army with losses in a protracted siege, Your Lordship. I beg your forgiveness My Lord for this unwanted sight."

Xerxes glared at him, but then stepped back, "No Hydarnes," and burst into laughter. "It is a joyous sight. I have every intention of gaining my revenge on these Athenians for the rape of Sardis. My only displeasure is I would have liked to have been here to watch them burn."

"My apologies, Your Highness," answered Hydarnes.

"You are forgiven." Xerxes looked around him again taking in the scene. "So few," he muttered. "Of what mind were these fools? Demaratus, these are your people, do you know?"

"Sire, these are Ionians, Athenians—not Dorians like myself. I know not why they stayed while all the others left. There seems no reason for an enemy of sound mind to die without causing harm to us."

"Well, they are of no account now. The city is taken, as was meant to be. We must prepare to continue the campaign. I will meet with my captains at Pharlerum in the morning." He wheeled then, descending from the parapet, and glanced back. "You two may stay, if you wish," he said, looking at me. "I will not ask you to bury these people, Demaratus. After all, they are not 'your own.'"

A luminary amidst a seething mass of fattened flies, he strode away—out the gate, down the hill, and gone.

Hydarnes turned to me with a grim smile. "Not forgiven yet, my friend."

"So it would seem." We stood there in silence. "Hydarnes, I wish to take leave to my tent."

"As you wish."

I thanked him and climbed down from the crumbling old wall, walking the length of the citadel and passing once more through the gate. I found myself alone on the Panathenaic way, heading back toward the Dipylon as twilight descended.

As I reached the entrance to the city, I caught a flash of movement to my right, down a narrow street that paralleled the wall inside of the gate. I turned and looked, expecting a donkey or some other creature. But it was a man. He exited a doorway and was walking away, a sword grasped in his right arm. I called after him to stop, but he did not. With a familiar gait I had trouble placing as I began to jog after him, he broke into a run and disappeared into a side alley. By the time I arrived there, no one was in sight. I looked for a moment down the shadowy side street, but feared getting murdered in a darkened Athenian gutter, even after having survived worse danger in my many battles on land and at sea. So I stopped and retraced my steps.

I came to what looked like the door he had exited. It was open, swinging on its post rod. I glanced inside and saw nothing but a standard Athenian house, wooden columns in the entrance hall, a large open courtyard, cisterns, and a small garden. Dim lamps were lit in the hall. I swept the area, my eyes searching for warnings. Seeing none, I moved inside, but right away, my sandals stepped into a sticky pool I had missed in the gloom. I reached down and touched the surface. It was blood.

I walked forward and swung the door closed. Leaning against the wall behind a carved column was the body of a pretty, dark-haired girl. Her throat savagely slashed, she lay in an ever-widening puddle of her own blood. Her full mouth was agape and her half-lidded eyes dull and lifeless. I stared. Long years of war had conditioned me to such brutalities, but this did not seem to be a killing by a lust-crazed soldier. This girl had not been abused in any other way. I continued into the house, glancing inside a bedroom to the right and the kitchen straight ahead, but in the gathering darkness, I saw nothing. Off to the left, another room beckoned. I peered inside. A single olive oil lamp burned in a recessed alcove. Beneath its wavering flame, on a sleeping couch, lay the bodies of a middle-aged man and woman. Both dead, stabbed through the heart. Blood soaked their clothes and still dripped from the couch onto the stone-flagged floor.

The room had been pillaged. Two fine cedar wood chests had been wrested open in the corner, their contents, tunics and linens, flung all over the floor. Clay pots were broken and a well-made shelf that held several valuable scrolls had been overturned. The scrolls themselves were torn to shreds. I leaned down to examine them: records of transactions, accounts and agreements, nothing more.

Leaving the bodies but taking the lamp, I retraced my steps, going back inside the kitchen and bedrooms. There I saw what I had missed before. Both rooms had undergone the same pillaging as the victims' final resting place. Whatever the killer had been looking for, he did not know where to find it. I walked back through the entry hall, passing the girl whose head had drooped further on her chest, and exited the house. It was getting dark now and I needed to take leave of the city.

Glancing behind me, and keeping a wary eye ahead, I walked back up the deserted street, my footsteps echoing against the city wall until I found myself back at the Dipylon Gate. I looked along the Panathenaic way, back toward the ruins of the Acropolis, still smoking, and knew Hydarnes would have charge over the burial and disposal of the combatants lost. Xerxes was right this time.

Better Hydarnes than me. I was growing weary of the sight of dead Greeks. I turned right, out of the city, all the while pondering the murdered civilians. Who were they? What had made them stay in this hopeless city when all about them had fled? Someone had the answer, and I thought I knew who. But what was he doing here?

I would have to wait to find that answer. Ahead, a column of troops marched back to their evening camp. I caught up with them. Being alone in a hostile country, even a conquered one, was dangerous. With all that had happened this day, I would be glad to return to my tent.

Lysis

We enter the city from the south. The home of Hippocrotes and Andronica is on the far side of the city near the Dipylon Gate. However it matters none since I will not be free of my escorts or of my mission to strike at other traitors. I know not what Themistocles wants my father to do. I have not sorted out my feelings about Androcles, not completely. I had expected to meet him after our arrival at the Piraeus, and have been preoccupied with what I will say and how I will feel when I see him again. While at Thermopylae, he had seemed almost omniscient. But my father has not greeted us and is nowhere to be found.

I had hoped to see him long before I ever arrived back in Athens. And now in a time of battle here in my home city I am not sure I want to appear in front of Xerxes. As one of his escaped prisoners, I am not certain he will honor a truce. I become nervous. Themistocles told Sicinnus to deliver a message to Xerxes, and I am to make sure I speak with my father alone. But I have not expected this.

The streets are quiet. Even the loud chatter of our small escort is muted as we enter the narrow alleyways of Athens. It appears the Persian soldiery have not yet been allowed within the walls to sack and pillage many of our homes. Wood-columned porches and looming terra cotta and thatch overhangs darken the dimly lit streets. As we walk, my mind fills with anger and nervousness.

Then I remember Demaratus. So far as I know, he is still here in the camp of the enemy, still serving the king, but he is also a man who has helped me escape to freedom. He did so on the strength of a lie, the assertion that he had killed me in the forest on the slopes of Callidromus. By proof of me being alive, his life will be forfeit, and possibly mine also. I begin to sweat.

As we near the intersection of the Panathenaic way, I feel called on to act. I can not see the king. Not now. I have made a terrible mistake in coming here. I have to get away. Sicinnus glances at me, sensing my agitation. I look back, willing him to understand I had to escape but he returns my gaze, puzzled.

I lean over and whisper in his ear, "Sicinnus, deliver your message! You will be with the gods. I cannot take leave with you. I must flee!"

With that, and before his startled face can register understanding, I bolt from the group, down a side street crossing the Agora that I have trod many times when a youngster. I race down its narrow path on the wings of the shouted curses of the Persian escort, who give chase but then fade from sight and sound as I dart in and out of the alleyways Hippocrotes and I had explored years before.

I have not been thinking straight, and hope Sicinnus will be safe, but there is no other path for me. I run until I reach the other side of the city, never seeing a single soul but hearing an occasional thud of sandaled feet on the dirt and graveled streets. I come upon the north wall and the road that runs along its length, right to the Dipylon Gate, and then make the short walk to the house of Hippocrotes and Andronica.

I am exhausted and irritated at the slow healing of my wounds here in the midst of the enemy army, in a ghost city, unarmed, and with little idea of a plan other than to stay hidden. I creep down the street, trying every door I come to. All are locked. The house of my former friend Hippocrotes, and his sister Andronica who was perhaps now my former love, is closer now. I can see it up the street, its red walls and four solid blue painted columns standing out. Two more doors, one locked, the other not. With caution, I push the heavy planked door open, peering around the corner. Twilight is near, and no lamps burn.

I enter the house, stumbling in the darkness until I locate a door that opens onto a small courtyard. The fast fading light of the day pours through, and in its dim rays, I locate a lamp but no flame. I will soon be shrouded in darkness. Seizing the time I have, I search the rooms that border the courtyard for anything useful that might aid my escape. In a long and narrow ironwood chest much chipped and scarred, I find a dagger. In a bedroom, I find only a filthy chiton, but again, perhaps useful.

Gathering my new possessions, I creep back to the entryway and look down the street. Still no one. I go back inside, leaving the door ajar, and lean against the entrance hall wall. I think of Andronica, perhaps yards away in the next house, perhaps anywhere in this vast land, anywhere in this new world the war has created. I feel an overwhelming desire to see her, to touch and feel her, to tell her how much I need her and love her. But I can not tell her that, not now, despite the cravings of my body and the need in my heart until I know the truth. I need to know if what she felt for me is real, untainted by betrayal. I need to know she is innocent in this treachery and not of many minds like her brother had been.

I grip the dagger in my hand and think again of the words of Hippocrotes and Andronica's father, words that told of my death sentence. Are they close, too? Can I have vengeance for myself and my family and still keep the love of their daughter? And what will become of me if she were as guilty as they? I can think no more. I need to move.

Back inside the house's courtyard, I pace, trying to untangle my racing thoughts. On the gravel outside, I hear muted footsteps. More than one? Several? They are rapid but precise. Then comes a rap on a door—not for the house in which I hide, but a nearby one. I move through the courtyard, masking my steps. From the direction of Hippocrotes' house, more noises—sharp crashes, loud words, voices raised in protest. I move closer to the door. A woman's stifled scream. Who is it? Andronica? Then I hear a door burst open and footsteps tapping again, this time moving faster, coming my way. I take cover inside, in the dimness tripping over a clay amphora, shattering it, sprawling it in pieces across the floor.

The footsteps stop, then move toward me. They are at the door that will lead to me. They thrust it open. I scurry to a corner of the courtyard, and crawl behind a broad-based stone cistern; my only hope, the darkness that envelops the house. They come inside, making a rapid search of the rooms, even climbing the ladder and peering into the second-floor chambers. I hold my breath. There are four of them at least, Persian soldiers. They say nothing and finish their search, satisfied that whatever they had heard is gone, and take leave.

I crouch there, stilling my breathing, of no mind to move, waiting until I am sure. Then, as I rise, I hear other steps, softer this time, more cautious. They come from up the street toward the Dipylon Gate. I approach the door of my hideaway, listening. My heart hammers, and I ache to see outside, but I wait, torn. After hearing nothing, I reach for the door, curiosity and anxiety overcomes my natural caution as I grip the dagger and step outside. From the Dipylon Gate comes the trample of many feet, a group of soldiers passing from the city.

Then, out of the blue-columned house, a man exits, looking north toward the gate, and carrying a broad-bladed sword.

It was my father.

When he steps into the street, a voice rings out from the Panathenaic way. "You, there!" it says. "Stop!"

Androcles whirls and hurries down the street toward where I stand, rooted in place on the threshold of the house. He sees me, surprised, but does not let his surprise disturb his commanding presence. As the voice continues shouting, he breaks into a run straight toward me, grabbing me and pushing me inside. He motions for silence and closes the door. I can hear the crunch of sandaled feet and the heavy breathing of a big man pass by close outside. The sounds continue, stopping a moment at the alleyway that runs on the other side of our hideaway. There is hesitation, then movement back past us. Then motion toward the blue-columned house.

We wait, saying nothing but staring at one another until we hear him exit the house and stride back to the gate.

"Lysis, for what reason are you in Attica?" my father gasps.

I am at a loss. Seeing my father once again, face to face, stuns me more than I have expected. He looks the same as when I had last seen him. His scars are still deep and angry, his eyes dark and challenging. But something about him has changed, something deep and to his core where only the gods can reach.

I say, beginning to calm down, "I came looking for you."

He pauses, that pained sense once again overtakes his demeanor. "You and many others, though the others are without good will and perhaps you are too. For what matter must you see me now? What have the gods asked of you since our last moments at Thermopylae? Have you had time to stoke your hatred for me even further?"

I cannot answer, not right away. He has hit right on the mark. But as my heart churns through a riot of emotions, I remember with a shock the screams next door. "From what does the disturbance arise in that house? And why is it of concern to you?"

"There are three dead bodies in that house. I went there to find answers, though we have seen with our own eyes that others seek the answers for themselves."

"Three dead...." I stammer.

He nods.

I push past him then, my heart pounds, my entire being is suffused with fear. He tries to grab me as I run out the door, but he tears only at the old chiton I have over my shoulder, dumping it on the threshold beneath the dark and empty street and the dull glimmer of the stars. In the air hangs the smell of cinders, ash, and the underlying stink of the fallen city. I run to the blue-columned house and push my way inside the open door. In the hall, a lamp sputters a flickering light struggles in a smoky cloud, etching out the outline of shadows in the night.

My feet tread in a pool of dark liquid as I turn and see her. There she is, sitting slumped against the wall, her head hangs to her chest, her eyes masked and shrouded in death. My stomach spasms in denial. Andronica? It has to be. I fall to my knees, bile rising in my throat, and reach out to lift her chin.

Oh! The gods be praised. It is not. The poor slave girl who has so borne her resemblance has suffered the fate I feared for my love. But where is Andronica? I rise, my heart thumping against my chest and step farther inside. Behind me my father enters the house and closes the door. I see Hippocrotes' bedroom, empty as before, the kitchen, dark and silent, and then the Andron, where I had met with Hippocrotes' parents. They are still there, but this time they rest together in death. I stare at their broken bodies for a long moment, feeling pity for them, even now, even after I know what they have done, or what they were prepared to do to me and to my family.

I search the room, and my eyes gaze over the disordered mess it has become.

"I was looking for something," interrupts my father.

I turn to face him. I walk to the far side of the room. "Was it a record of betrayal you were looking for?"

He nods and then meets my eyes. "So it was you who put those papers in my old chest?"

"Yes. I figured you would come to the house if you came to Athens. I thought you had a right to know."

"Yes, I did, though it is a hard knowledge to learn of.

"Yes, it is," I answer.

We remain locked in silence, he rooted to his spot by the door, me leaning against the Andron wall, my eyes closed in fatigue and confusion.

I say at last, "We honor these dead by leaving them. We must take leave."

"It is not safe on the streets yet Lysis, we can move when the army sleeps."

"What have you to fear? You are in the graces of Xerxes while I am the one certain to be beheaded."

"What I have to fear can be discussed another time. Now why have you sought me?'

"Why have I—" I feel exasperated, angry, and ready to lash out; the tension of the last hour surfaces. "I have come at the request of Themistocles," I spit. I push myself off the wall and stride toward him. "With devotion to all the gods in heaven for all time, know without doubt if it had been my decision I would not be here with you for even a moment!"

"I believe you son, but what interest has Themistocles in me?"

"A message..." I can not finish. My father's unruffled, stoic demeanor is what I have sought in my own desire to excise feeling, to remain detached. But his success feels as though it mocks my inability to control myself, and that increases my agitation. All at once, the desire to know what had happened to him those years ago, the desire that had been competing with the hatred of what he had become, bursts forth. "Why did you leave us? How could you be with these people?"

His face sets in stone, and his eyes narrow. "Come with me, we will talk in the courtyard." He reaches above and pulls a lamp from its alcove, leading me out under the sky into the open air of the courtyard. He sits down, and leans his back against one of the carved sea-blue columns and stretches his feet before him.

"Sit down," he says, placing the lamp by his side. "We will be here for a while. I will tell you what I can."

CHAPTER 13

Demaratus

Exhausted, reeking of smoke, and covered with flecks of ash I could not remove, I was awakened and told to report to Xerxes. I swung my feet to the ground and stripped off my dirty tunic, slipping on another more suitable for the king's presence. I could feel the weariness in my eyes, my brow pressing upon them as I struggled for awareness. The air was cooler when I stepped out into the night. The long, hot Greek summer was waning, and I thought *this campaign needs to move on.*

Why was I so tired? I was older, and the soft living of the Persian court had taken the edge from my former Spartan regimen, but it could not account for this bone-deep, even heart-deep, fatigue. I had marched more in my life, fought many more battles, seen cities fall, temples burn, innocents slaughtered. What was it here in Attica now that made such a difference? I thought of the Acropolis again, of the dead priests, of their faith in the gods. And then I thought of Thermopylae and of Leonidas' mutilated body, of the Phocians and their despoiled towns and raped and murdered women. I remembered our march through Boetia and the fall of the cities and towns there. All the while, Xerxes had led us onward, led us into Greece, closer and closer to my homeland. Is not that what I had wanted, to return to Sparta a conqueror? To avenge myself on my tormentors? Was not Xerxes giving me that?

Yes, he was, that and more. Xerxes was showing another side to my own ambition. An unpleasant side. In all the battles I had waged, all the peoples I had fought in my long years as king of the Spartans, I had done so as the head of my country and my peers. I had done so representing them, not myself. The results of my actions were sanctified by the gods and approved by the state but what I did now met neither standard. My own pride and need motivated my ambition to return to the land of my birth. I represented myself and myself only. *How individualistic*, I thought, *how Athenian.*

And here I was, in the land of the Athenians, the land of the city that celebrated individualism and individual achievement, having witnessed self-sacrifice for a higher cause of the greatest order. Their odds were as hopeless as at Thermopylae, maybe more so, making Athens pitiful in its end, yes, but glorious in its nobility. Were there now any Athenians left who could understand my pride and the wrongs that had put me here in the service of the enemy?

Xerxes had understood. And he had rewarded me with lands, honors, titles, and a place at his side. Did I not owe him my allegiance for that? Did I not owe him the same loyalty I had given the Spartan state? But at Thermopylae, the king had shown something, a fear that belied his power, an anger that diminished his own kingship. He did not keep his power by consent of the people he ruled, rather he secured it by his ruthless manipulation and unrestricted cruelty. If I followed him, was I any better? Yes, he had seen my plight. But could all the lands and titles in the world be worth the destruction of the noble man I was before?

I had been so certain of myself. Now, I was not.. Before, I had been a true measure of what it meant to be Spartan. Now, I, returning in triumph and honor, would reclaim not my legacy nor the chance to restore the Spartan state to its former glory. I was nothing more than the representative of a brutal conquering army, out to destroy forever the uniqueness of my own people. Could I stand by and see that happen? *No*, I thought. I could not.

Thus it was that I thought of Phracrtes, whose loyalty was also suspect, or could be, with my help. We could help each other, if it came to that, to redeem some of the pieces of who we were.

When I was exhausted like this, it was difficult to keep these dark and depressing thoughts from ruling my mind. Though not as difficult being the man, indeed the king, I used to be.

And here I was now, at the tent of the Great king of Persia, being called to serve his wants, called to advise against the Greeks. What would I say? Would I give the advice that came from my sense of honor and service?

Hydarnes, who had obviously not yet slept, greeted me at the entrance. Other generals crowded the tent, including Mardonious, who watched me with disdain. There was a man who could hold a grudge—a dangerous man, one not to be trusted. The king sat as usual in his chair behind the map table, where he waited, searching the assembled faces. I was the last to arrive. Xerxes leaned forward.

"Generals," he began. "Word has come to us from the enemy camp in the form of a messenger from Themistocles, admiral of the Athenian fleet, that the Greeks are ready for flight. Themistocles claims he will work with our naval forces in the event of an attack."

Several murmurs arose from the assembled, but no one spoke.

"What do you think of this, Mardonious?" asked Xerxes, glancing at his brother-in-law, the second in command.

"Sire, do we know if this message is spoken as truth?"

"It was delivered by a house slave of Themistocles," said the king. "He swears the enemy has decided to abandon Athens and retire to the isthmus. It makes sense that the Athenians, like so many others who have met our wrath, would make the choice to join us."

Mardonious dropped his chin, deep in thought. "If that is the case, Your Highness, it is wise to attack soon before they can escape."

"Yes, sire," said another, "perhaps like the hare, they will be startled by our approach and bolt!" A few snickers greeted this remark. The mood of the group was changing from fatigue to confidence. Xerxes turned to me.

"And my ever loyal Demaratus," he queried, "of what mind are you?"

I was not sure of Themistocles' battle plan, but doubted if it was as his messenger had said. I had seen how a few dirty paupers and ill-armed priests on the Acropolis facing certain death did not surrender, and thus found it hard to believe the entire Athenian fleet, some two hundred triremes strong, would change sides before battle was even joined. My impression of Athens and Athenians had changed since this invasion. What I thought was if we were going to fight here, we had best scout out the enemy, and not rely on dubious assurances of betrayal. Further, the better strategy would be to attack the Peloponnese by sea and choose the time and place of battle ourselves. Our ships would fare better fighting in the open sea, not in sheltered waters.

But, opposing the direction of the group would throw more suspicion my way. My assent would give the decision weight, no matter what Mardonious and the others thought of me. And so, for the first time in my counsel to Xerxes, I told him what was in my own best fortune instead of what was honest.

"I believe what Mardonious has said is true. We should attack here, and soon."

"Good, Demaratus, good, we are all in agreement then?"

There were nods and quiet grunts. Xerxes clapped his hands together and smiled. "We will meet in the morning as planned and on the beach at this harbor of Phalerum!" Standing, as all of us bowed low, he added, "You may leave."

I walked outside trailed by Mardonious, who soon came upon me.

"Demaratus," laughed the king's right-hand man, "You are among the enlightened now," but he had the look of a man not convinced of my sincerity. It is hard to lie when you are not practiced at it, I thought. It did not matter to me, what was meant to be would be. Craving sleep, I headed to my tent when Hydarnes caught up with me.

"There was someone else who came with Themistocles' servant," he said. The men in their escort were from my command. One of them claims he recognized the other Greek. He says he was a prisoner with us before Thermopylae."

I stopped and turned, "A prisoner?"

Hydarnes held my gaze and nodded, "A prisoner in your charge. The one who delivered the king's message to the enemy before the first day's fighting."

"Where is this prisoner you speak of?" A twinge of fear shot up my spine.

"He escaped into the city."

I thought again of what I had seen earlier. It was Phraortes running away from me, but was there someone else? There could have been. I struggled to reconstruct the memory, but my brain was too fogged. It did not make sense. Why would Phraortes run? And why would Lysis be in the city? That would bring an ill wind should Xerxes find him alive. I met Hydarnes' gaze, "That is impossible, I killed him at Thermopylae."

Hydarnes' eyebrows arched. "That is the news, yes." And his normally cheerful countenance welcomed a tight smile. "I will have my men search the city. I am sure it was a only a ghost."

Walking away, I said, "Yes, but if this ghost should be found, perhaps you would deliver it to me?"

"Of course," said Hydarnes.

Lysis

My father rests his head against the column and closes his eyes, allowing a wave of weariness to cascade over his features, sagging his scarred cheeks and turning down his lips. He looks much older than his age. I take a place opposite him and sit cross-legged on the cooling stone of the courtyard.

When he opens his eyes, he scans the home of my former best friend and his sister, my love. "You know of this house?"

"Yes, Hippocrotes used to live here, the one I told you about after I was first captured. He was…He was my best friend. We used to play here as children. And his sister, Andronica, she…well, she is the woman I would marry."

"I recall you talking of this Hippocrotes. But of your marriage… you speak of Andronica and seem unsure."

I try to gather my emotions. "With her I am as a pigeon in search of a nesting place, while falcons circle above and snakes gather below."

My father nods. "Ah, your heart brings danger, or so it would seem."

"So it would seem."

"Matters are never as they seem, never as you want them to be." He reaches out and grasps the lamp, gripping its ornate black belly and staring into the flickering flame. "I left, Lysis, because I was ashamed. That's the story of my absence. I was ashamed." He proceeds to tell me what my uncle had said about the uneasiness before Sardis, the push to try to be somebody he was not.

"I placed myself in much trouble, in much debt, and there seemed to be no way out. I journeyed on the expedition to Sardis to serve the city and make a name for myself, and also to find some fortune, some coins, that would bring peace to our home."

"Uncle told me that."

"He did, eh?" Androcles shakes his head, grinning. "Well, Laertes was always an observant one." My father rocks the lamp, swirling its oil and making the flame falter. Our shadows waver and sway on the courtyard walls.

"At Sardis I took a patrol one day to collect wood and supplies when we suddenly faced an attack by a group of Persian cavalry at a farmhouse. They were an advance guard from the army sent to relieve Sardis. Most of our men were killed right away, but I escaped with two others into the fields, at least for a short time." His eyes glaze over, remembering.

"When they caught us, I thought we were each to have a slave's life from that time on. But there was some blood lust in those Persians that day, and they gutted my two companions in front of my eyes. They screamed to the gods as their entrails spilled on the ground. They were to do the same to me when their commander approached and told them to stop. He dragged me back to the farmhouse where we sat, and talked." My father's expression hardens

227

now. "His name was Hystaspes, the father of Medarnes." He looks at me, "Yes, I bartered with Medarnes' father, but not for what he swears you are to die for."

The stars are dense overhead, and the smell of smoke has drifted away leaving in its wake the clearer scent of the summer flowers that ring the courtyard—flowers planted and tended by Andronica that are reminders of a happier and innocent time. Night is coming on and we will have to take leave soon, but I yearn to hear more.

"Tell me of the barter for which you betrayed your family and all of Greece?"

"He offered me my life, my freedom, and a fortune. I was but a sword's plunge from being no better than a stuck pig, and then this Persian offered me safety and the answers to all my woes."

"And you bartered in exchange?"

"All I had to do was supply information." He shakes his head purses his lips. His eyes gaze far away. "It was not betrayal, or at least I did not see it as such. It had no bearing on that expedition, and they seemed to already know we were not to stay. He sought information from back in Athens. He wanted to know of Athens."

My father gets up and paces the courtyard.

"In return, I would receive gold, pure gold, one talent a year," he says, still seemingly surprised at the staggering amount. "I accepted. What harm would it do? The Persians were never to arrive in Athens. And were I not to agree, the alternative was death or slavery. They kept me for a while. I told them all I knew, including everything about my family, everything about the city. After that, Hystaspes seemed satisfied. He sent me off, and I went back to my countrymen who were relieved to see I had lived while all others in the scouting group had been called to stand before almighty Zeus.

"Not long after we arrived home," he continues, "a fish merchant from Ephesus contacted me. He said he had cargo for me, and I was to accompany him to Pharlerum. I took leave, curious, and behold, he had my gold. Well, he and another had it, a passenger who was not a fish merchant. This man would not release it to me until I had written a detailed account of the activities in the city, including what I knew about our coin reserves, number of battle ready hoplites, that sort of news."

Father lets his head drop to his chest and lets out a sigh. "At the time, I was a man in great despair. Lords of commerce had seized half of our holdings, and the last harvest had been a disaster. I was falling into deeper debt than I wanted. There was no excuse, but still I fell. I wrote the report. He gave me the gold, promising more if I would keep sending news every three months. So I did. That's how it started, and that's how it kept going."

Father fingers the scar on the left side of his face. "He spoke of one other matter, though, one other matter. He said I would be watched. My family would be watched. Hystaspes had made sure of that. He said it would not be wise for me to have a change of mind.

"I did not know if he was a sorcerer or not, so I did not back out. I walked the streets of the city looking for people following me, for strangers turning up at the farmhouse, for anyone gazing upon me with mystery. I never saw or heard anyone, but it was hard; I was never sure, and so I stayed with the arrangement. For years, I paid attention to governance and decrees as I never had. But going to the assemblies when I knew afterward I would be informing a potential enemy became more difficult. I stopped attending, fabricated some reports, relied on information from other sources, and tried to turn my attention to the farm."

He stops his pacing and glances at me. "I never had talent for farming, and not much for commerce either. The more work I did, the worse it got. Even though I had all the coins I could use, I felt Hades filling my soul. I began to feel more ashamed, more like a traitor. I thought if I could work my way out of debt on my own, if I could learn to farm and turn a coin, I could restore my sense of honor, my sense of self. Perhaps then I could send word to Hystaspes that I had changed my mind. I would write the last reports, and we could end it. But I did not. Instead, I realized I was tied to that from which I could not escape. If I stopped, they would come for me and you, my family, any time in the night. And so, I kept reporting and the coins kept coming, and my skills at farming and managing never did improve."

My father becomes silent, staring straight ahead into the dark hallway where the dead slave girl rested. "You came along, of course, and your sisters and matters became more complicated. I did not want you to be son to a man who could not keep his commerce straight, who lived a secret life. Though I'd managed to stabilize the situation, by buying a few ships and trying my hand at trading, nothing worked. Still, we never lacked for coins. We were not poor. But many became distrustful of my commerce and I became... unhappy.

"Then word came that Darius was planning an invasion. He had, in fact, assembled an enormous land army and fleet as well. He had not forgotten Sardis, they said; only that he had put off revenge until he was ready. That's when my arrangement with the Persians became more dangerous. I suppose I had accepted the barter because it seemed I would ever have to pay a heavy price for it. Now it looked like I would. Athens was in an uproar. We began mobilizing, arming ourselves, training the light armed troops, asking for help from Sparta, Plataea, anyone with forces. I was part of this defense, but also part of the offense against our own people. I did not know what to do.

"When Hystaspes sent a message ordering me to betray my city, to open the gates from the inside once the enemy arrived on our shores, matters got worse. He threatened me and my family, you, with death if I refused. I had to take action with limited options. If I stayed and disobeyed the command, whether the enemy won or not, I was certain we would all be killed by some phantom; by an agent of the Persian king who walked the streets of Athens as if he belonged. If I obeyed," he paused, his voice for the first time betraying the agony he must have felt. "I could not obey." He turns to me, his eyes plead.

"I had to take leave and had to make it appear as if I were dead to you, dead to your mother and sisters, dead to my city. I had to make it seem to the Persians a treachery occurred that would made it impossible for me to carry out my task. Otherwise, you would all be killed.

"So, I told your uncle I was to travel to Siracusa, a journey I was sure would reverse my fortunes. I knew he did not believe me, but that was not my concern. More important was convincing my Persian masters I had to leave the city. I left you without knowing how to do that, but the gods intervened. A storm came upon us before we had passed Larium. The ship foundered and smashed against the rocks, killing all but myself. I was thrown clear, by the gods' fortune, and washed upon the shores of Euboae. Afterwards, I journeyed with a crew sailing east. We came upon the enemy fleet readying for attack against Attica, and I was brought to Hystaspes.

"He was angry I was no longer in Attica, but seemed to believe my story of the shipwreck. I told him I had evidence others knew of my reports, and I had thought it best to escape. This prevented him from sending me back to continue as he had envisioned for me. Thus it was that I saw the battle of Marathon from the deck of a Persian warship, escaping with my life as my friends and relatives descended on the beach, killing all in the way. I was proud of what we had done at Marathon, proud of our army and of Athens. But my heart had broken. I had betrayed my country, brought destruction upon them. I had abandoned my family, the children I loved, your mother..."

His lips tighten. "It was done. I was part of a defeated enemy force, sailing away from my city. I would never see my family, or any of Athens, again." He falls silent.

For all of this time I have been listening to him, the world seems to have stood still. The tale my father told was one of agony. It melts my heart, the fortress wall of my hurt and anger begin to breach. I can not help but be moved, though so much else remains to be understood. "Father, you could have come back. Why did you not send word?"

"Come back? How could I have ever come back? If I did, nothing would have changed. You would still be in danger. I would still be a traitor. The only difference would be my people knowing me for betrayal. It would get worse, not better. No, I could not come back." He gets up and paces again. "I did think of it and wish for it. I did, every day. I wrote letters…" and he pauses, as if he'd said more than he had intended.

"Then you did try to contact us?"

"I did," he answers. "I did, but I think none of my messages arrived. I'm sure now they did not."

"No, none of them."

He nods his head. Once again, we lapse into silence.

My father comes back to the column and slumps down, once again gazing into the flame, which now flickers, its supply of oil ebbing. I can see his pain through the scarring that did more than disfigure his formerly handsome face. Those scars are markings of emotions that are not truly his, that he does not feel. But this opening of his heart now imbues those scars with an unexpected softness, an unasked for welling of pity and understanding from my own seared soul.

But those scars? The behaviors he had shown long after he had left us, how could they be explained? How had he become the Butcher of Egypt? What was the genesis of the layers of hate he felt? I need to know that as much as I need to know why he had left us alone.

"Father, I sense you tell me only parcels. What else have you been silent on?"

His lips move, but no sound comes out. He wants to speak, to unburden himself, but he can not. "The army sleeps now," he answers. "It is time we take leave." He rises as the lamp lets out a last breath of fire, whimpers, and goes out.

"Please," I say, once again swimming in darkness. "Tell me. What are your secrets in Persia?"

"It is done," he replies, and he leans over to pick up his sword. He thrusts it into the tough leather scabbard at his side. "Done. My life is now. I can not change what is done, only what is now."

"Yet you are here," I challenge. "Why do you come to this house? What here is of concern to you? I left those papers in your old chest because I wanted you to know I was wise to your ways. Maybe you did not realize your family was being stalked, watched like prey for years. You said you were looking for answers. Answers to what?"

Androcles turns from me, his fists clench and unclench by his sides. "You are right. There is another matter, one of which I have not spoken of. I realized Hystaspes had placed someone here in Attica to watch my family, and that continued long after Hystaspes had died. I wanted to know who else was keeping watch. I still want to know." He looks at me. "Someone killed these people. There is a reason."

"Persian soldiers killed them."

"You saw them?"

"Yes."

"Did you recognize who they were?"

"It was dark, and I could not see much other than their red and gold felt headgear. I saw the same on Xerxes' guard at Thermopylae."

"Xerxes guard? "Are you certain?"

"That is what I saw."

My father smacks his hand against the column and swears. "By the twelve gods, the king's guard. I do not understand..." His voice trails off. Even in the darkness, I can sense his features hardening. " I have much on my mind but we must take leave now and can talk more on the way."

I nod, stand and stretch. I am stiff and sore. We have been sitting in this house of the dead, and I will be happy to leave it. I worry about Andronica's fate. She had not been here with her parents, and should have been. Have Xerxes' men taken her elsewhere, have they killed her? I know not how she fits within this, but I swear to the heavens I will find answers.

We exit the house finding empty streets and make our way along the back alleys toward the south gate, our journey illuminated by the stars overhead. Once or twice we hear parties of soldiers on the main streets, but they never come close enough to alarm us. We arrive at the gate, which is open and unguarded. I think how remarkable it is that these Asian levies have kept control in the face of a conquered and empty city. Athens is plentiful with potential treasure, waiting to be stripped clean. The army fears their leaders, though I have no doubt of the outcome if Xerxes gives the nod. The road runs ahead through the gate, down toward the harbor. On either side, the camp of the enemy is laid out before us. The army sleeps. Watch fires burn in the distance, but along this route, the Persians do not keep watch with a close guard.

My father has been quiet until we get into the open beyond the gates. "Lysis, we must get you to the harbor and aboard a vessel to your ship before morning. I can not be seen with you, and my help will be limited," he says, trying to keep his voice low.

I nod and understand. It is to be another escape. I have been doing some thinking of my own. "The ship sheds down by the Piraeus," I reply. "We store small boats there for running supplies out to anchored vessels in the harbor. They might be still there. I can be gone by first light."

"Good."

"And you my father? What awaits you?"

"Answers, I pray to why the king's guard was in the city for the purpose of murdering those people. I do not understand it, but I will." He turns to me and smiles, his teeth ivory in the starlight. "You have not yet told of Themistocles' message to me."

I flush, ashamed. I have forgotten my mission, consumed by my own cares. "He wants me to see of what use you could be to him. He asks you to remember Athens in her hour of need, and support whatever other messages might come from him to Xerxes." I pause, and look at him as he walks beside me, listening. "He feels there is still some good in you, father. He thinks you are positioned to help." I hesitate again. "Are you?"

He does not answer at first. We are approaching the town. "Xerxes helped me when I first arrived to the court at Susa. Hystaspes took me to Darius, who was so angry his men had been defeated at Marathon, he was of no spirit to help Athenian exiles like myself. Hystaspes was not much help either. It was Xerxes, who had not yet ascended to the kingship, who persuaded his father to reward me and the other exiles for our services. I suppose he felt we would be of some use in the days beyond. The king listened to Xerxes' arguments and bequeathed me with some fine estates in the Troad region. They were near to both Hystaspes and Demaratus."

I watch Androcles as he says this. I can see the shadows darken on his face as his scars twist in anger. "My lands abutted Hystaspes on one side and Demaratus, when he arrived, on the other. I am certain Darius commanded Hystaspes to keep watch on me, not that I had a mind to take leave. I worked my lands with as little success as before, and lived the life I could. I was lonely, and was not at peace with my choices. After a while I could not fight the demons any longer. I loved your mother and you children, and I thought perhaps I could explain the situation and you would come to understand my soul. So I wrote letters, handed them to my servants, telling what had happened and asking you all to journey to me. But no reply ever graced me. I could not blame your mother. I was a traitor. Why would she want me? How could she forgive me? How could anyone? I fell into a blackness so deep I could not even think with one mind, nor work or take care of myself. My servants became alarmed, so much so that the chief of my house servants finally revealed that one of the servants had confessed my letters were never delivered to whom I had intended. Every one of them instead had been delivered to Hystaspes.

"I was enraged. I sent for the guilty servant and had him accompany me to Hystaspes' estate, threatening to burn his eyes out the whole way. I had no mind to do such a horror. I was angry, yet not capable of such ferocity. Still, the slave thought I was, and remained in fear when we arrived. He was ready to stand with his confession, even if Hystaspes offered only denials.

"Haughty Hystaspes acknowledged he had made certain no letters of mine left his attention. He had kept a careful eye on me since we had first arrived and told me he did not trust me in the least. He had not trusted me since I had failed to carry out my mission in Athens, and it was only by Xerxes' insistence that he tolerated me at all. He reminded me of my plight, taking great pleasure that I could never return to my homeland.

Hystaspes said, "I could have spit you like the barbarian you are, and I will wager you wish I had. But you will have to stay here and live with the sins you have committed as the wretch you have become for the rest of your life. I am certain Xerxes thinks he can use you, but I do not."

By this time, I was both raging with fury and desperate because I knew he was right. Where could I take leave to? I could never return to Athens. We argued, and I probably threatened to kill him. I don't remember."

"Did you not?" I interject.

"What, kill him? No, I wish I had, but his death was not by my hand."

"Medarnes believes you did."

"I know. He was a child at the time, not much older than you must have been. He may have overheard his father and me at odds."

"Then who spilled Hystaspes' blood ?" I press.

He shakes his head. "I know not. Once I thought I knew, and then received word that Hystaspes' corpse was discovered in a ditch on the road to my estate, right outside my gate."

We walk within a few stade of the town, and Androcles halts. Ahead, a small watch fire burns. The port is being watched with more rigor than the city. I hear a stirring down the road, perhaps near the port but think that is to be expected. The stars are growing dim as the dark hours of the night draw to a close. Soon the eastern sky will begin to brighten. We do not have much time.

Androcles continues, though, faster now. "Lysis, I had been of mind to not tell you of these matters, and there is still much that I can not, or will not, but it is important you understand that which I do reveal."

"I know, Father, thank you."

He acknowledges my word choice with a strained look. "When I returned from meeting with Hystaspes, I was brewing with anger. I had resolved that whatever happened, I must take leave from that place. So I gathered up and left, heading north, intending to cross the Hellespont and make my way into Thessaly where I could settle in some other Greek city and plan how I could return home. As you can see, I have yet to make a plan."

Voices burst from the port, accompanied by the clatter of weaponry and the clink of armor. There is no one to either side of us, the noise is from up ahead, but it begins to get closer. My father breathes faster now, his movements become more rigid, and his composure falters as he continues the recitation of his story and ignores the danger.

"I was not with knowledge at the time that word had gotten out, from Darius, I suppose, that I had killed Hystaspes, and a reward had been offered for my severed head on a pike. A group of Egyptians picked me up before I had left the Troad. They seemed to know where I was and to where I journeyed."

Here, despite our urgency, my father could not go on. The agitation in his voice and demeanor has grown as he spoke, and it is clear he has reached some sort of despair in his tale. Breathing constricted, he continues, "They beat me at first, threatened to kill me. I did not know who they were. They were not common brigands and wanted none of my coins. They laughed at my pleas, taking pleasure in my fear. They gave me these," he says, and points to his scars. "Both of them." He pauses again, and then through gritted teeth, adds, "And other wounds."

"What other wounds? What else did they do, Father?"

I can see the glint of tears in his eyes. I think they are those of grief, and perhaps they are. But from what he says next it is clear that rage and hurt power his tears the most.

"They took away my manhood," he says, and his body trembles. "And for that, they will pay."

CHAPTER 14

Demaratus

Hydarnes woke me in the pre-dawn darkness. After so many days of heat, the cool air felt refreshing but still lingering with the familiar stink of an army.

"Demaratus! Wake up! I think we may have your 'mistake.'"

Groggy, I recognized the urgency in Hydarnes' voice. "What mistake?"

"Your former prisoner. Take leave with me. Our horses await."

That cleared my head. I rolled from the bed and stumbled after Hydarnes. So Lysis was here. Did we have him?

"Where is he?"

"Down by the port," answered Hydarnes. "But he's with some-one else—Phraortes."

"Phraortes! So he finally arose from hiding."

"Yes, and he must have some answers to reveal," said Hydarnes, with a look that said he expected an explanation from me. But that would wait.

Two saddled horses were harnessed outside my tent. I was never much of a horseman. We Spartans were infantrymen first, last, and always. But I had ridden in the past and learned to tolerate it. We swung up into the saddles and set off, the horses following a path through the campground until we reached the road to the Piraeus. The port was twenty stade or so away, but we kicked the animals into a brisk trot and their hooves avoided the grooves rutted from heavy carts. Such tracks seemed embedded in every Greek roadway, but more so in this one. All roads led to the sea for Athens, and the Piraeus, enclosed and fortified, was the gate to its bounty.

Lysis

I am stunned. Appearing angry and defiant, my father glares at me, his mood changed. I can now see in him the look that must have terrified thousands of Egyptians, the look that could kill, maim, and destroy. Androcles can see my horror.

"Yes, Lysis, that is what they did," he says, choking. "They were going to finish me, right there just before the Persian troops arrived; Xerxes' men. They killed and scattered the Egyptians and took me away. They had been following me since word had spread to them about Hystaspes.

"Xerxes hid me away until things died down. He came to visit me a month after. My wounds were mending, but I was at my lowest. I knew not who had attacked me, or why. Suicide seemed the answer I sought. But in the end, I could not take my own life. A spirit in me took hold, a resolve; it was vengeance. Yet, I had no target until Prince Xerxes arrived and named my enemy.

"He told me Hystaspes was conspiring to discredit me in front of the king. He was looking for signs I was a traitor to the king himself. That is why the bastard was collecting my letters. Xerxes said Hystaspes had hoped to acquire my lands and remove me. The prince hinted that Demaratus, among others, might also be involved. As a friend of Demaratus, he said, he could not confirm it, but there were rumors. The Egyptians had a special relationship with Hystaspes and someone sent them after me to avenge him."

The troops we'd heard before begin marching toward us.

"Father, we must take leave."

"I know, I am sorry. I am sorry for much, but you can see why I will not abandon Xerxes. He saved my life."

I do see, but I sense there is more yet to be told. "But what of those men I saw? The ones who killed Hippocrotes' parents?"

"I don't know, but on the grave of my own father, I swear to you, I will learn of their ways." He looks up the road at the approaching troops, then back at me. "Tell Themistocles my heart might be with my homeland, but I have no choice at this time but to remain loyal to another cause. I am of no mind to do otherwise."

I nod, my own heart breaking. I know not what to say.

"Lysis, you are in much danger now. I will stay with you to the port. Walk with confidence. Let me talk to them."

We begin to move toward the troops, swinging along with authority, as if we have a purpose. They surround us, their captain steps from their midst. He looks at us with displeasure, and frowns at my Athenian garb.

"Who wishes to pass?" he asks.

My father answers, "I am Phraortes, son of Hidalipus." Even in the darkness, I can sense the Persian captain blanch. "This is Lysis, son of Androcles, envoy to the king from the enemy fleet. I am escorting him to his vessel."

"We are looking for an Athenian," replies the Persian. "He escaped from us this afternoon." His gaze seems to pierce through my soul.

After a frightening silence, I answer "Yes. I am the Athenian you seek. A thousand mercies upon me sir, I became lost in the city."

"My men found him earlier tonight," says my father. "In the name of the Great king himself, I have been commanded to deliver him."

"I do believe you sir," the captain says, "but I am under orders from my commander to seize this Athenian."

"And your commander is?" challenges Phraortes.

"General Hydarnes, sir."

"Very well, captain. Let Hydarnes set forth to settle this matter between us. I will tell him myself of Xerxes' command and let it be for Hydarnes to defy the king's wishes."

The captain looks ill at ease, his expression droops. He sends off a runner who races back up the road toward the city with the message for Hydarnes.

"We sit down and wait," says my father, giving me a confident look. "This will not be long."

It was not. Before the blackness of night had been chased off by the pale blue morning sky, two riders canter up to us and dismount. It is Demaratus, who nearly falls off his horse, and another Persian general who must have been Hydarnes.

My father looks displeased to see Demaratus.

Demaratus

The two of them rose from the dirt road as we approached, Phraortes looking arrogant, eyes snapping fire, and Lysis calm. I remembered that from our brief time together that Lysis was a remarkable young man, and now more so having put himself back into the fray to volunteer once again for a mission such as this.

"Hydarnes," began Phraortes, "We have been stopped by your men here. They claim rights over this Athenian envoy."

"That is right. They are under my orders."

"This Athenian was in search of me," said Phraortes. "Now I must return him to his people to honor the agreed upon truce.."

"Questionable," sneered Hydarnes. "Of what mind would an Athenian be to have cause for the head of the king's sentries?"

"The king's fortunes," replied Phraortes, unruffled.

"Hmmph," grunted Hydarnes, looking at me. I had been staring at Lysis, who returned my gaze.

"Why is this man before me?" asked Phraortes, pointing at me. Hydarnes turned to me also with a curious look.

"Demaratus is here to check on a mistake," he answered. He then said to me, "Is this the Athenian of whom we spoke?"

I walked closer to Lysis, pretending to study him. I shook my head. "No. I know no one of his likes. The man I killed on the slopes of Callidromus could not have survived."

Both Phraortes and Hydarnes looked surprised. Although Phraortes said nothing, his relief was evident. It was clear he and his son had talked. They both knew than my part in what had happened at Thermopylae. This could work to my advantage.

Hydarnes, however, had grown confused and cross. "Demaratus, I am of no mind to hold this Athenian further." I nodded. Hydarnes signaled to the captain of the guard, who, relieved, bid the two detainees on their way. Hydarnes and I mounted and turned our horses, cantering back to the camp on a chilly ride.

Lysis

I have neither time nor Poseidon's winds to sail a small boat through the Persian fleet and back to Salamis. Thus, another plan is being forced upon us. My father does not seem worried though. As we leave the Persian troops behind and enter the narrow streets of the Piraeus, he is almost excited.

"Strange, was it not? Demaratus' reaction, I mean."

"Strange?"

"I thought him to be of a mind to take you captive and to burn me at the stake to save his own flesh. But now I wonder of what he dreams."

"Demaratus gave me comfort, Father. I know not of what dwells in his mind, but I am certain his thoughts are not ones born from an evil man."

"You know not of him son. He feasts as a hyena in a den of rabbits and that is why he remains in the king's graces, for all these years. I will never trust him."

I do not want to argue. I only want to take leave from the port, but not alone. "Father, I beseech you to journey with me."

"I can not Lysis. Even if I was of mind to do so, Athens will never take me into her bosom again. I have hurt her too much."

"And you are a god to know that with certainty?"

"I do know that!" he insists. "There's no herb I can smooth on to heal what I have injured. In my own country, I have no honor left to me."

By this time, we have reached the quay where Persian vessels are moored. I speak not a sound.

"Farewell my son." Androcles grasps me by the shoulders, and touches me as a father would. "I will board you on one of these vessels. They know my name and fear it. They will take you where you want. May the gods be with you, and may you have new thoughts of me that are better than those of yesterday. Perhaps we will see each other again when the war passes."

I nod, unable to speak. He smiles, his scars no longer formidable, but he also looks so unbearably sad. He leads me up the gangplank of a small bireme and bids the master take me wherever I ordered.

The sun peeks over the horizon and the still water's surface reflects the soft honey-gold and muted-red of the morning rays. They rise over Hymettus and fall to the west on the Isle of Salamis, a green and brown smudge. I turn to Androcles as the ship pushes off and the oars dip in unison into the sparkling sea. He stands on the quay, his back to the rising sun, moving not a muscle, saying not a word, but now being the father whose memory will sustain me.

Demaratus

"Was that not strange?" asked Hydarnes.

Hydarnes and I had not spoken since our morning ride until he broached the subject now on our way to attend Xerxes' council of captains.

"Of what do you speak?"

"You know of what I speak. I knew that Athenian was also at Thermopylae." He cocked his head. "My friend, I trust you. I am certain you know what you are doing, but I know not the plan you are to unfold?"

Hydarnes and I had grown close since Thermopylae. I had contact with him while still in Persia, but we had developed a strong friendship in the shared trials of this invasion. I knew how he felt about Xerxes, but there was only so much anyone should know.

"You remember the king telling us Lysis was Phraortes' son?" I asked.

Recognition dawned. "That was Phraortes' son?"

I nodded. Hydarnes let out a low whistle. "Therefore his interest."

"Exactly."

"Then you did not kill him on Callidromus," he stated as a fact.

"No. I did not. He escaped from me in the middle of the night. It is possible Phraortes had a hand in him reaching the Greek lines." All of which was true enough.

"Why did you lie to the king about this?"

"The king already suspected me of passing messages. Why give him further cause?"

Hydarnes grunted but looked satisfied. I felt bad about misleading my friend, but I did not have any choice if I wanted to keep the king's trust and cast suspicion on Phraortes. Besides, Lysis was safe and away, and with any good fortune, would not be in our camp for the remainder of this campaign.

"Come with me," said Hydarnes. "I would like to know what the king has in mind for this next battle."

We marched down the rise, making our way across the loose shale and rocks that bordered the beach of the Bay of Phalerum. Soon, we stood, along with Phraortes, Mardonious and the rest of the king's inner circle of advisors to the rear of Xerxes' seat. It was a few hours after we had left Phraortes and Lysis. Phraortes glanced my way, and his look was, as usual, venomous, but with a slight difference. Was it uncertainty? Hard to tell. It would come out though, soon enough. I planned to corner him later that day.

The king convened the meeting which included the commanders from the anchored vessels in the bay. "Honored guests and subjects of the Persian Empire, I have summoned you here to listen. To listen to what all of you, in your wisdom and experience, propose to be our best course as we continue our campaign to punish those who have opposed and invaded us. I trust in your faithful service and know you have the interests of our empire in your hearts. Do not fear to speak." The king looked to Mardonious. "Shall we begin?"

Mardonious bowed low. "As you wish, sire." He nodded to the king of Sidon, seated to Xerxes' right.

The king rose, bowed, and addressed Mardonious. "You may tell his lordship my ships are ready to fight, as I believe all of us are. The Greeks have shown good spirit, it is true, but we have all of our forces here to add more strength. Many who were not at Artemisium are in place among these brave warriors," he gestured to the assembled. "I believe in the greatness of Xerxes and the rightness of our cause. We should attack and destroy the enemy where they are and end their power without further wait."

Xerxes appeared pleased.

Hydarnes leaned over to me. "None will to dare to dissent in this group."

As Mardonious went around the gathering, stopping in front of kings, generals, admirals, captains, all leaders of their people, the answers, couched in language florid, simple, obedient, and blunt, all supported Sidon's view. All, that is, except for one woman, Artemisia of Halicarnassus, daughter of Lygdamis. She held a mere five ships under her command, but was of a mind to speak counter to the prevailing winds. She was a tall woman, strong and proud, and emanated an infectious spirit. Her dark hair was laced with grey and her weathered face spoke of a hard and fearless life. She was not afraid to displease the king.

"Mardonious," she said, stepping forward, "Tell the Great One he knows of my valor and the part I have played in the wars of this campaign. He knows I will speak the truth."

She looked at Xerxes. His chin rested in his hand, and he nodded.

"We risk ruin of this expedition if we rush into battle here. I know it is the wish of the assembly to do so, but I believe the enemy fights for their land and their lives. They have shown great skill at Artemisium and will show that again. If we wait for a short time, they will be forced to take leave from their position on Salamis. Alas, they have little store of supply. I believe if they take leave without battle, they will disperse to their various cities, like milkweed in a spring breeze, and we will have victory over all we desire without loss of treasure."

She stepped back as Mardonious turned to the king. All seemed to hold their breath, waiting for his expected rage. But it did not come. Xerxes' expression changed, a small smile creasing his lips. Mardonious studied him as the king drew himself up in his throne.

"Artemisia," he said, "We have heard your counsel, and we know of your valor. I receive it as a great blessing as I do your service for these many years."

There was a collective release of tension from the gathering.

"Would that all of my commanders could show the same!" Now, some in the group showed signs of displeasure. Jealousy? Were they looking to see the woman humbled, or worse?

Xerxes continued. "Despite your counsel Artemisia, I find favor with the majority of views. We will gather our forces and wait no longer. We will commence our attack both by land and sea."

The king nodded to Mardonious. "Order the fleet to sea and the army to march to the isthmus. We will battle the enemy tomorrow." He stood, rising from his throne straight-backed and square-shouldered, a picture of supreme-confidence. The guests and commanders of the assembly bowed low as he turned and took leave to his camp. Hydarnes and I moved to where a secret conversation would be safe.

"Tell me of your thoughts," said Hydarnes.

"I believe the Athenian Themistocles to be a clever man."

"You are of the mind that we are not ready?" he asked. I had my eye on Phraortes, who was beginning to follow the king's entourage, but I turned back to Hydarnes.

"I know not the ways of the gods in battle, nor their ways in peace. Yet, I sense an enemy hidden from sight. I sense our defeat."

Hydarnes shook his head. "Demaratus, you are always a surprise to me. Yet, you said no such words to His Lordship."

"And risk my obedience to him? No, I would not dream of it."

Phraortes was a stade or so away. I did not want to lose him in the mass of the army for another two days and delay my words, so I took leave of Hydarnes and hastened toward Phraortes.

Lysis

One of our guard ships stops the Persian bireme as we pass Psyttaleia, a small island that bisects the narrow channel separating the eastern spur of Salamis at Cynosura Point from the mainland.

The crew haul me aboard, and by mid-morning, I stand in the presence of Themistocles again. He is not happy.

"Lysis, in the name of all the gods, what became of you?"

I explain, begging forgiveness for bringing danger to the mission but also for not having surrendered from my decision.

He finally agrees I had no choice. "You have changed," he says. "On what other matter did you concern yourself."

"Sir, I came to know the soul of my father."

Those few words convey so much. But whom have I gotten to know? My father or myself? The walls I have built to shield myself from further hurt have crumbled to dust. Hope has replaced despair, yet fear has entered my heart and taken up residence. I fear for my father. No longer immersed in myself, I feel whole again yet in danger of losing it all just when the possibility of a new future dawns.

Themistocles smiles. 'That is good. And I have to ask, will he help us?"

"He is of a warm heart. He loves Athens, but he feels he can never be forgiven for his betrayal." Themistocles' smile fades. "Thus, I believe he is of no mind to help."

"That is as it must be. I am certain your father will find his own peace. It is for us, however, to do what we must do, even down to our last warrior."

He turns away, looking out to sea at the ships anchored in the bay, and then positions himself in a firm stance on the beach. The pounding of hammers and the rasp of saws fill the air as ships are made ready, hulls strengthened, bronze rams fitted tight, leather skirts tethered to the gunwales.

"We must battle here," he says "Our allies have decided to stay and fight, though that son of a whore Adeimantus made it difficult to gain favor. I told them we would stay and fight, no matter the cost. Adeimantus tried to point out that since we no longer had a country, we did not have a say in any decision made by those with lands. I reminded him and everyone present, however, that our fleet was the largest in Greece and we could land where we wanted, when we wanted, and take what we wanted. That silenced them, but they are nervous."

"What happened with Sicinnus?" I ask.

"He delivered my message to the king, who seemed receptive. We will see what the gods bring us, but I would wager the enemy will move soon. The question is whether we can hold our own warriors steady and not retreat from battle."

He views the hundreds of ships crowding the bay. "It is mystifying to me how difficult it is to gain agreement from a majority on such an obvious danger. They will argue until they are dead before acknowledging some benefit to the cooperation I have proposed."

He looks at me. "We may all be 'Greeks' in some ancestry, but it would not seem so to many. On sleepless nights I think being conquered by one power would not be bad. At least we would be united!" He looks down, and then into my eyes. "I beg your forgiveness Lysis, for those words were not of a pure mind."

"I understand, sir." We stay in place, immersed in our thoughts.

"Let us move," Themistocles says. *"Athena's Victory* is in need of your help. And you need some kit unless you would rather row?"

"As you wish sir. I am but a servant to the gods."

"Spoken like a true Athenian."

Demaratus

"Phraortes!" I came upon him as he prepared to mount a beautiful brown mare that had been harnessed for him. Gripping the saddle's pommel, Phraortes calmed the steed.

"What do you seek from me Demaratus?" he asked, turning to me.

"I must speak with you, now."

"Your words are of no importance to me. Now take leave from me!"

I grabbed his forearm in a powerful grip.

"Take your hands off of me traitorous Dorian!" he hissed.

"Listen to me! I wish to speak of your son!" I snarled back. His face went ashen. "What words have you?"

"You know what words Phraortes. I know Lysis is your son, and so does Xerxes." I removed my grip.

His eyes were wary, but his anger cooled. "Speak."

"Not here, we must gather where no others can hear."

"Very well."

Once again, astride the animal Hydarnes had brought me, I followed Phraortes up toward the city. We kept riding, taking the fork to the northwest that led around the city walls and toward the Thriasian Plain on the way to Eleusis. As we rode, we saw the fields and groves on either side of the encampment of the Persian armies. They were dousing their fires, arranging their gear, and preparing to march.

White clouds had moved in, their calm a sharp contrast to the beehive of activity set in motion by Xerxes' orders to get underway. Surveying the warriors' high spirits as we trotted along, I wondered what it must be like to be a god, looking down on the doings of men. Did the gods care? Did they interest themselves in our lives and deaths?

They had to see the masses of humanity armed to the teeth about to give battle. Pure Persians, Medians, Cissians, Hyrcanians, Assyrians, Bactrians, Indians, Arians, Egyptians, soldiers from all over Asia, Africa, and Europe. And Greeks from those cities that had not hesitated to give the gifts of earth and water. These were the troops beginning to arouse themselves for further invasion, the masses of vessels that swarmed the waters between Phalerum and Megara preparing for conflict.

Did the gods take sides, as Homer asked? If they did, which of them would take mine? I had ceased to pray to any god long ago. The oracle had deserted me, had expressed the wishes of the gods, or so it was said. I had not time for any fickle or unjust deities after that. Though I wondered if I ever needed them, would they remember I had turned away?

I shook my head to clear it of such thoughts and concentrated on Phraortes. He was leading us north now, away from the city. To our left, the vast bay of Salamis was littered with shapes that were the Greek fleet, waiting to do battle. Salamis itself rose against the sky, its green and brown slopes darkened in the shadow of clouds. More had moved in, their undersides black and forbidding as a fitful breeze began to blow and the waters of the bay showed flecks of white sea foam. Why was he leading me to regions so far from others?

"Phraortes!" I hollered. "We can stop here! Why journey such a distance?"

He did not answer. We rode on.

Soon the city lay well behind us, the steep slopes of Lysimachus lying off to the east and the rocky bump of the Acropolis fading in the southeast. As my endurance on the patient beast that bore me waned, Phraortes slowed his horse to a walk, reined it in, and dismounted.

A small shrine stood at the side of the road. Beyond that lay a tomb constructed of cut stone. It spoke of no meaning with its bed of overgrown vines, weeds, and barley grass swaying in the breeze. Phraortes walked toward it.

I came up behind him. "What is this?"

"A place where we can talk. Now say what you must and take leave from me."

I turned away and walked over to the stone gravesite. It was smooth and unadorned, but crafted with great care. Flowers struggled through the choking grass to reach the light. The tomb had not been tended to in ages. A shrine by the side of the road was devoted to the earth mother—it was a pair of crudely carved and painted wooden statues of two women, one holding a scepter, the other holding sheaves of corn. Both rested atop a piled stone altar. I turned back.

"You hold in your mind that I am your enemy," I said. "Your vision of me is that I have brought you only harm."

He said nothing, but his silence and tight lips conveyed all I needed to know.

"You believe I had a hand in your being deprived of your lands, deprived of your name even. Is that not right, Androcles?"

He said, with icy detachment, "You know my name. There are those in the court who do as well. The man I am today I was not before, but maybe I am not so hard to recognize after all."

"No, that is not true. Before I saw you in Greece, I knew not who you were. I had never met Androcles. I had never seen Phraortes. You did not exist for me."

"You do not need to know a person's name to steal his lands and take his future."

"I had no hand in either. From whose mouth did such lies spill? Whose?"

"The king," he answered.

"The king? For what cause would he stoke such a fire?"

"He saved my life and then wanted me to know who tried to take it."

"Why?" I pressed.

"I know not why," he answered, beginning to get flustered. "He gave me the sword to exact my vengeance against those who…those who…"

"Speak it Androcles!"

"If you know my name, you know what was done."

"I know not of what you test me on!"

"Enough! You torture me! It was you who conspired with Hystaspes to steal my lands! It was you who tried to kill me!"

"Androcles, you must listen to me, I had no hand in that! I had no cause to do so! But who would have cause to steal your lands, to bring death to Hystaspes, to pit you against me, to punish the Egyptians. Who would have cause to deliver you such agony?"

He spun away from me, agitated. Then stopped a few paces away and slapped his palms to his temple.

"It was the king himself. It was Xerxes who brought misery upon you. You have been tricked for years into doing what he wanted. You have been his perfect servant, his devoted minister."

Androcles dropped his head into his hands, but he was listening.

"Hystaspes was a staunch supporter of Xerxes' rival for the throne, Artobazanes. Those two fought out of sight for years. I later advised the course of action that gave Xerxes the throne. When I first arrived in Persia, however, it was Darius and Artobazanes who welcomed me, and I was loyal to them. So Xerxes considered me a threat. When I realized Xerxes was the stronger and was destined to win, I sided with him. Androcles, I believe Xerxes murdered Hystaspes and cast the blame upon you."

"Demaratus, you bark crude just as a jackal does!"

"Listen to me. Xerxes told Hydarnes and me that Lysis was your son. He was amused by the whole matter. He told me why you hated me. I knew not of you before then. What cause would I have to want your lands? Darius had already bequeathed me treasure. Xerxes told us you must be watched, that you were destined to a life of betrayal and intrigue."

"You are lying!" he said, but it was obvious his spirit was waning. I could see the struggle on his face and that he had other information. That this was not the first time his faith in his master had been shaken.

" I am telling you the truth," I pressed. Another thought struck me. "Androcles, tell me of Egypt."

"What do you know of Egypt?

"I know of what you did there, or what you are said to have done there."

He looked at the tomb, distraught. "They call me 'the Butcher of Egypt'," he said, never taking his eyes from the yellowed stone of the grave. "But it was not I who carried out the ruin that befell. At least not all of it." He paused and walked over to the shrine, placing his hand on the goddess' head. "We used to come here as children. It was a perfect vantage point from which to watch the procession."

"The procession?"

He watched me, puzzled. "The procession of the Eleusinian mysteries."

"Ah, yes," I said. I had not witnessed or been part of the "mysteries," but was familiar with them. People from all over the Greek-speaking world would come to Eleusis to be initiated into the cult of the earth mother, of Demeter, and Kore. They journeyed from

Athens to Eleusis itself, passing by this site, I presumed. It gave hope of wealth to those in life, and peace in the Elysian fields to those after death.

"My family built this shrine. My grandfather is buried here. He was a good man." He was initiated before he died. I suppose it gave him some comfort." His eyes were far away. "I wonder if it still does." He turned back to me. "There will be no procession this year. I suppose we have seen to that."

"I suppose we have."

He walked over to the tomb, wading through the wild barley grass caressing the cold stone. Then he said, "Xerxes told me the people who attacked me long ago were Egyptians. He knew by whose hands I fell. He gave me command of a troop of soldiers, well, more than soldiers. They were cold-hearted men, as cold as I had become myself. We went into Egypt on the heels of the army the king had sent to end the rebellion that had waged there for years. We were to take no prisoners if the Egyptians resisted, and if they did not, we were to sell their women into slavery and kill their men, except for those we took and, on the king's order, to castrate. So we did. Or at least, my men did. I only wished vengeance on those who had done the same to me. Xerxes seemed to know where they would be."

He looked at me.

"They were not the same men who had ruined me though. I will remember those bastards for as long as I live. But," and he shrugged, "I did release scorn upon them in place of those who truly were in my sights, and with the gods' mercy, I have carried no burden thereafter."

"Who were these men?"

"I know not, other than they were no commoners. No soldiers. They were men of privilege in their own country. They begged for their lives," Androcles snarled, "but I had no mercy. They asked me who had ordered this and I told them Xerxes." He gripped the stone of the grave. "They said they had been betrayed. They offered me coin, freedom, women, and wine, but I killed them where they stood. I cut them down. The gods have mercy on me, I cut them down."

I was silent.

"After that," his voice hardened, "I served the king faithfully. I tended to his wishes. I eliminated his enemies. I repaid the debt I owed him."

"Androcles, I know not of what debt to Xerxes you speak of, but I stand by my words. I believe your master betrayed you."

"Xerxes saved me from those men! They were about to finish me! He saved me!"

"Could it be that Xerxes sent those men to attack you in the first place?"

He gaped at me. "Why?"

"He obtained a loyal servant in you, did he not?"

Androcles stared. He did not want to believe. I could see that. He was struggling to give some sense to his life these last ten years. What would happen if all he had believed once more crumbled to sand? I noticed he was looking beyond me at the Thriasian Plain. I turned. In the distance, a rider was approaching; stirring up the dust on the dry flat, he was galloping hard.

We watched as the wind across the plain gained in strength, bending the grass at our feet sweeping it toward the bay. The rider was closer, pursued by powerful gusts and riding as if Hades was reaching out. I looked at Androcles. He was intent on the rider, but his face was a study of his own inner pain. The horseman rode straight to where we stood, and as the beast and its rider came upon us, I realized it was no man. It was a young woman.

She drew up and dismounted. The horse breathed hard. White foam lathered its face, and its limbs shook. But it stood proud and tall. I realized I had seen her somewhere before. She was of medium height, slender and shapely. Smooth-skinned, her raven hair fell about her shoulders and managed to keep its form, even in the wind. Her face was oval, her lips full, and her dark almond-shaped eyes deep and lustrous. The dust of the ride had coated her long

Andronica

cloak and sandals, but like her mount, she held herself aloof. She strode toward Androcles, letting go the horse.

"By what name do you labor under?" she demanded, pointing at me.

Androcles seemed taken aback.

"I am Demaratus, son of Ariston. I am of Sparta. And whose blood do you carry?"

"My name is Andronica. I am the daughter of Hegesander and Hegesipyle, who now lie dead in the city, slain by those they served."

I remembered her now. She looked like the young girl I had seen murdered in the city last night. The resemblance was eerie. I examined her. In those beautiful eyes were rivers of grief, dammed by anger and action but aching for release in some quieter time.

"Why are you here?" I asked.

"I might ask the same of you!" she said.

"She came at my request," said Androcles. "She has news for me." He looked at her. "Do you?"

"I do, but can he be trusted?"

Androcles was silent, struggling. "Yes, you may tell us both."

She spoke over the increasing volume of the breeze. "You told me to listen, and I did. I found them. They talked of it as if it meant less than a grain weevil. They had taken from the city, taken from our house." Here her tough façade began to crack, a glimmer of tears appearing.

"Who were they?" asked Androcles.

"They were who you thought. Xerxes' men. Part of his guard. They said—" A tear ran down her cheek and was dried by the wind. "They said Xerxes had told them to make certain those people never talked of their story. 'They are not going to talk ever again', I heard one say. I...I could not listen anymore."

She clenched her fists, trying to regain her composure, but the tears flowed now. Androcles looked helpless but then tried to embrace her. She pushed him away.

"I will be alright," she said. "I want to know how this came to be?"

"I know not, but I'm beginning to find answers." Androcles gave me a hard look, "Demaratus, I believe you. I know not the meaning of your words today or whether what you say is true, but I do believe you had no hand in my fall. And with the gods as my witness, I swear I will find more of the answers I seek."

"What will you do?" I asked.

"First, I know of one or two people I must find. And then may Zeus have mercy on Xerxes if what you say is true, for I will have none."

As he spoke these words, the gathering wind rose to a greater force. The horse reared as tufts of earth, pebbles and debris rose all around us, stinging and battering our exposed skin. Out on the plain, a dust cloud had formed. It swirled and circled, swayed back and forth, and expanded toward Eleusis. Then it began to move our way.

"What approaches?" cried Andronica. "Is it an army?"

Androcles, shading his eyes against the angry wind answered, "It is not."

As the cloud came closer, a strange wail emanated from its center. It carried across the plain, a chant or song that sounded almost as a man would as it pierced the air.

"It's the call of the mysteries!" shouted Androcles. "Iacchus! It says Iacchus!"

"Of what meaning does it bear?" I asked, straining to be heard.

"The gods have come to help the Athenians. Look! It moves!"

He pointed as the massive cloud scoured the flat land, moving toward the southwest. Shielding his face, he turned toward me, as Andronica held the reins of the terrified horse, whinnying and bucking in protest. Our own horses had bolted.

"Xerxes' army is in terrible danger!" he said. "The gods have come. If this cloud settles on the land, his army will be crushed. If on the sea, his navy will suffer!"

Devotion to the gods had left me long ago, but this display of divine power affected me greatly. I watched as the vast ball of dust swept up debris and migrated, passing over the highland and traveling with intent toward Salamis and the sea.

Lysis

A trireme battleship races toward us, rowing at full tilt, oars flashing and cutting the water with frantic precision. Yards from the beach, the ship holds water with its larboard oars and spins in place, directly opposite *Athena's Victory*, the trierarch leaping to the port shrouds.

"The enemy approaches!" he bellows.

His cry echoes across the beach. Heads snap around. Themistocles, who has been supervising work on strengthening the bronze-beaked ram that was the primary weapon of our ship, climbs to the forepeak. "From where?"

"From Pharlerum, Munychia, the Piraeus," the trierarch answers. "From everywhere!"

"In what strength?"

"A full fleet sir!"

It is late in the day, the sun low on the horizon. We have been working with a will for hours, jumping at false signals yet certain of the war to come. As time went on, we were of no mind the battle would commence today. It makes no sense that the enemy has decided to attack.

"They have landed troops on Psyttaleia!" the trierarch continues. "And they are blocking the channel!"

"But they are not sailing toward us?" asks Themistocles.

"No, they have not moved in. They are blocking."

The Navarch hesitates, then says to a captain before him, "Take your ship and the other picket ships opposite Cynosura Point! I will send another vessel." He begins to descend to the deck, but then thinks better of it. "I think they are of no mind to march," he says to the trierarch. "Not today, but stay at the ready if they do."

The captain salutes. In moments, the ship is underway, the rowers respond with alacrity to their commanders' shouted cries. Themistocles comes to the deck where I stand.

"Lysis!" he commands. "Deliver word to the trierarchs in the Yellow ranks. Tell them to launch at once and join the picket ships opposite Cynosura Point. Be certain they do not engage! Tell them we will support them as fast as the fleet can launch!"

I salute and make my way to the stern, slipping down the ladder to the beach and making my way toward the Yellow ranks. Behind me, bedlam has broken out. Vessels that had not yet unshipped their masts for storage on the land during the battle are endeavoring to do so. Ready ships move into the bay, their oars bite the sea and lever the warships into clear water where, one by one, they form into line, awaiting orders. I find Ameinias of Pallene, commander of the Yellow squadron, by his ship christened *Lightning*.

"Trierarch, the navarch's orders!"

"What does he say?"

I tell him, and he follows with a roar of his own commands. I wheel back toward my ship and clamber on board as she slides into the sea. Themistocles gives orders to the steersman on the stern. The ship lurches forward, and I brace myself against the rail as we gather speed. We dodge and cut through the other ships, the navarch braying out orders as we pass various fleet leaders. The other non-Athenians of the fleet trail far back in the bay, though they had been swift to launch.

"You must choose, warriors," I hear Themistocles mumble under his breath. "Join us or take leave."

He orders us forward, leading our own Red phalanx in line toward the channel entrance. With the sun diminishing, we reach the picket vessels and ships of the Yellow phalanx, which spreads in a line across the channel opposite Cynosura Point. Ameinias' ship sweeps alongside. The wind, sometimes growling with stormy force, has died to a soft breeze, leaving the surface of the sea placid. The two warships come together.

"They haven't moved," says Ameinias, "and they look like they are going to stay there.. I do not understand why they got underway this late in the day."

Themistocles looks thoughtful. "I know not why, either, but I am grateful to the gods for it. Though I am not sure we have all warriors ready for battle yet."

Ameinias looks disgusted. "If not now, when?"

"Indeed, we must be ready to fight alone if need be," responds Themistocles.

"We will be ready."

"That we will. Now, keep your ships here for the night and inform us of the progress of the enemy."

"I will do so, navarch. Will I see you in the morning?"

"One would hope so!" laughs Themistocles. "Time for us to return and make certain of our allies!"

Ameinias nods and salutes. Themistocles turns away and gives his orders. As Apollo's chariot continues its journey on the far side of the world, we reverse our course, the rest of the fleet following until we were again off the beach. Many ships remain afloat for the night, anchoring in the calm waters. We on *Athena's Victory* beach. Themistocles goes off to arrange a final council of war. We assume the battle will begin in the morning.

Chapter 15

Demaratus

I left Androcles and Andronica at the south gate of the city, riding on alone to find Hydarnes. The two of them rode into the city together. Following the dust storm, we had recovered our mounts and journeyed on the wings of the wind back toward Athens. I had not learned much from either one of them concerning Andronica's destiny. It seems they had met days before, when the army first entered Attica. She was the daughter of the murdered Athenians I had seen, and also Lysis' lover. How she ended up with Androcles escaped me. I was more concerned with what Androcles had told me about his Egyptian experiences, ones that had changed him forever. Somehow, Xerxes had manipulated the entire tragedy, calling for the attack that ended up castrating Androcles and then the whole ruse of a rescue. And the king did all of this, I assumed, so he would have a faithful servant who would serve at his pleasure. Yes, eunuchs tended to be faithful.

Why had Xerxes needed to kill those Egyptians, and how could I use that? Events were moving along well: Androcles would confirm what I had found out; he was already of mind to suspect Xerxes. He would be my own eunuch, if it ever came to that. I hated playing Xerxes' game, but I could see no other way to restore my honor.

I approached Hydarnes past midday while he was instructing his commanders. They were gathered on a rocky slope to the southeast of the city where the Immortals' general had made his headquarters. The wind abated somewhat, but the clouds raced across the sky, casting their shadows on the earth, and sending the sun in and out of sight.

The army was ready to march, and as I neared, the meeting broke. The captains of the Persian elite scattered to their commands, pulling on their gold filigreed felt caps, and issuing their orders. In minutes, the hillside emptied, but for Hydarnes and his servants.

"Ah! Demaratus!" he exclaimed. "I was looking for you. We are marching within the hour. I had hoped you would accompany us!"

"I would like to, my friend, but you journey to the isthmus to be met by a wall of Spartans. I have seen those battles end only when the last drop of blood has been spilled. I would rather watch the naval battle. Such a glorious view, you know, from the heights."

"True, and no doubt there will be a naval battle. The Greeks are but lambs to be fed to our hungry lions."

"On what belief are you so certain?"

"What? Have you not heard? The fleet is sailing around the island. By nightfall, their escape route will be cut off."

That was interesting. So the king had taken Themistocles at his word. If it was true, the enemy would be massacred, especially if the Athenians turned. The entire war could be over by morning. If the Greeks lost their fleet, they could not support their land army. Resistance would crumble. It would be worth seeing this battle.

"Then I suppose I will stay," I said. "If we are victorious, you will have little with which to occupy your mind, and if we do not—"

"If we do not, I would not want to be standing here," interrupted Hydarnes.

I had to agree. Xerxes in victory was bad enough. I could only imagine the opposite. And I would not have trusted Themistocles. Hydarnes strode toward his tent just as he was taking leave.

"You seek me?" Hydarnes asked.

I followed, limping along slower, still feeling my body from the unaccustomed riding. "Yes, I had a conversation with Phraortes."

"And?"

"Interesting, do you know of his time in Egypt?"

"Yes, I remember that. He was named the Butcher of Egypt for good cause. What did he say?"

"That he was following the king's orders, executing specific people."

"Not unusual, Egypt was a bloody campaign."

"Maybe, but these men were of fine breeding and expected favor from Xerxes."

Hydarnes halted, turning to me, head cocked. "What meaning rests in your words?"

"In those cases, people are killed because they know of matters that might be of concern to others. What might they have known of Xerxes that would weaken him were others to know as well?"

"I know not of what you speak!" replied Hydarnes, walking toward his colorful tent ahead, one of the last standing in the encampment.

"You are certain?"

Hydarnes wheeled, exasperated. "Demaratus, what cause do you have to badger me on this? I said I would support you with Phraortes, but this ground on which you tread now is more dangerous."

"Then you do know of these matters?"

He hesitated for a long moment, then said in a low voice, "The rebellion in Egypt was a surprise to most of us, Darius included. We were scrambling, trying to form a strategic plan to regain control, when Xerxes presented his own to us. He was ready with the measures, the decrees, whom to recruit, where to recruit, whom to ask for coin and supplies, all matters of battle."

"As if he had a vision in a dream of the rebellion?"

"Maybe more than a dream. Rumors were that Xerxes had barters with leading Egyptians and encouraged them to revolt."

"Encouraged them?" I said, surprised. "Why?"

"You know better than most, Demaratus. It was for him to gain position in the succession. Xerxes and Artobazanes were always trying to support their claims for the kingship upon Darius' death, and a military victory would bring favor to Xerxes."

"But he was already decreed to be the successor by that time!"

"To be decreed and to be accepted are two different matters, as you know well. Xerxes needed the mirage and the reality of power."

"So that is the tale you take into battle with you, perhaps to your end?"

Hydarnes shrugged. "I know not, no more than I know if clouds will smother the sun tomorrow. But those were the rumors. If you are not going to go with us, the least you can do is give me an account of the battle on the sea. I would appreciate that. May the gods be with you my friend. Knowledge is one step, action quite another." He pivoted away from me.

"Thank you, Hydarnes. Good fortune." He assumed his natural ebullience and turned to his servants. "To the ready!" Another lesson awaits the barbarians!"

I watched him go and thought about what he had said. It made sense. The earlier Xerxes could seize control of the military and make a legend of himself as a confident, aggressive leader, and the more who supported him, the more ease in which he could transition into the kingship. And poor Androcles was a slave to that desire. The men he killed in Egypt must have been those Xerxes conspired with for the rebellion. Who knew how long the king had planned that event? He never gave even a whisper to me in all the years I had known him. But it was obvious now he had little trust and closeness to anyone, even Mardonious, I would wager.

That made me wonder what would become of us if this invasion should fail. How many of us had considered the consequences of defeat? Up until now, we had experienced victory. What would the king do if events took a turn?

And yet, it was defeat I was after. Only in the defeat of this invading force could I journey back to myself and back to Sparta. It was vital I have a hand in bringing this loss to Xerxes. When I was at Thermopylae, I wanted Leonidas and his forces to be defeated and yet to escape. I thought how powerful it would have been to place before Leonidas a weakened Persian army in central Greece. He would know of it, and so would Sparta. Together we would return to our native land as heroes and liberators. Leotychidas, hiding at home, would be shamed as he had once shamed and humiliated me. My revenge would be sweet and complete.

But Leonidas died, and his death had made me realize so much more the beauty of my country, my culture. It was worth giving my life for sake of country. The gods had abandoned me, but not completely, as the Eleusis dust cloud had proven, despite my cynicism. All was not lost. I could save Sparta and regain myself. All the elements were now in place.

Androcles was on the edge of rebellion. Both of our purposes could be put to use. The king stood on the threshold of a battle, yet with what I knew, I could change the victor of that battle to be in favor of the Greeks. It was a matter of delivering my words concerning the dispositions of the fleet and army to Themistocles and the Greeks, of urging the Greek commanders to seize the moment. I no longer had a courier to trust in this role. I had no Lysis, no slave to send with a message. There was Androcles. He had to help! He could hide the origin of the message if it became necessary. I had to ensure his loyalty to the cause, and make victory ours. Should the Greeks win by virtue of what I provided, Eurybiades and Themistocles would make certain the Spartans and the entire Greek world knew it was so. I could return to Sparta in honor and glory, and Leotychidas would be without power to stop it.

Indeed, the gods must want me to succeed. Why else had they shown me the cloud of dust? To whom else were the portents of defeat so vivid? The thought heartened me. Deep down, I was angry at the deities who claimed to chart my life, but had they heard my anger rather than my disbelief? I would soon know at nightfall, down by the Piraeus, where I would meet Androcles and Andronica.

Lysis

The flames crackle and spark, consuming the dried driftwood piled high on the sand. Around its flickering light, the captains of the Greeks are drawn like moths, gathered for what many felt would be a final council of war. I am there, as the runner for the navarch, if necessary.

The meeting has not gone well. The sight of the Persian foe up close unnerves many of the Peloponnesian captains, and they renew their strident calls for retreat, or "reposition," as they like to call it. Themistocles had been right. The agreement he had forged earlier proved as delicate as the morning mist. Even the plan of our ships remaining and fighting is now uncertain.

"Go ahead! Kill yourselves!" some shout. "We will hold at the isthmus while your carcasses feed the fish at the bottom of the bay!"

I understand how they feel, remembering from Artemisium what it is like to face the enemy for the first time. But many of these men are like me. They have already discovered their own strengths and the weaknesses of the Persian naval forces. They should know better. As I listen to their fears, I begin to feel the hopelessness of our effort. To bring so many Greek states together for one cause has not been done since Homer's time. Will it happen now when we need it most?

We are outnumbered. The enemy triremes seem as numerous as grains of sand on the beach. The majority of them lighter, swifter, and more maneuverable than ours; Ionians crew many of their other ships that are larger, heavier, and slower; no one in this gathering is afraid of those. But it was the Phoenicians, the Egyptians, the Cyprians —in other words, the unknowns—that generate fear.

Still, Themistocles is right. If we can stand together in these narrow waters, the gods might gift us favor. But in the open sea we face disaster. The Navarch does his best, thundering forth the arguments, wheedling, persuading, castigating, humiliating. He joins in verbal battle with Adeimantus the Corinthian until tempers rage, but it is to no avail.

The assembled captains are not swayed. The danger that lurks in front outweighs the danger that might await them in their future. They demand Eurybiades move the fleet in total. If we refuse to come, we will rot, for all they care, and under this weight Eurybiades is crumbling. He dares not alienate his Peloponnesian allies, no matter what we Athenians want, even though he, as much as Themistocles, understands the strategic imperative of remaining where we are.

He looks at the navarch and draws jeers and insults from the crowd.

"Eurybiades! Who would have thought a Spartan to be the servant to an Athenian!"

"Who is the fleet commander here? I thought you Spartans were warriors!"

Just as it was becoming clear their argument will be victorious over ours, a man taps Themistocles on the shoulder. He is a fellow Athenian, a young trierarch I did not recognize. I assume his family's money fitted out his vessel for him, because he is too young to come to fortune any other way.

"Navarch, Aristides, son of Lysimachus has come, and would like a word with you."

I have not heard of this Aristides, but our commander has. He looks surprised but offers, "Take me to him." Then turns to me, "Lysis, stay here and defend my honor, again, should it come to that." He winks, and I turn back to the clash with all speaking over one another. Tempers are near eruption.

"Cowards!" shouts one of our Athenian commanders. "Of what mind are you to believe the isthmus will be any safer? Have you not listened to Themistocles?"

That draws a loud guffaw from the far side of the circle. "Cowards?" replies a rail-thin Corinthian trierarch. "We've courage enough to think for ourselves! Which is more than I can say for you!"

Eurybiades intervenes. "Warriors! This has gone on long enough! We will come to agreement!."

There are more shouts. The Peloponnese contingents are confident of the outcome. But as Eurybiades looks around for Themistocles and prepares to speak, the Navarch slips in by my side.

"Watch this," he whispers.

Off to his left, a lone figure steps into the circle of shadowy light. He is strong and handsome, his full, perfect beard stands out from his prominent chin. His eyes reflect the flames of the roaring bonfire, and his broad shoulders and brawny arms stretch his finely spun, deep red tunic across his chest. "Eurybiades!" he bellows.

The fleet commander, about to address the council, turns. "Announce yourself!"

"I am Aristides, son of Lysimachus, and I come bearing news of the enemy."

There is a stir in the crowd, as all look to this man.

"What say you?" asks Eurybiades.

Aristides stands firm, one foot forward in a trained speaker's pose, and addresses the council. "Men of Greece! I have arrived from the Isle of Aegina in support of our common cause. In the journey here, enemy warships nearly came upon my vessel."

"That is impossible!" cries a voice. "The enemy has been anchored since this evening!"

"I am certain of my account," he answers. "It is possible and has been done. The Persian fleet has blocked the Megarian Strait."

An uproar ensues. Shouts of "Liar!" and "Traitor!" rise above the bed of sound. But Aristides allows the tumult to die as he stands unmoved.

Eurybiades steps to the center. "Let him speak!" He turns to Aristides. "You have proof of this?"

"I do. My ship sailed by that lane near dusk. Several enemy ships pursued us, with the bulk of their fleet moving into position behind them."

"How was it you escaped then?" asks a voice in the crowd.

"They were unfamiliar with the waters in the strait and fell back. But I say with truth just as I say the tides will roll in tomorrow, your way to the west is blocked."

This last statement renews the general air of consternation and disbelief. If what Aristides says is true, the fleet must stay and fight. It is possible to attempt to break through the barriers, but in the face of a determined enemy in those narrow strait waters, there is little hope of success. The fleet is trapped. To our front is the main Persian force, right off of Cynosura Point; to our rear is the blocked Megarian Strait. Unless we abandon our ships and march over land to the Isthmus, a weak plan at best with the enemy's land army in the area, we have but one option.

"You must fight here," says Aristides.

The council flames into a panic, particularly the Peloponnesians, who do not understand the truth of Aristides' assertions. "Did Themistocles trick you into this?" asks one. "Are you not Athenian yourself?"

Themistocles stands with his arms folded and shrugs his shoulders.

"You may attempt to take leave, if you wish," says Aristides, "but if you do, be certain knowing you will be met with battle."

Now there is anger. "We were fooled!" cries Adeimantus. "This is an Athenian trick!"

"How can we trick you?" says Themistocles, with a grim face. "We have no state."

"There is no truth to this," Adeimantus hisses.

"Warriors," says Themistocles, raising his voice and addressing the entire gathering. "If you wish to wait for your own eyes to see the truth, it will arrive in the form of Persian rams in the morning. If they have blocked the front and rear, they mean to attack, and they mean to do so soon. We must prepare for battle."

He searches the assembly, but it has broken into factions, with captains arguing with each other, still seeking options.

To the Athenian and Megarian officers who gather around him, the Navarch speaks. "Captains! We must ready ourselves now. The others will join us in time. They have no choice. Our scouts will alert us of any enemy movement. In the meantime, feed your men, stock your vessels, and try to get some sleep. We will meet on the beach by *Athena's Victory* before dawn."

They salute and break off from the council, moving back toward their own ships and ranks.

Themistocles approaches Aristides and smiles. "Aristides, we have not always been friends, but I thank you for your words this night."

Aristides nods and leaves, following the other captains back to the beach. I stay by the navarch.

"Many are stubborn as mules," he says.

"They are afraid."

"Afraid, yes they must be. Within my own soul I am terrified," he grins. "But that is of no matter because Athens' heritage and generations to come are at stake. We have no other course. They will see this or we will force them to see it."

Demaratus

The sun dipped below the western hills of Attica, silhouetting the heights of Mount Aegaleos against a brilliant purple and red sky. I was standing by an Athenian ship shed in Zea Harbor at Piraeus, waiting for Androcles and Andronica. These ship sheds stood all around the littoral of the small, circular harbor. Their stone floors held triremes safe from the elements where they could be rigged, outfitted, and repaired in relative peace. I had seen sheds of similar style in some of the Phoenician ports I had visited, but these were new. Athens had spent the last ten years in a building frenzy, and it showed.

I knew not of these matters of commerce, but I could not help but be impressed. It was one vision to see the ships, though I had viewed them from a distance, but another to see the industry that supported their fleet. This whole seaport of the Piraeus was made for shipping and supporting the navy. Zea, Kantharos, and Munychia Harbors held the accouterments of naval warfare. Naval store sheds, warehouses, shipwrights, carpentry shops, rope and sail makers, oar repairs—all that kept a fleet on the sea was in this crowded collection of wood, unbaked mud brick, and stone structures. In Sparta, there had never been this level of industry and focus. We tended arms and armor, but this was different. The cost to build and maintain their two hundred trireme warships must be staggering.

The streets were empty—the bustling life of the port had fled with rumors of war—except for the Persian soldiers patrolling the waterfront and standing guard on the roads approaching the town. Dogs roamed the alleyways and rats skittered along the waterfront, dipping in and out of the posts, bollards, and piers that ringed the harbor.

Androcles had arranged to meet here by the small scout vessels tied up on the quays and anchored in the sheltered harbor, citing it as the safest place. I thought this wise given what I intended to do. He was late, however. Darkness settled on the town, and torches appeared in the sentries' grasps. I grew impatient. After Hydarnes left, I made my way toward the king's encampment in hopes of finding Mardonious and gaining the information I needed. I arrived at the end of a meeting that Xerxes was having with his commanders. The fleet was already putting to sea and beginning to blockade the channel. The admirals of the various forces were receiving orders as I slipped into the crowd standing behind the king, nodding my greetings to Mardonious.

I felt a flash of irritation at his disdain but this was not my concern. Mardonious was the most ambitious in the Persian court. The king's brother-in-law, he had always been a strong advocate of invasion. It was obvious he hoped to rule Greece himself as a satrap. I was an annoyance to him, and when my counsel was well received by the king, I became more of a threat to his influence. But now, being the closest to Xerxes, might be an advantage for me in victory.

The admiral in charge of the meeting was Ariabignes, son of Darius. He was dressed for battle, resplendent in his green long-sleeved tunic and pants, iron-scaled breastplate, gold filigreed felt cap, or "tiara," they called it, and jewel-encrusted scabbard. He commanded the Ionian and Carian forces, but had been anointed by Xerxes with the task of overall fleet strategy. The council was attentive and quiet as his full voice boomed: "Commanders! The order of battle is as follows: The Phoenicians will gather on the left wing and center of the fleet, the Ionians the right. The Cyprians and Cilicians will be in reserve. Taking their ships south and west around the island of Salamis, will be the Egyptians, the Carians, those designated Ionians, the Lycians, the Dorians, and the Palestinian Syrians. The last will block the Megarian Strait and prevent the enemy's escape."

Heads nodded and murmured in agreement, all eyes on Ariabignes.

"You have your orders. We will begin the attack after daybreak. The fleet will advance in line of battle into the channel where we will meet the enemy should they elect to die. Their ships are in sight across the bay, so unless they attempt to flee, we will commence battle after we pass Cynosura Point, the spur of land west of the small island in the middle of the bay.

"We will have marines on that island to attend to any Greek survivors who wash ashore." He smiled. "I am certain none of you will have such need of rescue."

Nervous laughter rose and fell.

"Questions?"

Heads turned looking to one another. No questions.

"Wait Ariabignes," said the king from behind him. The admiral stepped aside. Xerxes rose from his chair, arranged his robes, and gazed upon the group. "You are my fleet and my kin. I know you are as confident of victory as am I. I will be watching you from the heights of Mount Ageleos, witnessing the ultimate triumph we all expect."

The war council bowed as one. Xerxes turned and took leave as Ariabignes resumed his post. "You are dismissed," he said.

Should the Greeks come upon this information, the battle might be turned in their favor. I was eager to try. I scurried off and made my way down to the seaside, watching the fleet as hundreds of ships slipped into the water or pulled anchors up through the surf, all heading south and west toward the lowering sun. The general mood was confident, most believing by nightfall tomorrow, the battle would be decided. I took in the entirety of the view, noting with interest the differences in skill and speed exhibited by the various sailors: the Phoenician ships slid through the sea, their dangerous rams parting the waters in measured rhythm, while the Lycians jerked their vessels along with rowers slamming at the wave tops; its marines looked seasick.

Once the warships had cleared the beaches, they gathered themselves into columns. By sunset, they were out of sight. I turned and walked to the Piraeus, intent on my plan. But now that I was here, there was no Androcles. What had happened? What had delayed him? I began to worry. I paced around the circle of ship sheds as the gloom deepened. In the distance, specks of light indicated the fleet at sea, an unaccustomed position for ships at night. They preferred to lie safe on a beach or in a protected harbor. The king's late orders had sent them there, and despite their confidence, that open position would steal their rest.

A wavering torch advanced toward me. I heard a low whistle, the pre-arranged signal.

"Androcles?" I said.

"No!" replied a high-pitched voice. "It is Andronica."

"Andronica!" I answered, startled. "Where is Androcles?"

The young woman appeared out of the blackness, the torch before her. She brushed the hair from her eyes and looked around. "He is not to arrive."

"Not to arrive?" I asked, anger beginning to build. "For what cause has he not shown himself? And why are you alone here?"

"I am not alone. Androcles sent a servant with me, a eunuch. He stands behind, over there." She pointed to the corner of a ship shed. I could see a dim figure outlined against the lighter wood of the building. "He counseled me to wait here for him."

"What news have you?" I asked, impatient.

"After you left, we traveled into the city. I wanted to see my parents. Their bodies were still there, where those murderers had left them." She sobbed, "I wanted to stay with them, but he said it was too dangerous. Androcles made me come with him."

"At least he was of one mind," I said sarcastically.

She glared at me. "Androcles saved my life when the barbarians first arrived."

"I beg your forgiveness. Tell me where he stays."

"He took me back to the camp where I waited in his tent. He was gone for most of the afternoon, and when he came back, he was in a foul mood."

"So, he must have confirmed what I told him."

She nodded. "I suppose he must have, though he did not say."

"What did he tell?"

"That he was of mind to kill Xerxes."

Lysis

The full moon bathes the beach in a soft light, settling along the lines of hulking warships that float on the sea and rest on the sand. Delicate eddies wash onto the strand, roll down the length of the wooden hulls and emphasize the quiet that has descended on the fleet.

I have stolen for myself a bare patch of deck amidships trying to get some sleep. Around me, rowers, sailors, and marines are in the same strait. Some, seeming without fear, and nerveless, snored. How can they sleep while all around the rest of us lay staring at the washed-out stars? But sleep they do.

I roll over onto my woolen cloak, a himation given me by a sympathetic marine whom I had, for the tenth time, importuned for arms and armor, all to no avail. It seems I will have to wait and scavenge in the course of battle. Should my station worsen, I can stand as an aide, of sorts, to Themistocles. Or at least a messenger. If the Navarch grows tired of me, I can always take my place in the galley among the oarsmen. No one would begrudge me that. I would not be at war as I have wanted to be, but I will be helping the cause, and that will be enough.

I pull my knees up onto the cloak, feeling my bare skin scrape against the oaken planking. The deck is clean. Themistocles insists on its daily scouring. But the powerful smell of sweat and unwashed bodies make a stench anyway. Fresh air below deck is never plentiful and though one gets used to the wretched odors, I grimace with disgust.

Images race through my mind of my father, Thermopylae, Leonidas, Demaratus, a host of jarring visions that seem to fill my gut with worms moving about. Round and round they go in the endless wheeling of my thoughts. In their midst, like a splash of ice-cold sea water, I think of Andronica.

I do not think of her as once I had. She is no longer the woman who gave life to my dreams, nor the warm and passionate lover I had embraced. My heart wants to make her so, but pain and caution forbid it. I know not where she is or of her life. I know not what is in her heart anymore and I might never find out. She could be in the heavens or destined to Hades in the service of the enemy. Mulling on that idea, I can not believe it of her. I have known her for what seems my entire life. Can she have hidden from me, as her brother did, the true nature of her feelings? Was I such a lamb that my innocence kept me from the possibility?

And so it is that as the moon begins to set and the heavens turn above the earth, I hang on an endless row of horrid imaginings, unable to calm myself and sleep, unable to think and plan. I am awake still when a messenger arrives on the ship, stepping over the reclining bodies and heading to the bow, where the Navarch has taken his station. I hear him announce news to the commander that a ship of Tenians has deserted from the Persian cause and confirmed for the Peloponnesian captains the truth of Aristides' claims. Eurybiades and the rest will be there when we awake. The battle will begin in the morning, and we will not be alone. The whole fleet will now fight together. I feel a lightness in my breast, and the tenor of my thoughts loosen. I feel myself relax and I drift off to sleep.

CHAPTER 16

Demaratus

I was stunned. Androcles planning to kill Xerxes? Had he gone mad? I did not expect this turn of events. Though there was ample evidence the former Athenian acts without cause, I did not want to believe he was of a mind as is a squirrel, or worse, of many minds. I grabbed the woman by the elbow.

"Where does he stay?" I demanded.

Fear filled her dark eyes. "I know not! He called for his servant and counseled me to find you." She pulled a small tablet from her chiton belt. "I am to give you this."

I grabbed the wax writing tablet from her trembling hand and opened it, pulling down the torch and shedding light on the scrawled symbols in Androcles' hand.

"You have freed me from my bad dreams," it read. "You were right. I owe not a morsel to any man. This king must die. He will do so tonight."

He *was* of many minds. If this woman had been caught...it did not bear thinking. And my plans had now come to matter not. Androcles could have borne the information I had gleaned from this afternoon's war council to the Athenians and their allies. He could have saved us both. I was hoping to tell him of that here. With his name alone, he could arrange passage to the other side.

Then a thought seized me. Did I need Androcles? I could go to the Greeks myself. I, a former king of the Spartans, could be the messenger of victory. Imaginings of glory bloomed in my mind. I would be welcomed, as I had hoped to be, as a savior of Greece.

I would be the man who turned the tide of the war. I could even command a portion of the fleet. Eurybiades would come to me with arms wide, praising me to all of my Sparta. Redemption was close, if I chose it.

Then another, more somber thought intruded. What would become of me in defeat? Xerxes would have no mercy upon me. What about the Athenians? Could I trust myself to have understood Themistocles correctly? Might he turn on the other Greeks? Might this all be a secret plan? If so, I would be a fool, one tortured until dead at that. No, I had picked Androcles for a reason. Better for him to fulfill his destiny and in so doing help mine. Thus, there had to be another passage.

Another messenger! Of course. But who? I looked around. Androcles' eunuch? Andronica? A surging moment of hope. No, no, of course not. They would not arrive in haste unless upon a swift ship. Yet, they had no power and could not commandeer one, and I could not be seen to do so. An impasse once again. It had to be Androcles. I had to find and stop him before it was too late.

Lysis

I feel a sharp kick on my shins and open my eyes into darkness. I have pulled the himation up to my chin and am curled in my sleeping position. The night air has grown cooler, even in the few hours I must have slept. I hear the sounds of a warship coming to life, the sound of two hundred men awakening, the mutterings while they stretched cramped limbs, and the occasional curse.

The marine who has initiated me into the new day smiles. "The navarch wants to see you."

I brace myself and throw off the cloak, rising to my feet in the predawn shuffle. Stiff, my eyes full of sleep, I can see Themistocles at the bow. I feel a thrill of fear, remembering what this day will bring. I approach the bow, more alive now that my worries have awoken. The commander turns at my arrival.

"Good morning!" he says, upbeat. "You rested I hope?"

I nod, stifling a yawn.

"Hmmm. Not enough it seems. Lysis, I need you to make a quick round of the fleet. Gather the trierarchs and the captains of marines, as many as you can. I have been to see Eurybiades. In case you have not heard, we are trapped!"

I manage a grin.

"Good! I am happy you are awake enough to appreciate that. On your way now."

I salute and make for the stern, slipping down the handholds on the hull and dropping to the sand.

Every ship I pass, I shout to the steersmen at the stern, most of whom are adjusting their rudders, tightening lines, or searching for breakfast. When each acknowledge, I go onto the next, recruiting other runners as I proceed. In no time, I manage to pass the word to everyone. They have been expecting the summons. I imagine Themistocles is more anxious than he looks, eager to wage battle. I return to *Athena's Victory* leading, what appears to be, half the fleet.

The navarch has stationed himself on the beach near a large boulder. I stop a few fathoms from him where the others have congregated and wait. It occurs to me I have not eaten since noon the day before. Famished, I look around, intent on food, but there is none. The others seemingly have more on their minds. Themistocles waits until the crowd has swelled close to one thousand men. He mounts the boulder, beckoning us in close. The stars have fled the dawn's sky, and the sun announces its arrival in a breathtaking mosaic of color. Themistocles smiles and looks across the multitude.

"Heavenly Zeus and sun-shielded Apollo smile on us today my fellow warriors!" he says, his voice, practiced and powerful from long use in the ecclesiasta, pitching to the back rows. "The omens have been taken. The gods have spoken their desire. While all of heaven looks down on us today, it is Athena who yet bids us to remember who we are. Pallas Athena, protector of our city, guardian of our sacred hill, long prophetess of our 'wooden walls'. It is she who this day smiles upon us, she who shows us the way to our inevitable victory."

He raises his voice then, imbuing it with passion and intensity. "For victory we will have this day, citizens!" he roars. "A victory borne of justice and righteousness, of faith and freedom." He pauses and looks around, and when he speaks again, he is quieter but no less intense. He is focused, speaking to each one of us as individuals, as members of the greatest city in all of Greece.

"There are two natures to man. The nature that will live only in freedom, and the nature that will be free only in death. This side, our nature, has chosen the path of freedom. Over there," and he sweeps his right hand toward the still darkened west, "they do not love the way they live, yet they choose to live it. That is the other nature of who we are, the side that would succumb to the tyrant's lash, suborn the natural urge of man, and exist in darkness and fear rather than rise up against the tide of despotism and throw off its chains."

Themistocles leans over and seems to stare into each of our souls. "We have made the choice to live in freedom. And here we stand because of it. It was a choice many of us made by birth, or made for us by chance. It may have been a choice that was handed to us, not one we had a hand in making. But now, we have come to it at last. The great trial of our lives. This is our opportunity. The choice is ours to make, and today we make it.

"Is it in your nature to choose the course of darkness, to submit your mind and heart to the cruel whims of tyranny? Or is it your choice to grasp with fervor the gift of freedom given us by the gods of our city, given us by Zeus, by Apollo, by Athena—given us, dear citizens, by ourselves! Will you be like the barbarian, poor, shackled, and soulless, fighting for false causes, doomed to detest the life he has chosen? Or will you rise up and fight in the name of all that is human, of all that is sacred and possible? Will you choose to lead the life you love?"

His voice soars, echoing across the bay as his fists clench and his beard shakes, willing the gathering and filling us all with his fervor. In response, we erupt. A thousand voices rise in one powerful, uplifting shout of resolve.

The navarch is exultant. "To your ships! For Athens! For Victory!" Then he leaps from his perch and wades into the masses, leading us back toward all that is left of our city.

Demaratus

I left Andronica with Androcles' servant, cursed not having a horse, and raced back toward the encampment and Xerxes' tent. That fool of an Athenian could accuse me as well as get himself killed. Only the gods knew what laid in his mind.

I stopped short in recollection. Damn! Xerxes was on the march. He had left for the foot of Mount Aegaleos before dusk where he planned to set up camp and watch the battle from the heights. Androcles knew that. He must have intended to intercept the king along the way or maybe try to wait until morning at first light. I would never arrive there in time on foot.

I spun back and ran to the waterfront. I found Andronica and the eunuch where I had left them, huddled against the ship shed wall. They were startled to see me.

"Let us take leave!" I barked.

"To where?" asked Andronica. "Androcles told me to wait here for him."

"Androcles is not to arrive here, at least not if he intends to do what he told you."

"But he told me..." she hesitated.

"What were his words?"

"That he would get me on a ship to Salamis."

"What I offer you now is the only hope for that," I said. "Follow me."

Andronica looked confused, but she seemed a strong woman and made up her mind. She nodded to the eunuch, who seemed torn as well.

"Eunuch, do you wish to save your master?" I asked. "If you do, take leave with me."

They both followed. We ran along the quay toward a small, stoutly built, twenty-oared vessel I had seen earlier. A dozing guard was stationed along the rail, and our rapid approach woke him from his stupor.

"Stop!" he said, as I came aboard. He fumbled for his dagger as I searched the vessel. Two other men were aboard, both curled up on some coiled lines in the stern.

"Stay your hand! I am Demaratus, son of Ariston. I am on a matter of great urgency for the king."

The men in the stern stirred and then sprung to their feet, alerted by my presence. The guard looked at all three of us, his blade poised at the ready. "Upon whose authority do you stand before me?" he queried.

"My authority comes direct from Xerxes. If you want to save your head, you would be wise to obey. Where is your crew?"

"Asleep. Over there." He pointed to a low-slung warehouse that hugged the waterfront along the road to the town.

"Bring them," I ordered. "The king is in great danger. We must take leave now!"

Andronica looked at me, surprised. I gave her a warning glance. She said nothing. The guard responded. "Bring forth the others!" he shouted to the two men. "Make ready to get underway!"

One of the sailors pulled on his sandals and raced down the quay. There was a shout, and then tumult. Bodies came tumbling out the door of the warehouse, rowers still in various stages of dress fielding curses and screams from the sailor. The crew hurried to where we stood, imperious and impatient, amidships.

They pulled in the bow and stern lines and shoved the ship away from the stone quay. They rowed her around and turned into the harbor, laying into their task with a will while the steersman guided her out the mouth of Zea Harbor. They turned south as we exited the mole, and the moon rose overhead to light our way. It would be a long pull to reach the king at Aegaleos before dawn.

Andronica sidled up to me as the vessel heeled underneath on the turn. "You spoke to them of our secrets," she accused.

"There was no other way," I whispered. "Androcles cannot succeed in this. Unless we arrive to him first, none of us will ever see home again."

Lysis

The tide is ebbing its last fingers as our battleships launch, riding the receding eddies out into the low surf. In the stern of each ship, below decks and between the steersmen, the flautists play and set the rhythm of the crew, the stroke oars on either side swing to the skirl of their pipes. The fleet advances to the center of the channel, forming into columns as it turns eastward.

Ameinias' *Lightning* leads the Yellow squadron on the far right, or southward end, of our line. On the far left, Eurybiades has stationed himself with the Peloponnesian forces and is advancing in similar formation. The bay here is wide, but it narrows as we bring our vessels between Salamis and a small isle off Paloukia Bay, where we had beached. Our left wing skirts the mainland, avoiding the reef and small island at the foot of Mount Aegaleos. The water is shallow between the island and the mainland and will prevent enemy ships from flanking us on that wing.

Ahead, through the morning's low-lying mist, we can see on the water the enemy fleet, the tops of their hulls revealing their line, stretching from shore to shore.

I follow Themistocles to the stern and peer west. The sun has not yet risen over the hills of Salamis, but the scene is lit like the most magnificent painting imaginable. As we row out from the protection of the island, our wings join with the center, and we advance in one unbroken line. Each wing advances in column formation and both are stronger than the center. The center itself advances, not as deep as the wings, but still holding a similar line.

Our ships, beaked with red, green, and blue, slice through the bay with precision, our weightier hulls riding steadily. We row with ten fathoms between the ships on either side and double that to the ships ahead and behind. Hoplite marines crouch low beside each

The ship flew under the measured cadence of 170 oars

Three banks of oarsmen, thranites, zygites and thalamites, moved as one

bow rail. They hold their four-foot shields braced against the deck, their polished bronze helmets and fluttering plumes peer above the shield rim, poised for battle. Behind them kneel the archers, rocking to the rhythm of each crew and fingering their arrows as they wait to come within range.

Suddenly, a voice rises in song from deep within our own ship. It begins as a lone achingly beautiful melody singing Apollo's paean to victory. It rises powerfully above the creak of oars, the stretch of leather, the splash of blades to the water. It pierces the held-breath silence of our fears and begins to spread. The oarsmen, backbone of the fleet, solid citizenry of our country, join with it, supporting, uplifting that single voice, coming together in a rippling, exultant swell of determination. Their chanting builds, voice upon voice, deep bass to soaring tenor. And from those voices, from that chant, the hymn of victory springs forth. The one hundred-seventy men who strain at our oars chant the paean, singing together, inciting the others on either side of us until the sky turns blue and the sea parts in front of us, the entire fleet having taken up the song. We fill the air with the music of our land and the determination of our people.

With my heart filled to bursting, I look to Themistocles. His eyes mist and his visage, grim and ferocious in the dawn, lightens with the morning's arrival. The enemy become more visible now, through the tendrils of vapor that drift from the sea. The Persian ships crowd together with little room between the tips of their oars, but their fierce rams cut the sea, searching for prey, hoping to sink their bronze-sheathed iron heads into the soft underbelly of our hulls.

"Look, Lysis!" Themistocles called. "Eurybiades gives the signal!"

From the Spartan's ship, an enormous, bright red flag snaps up and down three times. Sharp commands ring out across the water, and almost as one, the oarsmen dig their blades into the sea, and make their ships motionless. The entire fleet halts, singing with pride. I steady myself against the low rail, imitating the marines up front, several of whom fall, but even so, the voices never falter.

We are at slack tide now, and no one moves. We watch the enemy approach, two or three stade now, close, their impressive line unbroken and dangerous. Their oars grab the water together. Marines, with the plumes of their helmets rising above the rails, pack their decks—Persian marines, but this time on Phoenician ships. Themistocles continues to look north.

They are almost upon us. What are the commanders waiting for? My stomach churns. I see individual faces now, the backs of individual rowers naked, bronzed, and straining. For the first time, I remember I am unarmed. Up to this moment, that has been constantly on my mind. Now I feel exposed, nothing but a straw target for some Persian arrow. I want to run, to hide below decks, and escape the forthcoming hail of missiles that will rain upon us, even if our vessel avoids the formidable rams. But the sound of the voices steady me, lift me up We are singing louder.

"There!" shouts Themistocles, pointing. Again the flag, again the signal from Eurybiades. "Back water!" booms the navarch. "Back water!"

Every ship in the fleet begins to back, the center more so than our wing. We had been ahead, but now the center recedes farther to our left. Backing water is a difficult maneuver for inexperienced crews, but our entire force follows the command without hesitation. Even above our singing, I can hear a rolling cheer from across the water as the Persians increase their pace. They must think we are retreating. They spring forward, racing into the abandoned center.

I can feel the water move underneath me. It is slight, the warning of some larger event to follow. Yes! There it is! The tide comes in on a huge swell, as so often happens in these narrow waters, sweeping through the enemy fleet from west to east, taking them by surprise and lifting their steering oars clear of the sea so that Persian ship is flung into Persian ship. Packed together, many can not keep themselves from smashing into each other, their rams crush banks of oars and vulnerable timbers. Many are swept ahead of the main formation, swinging sideways, and exposing their tender sides.

Then the swell moves to us, yet we sail at the ready.

"Attack, you sons of Greece!" yells Themistocles. "Free your native land! Free your children, your wives, the fanes of your fathers' gods, and the tombs of your ancestors! Now you battle for your all!"

The rise dips under us, but our oars dig deep and rock us forward. I hold the rail, gazing across the line. As one, the Greek fleet advances.

Demaratus

We reached the foot of Mount Aegaleos by sea near dawn. Forced to labor in two short shifts with minimal rest, our crew was prostrate and close to its end. I showed no pity. Three-shift work would have been more efficient, but we had no time. And with the fear of Xerxes at their backs, they gave me what I wanted.

Our arrival made no difference, even so. The entire Persian navy had already rowed into the channel ahead of us. As I stood on the bow, I could see their sterns disappearing into the mist. The battle was about to begin and I felt a surge of anguish knowing events were out of my hands. The fates had spoken. The gods had abandoned me. The mountain appeared against the lighter blackness. Xerxes was there, somewhere, and so was Androcles. What kind of man had I become that my hopes for the future rested on two like them? They both deserved to die, to rot in Hades.

My bitterness and anger increased as the ships of the Persian armada receded into the lightening east. The best I could wish for was to forestall Androcles and prevent my possible betrayal. That could turn out to be a forlorn hope. What would happen if Androcles spoke of me?

"Demaratus," Andronica said, her exhaustion evident. She had not slept either. "What destiny befalls us upon landing?"

"We will be killed," I answered.

She gaped, openmouthed. "Killed? Are you sure?"

"Sure?" I hurled back at her, forgetting myself. "I am not sure! I am not sure of any matters!"

She recoiled, but I was not done. I leaned over her, trapping her between myself and the gunwale. "Androcles has doomed us! They will catch him and torture him, and he *will* speak of us!"

"Then why do you sail there?"

I took in the straining oarsmen, the Persian officers, and spread my arms. "Do we have another road to travel?"

She hung her head and slid away, slumping to the deck.

I felt remorse. "Andronica, I'm sorry. I know not of tomorrow. I am angry at myself for revealing secrets to Androcles."

She looked up. "It is not for you to have a heavy mind, especially since he knew of a greater barter."

"Of what do you speak?"

"He knew of Persian spies who watched his family. And he knew Xerxes' soldiers killed those spies."

"How did he come to this knowledge?"

"Those spies...those spies were of my family. It was my family they killed." She crossed her arms over her head and hid her eyes.

I turned and gazed across the water. What she said made sense. Androcles had learned before I came to him that he had cause to suspect Xerxes. This made me feel better, though not much. I had pushed him over the edge. I had tricked him as much as Xerxes had. But all had not turned out as I expected.

We drew up onto a rocky beach inside a narrow cove that lay at the southern slope of the mountain. To the west, I saw a promontory jutting into the bay on which sat Xerxes' camp. A trail lined with scrub brush and stunted trees wound along the shoreline and became more visible as dawn crept upon us. I departed the craft, making my way over the stony surface to where I could access the road. When I heard rustling behind me, I turned. Andronica struggled out after me and followed.

"Stay here," I whispered.

"I can help."

"You will be of trouble in this way. I will return for you."

She was brave, this woman, and determined, but I also realized she must be suffering. She and Lysis were together, but her family had been tasked to kill Lysis' family. Now she saw her prospective father-in-law in the enemy camp and attempting suicide. Not a good beginning to a long life together with Lysis.

"Bring him back," she said, as she heeded my instructions to return to the boat.

"The gods have little will for that." I shook my head, then took leave of her and proceeded along the shore.

The trail climbed onto the lower slopes of the craggy hill, and from my ever-ascending view, I watched the opposing fleets as they closed with each other. This was the nearest I had ever been to a major naval battle, and the scene was awe-inspiring. Nearly one thousand ships coming toward one another in the tight waters of the bay with more than 150,000 men on those vessels.

In the dim morning light, the dip of hundreds of thousands of oars looked like the movement of flocks of seabirds, up and down, up and down, slower but more deadly. It was hard to keep my eye from wandering to the vista, but I had more pressing matters. I labored up the path as fast as I could go, hoping I was not too late.

Twenty fathoms or more above the sea, I dipped in and out of the small promontories that molded the pathway. Ahead I could see activity on a flat outcropping that spread in a grassy plateau, sloping down to the bay. Hundreds of forms moved around a great throne set up overlooking the waters of the bay; I was but a stade from the king's encampment.

I heard shouts, alarmed and strident. They echoed off the cliff sides, disturbing the gulls nested in the crags and sending them bolting into the warming air as the sun peeked over the hills of Salamis.

I increased my pace, heart thumping. Was I too late? I heard footsteps, running, sprinting down the path. A boulder that had lodged itself against the side of the mountain, impeding the way, lay ahead. From around it, pouring blood and slipping and sliding on the narrow road, came Androcles.

Lysis

The enemy has been caught in our trap. Their center has raced into the gap left by our retreating ships and the swell has confused and disoriented them. Our triremes sweep forward, impelled by the will of our commander. Up ahead, Ameinias is the first to engage. The leader of the Yellow squadron catches a Phoenician vessel at a sharp angle, his ram smashing into the unprotected side of the enemy but becoming entangled in the ensuing melee. His whole column continues to advance, breaking through the Phoenician line as they sweep by, so close to the southern shore that they drive some of the enemy onto the rocks.

We follow, hugging the tail and the larboard side of Ameinias' ships, driving a wedge between the shore and the main body of the Persian fleet. Ours is a classic "diekplous" assault. We have broken their initial line and can now charge from the side at will. We have room to maneuver, while they, hemmed in by their large numbers, have none.

This must have been what the allied commanders had met about. This must have been the strategy. And it is working, at least on our side. Eurybiades on the north shore is trying the same thing while the center holds back. We continue this way, advancing straight east, right through the enemy line, pushing and crowding their craft closer and closer until we choke their freedom of movement.

The grand view I have of the battle degenerates into a tunnel of focused survival, ship against ship amidst unimagined chaos. The entire bay between Cynosura and Mt. Aegaleos is packed with warships of both sides trying to break into an open area where they can maneuver and prepare to attack or defend. That is not to be, however. The fighting is too close for the hemmed in Persians. Then my gaze narrows to my ship and the enemy vessel we are engaging.

The enemy's archers and javelin throwers arise and cast, sweeping our decks and killing and maiming half the marines and several sailors. I dive beneath the stern rail in time to avoid a pointed and well-aimed javelin that almost slices my head open.

Themistocles never flinches, looking down at me and flashing a broad-toothed smile. "Too close for you, eh, Lysis?"

I say nothing but scramble to my feet. The navarch bellows out his next command. "Hard to larboard! Prepare to ram!"

He has spotted a pair of entangled galleys, trying to get free, half a stade distant. The steersmen lean on the rudders, and *Athena's Victory's* first mate relays the maneuver to the rowers. In a flash, larboard side eases power and starboard lays into it. The ship spins, pointed broadside toward the enemy vessels.

"Full ahead!" shouts Themistocles. "Maximum speed!"

The oarsmen respond, standing on their foot boards, hurling their backs as one against the oars. Feeling the speed build underneath them, the stroke oars measure the rhythm of the crew and increase the rating with the others. There is no time to attain full speed, but it is enough.

Our bronze-sheathed ram parts the sea, flinging white-rimmed water to left and right. Twenty swift strokes and we will be on them. Pandemonium reigns on the enemy trireme. Marines line up on their larboard side, preparing to cast their weapons upon us as we come within striking distance. I can see their strain, feel their fear. It echoes my own. Themistocles is shouting. Our own remaining marines and sailors crouch low against the rail, anticipating. I stand unmoving by the navarch's side. Right before impact, he turns to me.

"Now that's better, Lysis!" he shouts laughing. "Let's see how they take this!"

I brace myself. Moments before impact, the enemy marines let fly a torrent of javelins and arrows that whistle through the limpid air and slam into the hull, splintering against iron and bronze, or finding their targets in soft flesh; I listen to the horrible screams of the impaled while several projectiles whiz by my ear. I seize weapons from a felled marine as Themistocles, unharmed, roars his approval and at that instant, we strike.

I hold the rail as our beak buries itself right up to the ferocious black and brown eye on the prow of *Athena's Victory*. There is a satisfying crunch of timbers as the enemy's hull collapses like a broken eggshell. Pushed over to her starboard side by the impact, she collapses back to larboard, back onto our ram. Most of the Persians and Phoenicians on deck have been thrown off their feet or hurled overboard. Themistocles and I, along with every other non-rower aboard *Athena's Victory* rush forward, attempting to drive our own bow down as the oarsmen begin to back water. This is the assault we have practiced a thousand times before. We back out of the jagged hole and watch as the barbarian ship fills with the sea, settling to deck level. Many of the enemy are trapped and drowned, while some rowers on board are able to escape from their stations and scramble topside, though their former warship has become a splintered raft.

We are a navy trained to use the ram, thus boarding the enemy ship is not possible and we will see to their survivors later, if any remain. Themistocles pulls us back and looks for another enemy vessel. The other galley that had been tangled with our victim frees itself from its sinking erstwhile companion, It tries to extricate itself from a similar clutch on its starboard side.

The navarch whoops. "Time for another one, men!"

Again, he orders the trireme forward. Again, we use the ram, pounding the enemy straight on amidships to the cheers of our rowers and the other Athenian ships, and to the consternation and disruption of the Phoenicians. This time, though, their marines wait until impact before recovering and attempting to wreak havoc on our vessel while it is still entangled with theirs. Our own hoplites rise to throw and are met by a wall of enemy javelins and arrows appearing in a rush from every point, felling in an instant most of our warriors.

We rush forward again, and as we arrive to the bow and begin to rock her to free ourselves, I see the whir and flash of an object to my right. I feel a great blow, like a solid right hand fist to my shoulder. I stagger and fall like a sack, searing pain pouring through me. I stare at the blood gushing from my shoulder before I can drag myself to the protection of the forepeak. Meanwhile, we have somehow managed to clear ourselves of the Phoenician trireme, and Themistocles is once more in charge, swinging the ship around, looking for another enemy ship to bring down. I shake my head, trying to gather my thoughts amidst bodies, blood, gore, and screams.

I am sitting against a poor marine who lays motionless, a javelin piercing his neck. His life blood spurts in an ever-diminishing stream as his terrified eyes lose their focus and dull into the cave of gods. Other men attempt to crawl away, crawl anywhere but where they find themselves, holding their wounded bodies against the rock and check of the ship. I can feel we are not as smooth of a crew below decks. The rowers must have lost men as well. Themistocles' next command confirms this.

"Clear the dead and wounded!" he bellows. "There is no time for retreat! Clear! Clear!"

The healer on *Athena's Victory* is the navarch's personal servant, and he must have been born in the good graces of the gods for he slips from man to man offering help to the wounded where he can, comfort to the dying where he must. As the ship knifes through the water, and the chaos and roar of battle surge all around us, he comes to me. "Ah, Lysis, a battle wound to tell your children of one day?"

He is still in my eyes' vision. That is good. Maybe I am not going to die after all. I manage to tear off a piece of the dead marine's tunic and stuff it in the wound, at least staunching the flow of blood some, but the arrow is still buried within. I try to smile.

"Heroics, eh? Well, we have seen those before from you, have we not?" He removes the rag. "We will have to pull that arrow out." With great precision, he breaks off the shaft head of the arrow near the wound, causing me to scream, and in one swift motion pulls it out from the point. I feel myself nearly faint. The pain is overwhelming. A fresh gush of blood follows, but he stems it with his firm hand applying pressure and a tight clean linen bandage he has unrolled from his bloodied sack.

"The gods have smiled on you. It missed the major blood flows. you will be alright."

I nod, too stunned to speak. He moves to the next man, while above me, the navarch's voice echoes and the din of battle rages on.

Demaratus

Sword in hand, Androcles was a bloody mess. His arms and chest were a crisscross of deep cuts that leaked his life force like water oozing from a well. We saw each other in the same instant. Behind him, on the narrow trail, I could hear the stamping of many feet. The fugitive had little time.

"Demaratus!" he gasped.

"Androcles, what have you done?" I rushed forward as, weakened, he fell at my feet, dropping the bloodied sword.

"I tried to kill the king...I failed." When he looked up at me, his scars were deep and pronounced, his eyes cavernous pools of misery. He gripped my arm: "Give this to my son, please," he choked, ripping off the long, beautifully crafted silver amulet around his neck. "Give him these words: I am sorry."

"Androcles—" but his eyes begged me to listen. So different, that look, from what I had known of him. Such hopelessness and self-loathing.

I took the chain, swallowing it in my fist as his pursuers rounded the boulder. He collapsed back onto the trail, dropping the sword. As it clattered to the ground, his head lolled, but he kept his eyes on me. "My son, give it to my son."

Then they were upon us —members of Xerxes' personal guard— and they had murder in their eyes.

CHAPTER 17

Lysis

My shoulder flames with pain, but it could have been worse. I can move, I can function; I am not an invalid. The ship heels to starboard beneath me as Themistocles orders another hard turn, avoiding a shattered Ionian hull and the wreckage that surrounds it. Men flail in the water, trying to get away from our thrashing oars, but to no avail. The navarch has no pity. As we sweep by, the few on our decks who can still fit an arrow seize the moment to fire down on the beleaguered survivors. Our rowers slash at the poor swimmers, clubbing them senseless as I watch our wake swallow them up and send them swirling beneath the formerly placid waters of the bay, now churning shore to shore.

Other missiles fill the air on either side impacting our hull or tearing through the protective canvas screen to wound a straining rower. The battle has been waging for what seems like eternity, but the placement of the sun denies that. I crawl aft, willing myself back into war, while under my palms and knees, the deck shivers and shakes with power.

When I stagger to my feet near the stern deck, I am promptly pulled back.

"Get down, you fool!" shouts a marine, huddling below the rail as arrows from a passing Phoenician ship whistle by. "Do you think you're Themistocles?"

I do not think I am the commander, but I do want to be where he is with the enemy at its thickest. He stands between the rudders, stern and unmoving one moment, and laughing like a mad man the next. He directs, cajoles, and encourages the crew, whipping the oarsmen into a disciplined frenzy. He plays the ship and its crew like a fine flute, knowing every note of its tunes and imperfections. It fills my soul with fervency, my heart with fire. I look down at the crew, citizens all, and know they feel the same. Even through their exhaustion, they rise to every demand with the courage and inspiration of our race.

But Themistocles, while driving the men, is wise beyond measure. He knows their limits, knows they can not keep this pace all day. "Hard starboard!" he orders. We head toward shore, passing through a column of our fellow Athenian vessels that are turning the other direction, pouring into the exposed flanks of the enemy. The navarch looks around him.

"Easy all!"

The rowers go to up oars, grateful for the pause. They collapse over their oars as the ship runs underneath them, clear for the moment of danger. Behind us, the awesome spectacle of the fight continues. Ships torn asunder—Ionian, Phoenician, Athenian, and allied—already the ruins of battle choke the surface of the sea. This is a hundred times worse than Artemisium.

A west wind has sprung up, spreading out the fleet commander's pendant that hangs on the stern peak, and as the tide slackens, we find ourselves drifting to the east, toward Cynosura Point. I draw myself up beside Themistocles, and as I do, so does another trireme. It is Ameinias, captain of the Yellow squadron with half his ship's oars shattered. Blood drips from the prow, painting with vermillion streaks the menacing hooded eye on the bow.

"Navarch!" he shouts over the din. "News from the south! An Aeginian ship reports the enemy has taken the Isle of Psyttalea!"

"In what force?" asks Themistocles.

"Infantry, but significant."

That is bad. With this wind, and when the tide turns, the wrecks will drift east, down upon the island. Occupied by Persian troops, any of our survivors will be at their mercy, while any Persians with enough fortune to escape the carnage will receive aid.

"We must deliver word to Aristides!" says Themistocles. "He must retake that island!"

"Sir, your command is my duty," replies Ameinias.

Themistocles is decisive. "Pull our ships together! Give me all capable marines and archers at the ready. I will give you the wounded to take ashore. Send word of our plans to Aristides at Ambelaki."

"Yes, sir!"

Themistocles turns to me. "Lysis, gather the wounded and take them aboard Ameinias' ship. We will see you after this is over."

I do not want to go, do not want to leave the fight, but the world is already swimming in front of my eyes. I do not have much choice. Themistocles needs men who can fight, not wounded ones like me. I work my way back forward, calling for those marines, sailors, and rowers who are in similar straits.

We complete the transfer, the healthy leaping the gap between rails, the invalids being handed over. I make my way to the stern, this time of *Lightning*, as *Athena's Victory* bears off, back into the battle. Ameinias does not hesitate.

"At the ready! Row!"

We are underway, heading east at a solid clip, without able fighting men and down to half of our rowers, but determined. A tangle of ships bar our way ahead. One of our triremes is engaged bow to bow in a death grip with an Ionian ship. The Ionians have managed to board, and the screams and shouts of the fighting echo across the water. As Ameinias searches the sea, another Ionian ship appears from behind. It seems to hesitate, as its bow swings to larboard, ready to fell our fellow Athenian trireme. But then it must have seen *Lightning*, since it changes course and gathers speed straight in our direction.

Demaratus

Xerxes' men surrounded Androcles, shoving me aside. They raised their swords, ready to plunge them into the desperate, shallow-breathing man, and his bloody head.

"Stop!" shouted a voice. It was Mardonious. "The king wants him alive."

The guardsmen lowered their blades. They reached down and lifted the unresisting Androcles to his feet, cuffing him across his face. His eyes were beginning to glaze over.

Mardonious noticed me, his brows rising in surprise. "What cause brings you here?"

"I took to a ship to watch the battle. We are moored back off this trail and I have only come upon him by chance."

Mardonious sneered, "You are late then, Spartan, the fun has already started. You may want to follow us, though, and see of what mind the king is in for this one." He indicated for the soldiers to drag Androcles away.

"Tell me of this, Mardonious."

"The fool worked his way to the king, but one of the guards saw that matters were amiss and tried to take his sword. He drew and went mad. Most of us were taken by surprise, but he was not to move close to his lordship. Enough reacted."

The Persian general looked over the escarpment, taking in the enormous expanse of the battle laid out before us. He seemed to hesitate for a moment. "It was odd, he was screaming about betrayal, accusing the king of the most horrible things." He glared at me. "Demaratus, what do you know of this mad man's rant?"

I stared back. "Mardonious, the king and you master your own affairs, not I."

He said nothing further.

We traveled to the plateau where Xerxes held court. The soldiers dragged the limp form of Androcles onto the level ground where the king sat on the throne overlooking the battle at sea. His face was dark and thunderous as a storm cloud. He seemed shaken.

"Bring him here!"

His guard complied, pulling Androcles toward the throne.

"Make him stand!"

They pulled him to his feet. Xerxes erupted. "You dog who gives no thanks! I saved you from your tormentors. I gave you life when you had none, lands and wealth that defied your dreams!" He stood. "This is how you honor me in return?"

Androcles' head lolled from side to side. He was trying to speak. The film that covered his eyes melted away as awareness returned. "You gave me a desert," he whispered. "A desert. You took away all I had. My life, my family, my manhood. You are but a snake."

The king seized the hair on his would-be assassin's head. "A snake who gave you a desert you say? Then I will give you now what you deserve. You may not be a man beneath your tunic, but the sea beasts will not care. They will be more than hungry for what they can find upon you!"

He wheeled to Mardonious. "Take this man to the shore and tie him to a post where the fish and the crabs can have their feast, and where he can watch the defeat of his former homeland!"

Mardonious bowed. "As you wish, sire."

Mardonious waved his arm and the guards dragged Androcles away, across the plateau and down the steep hill that led to the sea. As they did so, I caught Androcles' eye one final time. Even with their light fading, they had enough force to plead to me. I nodded, feeling in my sweaty palm the silver amulet and the long, beautiful chain.

Lysis

"Hard larboard!" shouts Amienias to the steersman, and to the rowers "back larboard, hard starboard!"

The ship spins in place as *Lightning*'s captain puts the trireme's bow on to the enemy vessel. We keep turning, forcing the Ionian to adjust its course, frustrating its attempt to ram broadside.

"We can't hold this!" yells the first mate. "She's faster than we are!"

That is true. Eventually, the other ship will catch us at an angle, and we will be doomed. But we do not have other choices.

"Best to arm yourself Lysis. They'll be aboard soon," says the Yellow squadron captain. I look around, staggering toward a discarded eight-footer that lay amidships beside a pile of dead hoplite marines. I reach for it as another voice booms over the water.

"Do not fear, Amienias! We will clean up for you!"

Another Athenian ship races by. As yet not battle worn, she is fresh and new, charging ahead at a speed we can only dream of.. Amienias laughs with relief and waves.

"We would have taken her, you son of a whore!" he shouts back. The other trierarch throws back his head, roaring with laughter as his black and red horsehair plume rocks and sways with his helmet. His ship catches the Ionian flush on the stern, splintering the larboard steering oar and spinning the battleship on its keel.

Amienias cheers as the enemy vessel and her crew sink into the blackness. "Drive it, now! Forward!"

The oarsmen dig in again, and we are off, hugging the shore, trying to stay out of the fight on our left.

Time seems to race,. The sun has climbed to mid-morning, and the sky is fresh and clear blue, almost as a dream opposite the nightmare of events on the surface of the sea. We have exited the maelstrom of battle and snap the taut rope that has held us all in tension and fear. The fog that has kept us enshrouded in the moment falls away, and I can feel myself loosen. In doing so, the pain of my wound returns with a vengeance. I sit on the stern deck, my back braces against the rail, my hand pressing my bandaged shoulder as I try to be of mind away from the throbbing ache.

Ahead is the promontory of Kamatero Point and the rear of the packed enemy fleet. Soon, we round it and are rowing hard almost due south. The bay here is wider, opening out to Cynosura, and I can see with a thrill the warships moving toward us. I hold my breath for a moment, not sure if they are friend or foe. Then I can see, standing out in the westering breeze, the pendants of Aegina and the insignia of Athenian vessels. Our crew erupts in cheers.

That is where Eurybiades and Themistocles had hidden the rest of the fleet. They must have been concealed deep in the inlet by the early morning darkness and mist. Now, they come charging from their hidden cove, sweeping down on the flanks and rear of the enemy force.

Aristides is an Athenian exile who has made his new home on Aegina. He might be with that force. Ameinias has the same thought. He orders a turn to starboard, aiming for the left wing of the phalanx where the Aeginian ships are thickest. We close, signaling for a word together. The lead vessel heeds our frantic waving and goes up oars, letting the ship run out. We hold water, coming to a dead stop as the Aeginian trireme glides alongside and also holds water.

"We are looking for Aristides!" shouts Ameinias.

Aristides arises from the bow behind a rank of marines. "As is my father's name, so it is mine! Who calls for me?"

"Ameinias of Pallene, I speak for Themistocles."

"Speak then!"

Ameinias explains of Psyttaleia, endorsing Themistocles' request. The entire left wing of the phalanx is at a standstill, waiting for Aristides' ship to lead. The rest of the force is swinging into the Persian left flank.

Aristides hesitates, but his eyes tell that he wants to join the fight. He finally says, "We will sail to Kamatero. There are hoplites there, stationed to help our men. We can take them to the island. That will be enough." Once he makes his decision, Aristides moves fast. He orders the wing to larboard, directly for the open beaches of Kamatero. "You can help too, Ameinias! You have plenty of deck on that now!"

Ameinias agrees, and we follow the other fifteen triremes into the strand, where an anxious group of hoplites, unsure who was bearing down on them, are drawn up in loose formation on the high ground inland,. In swift succession, our ships stop, turn, and back onto the beach. We moor next to the Aeginian flagship and watch Aristides leap off, waving to the hoplites who, relieved we are friendly, advance to meet us.

"We arrive seeking help!" says the Athenian exile. "Can you gather hundreds of warriors? Now?"

The phalanx commander, a squat Megarian, nods. "In a war against the Persians, we are prepared to die,." He eyes the ships uneasily. "I never had visions of being a marine though."

Aristides laughs. "Not to fear Megarian. We will land you on an island crawling with Persians to kill, lest they kill you."

The hoplite smiles, showing yellowed and missing teeth through the face guard on his helmet. "If the gods favor me, I will live!" He turns to his men, ordering messengers to gather more warriors.

I collapse once again against the bulwark, secure in the knowledge that we have carried out our orders but feeling light-headed and hungry. As if in answer to my thoughts, the ship's cook, along with a healer of sorts, doles out wineskins and loaves of bread. The healer tends to the wounded with rough care, rewrapping bandages and drawing pained cries from the men. He does not have the training of Themistocles' healer. When they come to me, I accept the wine, guzzling a bit and then tear off chunks of barley bread. I take some goat cheese the cook brings from out of a leather shoulder sack. The healer seems pleased with my dressing and lets me be, moving with the cook through the ship, neither having interest in the activity around them.

Hoplites begin to arrive and are clambering aboard the ships, passing up their great shields and spears, aggressively grabbing onto the handholds. *Lightning* rocks and leans as she takes on the extra weight. Then we enter the shallow water for battle again.

I look over the rail toward the north and west. I see the battle four or five stade distant. Racing ships and flashing oars fill the straits, and tens of thousands of men fling themselves one upon another with desperate fury. Over the water comes the roaring sounds of their struggles—screams, the crashing thunder of iron against wood, and the splintered moan of the result. The flautists skirling their call to rhythm never ceases, though all around them, the din of a different kind of chorus soars. The staccato patter of arrows hitting their marks are as ill-timed drumbeats weaving through the haunting melody of the flutes.

Demaratus

I stood behind the king and watched as Mardonious' men dragged the unresisting Androcles into the low surf. Other men were tying a series of long poles, lashing spears, together for the effect. They followed the prisoner into the water and then, when chest deep, drove the poles into the murky bottom, setting up a rough trellis on which they strapped the victim. He hung there, alive, splayed across the poles, chest awash, head hung low.

Xerxes, still shaking in shock and anger, growled in satisfaction. "Let him rot in this place, for all to see." He turned to me. "You see, do you not Demaratus, the fate of a traitor?"

"It is a kingly thing you do, sire." My voice dripped with contempt, but he did not seem to notice. "His fate was fixed by the gods long ago and now you have honored their wishes."

The king attempted to pierce me with his gaze, but I did not waver. He turned back to the battle and to the sad form of Androcles. "He was a foolish man," he muttered. "A foolish, foolish man." Gripping the gilded armrests of his throne, he cast his sight over the expanse of the bay.

It was a breathtaking sight. From our lofty perch, we beheld the entire spectacle, real, but also dreamlike. Separated from man's natural home and suspended on Poseidon's oceans, the great slashing ships drove at each other in a riot of focused ferocity. Their wooden hulls were painted and decorated with fierce symbols and menacing threats in all colors of the rainbow. They were the shields of their crews, and like a hoplite's protection, gave identity to who they were. Once I recognized this, my thoughts on the fight changed; it was an extension of Spartan tactics on land. I could see the Athenians and the Lacedaemonians attempting to draw our forces into the center while they struck on the wings, an attempt at a two-sided assault. My admiration grew for their tactics.

Once battle was joined, it was difficult to tell who was friend or enemy, but Xerxes' naval advisors offered expert counsel until all became clear. The larger Athenian ships did not carry the same force of marines as our Persian ones. The king brought his hands together in satisfaction when enemy ships were boarded and taken, our marines pouring over the decks, sweeping them clear, and sending the enemy cascading into the sea with screams echoing across the water.

"Those will come to a bad end!" he exclaimed.

"Indeed, sire," confirmed another. "Even should they escape the perils of the sea, they will float down upon our men on the rocky island."

I searched the strait where he pointed and saw, outlined in the sun, a knuckle of earth plopped down in the middle of the bay to the southeast; the island Mardonious had mentioned in the council one day earlier.

Individual ships and captains could be identified by the pennons that hung fluttering by the sterns or by the colors painted on their fierce prows. As the battle raged, I detected a disturbing pattern—one that the king's advisors must have noticed but were not telling him of.

Our ships were being squeezed into the center. The ones on the outer edges of the battle had some freedom of movement, though only little. They were being attacked by the enemy triremes as if they were fish caught in the outskirts of a net, speared, and left to die. The ones in the center struggled for any movement from side to side, and were being pushed forward where lines of enemy triremes waited, ramming from the side those that moved ahead, thus sowing even more confusion in the ranks behind. This battle at sea was looking like infantry encounters on land I had the pleasure of winning. Many of our ships in the rear pressed forward, having not yet understood the importance of backing off to give the rest of the fleet maneuvering room.

There were encouraging signs, too. Individual ships and captains stood out, primary among them Artemisia of Halicarnassus, Xerxes' new favorite. Her ship had been in the forefront of the first advance and was having success skimming across the bay, taking advantage of the open seas.

As we watched, an Athenian chased her trireme while she rammed and sank another of the enemy. The gathering shouted, even as the crunch of shattered timbers from others of our fleet showed her success was not for all to reap.

"Your Highness," said a courtier, "Look! Artemisia fights well! She has sunk an enemy ship."

Xerxes strained to see, the others pointing out the victory. But the king did have his eye on the overall battle and could sense the tide. "True, but it seems she is alone. My men fight like women and my women like men!"

The advisors were silent. I had been absorbed in the battle, but the king's remark awoke me from my reverie. I felt, cold and solid in my hand, the silver amulet of Androcles. My gaze drew to him, bound and listless in the strait, awaiting his fate in the wash of the tide.

And what of my own fate if we lost this fight? It was one matter to have a hand in victory with the near assurance of a warm welcome from the king. It was quite another to be on the losing side when blame was meted out. Artemisia fought well, and good for her, but what of the others? What would be their fates? Androcles, though a traitor, could be but a signal for more of the unpredictable moods of this king. If such was true, and suspicion fell upon me, I would bear my own fate like a Spartan. I had taken a course and stuck by it. Should I be called for it, that would be my fate.

But there were others who did not deserve such a fate, people who, in their innocence, would have helped me. Androcles, lying in the surf, his life a ruin, was no innocent. But Andronica could still be saved. I had enough heart within me to see to that, and enough honor left to seize upon Androcles' request. In doing so, I would help Lysis, who had helped me and deserved help in return. For Androcles I felt pity, though I would have used him to the end, if that had been needed. He had led his life with fear, betrayal, and lies. He was tasting the fruits of his own choices, as would we all.

The king alternated between fear, anger, and frustration watching his fleet. Around him, his loyalists stood silent, and I stole away. I made for the coast path, striding toward the ship that had landed me here. I passed ranks of soldiers, hundreds of camp followers, thousands of souls, witnessing the life and death struggles of those on the sea..

I reached the ship. Many of the rowers had climbed to the top of the path to watch the fight, relaying descriptions. Others were curled up inside the ship, exhausted and dead to the world. Andronica sat on a rock, her head in her hands. I hurried up, catching them by surprise.

"Orders from the king! We must get underway at once!"

They gaped at me. Andronica started.

"Underway?" asked the boat captain. "But the battle goes on!"

"To Athens!" I snarled.

The crew looked from one to the other with confusion.

"Now!" I commanded. "Or would you rather face the king's wrath?"

They rose from their stupor, muttering, and boarded the vessel. I moved to Andronica. She looked up at me, brown eyes glistening, lips opening in a silent question. She searched behind me and seeing no one, dropped her shoulders. I came close to her and took her hand.

"Take this to Lysis," I opened her fingers and pressed the amulet into her palm. "Tell him his father begs for forgiveness."

She looked down, and her hand flew to her mouth. "Of what do you speak?" she asked, quivering.

I told her all. "Androcles has earned his penance. Lysis will understand."

She nodded, too numb to speak.

"Now take leave to Athens, move into the country, disguise yourself, and stay out of the way. It may be a while, but we will not be here forever. If Lysis is still alive, he will return to the city." I touched her cheek. "And tell him I'm grateful for Thermopylae. He's a good man."

She looked confused, but embraced me, her silken hair upon my chest. "Thank you," she whispered. "I will never forget you."

I felt an unexpected opening of my heart, a reminder, I suppose, of my own family left behind these many years. "May the gods be with you."

She nodded once again and turned to board the ship. "Keep watch of her!" I warned the captain. "She is the king's messenger. If she is hurt, you will suffer the lordship's answer to it!"

The sailor acknowledged my threat. "Shove off!" he ordered. The crew pushed the vessel into the cove and hopped aboard, manning the oars. They bent to their task, pulling and levering out of the inlet, into the open waters of the bay. Ahead of them, the battle raged, thus they crept along the shoreline to avoid being seen as a fat, slow target. Maybe the two navies would be too occupied with each other to notice. I hoped so.

Andronica stood in the stern, looking aft. She raised her hand and waved. She looked beautiful. I wondered if Lysis would ever see her again. I bowed low and wheeled, my long red cloak sweeping behind me. I had done all I could do. Now it was back to Xerxes, back to the battle, back to the fate that awaited me.

CHAPTER 18

Lysis

In two columns, our force dashes out of the confines of the cove, rowing hard due east. We keep close to the coastline of Cynosura Point, covering the distance to its tip. To our left, the enemy is in confusion, surprised, and angry by the sudden attack of our forces on their flank and rear.

Ahead, the results of the battle are visible for both sides. Remnants of the savage conflict float down the strait, drifting on the outgoing tide and the westerly wind. Overturned hulls show their barnacle-and-algae-smothered undersides to the sun, while other ships, decks awash and level with the sea, grind into each other or swim alone as wrecked and shattered remains of their once proud selves.

Sailors are aplenty also, hanging onto the rails or lying in the stinging salt water. They will suffer as the day draws on. Sharks will notice, the sun will blaze, and more than all else, humans will finish what they started. Were we not in haste, Aristides no doubt would have stopped to kill off the Persians wailing for help, and aid the allies who cry for vengeance.

But there is no time. The sun says midday, and the battle has been waging for hours. These wrecks and their cargos of misery will soon be landing on the beaches of Psyttalea where the Persian soldiery will send them off in their glory or shame to Zeus or Hades. Better it is we who do the finishing.

We round Cynosura Point and head southeast, making for the far side of the island. Aboard *Lightning*, our diminished crew leave us lagging at the rear of the left column. We see the island ahead, small, rocky, and low-lying, except in the south, where a series of hills rise against the sky. Aristides steers for the beaches, the place where the wrecks will land.

Off to my left, I spot a Lacedaemonian trireme bearing down on a hapless Persian vessel with its twenty oars slashing through the water as it tries to escape its fate. The trireme has broken free of the main fight, flushed its prey, and rather than return, begins advancing on this small prize. I feel sorry for the poor enemy sailors, as theirs is not a warship. But I harden my heart certain the Persians will spare no mercy upon us were we its prey.

The chase ends. The victims' oars cease moving all at once, dropping to the sea as the battleship's ram catches the small craft amidships, breaking its back and severing one half from the other. We sweep by, intent on our own mission, but above the sounds of our own splashing oars, grunting rowers, and creaking leather, I can hear the despairing cries of the enemy's wounded and abandoned.

The trireme's crew is not silent either, heaping insults on the struggling swimmers and firing down into their soft bodies until, as we leave the drama astern, movement ceases on the surface of the sea. I turn a final time, noting the Lacedaemonians steer their ship west and head back toward the bigger fight.

Aristides signals for line abreast and we take position, the archers crowding the bows of our ships, facing the island that looms ahead of us. On the beach, the surprised Persians are gathering in formation, ready to engage. We come to within half a stade of the strand, and the enemy let arrows fly. Their poorly aimed shots plunk into our stout sides or fall to the water. Our reply is devastating. Our light armed troops unleash a torrent of fire on the beleaguered enemy. They stagger, dozens screaming in pain, as they drop in their tracks or reel from the ranks.

We keep up a dense covering fire with our ships turning in place, again showing the extraordinary discipline of our citizen navy as the hoplite marines scramble aft. The oarsmen back and our sterns impact the sand. Our warriors drop to the water and wade ashore with shields held high and spears at the ready as the enemy, distracted by our hail of missiles, try to mount a counterattack.

The hoplites, some four hundred of them, including the various marine forces, assume the phalanx formation and advance across the narrow, amber beach. They level their long eight-footers and drive into the ranks of the enemy, whose numbers have swelled with the arrival of reinforcements. They have not been expecting this sudden onslaught. Alas, they believed they would be facing deranged, wounded, and helpless sailors, defeated men arriving on sodden wrecks, not an armed, angry, and vengeful hoplite soldiery.

The outnumbered and poorly armed enemy fight desperately. They break as our phalanx rolls into them, slashing at our cornel wood spears, and hurling their javelins upon us at close range, but to no avail. We overwhelm and ride them into the sand, which takes on a different stain, one I had seen at Thermopylae. The survivors bolt into our trap, pursued by our light troops and a large force of hoplites which will hunt down and kill them to the last man.

Aristides leaps from his ship and runs over to *Lightning*. "Ameinias!"

Our trierarch comes to the rail. "Sir!"

"Can you take a party and collect some water? I see there's a stream by those rocks." He points to a cluster of boulders nested together where the sand meets the earth at the beach's edge.

Ameinias salutes. "And then?"

"We will leave the hoplites here to salvage, and bring aboard our marines to rejoin the battle. That should work."

Ameinias beams. "Yes indeed, as long as I can battle with some of those marines by my side as well!"

"The gods give you their blessings!" Aristides sprints away to his ship. Through the noontime heat comes the sound of unequal battle from the small isle, a local picture of the far greater conflict thundering less than five stade to the west.

Ameinias comes to where I sit in the stern. "Lysis, take leave with the others to collect water for our men."

I nod. The pain in my shoulder is still intense, but I have drunk enough wine to not be afraid of it. Ameinias smiles and moves forward, collecting some of the other walking wounded. I stagger to my feet and feel the blood rush to my head. But I know the others are in no better shape, and I understand we must keep the able-bodied men ready for swift flight. In the midst of the enemy, a trireme battleship must move like a hummingbird, never holding in one place too long. So I lean against the rail, regain my mind, and step over the stern rail, making my way down the side of the hull ladder and splashing into the shallow water. I wade ashore as others follow bearing ample amphorae for the task. Aristides has collected other men from the force, and they tramp toward us toting clay jugs.

Walking up the beach to the rocks Ameinias has pointed to, I notice a steady flow of water leaking between the stones and gathering in a deep pool at the base of the boulders. We head for that, eager to fill our jugs and be gone.

A shout comes from *Lightning*, the last of the ships in line on the beach. "See," cries the voice. "The enemy arrives! But not so proud now!"

We turn our heads to witness the first of the wrecks bearing down on our island, driven by the wind to the far side of our strand and nearly, but not quite, missing the middling rock. A Persian ship, its hull shattered and the sea lapping over its submerged deck, holds a cursed group of sailors. When the craft shudders to a halt a few fathoms from the shore, its wide-eyed survivors stare in terror at the hoplites. There is to be no mercy as the Greek soldiers wade into the water while our rowers holler.

"Behead them!" the oarsmen shout. "Behead them all!"

The weakened Persians attempt to escape, moving to the water. Those who make it overboard can be seen thrashing in the sea, their efforts smothered in a watery death. Those who do not flee await their fates, putting up feeble resistance as our men spear them, Like wild boars, the enemy's wails echo from the isle's rocky heights.

They are the first of them to leave bodies behind, without souls. As I wait to fill my jar, the breeze wafts the smell of death past my deadened nostrils, and the detritus of the enemy fleet keeps coming, piling up, and spreading all along the shoreline. The same end awaits every single Persian ship to wash into our grip.

Though deep in my heart I feel pity for their wretched plight, I also remember the burning of my own city. I remember Thermopylae and the arrogance of Xerxes. I turn away, preferring not to look. I stoop to the pool, filling the pot partway, then take leave for another to partake in the fresh water, and turn to slog back down the beach toward *Lightning*.

As I do so, I hear another shout. "Come! T'is a horror!" cries a soldier, knee-deep in the surf a stade up the strand. I look up but have to shade my eyes against the sun, now beginning its descent to the west. The hoplite waves his arms, excited as other soldiers run toward him.

"What?" one shouts. "What have you?"

I place my pot in the sand and sit down, awaiting the answer to the riddle. A small force has now gathered by the single soldier. His cries are soon joined by their own. A few wade further into the strait, dragging closer to shore what appears to be a large piece of driftwood. A limp form clings to the debris, and it is this that commands their attention. The soldiers close in, not as executioners this time but, as saviors. They pick up the body and begin to bear it to our ships.

Curious now, despite my aching shoulder, my semi-delirious condition, and the hot sun, I rise to my feet. The other water-bearers have paused in their task, like me, wondering what the loud voices were about.

Seeing our attention, a hoplite shouts. "A woman! A woman washed ashore, right over there!"

A woman! How could that be? There are no women on our ships, though we had heard the Persians had women on some of theirs. What was the name? Artemisia? Can it be her? Could we have captured the famed Halicarnassian man-hater? That will be a prize indeed! I pick up the jug and feel a sharp stab of pain in my wounded shoulder.

By the gods, that staggers me, and I almost drop the water. The world swims in front of my eyes as the gang of chattering hoplites come closer. The noise attracts Aristides, who has been keeping watch of the flow of the fight from his own ship. He bounds over.

"What have we here?" he says, approaching the crowd. The rest of us close into the group, gathering around, and straining to catch a glimpse.

"A woman, sir," replies the soldier who has found her. He points down the shore. "The waves brought her over there."

Aristides parts the men. I can not see, my view obscured by the mass of the curious. "Indeed!" I hear him say. "Not a Persian is she, but one dressed as an Athenian; and alive."

Athenian? I lean closer. The ranks part, and I catch a glimpse of a soaked and salt-caked form lying in the arms of the hoplite marine. Athenian all right. No others make chitons like hers. The Athenian's face is turned away, buried in the soldier's chest. She chokes, coughing up water, and moves her head toward me, her sodden raven hair dripping the sea. It is Andronica.

Demaratus

The day was well spent, the heat lifting somewhat as the shadows lengthened on the plateau of Mount Ageleos. The battle had been lost. The fleet was in retreat—or those who survived were. All day, the king switched between fits of rage and black depths of despair. He clung to individual victories even as he mourned the general tenor of the battle. Mardonious fluttered over, whispering in his ear, breathing encouragement, stricken beyond fear for his own safety. After all, Mardonious was a prime commander in the expedition and his blood relation to Xerxes offered no sure protection. My own fears over Xerxes' unstable nature were confirmed during the course of the day, the latest being his order to sever the heads of his Phoenician captains who tried to blame our ill fortunes on the Ionians, claiming the conquered Greek cities were partial to the Athenians and had thrown the battle.

Xerxes had witnessed the success of the Ionian ships against the Lacedaemonians and the futility of the Phoenicians pitted against the Athenians. He was unimpressed. He ordered the godless commanders to be taken to the beach and decapitated. He ordered their heads tossed into the sea, where they bobbed in wakes thrown up by the speeding hulls of hundreds of trireme battleships. They would accompany Androcles in his long journey to Hades now so close.

Androcles himself hung on the trellis, his position unchanged. Perhaps he waited for some release. Perhaps he was already dead. Either way, he, like so many, had met his end on these Greek shores, the land of his birth. In that way, at least, the gods had favored him. I wondered if they could do the same for me.

As I stood by the throne, witnessing the destruction and ruin of a large part of our fleet, the king turned to me. "Demaratus," he said, in one of his black moods. "Approach."

I strode to his side, passing a glowering Mardonious, and bowed. When I met the king's gaze, I saw there the brimming darkness of defeat. How remarkable, I thought; how he changes from a conquering, arrogant despot to hopeless victim. Is this king not only cruel, but weak?

"You had a vision of this," he said. "You said we must not fight here."

"Yes, Your Highness. We have fought here, though it is not the end."

He shook his head, not hearing. "You have always given me wise counsel. Have you not?"

"I have done my best my lord."

"Others have not given me such wisdom." He glared at Mardonious, who shifted.

"It is not easy, Your Highness, to give good counsel. There is much that is unknown."

"That is noble of you to say Demaratus. Perhaps this court will listen to you now, while we still can. There is much you wish to say, eh?"

"In time your Highness," I said, stepping away. "I remain at your service."

He returned his attention to the battle that had by this time degenerated into a spirited pursuit of our ships by the enemy, skipping over the surface of the strait like giant, stinging water bugs.

Our fleet, superior in numbers, maneuverability, and training, had thrust themselves into a noose, and the Greek allies had tightened it, breaking through our line on both flanks and crowding our ships together to limit their mobility. It was a brilliant tactical ploy, admirably executed. The result was what we saw before us, a day-long, losing fight ending in a humiliating retreat. We still had more ships than the enemy, despite whatever losses we might have suffered. After all, the Egyptians were not involved, and our reserve squadrons had never come into the fight. Even so, this was a bitter and decisive setback to the king's hopes for a quick victory and a crushing blow to the morale of our warriors.

The king understood this. He watched the now unequal fight for a while longer and then stood. "We will return to Athens," he said to no one in particular. "There is only an empty well here."

His attendants bowed. I stood silent as the king of Asia turned, squared his shoulders, and strode toward the waiting horses without another word. Mardonious was quiet, his own face distorted with fear rising inside him, though as he turned to follow, our eyes met. I could see his hatred. Ah, but the birds will still fly, the trees will still grow; he was of no matter, as I still must live with this man and the king, at least for now.

As if hearing my thoughts, Xerxes, mounted, called to me. "Demaratus, you will ride with us. I seek your counsel."

I bowed and walked to him, turning to cast my eyes over the deepening blue of the sea and then over the strait from end to end, taking in the shattered remnants of our defeated navy and resting, finally, on the sad form of Androcles. He was pinioned to a pole, swaying in the surf, his choice made, his fate finalized. Courage or madness? I was not to judge, however, for my own fate remained adrift, awaiting choices I loathed to rest with.

Lysis

The sun is low over the hills of Salamis as we approach the narrow beach at the foot of Mount Ageleos. The enemy fleet has been driven from the bay in disarray, and all around us floats the detritus of battle. We row our way through hundreds of shattered trireme hulls and thousands of corpses. The ones that have not disappeared into the depths bob in the waters that lap the sunken wrecks. The choking smell of death lay in the late summer air even as the setting sun paints the strait with the color of honey.

It is a bloody end to a glorious day for Athens. It has been a glorious day for all of Greece. The gods have bequeathed us this gift, and as we pass through the surging columns of our own fleet, the paean once again rises into the evening sky, this time as a joyful song of triumph.

The ranks of rowers on *Lightning* join in the singing. Thranites, zygios, and thamamios all raise their voices, their fatigue wiped away by the heavenly knowledge of unexpected victory.

It has been a long, hard fight. After we secured the isle of Psyttaleia, we reembarked, brought aboard Megarian hoplite warriors and jumped back into the fray. Ameinias was cautious, even so. We had lost a number of thranites on the top level, and the ship did not quite have the pluck and quickness a trireme needed to control a battle. We followed the Aeginian ships toward the rear of the Persian fleet, helping to kill off enemy strays along the way.

I sit with Andronica in the stern, in the small deck beneath the trierarch's chair, and try to coax her back to one mind. The shock of seeing her in such a state has staggered me. I explained to Aristides and Ameinias who she is, but none can answer from where she had come.

She comes awake as the ships are loading, preparing to depart. Ameinias has ordered me to stay on the island with the other wounded, and this time I had not objected. Andronica is given to my charge, and I take her to the shade of a large plane tree near the stream. I cradle her head in my lap, and ignoring my own pain, minister to her as best I can. She has a bad welt on her head, and razor-sharp cuts cover her body. I wipe her beautiful face, wrap her in an oversized wool himation Amienias loaned her, and clean her cuts, all the while fearing the words she would speak once she has regained her strength. Nor am I sure of what words would pour from my own lips. How had she gotten here? And why?

It seems she has been on a Persian ship, not a Greek one. The more my thoughts work on this mystery, the more my initial joy gives way to sorrow and suspicion. Even though the war in my own heart rages anew, I feel the welling of relief and happiness that she is alive, and with me now, no matter the truth that lay buried within her.

As these thoughts race through my mind, she coughs, opens her eyes, and studies me. Her lids open wider, and her dark orbs struggle for recognition. She grabs my arm and tries to sit up—

"Rest Andronica."

She replies, gasping. "Lysis, I—"

"Rest."

"Your father," she says. "He's in trouble...he needs you..."

"My father? Of what danger do you speak."

"The king..." she struggles to speak.

"The king?"

"Your father ... in the sea... off Ageleos...delivered to death's door..."

Andronica can speak no more. Her eyes flutter shut, and she lapses back into a mind of other worlds. Her breathing is steady—she will not die—but she will not have words for a while, either.

What is she saying? My father? Death's door?

I lay Andronica's head down on the himation and lift myself to my feet. The ships are shoving off from the beach, with Amienias directing *Lightning's* seafaring.

"Trierarch!" I cry. "I must go with you!"

"We have no need for wounded or cripples, young Lysis," replies Amienias, "noble as your desire may be."

"Sire! I beg of you to hear my cause!"

Amienias cocks his head. "Speak man! Speak! We have no time for lambs among us."

"Trierarch, a great friend of Athens has fallen to the Persians. Xerxes has planned to bring death upon him, yet we can bring the power of the gods and change destiny!"

"Many friends of Athens have fallen this day, Lysis. This man you speak of. Is his life more important than another friend's?"

"The navarch thinks highly of him, sir. I am certain he would grant you favor for your help."

Amienias notices my struggle. "I hear all of what you say, but cannot see what else you hide."

I raise my chin and look the trierarch in the eye. "He is my father, sir. The Persians have left him in the sea near Ageleos. I beg of you for help. Will you?"

Amienias is taken aback. He looks over at the still form of Andronica under the tree and glances at me. "The gods have already blessed you with a great fortune today, Lysis. It is not wise to fill another supper plate when you have a full one before you."

I hold my ground. "Please, sir."

The trierarch turns away and pauses at the shoreline. "I give no oath, but if the gods blow the winds as you wish, we will obey." He strides to the ladder and, grasping the rungs, pulls himself up.

"What are you waiting on? Let's set our course Lysis!"

"Sir. Andronica knows of his place. Can we board her as well?"

"You test my patience!" he cries, irritated. "Now you risk more, but it is your life, not mine. Bring her if it pleases you."

Amienias is right. The rest of the day is spent in an agony of near misses and terrifying moments. A battle is different when trying to protect another. From my position in the stern, I can see straight down the middle deck, or zygios, where the flautists hold court, pipes whistling to the beat of the oars. We are shorthanded on rowers, but the spirit of those remaining never wavers. They answer the call for speed or maneuver with loyalty and determination, which is fortunate, as they are called upon often.

We only have recourse to the ram once, crashing into a fleeing Persian vessel in even worse shape than we are and filling her shattered hull with Poseidon's waters. The rest of the voyage, Amienias weaves among sunken wrecks, debris and any of the enemy still willing to fight. They fling missiles by the score onto our protective screens, canopy, and exposed deck. It is here that anything can happen. Indeed, more than one of the enemy's barbed arrows is still lodged in the stanchions by my head.

But nothing does happen. There is no sea change, at least not for me and not for Andronica. We make it through the fight, and now find ourselves on the other end. I lean against the solid wood of *Lightning* and allow myself, for a moment, to drink in the overwhelming feeling of joy that permeates the fleet. Thousands of men are singing as the last vestiges of the enemy are driven from the strait, and our victory penetrates even the most pessimistic minds.

The rowers on *Lightning* smile, laugh, and cry at once, even beyond their pinched and narrow faces, their exhausted bodies. Those not wounded topside raise their spears and arrow-pocked shields in triumph to others of our ships passing by. The drained deckhands and officers sit limply on the deck while Amienias stands by his chair and the helmsman's rudder.

As the trierarch gazes upon our victorious fleet, he looks down at me and smiles. "Alright, Lysis, the gods are calling us to your father."

We row toward the foot of Mount Ageleos. Though Andronica has not yet found her presence, a passing Lacedaemonian vessel tells us of Xerxes' high seat and the beach in front of it. They know not of the Persian tyrant still being there, but we will know this answer soon.

The hills seem deserted. We cautiously approach with scouts in the catheads, alert for any movement, any sound. There is none but the now-muted and gentle sound of the thranites' oars looped around their tholepins. The other two levels rest, their oars shipped, as we creep to the beach.

"There! In the water!" A scout shouts from the starboard cathead. "Two points to starboard."

Amienias orders the course change, and we swing around toward the sighting.

I leave Andronica where she lay and move to the bow. Off to starboard, a figure rises out of the water near the beach. It is a trellis of sorts. Between the poles, splayed out like goat meat hung to dry, is the limp form of a man. Amienias orders the ship to drift alongside.

I look down on a painful and pitiful sight. The body is submerged. The face is cracked and swollen, the arms burned and blistered. The wrists have been tied to the poles, and they ooze blood and fluid. The tunic is torn. The head hung low over the water. But I know who it is.

My heart swells like a river close to bursting as tears push from my eyes. There is no movement from that body, no life in those limbs, but still I dare to hope.

"Free him," I say through clenched teeth as Amienias comes up beside me.

"Cut him down!" shouts Amienias.

Two deckhands jump into the water and swim to the body, slashing the chords and dragging the violated husk of my father back to the ship. Willing hands reach over and pull his lifeless form up onto the stern deck by the trierarch's chair.

The healer puts him down with his face to the darkening heavens, his deep scars now looking at home amid the wreckage of his physical self. I lean over him and will life, wanting it. But there is no movement. No breathing. There is only death.

I cry over my father. I know not the king's cause for this death, nor do I care. It is of no matter now how he has lived or died. He is my father, and now, he is in the chambers of Zeus, Poseidon, Hera, Hestia and Demeter. And that is all that can ever matter. I arrange his body, laying together his devastated arms, bringing up his mangled legs, attempting to hide the cuts in his chest that have long ago ceased exuding his life force.

His eyes are closed and his face bears the marks of long suffering, yet still he appears at peace. Above me, Amienias speaks. "I am sorry, Lysis, I wish it was not so."

I nod my head. This is not his failing. This is not anyone's failing. My father was dead long before Andronica spoke to me of him.

I believe I sensed he was already dead when I left him at the dock in the Piraeus. He was on a path only he could control. That much was always true.

As I sit looking at him, I realize more than ever the same is true for me. The path I choose, only I can control, only I can ever truly know. When we row back over the bay, back toward Salamis, I am deep in my own grief, though all around me, shouts of joy peal out into the evening.

Amienias beaches *Lightning* in the darkness at Paloukia Bay. We had launched from there this morning, but it now seems like weeks ago. The drunkenness of triumph has worn off for our crew, who sit slumped over their oars trying to recover, remembering the terror of battle even in their joy of having survived. They rise from their seats, stretching their spent limbs and filing to the stern to climb down the ladders and splash into the calm water. Once on the beach, they gather, looking around for friends no longer with them, or speaking with concern of the wounded who are bedded in the vast array of warships.

I remain with Andronica, who shows signs of waking. My father lay on the stern deck where I have left him, supine, and deep in eternal slumber. Amienias sets the watch for the night and makes his way over the side toward me.

"Lysis, I will tell Themistocles you have survived the day. He will be happy to hear that." He pauses, gazing at the body on the deck. "I will tell him also of this hero of Athens."

I thank him, and he swings himself over the rail and clambers to the sand. Except for the silent watch, I am left alone on *Lightning* as night falls upon the earth and the brilliant stars appear in a full harvest, distant evidence of the gods' eternal presence.

On the beach and in the distance, the sound of exhausted celebration rolls over the fleet, sweeping by the grounded warships, and echoing out over the bay. The noise pursues the enemy one final time down the long strait and perhaps, at last, laps in exultation against the limping masses of the invading horde.

Deep within me, I feel the joy. How can I not? We have won a great victory, for now. Athens is here. My community is within these ships. They are I, and I am them. Together we have come through fire and water and emerged on the other side, bloodied, but triumphant.

I also feel the void left by my fresh wounds of abandonment. Though my father has been physically dead to me before this campaign began, in my mind he has lived as an image of greatness, a vision to be emulated. The truth of his existence comes as a shock that rocks and confuses me just as the pounding sea tosses a solitary ship adrift at sea.

I have not found him until these last few days. I have not opened to who he really is. And then, when I did, to lose him again, and forever, seems more than I can bear. I know where my city is. I know we have survived this day and will live to fight again, but where am I now? What does my future hold?

I look down at Andronica, and she stirs again. This time, she opens her eyes. They are clear and calm.

"Lysis," she whispers. "You are here."

I answer, stroking her hair, "As are you."

She nods, and closes her eyes again, her breathing gentle. "I was of a mind that the gods had delivered me to my end. I knew not of the world swirling around me… the ship…the ship sinking so fast, and the arrows…"

I tense, remembering her arrival in my arms. She feels it, and her eyes open again.

"What troubles weigh on you, Lysis?"

I struggle to speak, unwilling to break the illusion of peace. I have no choice. I have to have the answers.

"Andronica, from whose ship were you cast into the sea?"

"An enemy ship."

"An enemy?"

"Yes, I was on a Persian ship." She seems to sense what I am digging for, but she waits.

"Why?" I ask.

"In obedience of a command by Demaratus. He said it was the will of the gods that I find you."

"Demaratus did?"

"Yes, he gave of himself to help us escape last night..." Her eyes lose focus. "Was it last night?"

"You choose the word 'us'? Was my father to take leave with you?" My heart races in agony.

"I believed he was. But he was not to appear at the Piraeus. Instead, he gathered his wrath so to kill the king."

I am stunned. My father had tried to kill Xerxes, the king of Asia. It is not even of a dream I can have imagined. I know then why Xeres delivered his end in the sea.

"What cause did my father have to bring such rebuke upon himself?"

Andronica hesitates this time. "He learned of matters, I think, about how his destiny had come to be. About how he had been lied to by Xerxes. Demaratus spoke of this to me."

There is another uncomfortable silence. Above us, a watchman walks the deck, his measured tread mimicking his counterparts on three hundred other ships, beached and anchored.

"Andronica, what turns in your fate led you to Demaratus and my father? What cause did you have to rest in the camp of the barbarians?"

Her eyes grow moist and she turns her head away, dashing away the tears before they can run down her cheeks. "I was looking for you," she says. "I could not stay in Eleusis. I heard from a runner who came from the city that the fleet had returned. I walked all the way home but, alas, arrived after you had taken leave. Distraught, I grew into ill-spirits toward my parents."

The tears flow now.

"I knew not of the way they had betrayed you...as if...as if... you had killed Hippocrotes. As if you were the enemy. They told me to cleanse my mind of you. They said you were but a small fox and I best cast you to the wind for all eternity, and that a noble lion awaited me to bear his children."

As she speaks, I feel my heart begin to lighten. I feel the strained chords loosen within my gut.

"I spoke of finding you. They forbade it. They locked me in the house. I bribed Hegisipyle..."

"The slave girl?"

She nods, dabbing her eyes with the himation. "Yes, she opened me to the dark night and I ran through the deserted city."

"I know."

"I ran to your house and almost to the mountain!"

I nod, and stroke her lovely, dark hair.

She continues, "When I got there, the house was empty."

"Yes, we had taken leave that afternoon. The enemy was nearing us."

"They were already upon Athens. At least Androcles, I mean, your father, was. It was dark, and I was afraid." She shivers at the memory. "I carried a lamp and called for you, but he came instead, from the fields. He was alone. He asked of my family name, of my destiny, and I spoke to him of truth. I knew not he was your father then."

"What did he do?"

"He looked around. He looked in his old chest. That is when he found..." She stops, and now the tears gush.

I hug her closer.

"He found the papers," I say.

"Yes. That moment will be in my visions for eternity. His face went pale. He dropped them and walked away. I picked them up. I... I... I... my heart turned to stone. My parents, my brother..."

"But not you."

"No, Lysis! Not me! I knew not a morsel of their plot. I was so ashamed."

"But it was not your fault?"

"No...but I wished it could be another way. I wish this whole matter would wash away like tides over sand."

She buries her face in the himation for a moment, sobbing. "My parents..." she cries, "my poor, poor parents."

I hold her and rock her, as she unleashes her pent-up grief. I let her cry herself out, giving her release. Finally, like the last whisper of a dying storm that stirs the sails one more time before fading away to stillness, she ceases her tears and lay spent in my arms, her eyes deep pools of sadness.

"Your father told me of his life. He asked if I wanted to return to the city, but I did not. I could not. Not then. Besides, I did not believe my parents were in danger now that I was with knowledge of their pact with the enemy. So your father sheltered me and delivered me back to the barbarian camp. He told the others I was but a slave he had captured."

She reaches up to brush my cheek. "He treated me well, once he knew how much I loved you."

My heart sings. She loves me now, as I had hoped she would always love me. There is no deceit within her, no betrayal. She clings to me now as I had hoped she would always cling to me, and I to her.

I listen as she recounts her days with my father, his alliance—surely blessed by the gods—with Demaratus, the Spartan king's attempt to save both of them, and the last desperate act of my poor father. I know not, in the end, why he had chosen this journey. I know not if it was for redemption or for vengeance: I know not, nor would for eternity, nor need to. I know of him what I had always known of him. He is my warrior hero once again. He is my Achilles. To me, in the end, he has truly come home.

Andronica pulls from within her chiton a long silver chain, finely-crafted, light and smooth to the touch. On the chain is an amulet of the purest silver and engraved on the surface of the oval charm is the letter "Alpha." She lay watching me. "Lysis, Demaratus bequeathed this to me. He said it was from your father. He told me to tell you your father said he was sorry." I take it from her, rubbing it between my calloused fingers and feel, again, the well of my own tears rise to the font. But I have cried enough. At last, it is over.

I give the amulet back to her, putting it around her neck and locking the delicate chain. "It is to be yours. My father, I think, would have wanted it this way."

She throws her arms around me.

And that is how Themistocles, navarch of the Athenian fleet, finds me at last. In the first watch of the night, I am wounded in both heart and body, but content somehow, deep to my core.

Chapter 20

Demaratus

"I must return to Susa," said the king.

We stood by the port of Phalerum—Mardonious, me, and Hydarnes, who had been recalled with his forces before they were halfway to the isthmus. The king had finished an audience with the surviving captains of our fleet, an audience that had not gone well. He had settled his temper from yesterday's defeat, and his new spirit was fortunate for most of the navy. I had expected a blood-bath, but Xerxes was moving forward.

He arranged for the fleet to return the same way it had arrived. He would accompany them himself, speeding his way back to the capital. Xerxes was unwilling to stay in Attica for the winter while news of the defeat at Salamis spread throughout the empire, possibly sowing seeds of insurrection.

He also learned the fleet was in ill-spirits from the results of the battle. They had expected an easy victory and crowded into the fight, hoping to gain the favor of their monarch. Instead, despite their efforts, the Greek allies defeated them in as mismatched a contest as anyone had ever seen. Although they expressed their willingness to attack again, and indeed still outnumbered the enemy, Xerxes could sense their confidence was shattered. The king could not risk losing his entire fleet with the prospect of a long retreat ahead of him. Without support, the entire expedition would be lost, swallowed up in a foreign land without hope of mercy from its ravaged defenders. No, he would not go forth with that.

I was surprised by this decree. The fleet was capable of staying. We could winter here, drawing reinforcements from the Ionian cities, the Egyptians, and the conquered cities of northern Greece. As I had reminded him on the day of battle, this was not the end. Yet for Xerxes, it seemed it was. He was more eager to secure his conquests and his throne than to march into hostile land and risk annihilation. He was weak, an elephant against only mice.

Xerxes looked at us with his chin raised high, displaying the haughtiness of his position, but to no effect. We knew of him too well. His bluster and feigned decisiveness hid the panic that lay under his surface. These Greeks, united in their desire to defeat the common enemy, were a foe he had never faced. It seemed in the king's mind, the enemy had assumed magical forces.

"Mardonious!" he commanded. "You will lead the army through the northern part of this forsaken land and return them safe across the Hellespont. It is to be your own head were you not to deliver them safely!"

Mardonious, staggered by our defeat, knew Xerxes blamed him for it. He was of one mind: make amends. He knew his future lay here, in Greece, not back in Susa. Without victory, the poisoned barbs of ridicule, rumor, and blame would fall thick and fast about him back at home. The path for Mardonious was clear.

"Your Highness," said the beleaguered general, "I am devoted to your return home. It is a wise plan. But Your Highness, I beg your answer: Is it wise to give up our campaign after this small reverse? Can we not turn the war in our favor?"

Xerxes peered at his brother-in-law. "Of what do you speak?"

"Your Majesty, grant me command of the best of our warriors. Let me winter here, in the home of the conquered. In the spring, I will draw the enemy's land forces out in the open, where we can use our numbers and our cavalry to defeat them. I will give you Greece, for these Greeks can never stay united for long. Glorious victory will be yours and remain so under your guidance and leadership."

Xerxes examined all of us. He returned his attention to Mardonious, as aware of his general's dilemma as the rest of us.

"I will grant your request. Take what you need to complete this campaign. Keep me with knowledge of your victories. I need not remind you of the price of failure."

Mardonious bowed low, so relieved it almost made me laugh. They both deserved my contempt, not my humor. Xerxes was happy to place the burden for ultimate triumph or catastrophe onto the shoulders of a surrogate. By the spring, he would be safe in Susa, able to claim his army was marching onward and with confident claims of his future victories. Should Mardonious fail, the one to behead would be clear. It made me sick.

But what about my own part? What was I to do? If I stayed in Greece, another path might open to secure my place among the Spartans. Perhaps in a land battle, the information I could provide would be decisive. But I could feel the enthusiasm for such a course die stillborn within me. The gods had not favored me, and through the nightmare of this campaign, I had come to believe that they did exist and were speaking to me. I was not to return home with honor by corrupting the house that had given me succor, despite the unworthiness of the host. If there was another way, it would be revealed to me, in time.

No, I would not go that way any longer, and Mardonious and I were, but for in the field of battle, enemies to each other. He would neither be pleased by my presence nor heed my advice. Though the king had not addressed the fate he intended for me, it seemed I was not destined to spend my time here, in Attica.

The king turned to Hydarnes. "The commander of my Immortals will return with me. And you, Demaratus, will accompany me. We will plan our next campaign."

I did not try to dispute the order. I accepted my fate. I put my future in the hands of the gods. The king strode away, heading for his encampment. "Let us make haste," he said. "The autumn storms will be upon us. This fleet must set sail."

We all bowed as one. Mardonious stood and watched him take leave, finally swinging his bright eyes upon me. "You have cast the light as does the full moon. The king trusts you now."

"I have no say in whom he trusts," I answered. "Nor do I wish it. I counsel him with what I know to be true from within."

"May you keep your head as you do so," he said, walking away.

"May you keep yours," I answered, to his back.

Hydarnes smiled, his old humor reasserting itself. "Ah, loose heads! This talk can make a man weak. Or hungry."

I laughed. "Hydarnes, as I am to travel a long voyage with the king, I am glad you will be near."

"As well to you sir," he replied, slapping me on the back.

We steered our course to the north and up the port road toward what stood of Athens. This war was far from over, but for me the end had arrived. I was to go home, but not to Sparta.

CHAPTER 21

Lysis

While our ships watch the enemy huddled in our former harbors, the commanders of the fleet preside over the funeral rites for the dead. With the Persians still occupying the city, the fallen can not await their interment for quieter times. So they are buried like the heroes of Marathon, near the battle where they fought and died.

Many find their final resting place in the arms of the sea, intertwined with the slain of the barbarians. Nature eventually separates all that is corporal, and these dead will drift alone on Poseidon's waters or sink to the depths, unfound in this mortal life, but not unmourned. The cries of the women who circle the graves, wailing and gnashing their teeth, speak for all the lost who cannot speak for themselves. Their grief is terrible to behold, heartrending and ferocious like the violence that has laid these warriors low.

The poor sacrificial goat, its trusting brown eyes half-lidded in the whipping wind, bows its head when Themistocles does the honor of sprinkling clean water drawn from a nearby spring on the animal's pure-white nose. I think again of the day's early morning, remembering the procession from the shore, the ship's crews bearing the burden of their fallen heroes, each one laid out upon a bier of wood and flaxen canvas, each one covered in colorful himation or the rough wrappings of the dockyard.

The enemy has not moved in two days, and the citizens who had transferred to the island, fearful of the end, come down in droves from the hills. Some to claim their own, some to rejoice in victory, and some to pray for the future. All join in the slow funeral ritual to give honor to the dead. They surround the gentle rise upon which the graves have been dug, and watch. The women, relatives of the slain, come forth from the crowd and stand together, their sorrow finding its release in their fallen tears and piercing wails. Soldiers and sailors lower the bodies to the earth, fold the dirt back over their remains, and stand back as the last shovelfuls empty.

Then, in the silence of the end, as the mournful cries dampen to rasping sobs and the comforting grasp of family and friends, Themistocles stands to speak. He strides to the fore and turns his back on the newly interred to address the living, finding in tragedy the greater realization of continuity, victory, and hope.

"Citizens!" his voice carries across the strand, echoing against the hundreds of hulls drawn up upon the beach, the sound rolling across the water even to the picket ships that keep their watch on the sea. "We cry for these men and mourn their passing as it should be. They were our friends, our family, our countrymen. They will be missed for all they might have been, as well as for all they were."

He pauses, sweeping his eyes over the gathering, lifting his chin, and breathing in the salt-laden air, his gaze resting on the gulls that circle overhead in the uncertain breeze.

"But even in your grief, remember this: by their sacrifice, they have given to us a mighty gift, a gift that can be gained by no other means. It is a gift that many of us, in the quiet of our peaceful years, take as a right rather than a privilege, a demand wrested from the gods in the arrogance of power rather than a treasure gratefully possessed and guarded. This gift is for all of us. It is for all Athenians, prized above every other, and the envy of the world. This is the gift of freedom. For freedom, these men gave their lives, so we might enjoy in this life what they have found in the next."

I listen with my arm around Andronica, my mother, and my sisters, with my uncle by my side. They had arrived with the others the previous night and had found Andronica and me tending to my father's corpse, laying him out for burial. My mother had burst into tears. Even with his scars and wounds, she recognized the physical essence of the man she loved. There is much to explain to both her and uncle, and they listen to our tale with mounting grief and wonder.

My mother's eyes glisten as she reaches across to Andronica, touching the silver amulet. "The gods have blessed you, son," she says, her other hand going to her own throat. "It is the match of this amulet, the one your father gave me many years ago, when we were married." She turns to Andronica. "He would have wanted it for you."

Andronica smiles in thankfulness and seizes my mother's hands. "You are my mother now."

They embrace and hold each other.

Concerned over my latest wound, my uncle asks about the battle. He and the others had watched from the hillsides above the town of Salamis as their future was decided in the narrow waters of the bay. They had cheered and agonized over every maneuver, every blow that sank an enemy ship or drove one of ours to the depths. Defeat would have meant at best, another exodus, at worst, slavery or death. Uncle notes with approval our tactics while his aging body appears to ache with desire to strike a blow against the invaders with his own hands. "And this Themistocles," he inquires, nodding toward the speaker, "he commanded well?"

"Yes Uncle. Honorably at all times, tender in calm and fearless in battle."

Uncle smiles with approval. "Good. We need leaders like him. Our fight lives on."

Themistocles continues, "Those who have given their flesh thus far in this war have done so knowing they would be remembered for their sacrifice, knowing that their friends and fellow countrymen, the soldiers and sailors of Athens whom they knew their entire lives, would not desert them in the end. And they gave themselves to this cause knowing we would continue this fight, give meaning to their death, and give them passage to the heavens."

These words make me think again of Hippocrotes, my boyhood friend. The night before, I had looked at the papyrus scroll intent on burning it to ashes. But something inside told me to know the full story now that it was over. I would put behind me what I could and bear what I must.

I had unrolled the scroll's final sheets, reading with pain the rantings of the old man, even as I came to the end, where a different hand had taken over. I recognized the awkward strokes of Hippocrotes, his lettering, like his physical self, large and bold.

"We go tomorrow," he had written. "The fleet takes leave for the north. The Persians have come at last, and father is happy. But my own heart is torn, though he will not know of this for all of eternity. What will this hold for me now that today has at last come? Lysis and I go to war, a war I've known my whole life we cannot win. And yet I say 'we'.' Whom do I mean? The faraway cousins of my line who come to conquer my adopted homeland? Or, this home I have come to love?

"I think that for me, the answer now is clear. What I have gained by deception, I have earned by right, the love of my friend, the tug of this, my true home. Lysis need never know the anguish of my falsity, for now it is done. I must see what has been true these many years. I go to war with the best friend I have ever known. May it always be so."

I bow my head in grief, my memory restoring to glory the tarnished image of my friend, placing him in the pantheon of heroes that would forever fill my heart.

The breeze ripples across the water's surface and grows, swaying the ship's rigging and snapping blocks against masts. The loss I feel can not diminish or silence the navarch's message.

"The enemy, dangerous in their despotism, lies across from us licking their wounds. They have battered themselves against free men and been found wanting, but they are there. They still demand our might. They still challenge our courage. Should they wage war again, we will answer them, as we did ten long years before at Marathon and as we did here at Salamis. We will answer them as much for the dead who lie here, who would reproach us for any other course, as for ourselves who deserve no less. We, the free citizens of Athens, have not chosen this fight, yet we choose to defend ourselves and our city. May we always be worthy of the hopes these dead held for us. May we always be willing to pay the price such hopes demand."

He finishes and turns in silence back toward the long row of bodies, bowing his head. We echo him in our quietness, moved by his eloquence, lost in our own sadness.

Afterward, I find Themistocles on the deck of *Athena's Victory*. He worries over the fitness of his ship, preparing for what we all think is the inevitable Persian attack.

"Navarch!" I call, craning my neck to the trierarch's chair where he holds court.

"Lysis! You have come to sail with us again?"

I grimace. "Not right away, sir. Maybe the enemy will let me heal?"

He laughs. "Not likely, though only the gods know. What cause brings you in want of an old sailor?"

"I am to bury my father, and would be honored for you to bear witness with me at his grave."

He looks around, sniffing the air, studying the rough waters and whitecaps of the bay. I can feel the wind tugging at my tunic as it whips the lines in their blocks and rattles the shipped oars that lay athwart the trireme's decks.

"I will do as you wish, the enemy will not move today."

Themistocles shouts for the pilot and mate, gives them orders, and joins me on the strand. We walk up the beach to a rise that beckons inland.

"I grieve for you," the navarch says. "In the end, your father did what was noble. He remembered the land of his birth."

"Yes," I reply, thinking it was not to be that simple, "I suppose he did." But in the end, not I, nor any other, can know of the mysteries in his mind. Had he remembered his homeland or tried to avenge himself?

"For now, I believe that is enough to honor him."

We bury my father on a hill overlooking Paloukia Bay on the isle of Salamis. The wind howls across the water and trees creak and moan, lashing back and forth with the leading edge of an autumn storm. We huddle together, our himations wrap about us as the air swirls and fills with debris: tufts of grass, sand, dirt, and the deep, tangy salt of the sea.

Themistocles and my mother are here. My uncle supports Andronica and my sisters as I lead the small, shivering goat to the lip of the grave and draw my dagger for the blood sacrifice. It is apt, we have decided, that Androcles be honored in this way. In the end, none of us could have known what drove him in his final hours, but his deed was that of a warrior, a defender of his city. Therefore, will we deliver him to the fate that awaits him in the dark underworld with all the honor we can bring to an exiled life.

Maybe my father, like my grandfather, will find his soul's peace in the unknown "blessing" of the Eleusian mysteries rather than wandering in Hades' domain. On Salamis' windswept slopes, I hope that for him as I consider the words of Achilles: "I'd rather be a day laborer on earth working for a man of little property than lord of all of the hosts of the dead." We the living, of course, will never know our ends until death's cold breath beckons, offering either knowledge or oblivion.

We honor my father and perform the rites for a lost son of Athens, gathering around the burial of his mortal remains and bringing to him the symbolic blood sacrifice reserved for the gods and heroes of the city. I know my father would be pleased and proud—surprised, maybe cynical— but in the end, relieved of his burden and shorn of his guilt. It was for us to free him of our own disappointments, bitterness and loneliness of lost years. Were we to find this freedom within ourselves, his soul might find its own repose.

With my bright dagger hanging at my side, I search the faces of those who share this moment. My mother, her tears dried, gazes at the freshly turned earth with a sad smile, remembering. My uncle and sisters hug each other, pressed close, against the wind. Andronica observes me with love and, as with me, scars from so many losses. Themistocles stands like a rock, looking at my face, as if asking whether the gods had deemed this the end of my heartache.

I hold the animal by the scruff of the neck and think of my father, the hero of my youth, and the curse of his own existence. He was a man who, despite his own life, had never forgotten those he left behind, never ceased loving what he could no longer possess except in memory. It is enough, I find, that he ended this way. It is enough for me to continue. My father deserves my love, my respect, and the honor I will give him from this day onward.

I complete the ritual, spilling the offering onto the dirt as the grave absorbs the blood—not as a stain on the earth, but finally, as a mark of honor.

CHAPTER 22

Lysis

The Persian host does not come against us. They menace us. They show their teeth. But that is all they do; a snarling, snapping dance of a wounded cur, hurt and confused, they seek to cover retreat. They attempt to build a bridge to the island of Salamis using merchant vessels, wrecks, and transport ships. It seems Xerxes tries to force us off balance while he packs his kit and takes leave.

He withdraws his navy and much of the army, and leaves a force of the best he had under Mardonious, while he himself returns to Susa to quell unrest and answer disbelief. We return to pick through the ruins of our devastated city. We are eager to rebuild, but we can not—not while the enemy lay in wait to the north for better weather, gathering themselves for what they perhaps hope will be the final crippling blow. No, the last act of this play is yet to unfold.

For Andronica and myself, life has begun. In the ruins of the old, we seek promise for the future, blessed as we are with one family now and one path to follow, no matter where it may lead.

THE PLAYERS:

The Greeks

Ameinias – trierarch of the trireme 'Lightning' and commander of the Greek Yellow squadron during the battle of Salamis

Andronica – Sister of Hippocrates and girlfriend of Lysis. Andronica emigrated from Persia with her family when she was 8.

Androcles – Father of Lysis

Aristides – Athenian trierarch and son of Lysimachus

Calliades – The Archon, or leading citizen of Athens and elected head of the Athenian assembly.

Cleomones – Spartan king from 524 to 490 BCE. Cleomenes was exiled from Sparta in 490 when his plot against his co king Demaratus was discovered. He returned and later died in prison in Sparta. He was the father of Gorgo, wife of his successor king, Leonidas.

Hippias – The last Athenian Tyrant ousted prior to the formation of the Athenian Democracy

Hippocrotes – Boyhood friend of Lysis

Leonidas – Spartan king leading the defense of Thermopylae

Leotychides – Spartan King from 496 to 476 BC. Leotychides was co king with Cleomenes. He reign ended when forced to flee Sparta after having been accused of accepting a bribe from Thessalians who had purportedly aided the Persians during the invasion of Greece.

Lysis – son of Androcles and young Athenian hoplite warrior. His girlfriend is Andronica and his best friend is Andronica's brother, Hippocrotes

Menilius – Pedagogue, or teacher, of young Lysis

Miretus – trierarch of 'Winds of the Gods'

Patrocles – Captain of Hoplite Marines on the Athenian trireme 'Winds of the gods'

Themistocles- Leading citizen of Athens. Themistocles commands the Athenian contingent of the Greek allied fleet at Salamis.

For the Persians

Artemisia of Hallicarnasis.- Artemisia commands a small fleet of triremes from Hallicarnasis and comes to the attention of Xerxes during the battle of Salamis

Cyrus – Persian warrior and confidante of the Spartan king Demaratus.

Darius – King of the Persians prior to Xerxes.

Demaratus – One of two Spartan kings chased from Sparta who has defected to the Persian cause. Demaratus is an advisor to King Xerxes.

Hydarnes – Commander of the Immortals and friend of Demaratus

Hystaspes- Father of Medarnes. Hystaspes captured Androcles and made sure Androcles was watched while in Athens and reported on Athenian readiness for war.

Mardonious – Brother in law of Xerxes

Medarnes – Son of Hystaspes. Medarnes swears revenge against Androcles for purportedly killing his father, Hystaspes

Phraortes – Head of Xerxes Secret Police

Xerxes – Great king of the Persian Empire and ruler of such from 486 to 465 BCE.

GLOSSARY

Agoge – The brutal training program required of all male citizens of Sparta except the firstborn son of the ruling classes. The agoge was primarily concerned with fostering the Spartan warrior culture, but included all aspects of an individual's schooling.

Akamantion – a member of one of the 10 tribes of Athens. The tribes were delineated by the Athenian statesman Kleisthenes in 507 BCE to help prevent the concentration of power in one geographic location. Each tribe had members from the coast, the city, and the inland areas of the Athenian state. Political positions, military obligated service and other civil duties were differentiated by tribe.

Angre Mainyu – An evil and destructive spirit in the Zoroastrian doctrine of Persia

Askoma – The leather sleeve fitted to the oar port of a trireme to minimize water taken aboard and to protect the rower.

Balbis – The stone starting blocks at the Olympic Games in Olympia Greece for the **Stadion** running race. Grooves, approximately 4 inches apart were carved into the blocks to help runners anchor their toes prior to the start.

Chiton – A form of wool or linen tunic, fastened at the shoulder and worn by both men and women in ancient Greece. The chiton was longer than the height of the wearer. A belt was used to gather the excess fabric either high (below the breast) or lower (around the waist)

Dahaka – Persian god of death. Dehaka is often shown as three headed with lizards and scorpions crawling on his body.

Diekplous – A naval tactic designed to penetrate an enemy's line between their ships and then turning and attacking with rams the enemy's vulnerable sides.

Elatai – The name given to the oars of ancient Greek triremes.

Eleusian Mysteries – An annual secret initiation into the cult of Demeter and Persephone held at the Sanctuary of Elefsina near Athens. The mysteries were based on a retelling of the abduction of Persephone from her mother, Demeter, by Hades, the god of the underworld and the eventual return of Persephone to her mother. They were symbolic of the eternity and rebirth of life.

Ephebe – A young Greek man of between 18-20 years old undergoing military training.

Ephors – One of five magistrates in ancient Sparta elected to oversee the actions of the Spartan kings.

Helots – The equivalent of serfs in ancient Sparta. Helots were above slaves, but below Spartan citizens.

Himation – A large rectangular piece of woolen clothing worn as either an outer garment or as a single garment in ancient Greece. It was used as a robe or in the case of women, a shawl or outer wear over a chiton. The manner of wearing depended on the wearer, but was capable of covering the entire body.

Hoplite – A citizen soldier of an ancient Greek city state. The hoplite was expected to provide his own armor and weapons and fight in the Phalanx. Most city states could field hoplites representing up to ½ of their adult male population.

Kekropis – One of 10 Attic tribes explained above.

Kynosarges Gymnasium – A temple and gymnasium dedicated to the god Heracles. Greek gymnasiums were used for athletic training such as wrestling, boxing, equestrian activites and military training.

Marathon – A beach site 25 miles from Athens where a large Persian force sent by the Persian king Darius in 490 BCE was defeated by Athenian and Plataen hoplites.

Mount Hymettus – A mountain range about 9 miles east of central Athens extending north to south for approximately 10 miles with a maximum elevation of 3,300 feet.

Munychia – The port of Athens and home of the Athenian fleet

Navarch – The terms used by the Spartans to describe the Spartan 'leader of the fleet'. In 480, the Spartan Eurybiades commanded the combined Greek fleet at the battles of Artemision and Salamis

Panathenaic Games – An athletic series of events similar to the ancient Olympic games held every four years from 566 BCE as well as a religious festival honoring the goddess Athena, patroness of Athens.

Pankration – An athletic event in the ancient Olympic games combining martial skills such as boxing, wrestling, and kick boxing.

Pentathlon – A series of five athletic events held in ancient Olympia as part of the Olympic games. The pentathlon consisted of the stadion (210 yard sprint), javelin throw, discus throw, long jump and wrestling.

Phalanx – A tactical formation of heavily armed soldiers (in classical Greece called Hoplites) in close order bearing long spears, large heavy shields and protective armor. The phalanx was difficult to defeat head on, but lacked maneuverability and flexibility.

Plethron - A unit of measurement equal to about 100 Greek 'feet', or about 30 meters.

Pnyx – The hill in the center of the city of Athens utilized in classical times for political assemblies of all male citizens of Athens from 507 BCE

Stade (Anglicized) – A unit of measurement also termed 'stadion'. The plural is 'stadia'. It is a unit of 600 Greek 'feet'. In this work, the Olympic distance for a stade is used which is about 210 yards.

Stadion – The penultimate race in the Olympic games in Olympia Greece. It was approximately 210 yards in length.

Strigils – A curved bronze tool used to scrape oil, dust, and dirt from an individual.

Talent – A unit of measure of weight. One Attic talent was equivalent to 26 Kilograms, or 57 pounds

Thalamite – A rower in the lower tier of a trireme

Thranite - A rower in the top tier of a trireme

Trierarch – Captain of the trireme

Trireme – A war vessel with three banks of oars manned by 170 rowers in three tiers. Each rower manned one oar. Upwards of 30 other crew members served the sails and rigging, steered the ship using a large stern rudder and served as archers and marine for close in fighting. The triremes were the primary 'battleship' of ancient fleets for upwards of 500 years.

Zygite - A rower in the second tier of a trireme

FALL OF HONOR

Synopsis

In the summer of 480 BCE, Xerxes, the Great king of the Persian
Empire, intent on absorbing the Greek city states into his domains,
invades the Greek mainland with the largest army ever assembled
and encamps in front of the narrow pass of Thermopylae, where
5000 Greek Hoplite soldiers, led by King Leonidas of Sparta and
the 300 elite soldiers of his guard, block his advance and await his
assault. In the waters that lap against the shore of the Greek position, hundreds of Persian ships face off against an equally determined Greek trireme fleet.

Nervously awaiting the Persian Naval assault is Lysis, a young
Athenian marine along with his boyhood friend, Hippocrotes. Lysis
is fired not only by his love of country and his beautiful fiancée,
Andronica, sister of Hippocrotes, but forever by the memory of
Androcles, his father, long feared lost at sea, and the need to be
worthy of the hero he holds in his heart. Meanwhile, the volatile
Xerxes counts among his closest advisors the former Greek Spartan
King, Demaratus, who is driven by an insatiable need to recover his
lost kingship and prove himself worthy of his Spartan Heritage.

The fleets clash and in the melee, Hippocrotes is killed but gasps
out a puzzling request with his dying breath. Lysis is captured and
finds himself an unwilling messenger from Demaratus to his former
co king, Leonidas. Demaratus hopes to betray the Persian cause in
an effort to return to Sparta with honor. While in the clutches of

the enemy, Lysis learns of his father's true fate and is stunned to find that not only is Androcles, now known as Phraortes, still alive, he is the head of Xerxes secret police, slavishly loyal to Xerxes, and has long suspected Demaratus as a potential traitor to the Persian cause. Lysis is devastated and convinced his family has lost all honor. Disavowing his father, he is helped by Demaratus, who claims Lysis is slain, to escape into the Greek lines at Thermopylae.

Leonidas' passionate leadership is in sharp contrast to Xerxes and the fear he engenders. Inspired, Lysis is determined to die in partial payment of his father's betrayal and stays to fight in a doomed cause, as the Persians have found a route around the Greek position, cutting off their retreat. Leonidas orders Lysis to leave and take a message to the fleet. Lysis initially refuses but then, humbled by the king's bravery, escapes to Themistocles, the leader of the Athenian fleet, while behind him, Leonidas and his Spartans meet their end.

The fleet retreats to Athens in the face of the Persian command of land and sea, and Lysis is reunited with his family, informing them of his father's betrayal. Andronica is nowhere to be found, and her family treats him with near hatred. While there, Lysis discovers Hippocrotes and his parent's secret life as Persian spies ordered to watch over Androcles' family and to kill them at the first sign of betrayal from Androcles. Lysis cannot believe that Andronica is part of the plot, but sees no other possibility, even though Hippocrotes final words in his personal diary reveals he was committed to Lysis as a friend. Nevertheless, surrounded by the crumbling of all he has known and believed, Lysis commits to the defense of his city under the leadership of Themistocles as his only solace.

Summer has given way to fall, and the Persians take Athens and kill the final defenders on the hill of the Acropolis, even as the Athenian fleet retreats to the isle of Salamis to plan strategy in an attempt to defeat the massive Persian forces at sea. Themistocles is masterful in persuading his Greek allies to stay and fight at Salamis rather than retreat. Demaratus continues his attempts to subvert the Persian cause, and in doing so, exposes Androcles to the truth of how he has been cruelly used by Xerxes. Themistocles uses Lysis once again as a messenger, this time to Demaratus seeking information on Persian plans. Lysis is recognized by the Persians as still alive and is forced to escape into the city. There, he once more meets with his father, who is in the process of verifying Demartus' claims of Xerxes lies. They reconcile and Androcles tells his story, revealing his character flaws but also his determination to make things right, even while admitting he can never go home again. Lysis returns to Themistocles never having met Demaratus.

Meanwhile, Andronica has also realized the truth of her family's role and comes together with both Androcles and Demaratus, who is desperate to help the Greeks in the upcoming fight. As Androcles departs with vague assurances of support, they arrange to meet later, but Androcles never shows up. Andronica reveals that Androcles has vowed to kill Xerxes. As a result, Demaratus is forced to take ship to prevent this, but they are too late. Androcles' attempt has failed, and he is severely wounded, captured, and hung on a trellis in the rising tide.

At sea, Lysis and the now united Greek fleet engage the Persian armada at the Naval choke point at Samamis. The Persians are defeated. During the action, Andronica's ship is sunk, she drifts to a Greek held isle, where Lysis, himself wounded, finds her. She tells him of Androcles' fate and professes her love. Lysis rushes to try and save his father, but is too late. They retrieve the body and his family buries him, with his honor restored. The Persian invasion is turned back, Demaratus realizes he has chosen his path and must remain where he is, and Athens is once again freed.

ACKNOWLEDGMENTS

I finished the first draft of this work in 1998. I obviously experienced some distractions since then. I would like to thank the people who have made certain that those distractions were not eternal.

First, to Valerie Ormond, who was my first and most patient editor and a constant positive force. Next, to Ken Kales and Josh Freel at Waterside Productions whose editorial efforts added a rich texture to the language.

I'd like to thank my two wonderful children, Anna and Danny, for their own patience and over the years the many bedtime stories that had more than a thread of the ancient world within them.

And finally, to my lovely friend, partner, and wife, Bobbi, who got to hear more about the ancient Greeks than she could ever have imagined (or desired) and whose steady attention to detail not only finished the final edit, but ensured the book would finally see the light of day. I am grateful to her and for her love.

www.ingramcontent.com/pod-product-compliance
Lightning Source LLC
Chambersburg PA
CBHW022147010726
47493CB00002B/376